He found
and
D0196710
GRIFFIN

At the Duke's Pleasure

"Would you like to be married here in your home parish or at Braebourne, perhaps? There is a fine chapel on the estate that I imagine you would approve."

She swallowed and said nothing.

"Or would you rather the ceremony take place in London? St. George's is a most popular choice."

Again he waited.

Finally, she turned her gaze to his. "Actually, Your Grace," she said, forcing herself to speak in a strong, clear voice, "I am afraid that none of them will suit."

"You have another place in mind?"

"No. You see, it's just that I'd really rather not."

"Rather not?" he repeated in clear confusion. "Rather not what?"

"Marry. I do not wish to be wed."

By Tracy Anne Warren

AT THE DUKE'S PLEASURE
SEDUCED BY HIS TOUCH
TEMPTED BY HIS KISS

Coming Soon

WICKED DELIGHTS OF A BRIDAL BED

Tracy Anne Warren

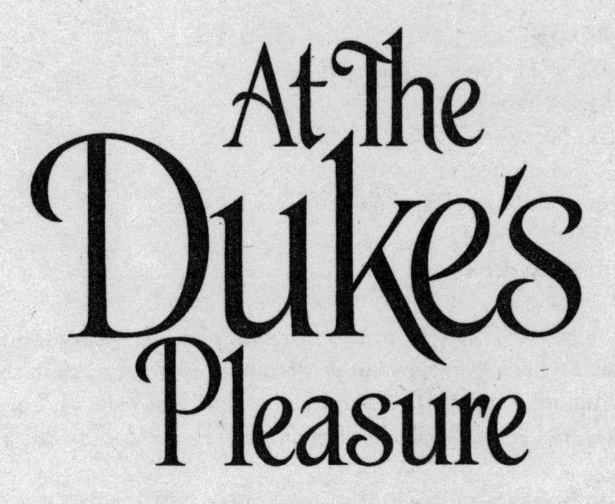

AVON

An Imprint of HarperCollins*Publishers*

This is a work of fiction. Names, characters, places, and incidents are products of the author's imagination or are used fictitiously and are not to be construed as real. Any resemblance to actual events, locales, organizations, or persons, living or dead, is entirely coincidental.

AVON BOOKS
An Imprint of HarperCollins*Publishers*
10 East 53rd Street
New York, New York 10022-5299

ISBN 978-0-06-167342-9
www.avonromance.com

First Avon Books paperback printing: January 2010

Printed in the U.S.A.

10 9 8 7 6 5 4 3 2 1

To the Friday Night Dinner Crew—
Jacque, Gail, Sue, Jeri, Barb,
Laura, Sheila and Leslie.
Thanks for all the fun and laughs
and for reminding me to take a break
and get away from my computer
every once in a while.

Prologue

Marsden Manor
Nottinghamshire, England
June 1789

The crack of a cricket bat and ball split the humid afternoon air. A triumphant round of whoops and shouts followed, as a group of boys raced across the immaculately manicured lawn to see who could capture the most runs.

Above them, inside a second-floor drawing room, stood Edward Augustus Joseph Byron, Marquis of Hartsfield. He drew an encouraging fist at his side as he watched his younger brothers play, observing the game's progress through one of many lead-paned, Tudor windows that lined the west side of the Earl of Edgewater's grand manor house.

Stifling an envious sigh, he leaned closer to the open window, the scents of oak pollen and ripe summer breezes redolent in the air. How he wished he could be down there with them now.

Racing over the grass.

Feeling the grip of the smooth-handled willow bat in his hands, his arm muscles singing as they absorbed the impact of a fresh hit.

The score wouldn't be so evenly matched, he knew, if he were among them. Not that Cade and Jack weren't holding their own—and admirably too—considering the size and age of some of the other boys playing. Twelve- and thirteen-year-olds against the Byron brothers' ten and eight.

Even four-year-old Drake was doing his utmost to insert himself into the action, ignoring the strictures of his nursemaid as he raced to collect the occasional out-of-bounds ball.

Were he anyone else, Edward knew he would have been free to join in like the other children of the guests assembled for today's christening celebration. But even at the youthful age of eleven, he understood that the heir to the Duke of Clybourne had far more important duties to attend to than an afternoon spent playing cricket—no matter how tediously boring those duties might be.

On the grounds below, Cade stepped forward and shook out his lanky arms with great fanfare as he prepared to pitch the ball. Edward grinned and silently cheered him on.

Suddenly a large male hand wearing a gleaming emerald signet ring cut across his line of sight—a strong adult hand that reached out to draw the window closed with a soft snick of the latch.

Edward stepped back, the noise of the game grown dim beyond the sealed portal. Shoulders straight, he turned a respectful gaze on his father, eyes moving upward to the powerful man, who wore a mature version of his own features.

Everyone said one day Edward would look exactly like

him. Sometimes when he gazed into a looking glass, he found himself wondering if their predictions would prove true.

"Those boys make a great deal too much noise," the duke observed. "I could hear Jack shouting all the way across the room."

Not sure how best to respond to such a remark, Edward stayed silent.

"Ought to send down word and tell them enough's enough, but I suppose they are only boys and know no better."

And so they are. So too am I.

Wisely, he kept his thoughts to himself.

"What's the score, then?" his father asked.

Edward's stance relaxed slightly at the casual inquiry. "Cade's team is down by two, but I think they'll make up the necessary runs during the next at-bat."

"I trust they shall. Well then, come along, Edward," his father said, laying a hand on his shoulder. "Important matters to discuss. You can watch the game later."

"Yes, Papa."

As he turned to follow the duke's lead, he caught sight of his mother watching them from across the chamber where she sat among a group of other elegantly attired ladies. Faint lines creased the smooth plane of her beautiful forehead, her soft lips drawn together. His gaze met hers and the lines vanished as though they had never been, her mouth turning upward as she sent him a gentle, loving smile.

He smiled back, puzzling for a few seconds over her initial look. Then he forgot all about it, as he hurried to keep pace with the duke.

They drew to a halt in front of a trim gentleman of moderate height, his thick blond hair brushed in careful waves, a diamond pin winking from the folds of his precisely creased neck cloth.

"My lord," the duke began. "Allow me to make you known to my son and heir, the Marquis of Hartsfield. Hartsfield," he said, nodding toward Edward. "This gentleman is a great friend of mine. Make your bows to the Earl of Edgewater."

Well versed in his manners, Edward bent at the waist. "How do you do, my lord? Thank you for inviting me to your home today, and on such a happy occasion as the christening of your new daughter."

The earl bowed in return, smiling as he straightened. "You are most gracious, my lord, and most welcome, though I would expect no less based on everything Clybourne has been telling me about you. I must confess I am vastly impressed. Understand you took top marks at Eton this past year and are even now being considered for early admittance to both Cambridge and Oxford."

"He'll be at Oxford outside of two years, and make no mistake," the duke stated in a firm tone, as if the matter were already settled. "My duchess thinks it's too early for a boy his age to be considering university. But she's merely being a cautious mother hen, who doesn't want to see her chick fly from the nest too soon. Hartsfield is up to the challenge, though. Aren't you, son?"

"Yes, Your Grace," Edward murmured, swallowing against the sting of nerves in his chest at the reminder—and the expectations.

"But come, Edgewater, we didn't bring the boy over here to discuss his educational prospects. We came to tell him the good news."

"Yes, yes, of course," the earl agreed, puffing out his slender chest with obvious anticipation and pleasure. "Should you like to do the honors, Clybourne?"

The duke waved a languid hand. "No, go ahead, Edgewater. It was your idea, after all."

"But you set me to thinking on it, so the credit must be mainly your own."

Standing between them, Edward forced himself not to show any reaction to their mysterious exchange. Whatever the "good news" might be, the sooner it was revealed, the sooner he would be able to find a way to escape outside and join the game.

"Perhaps you are unaware," the earl began, turning his gaze on Edward, "but a section of my property here in Nottinghamshire and one of your father's lesser estates share a common boundary."

"Yes, your lordship. The line runs contiguous for a few miles along the southernmost edge, I believe," Edward stated.

The earl beamed, a twinkle in his gaze. "Just so. You've taught him well, Clybourne."

"Of course. The title and land shall be his one day. He ought to know the extent and locations of his own holdings."

"What you may not know, however," Edgewater continued, turning back to Edward, "is that your father and I have been friends since boyhood. We went to Eton together and then to Oxford. For years it has been his dearest wish and mine that our two families might be even more closely and permanently allied. Which is why we decided to come to an arrangement."

"What sort of arrangement, my lord?" Edward asked, unable to keep from voicing his thoughts aloud this time.

"You shall see, Hartsfield. You shall see. But first, come meet my new daughter."

Edward frowned, wondering what the baby had to do with this particular conversation. But he supposed the earl had some purpose, if for no other reason than the pride of wanting to show the infant off.

Following behind his father and the earl, he made his way across the room to a place not far from where several of the ladies were gathered.

"Just going to borrow her for a moment," the earl informed his wife, as she cast him an inquiring look.

The infant, who until now had been peacefully sleeping, roused with a startled cry at being jostled awake. Her cries grew louder as the earl lifted her out of an immense rosewood cradle that had obviously been carved sometime in the last century.

Unfazed, Edgewater set her in the crook of his arm and brought her across to Edward. "Here she is, my lord. What think you of my Claire?"

Having worked herself into a near tantrum, Edward thought she looked as red and wet and angry as a lobster that had just been dropped into a vat of boiling water—her tiny features scrunched so tightly together that he couldn't tell if she even had eyes.

She sure has a mouth though, he mused ruefully. *And a fine pair of lungs. The next time the earl has reason to sound an alarm, he should prod this one awake again.*

"She's . . . um . . . quite healthy," Edward observed.

Edgewater chuckled. "That she is. Proof she'll grow into a fine young woman someday. Here, Hartsfield, why don't you hold her?"

Hold her! I don't want to hold that furious, squalling little creature.

But before he could refuse, the baby was thrust into his arms, leaving him no choice but to take her. She settled against him—warmer, softer and faintly heavier than he'd expected. Her tiny fists waved like a pair of batons in the air, her misery clear as she continued to wail.

Then, as abruptly as her crying had begun, it ceased. Blissful quiet descended once more over the room. As he watched, tension eased from her face, her fury-rouged cheeks standing out like burnished coals.

Her eyes popped open, her irises an entrancing pale blue that reminded him of a robin's egg he'd once found dropped out of a nest. They were red-rimmed, those eyes, and glistening wet with tears. She was staring now, her interest fixed on him as if he were the most fascinating thing she'd ever observed.

She sniffed and made a burbling little cooing noise, then waved one fist again, but not with anger this time. Instead, she seemed to be reaching out.

For him.

Bemused, Edward stared back, amazed at the change in her countenance now that he could adequately view her features.

Not so awful, he mused. He supposed he might even say she was pretty.

For a baby.

He'd been around babies all his life, as one brother after another was born. But he certainly wouldn't have called any of them *pretty*.

She waved her tiny fist again and blinked, her mouth curving in a faint smile.

"Well, look at that," the earl said in an amazed voice. "She's taken a shine to you already. I knew how it would be."

"Knew how what would be, your lordship?" Edward asked, still gazing at the baby.

"That the two of you are meant for each other. My Lord Hartsfield, meet your future bride."

"*What!*" Edward's gaze flashed up to meet the earl's, his hold wavering so that he nearly dropped the child lying so trustingly in his arms. Clutching her against him, he stared at her father.

Surely I cannot have heard him right? Surely he hadn't said bride!

"Your father and I have agreed on a betrothal between you and Claire. There's a parcel of unentailed land that will come to you through her dowry. Some excellent pasture which will increase your own holdings in this part of the country."

Land! What do I care about land? What about me? I didn't agree to this!

A heated refusal trembled on his lips, a violent protest that would denounce this appalling scheme. But then he caught his father's eye and knew any objections he offered would be completely useless. He would only create a scene, embarrass the earl and draw his father's ire. Besides, as he knew only too well, once Papa made up his mind, there was no trying to change it.

Swallowing past his anger, he held himself steady, jaw pulled taut as a rope. The baby shifted contentedly in his arms, oblivious to the turmoil at war in his chest.

"This union is years and years away, Edward," the duke reasoned in a quiet tone. "So think nothing more of it for now. When the time for the marriage arrives, you'll see the wisdom of this alliance and be grateful to have your future so easily arranged."

Grateful! How was he supposed to feel grateful when his entire life had already been decided for him? When he had no say over his own destiny?

Suddenly he couldn't bear to stand there another moment, fearing he might start screaming or something equally inappropriate.

Luckily, Lady Edgewater chose that moment to approach, halting beside him as she gazed with shyly loving eyes at her now sleeping infant daughter. Without a word, he pushed the baby at her, uncaring when he heard the child awaken again and begin to cry.

Pausing only long enough to execute a clipped bow, he mumbled an excuse and turned on his heels. He half expected his father to recall him, but he did not. Yet even if the duke had ordered him to return, he would not have obeyed. No punishment, he knew, could be worse than remaining now in this room.

Striding toward the door, he moved out into the corridor, his pace quickening with every successive step. He flew down the main staircase, then past a pair of footmen, who cast him curious glances but made no effort to impede his progress.

He burst outside into the moist summer air that clung to him like a suffocating hand. Or maybe it was his cravat that was doing the suffocating? All he knew was that he couldn't quite catch his breath. Couldn't slow the breakneck speed of his heart.

Stripping off his neck cloth, together with his coat, he dropped both garments on the lawn, forgetting them in an instant. From just over the rise, he heard sounds of the cricket match, as the game continued on.

Rather than going toward it, though, he turned away, staring across the surrounding grounds—out across the wide green fields, the manicured gardens and the nearby forest with its mass of towering trees.

Without any conscious sense of choice, he moved toward the forest, wanting to lose himself inside those sheltering branches and leafy boughs.

He went faster, then faster still, until he was running.

Running as if he might never stop.

Chapter 1

Marsden Manor
Nottinghamshire, England
January 1811

Lady Claire Marsden drew her dark blue woolen shawl tighter over her shoulders and thought about adding an extra log to the fire. She would have liked to light a candle as well to better see the fine stitches in her embroidery, but Papa frowned on the use of candles during the day. Not because the household couldn't afford them. Quite the reverse actually, since the Earl of Edgewater was a wealthy man. But he abhorred waste of any kind, and the burning of candles in daylight hours was chief on his list of forbidden indulgences—even on dim, dreary winter afternoons, such as this one.

Snipping off the end of a thread with a scissors, she listened with half an ear to her sisters bickering.

"Give me back that lace! I'm trying to trim my hat."

"Try all you like," taunted fourteen-year-old Nan. "But it

shall do nothing to improve the ugly thing. I've seen canine rectums that had a prettier shape and color."

"Did you hear what she just called my bonnet?" demanded Ella. "She said my velvet hat looks like a . . . a . . . a dog's bottom! How dare you, Nan Marsden. How dare you say such a horrid thing to me."

The younger girl smirked at her sixteen-year-old sister as she danced around the family sitting room holding the stolen lace high above her head. "Can I help it if you have wretched taste? Truly, you should spare all our eyes and toss that monstrosity in the fire. The brown color alone is enough to put one in mind of—"

"Why, you little fiend." Reaching out, Ella made a grab for the lace and bumped into an end table instead, nearly oversetting the vase on top.

"All right, you two, that is quite enough," Claire admonished. "And you'd best not let Mama hear such talk or you'll both be scrubbing the taste of soap off your tongues for a week. Now, Nan, apologize to your sister for your rude remarks and give her back her lace."

"But Claire—" Nan protested.

"No buts. Apologize now."

With a grumble, Nan did as she was told. Begrudgingly, Ella accepted her younger sister's words of regret, giving a stiff nod as she reclaimed her property.

Claire bent her blond head over her stitchery and hid a smile. "As for that bonnet, Ella," she remarked a moment later. "You really could do much better. It's woefully in need of a proper burial."

"I don't much care for it either," Ella confessed, "but Papa won't give me the money for a new one. You know how he is about allowances and I've already spent mine this quarter. It's this or nothing."

Claire knew the feeling only too well. She was considering alternate possibilities to suggest to her sister when a knock sounded on the door.

"Excuse me, miss, but a messenger just come with a letter," the servant explained with a quick curtsey. "Thought I ought ter bring it up direct-like."

"Lady Edgewater is lying down in her room. You may leave it over on the table and I shall see she receives it directly."

"Oh, but it ain't fer her ladyship. 'Tis addressed to you, Lady Claire."

"Me?"

Normally Claire didn't receive a great many letters, and none by messenger that she could recall. Curious, she reached out a hand for the missive.

The first thing she noticed was the elegant vellum paper and the thick red seal affixed on the reverse. Her heart beat faster as she stared at the design with its three overlapping heraldic shields hardened diagonally into the wax.

Fighting a sudden urge to tremble, she forced herself to flip the letter over. And there it was, her name and direction penned in a rarely seen, but never forgotten, hand.

His hand—the flawless script flowing with a dark sophistication that made all the memories come flooding back at once.

What very few of them there might be, she mused with a rueful tilt of her lips.

So, is my time up, then? Has my summons finally arrived?

Breaking open the seal, she scanned the contents and found her answer.

"Who's it from, Claire?"

Her sister's innocent question shattered her reverie, her head coming up with an almost guilty jerk. "Oh . . . um . . . no one. No one in particular, that is."

Unless, by particular, you mean the man to whom I've been betrothed for nearly the whole of my one-and-twenty years.

Growing up, she'd always known two things. First, that as the eldest daughter she was expected to always do her duty. And second, that someday she would become the Duchess of Clybourne.

Her sisters knew about the arrangement, of course; the entire family did. Every so often, the topic would arise and be discussed for a brief while before it faded into obscurity once again. And as the years had gone by, she'd been content with the arrangement.

But now he had written to her.

Now everything was going to change.

Ella gave her a quizzical look, and Nan as well. But she didn't want to talk about it. She couldn't, having learned long ago to lock away her feelings on this particular topic.

Still, the girls were clearly waiting for her to say more. Fingers tightening on the paper, she shoved the letter into the cushions at her hip. "Ella, I had a thought about your bonnet. Why do you not simply borrow one of mine? You can use your lace to remake the style entirely and no one will ever suppose it's anything but new."

"Really?" A huge smile lit her sister's face, her attention instantly diverted. "Are you sure?"

"Of course. I'll even give you a length of my pink silk ribbon. Now why don't you and Nan run along to my room and pick out the one you'd like."

"Any of them?" Nan chirped. "Any except your new chip straw, that is."

"Even my chip straw, if that is the one Ella prefers."

Ella paused for a long moment, then raced across the room to envelop Claire in a fierce hug. "Oh, you're so wonderful! The very best of sisters. And not to worry, your chip straw is safe."

Claire laughed, then shooed them out.

When she could no longer hear their footfalls, or the staccato rhythm of their excited chatter, she reached again for the letter. Smoothing it out, she reread the words, pausing on the most important passage:

> *. . . I hope to renew our acquaintance. Should it prove acceptable, I shall wait upon you in a fortnight hence. I have taken the liberty of apprising your father of my intentions as well. Pray be of good health and felicitous spirits until next we meet.*
>
> *Yours,*
> *Clybourne*

A fortnight. A mere two weeks that would pass by in a flash, and then Edward Byron would be here.

The duke was coming to claim his bride.

You don't have to do this, you know.

The words repeated themselves in his head as Edward Byron, tenth Duke of Clybourne, drove his curricle up the country lane that led to the Earl of Edgewater's estate.

Oh, but I do, he thought in reply, barely aware of the winter-dormant fields that surrounded him on both sides, or the trees that stretched their bare limbs over the frozen earth like clusters of dark, bony fingers.

The sunny blue skies overhead were what had tempted him to ignore the January temperatures and drive himself today, rather than relying upon the wiser—and far warmer—option of traveling in his coach-and-four. His need for solitude had taken preeminence—the cold barely seeping through his heavy black greatcoat, leather gloves or hat, as he sped toward his destination.

Additionally, driving himself provided a soothing measure of distraction—one he found himself uncharacteristically in need of today.

"You realize, sweetheart, that you aren't obligated to honor this betrothal," his mother had told him a few days ago after learning of his plans to go through with the decades-old promise. "This was your father's doing and I have never approved. As much as I loved my dear Robert, he was wrong to force this arrangement on you two children."

"I'm three-and-thirty, Mama," Edward replied. "Hardly a child now. I know what I'm doing."

"Do you?" she questioned in a soft voice, concern dimming the clear green of her eyes. "And what of this girl? What of Lady Claire? Even after all these years, the pair of you are scarcely more than strangers. How many times have you even met her? Once? Twice?"

"Thrice," he defended, deciding not to mention that the first time had been as children and the last occasion when she'd been a girl of sixteen.

"I implore you to think about this before you proceed," Ava Byron had continued. "Consider how this will affect not only your life, but hers."

He had thought about it—a very great deal, in point of fact—spending the past several months mulling over the advantages and disadvantages of proceeding with the marriage.

As a boy, he'd reviled the idea of the match. As a young man, he'd chosen to ignore it altogether. But now that he was mature, he could see the merit of his father's actions—no matter how high-handed they might have been. In the end, he'd decided that his father had been right, and that Lady

Claire Marsden was the most logical, most expedient choice of bride.

She had an excellent pedigree, for one. She was pretty and—if past observation was to be relied upon—gracious and biddable, even if a bit shy. She carried herself well and had been trained from birth in the duties that would be required as his duchess. She was reported to be in excellent health and should be able to provide him with robust sons.

In return, he would provide her with a comfortable life—more than comfortable, since he was one of the wealthiest men in the country. With him, she would never want for anything.

As for love? Affection would come with familiarity, he was sure. And if it did not? Well, theirs would be no worse than most Society marriages, based on mutual respect and lineage.

It was true that two of his younger brothers had recently fallen in love and settled into extremely happy marriages. Cade and Jack were deuced lucky, he judged. That or foolish, since in spite of his admiration for their choices of bride, he didn't know if he cared for the idea of ever letting himself be so completely vulnerable to another person. Of opening his heart and mind to someone else and giving her that kind of power over him.

Then too was the unassailable fact that out of the literally hundreds of women he'd met over the years—and the more exclusive number with whom he'd chosen to be intimate—he'd never met a woman he couldn't walk away from. A woman he couldn't easily forget.

No, since his title required him to take a bride, he reasoned she might as well be Lady Claire. It's what his father had wished. What her father still wished. And what duty demanded.

As for Claire herself, he didn't think it was conceit that

led him to believe she'd always liked him. Based on her clear affection for him as a child, as well as the rapt glances she'd given him the last time they'd met, she should be ready, even eager, for the long-awaited match.

Drawing his horses to a stop in front of the earl's sprawling Tudor mansion, he realized he would very shortly find out.

"He's here, he's here!" Claire heard Nan exclaim, as her sister hurried into her bedchamber in a breathless rush. Ella followed at a far more demure pace, although her face shared Nan's excitement.

"The duke's in with Papa now," Nan continued. "Mama says you're to come down to the drawing room as soon as may be, so as not to keep him waiting."

No, Claire mused wryly, as she returned to gazing out of her window. *Heaven forbid we should keep His Grace waiting. After all, he is the only one permitted that particular luxury.*

But she hadn't needed Nan to inform her of his arrival. She'd been standing at the window when he'd alighted from his curricle. Her pulse had pounded at the sight of him, unable to help but notice, even from a distance, that he looked every inch as tall, dark and urbane as ever. The past five years had done nothing to lessen his devastating good looks. If anything, they appeared to have improved upon them. But she supposed she would have to verify that for herself once the two of them were standing in the same room together again.

She smoothed a hand over one of her best gowns—a long-sleeved, pale blue velveteen with navy ribbons at the high, empire waist and lace on the cuffs and collar. Then, taking a deep inhalation, she turned from the window. "Wish me luck."

Both girls smiled and moved to give her a hug. "Luck!" they called.

But somehow, as she left her sisters behind and descended the staircase, she didn't think the nature of their wishes was quite the same as her own.

Inside the drawing room fifteen minutes later, she was listening with only half an ear to her mother's harmless chatter when the duke appeared in the doorway. Thankfully, she was already seated, otherwise, she feared her knees might have betrayed her. With her heart beating fast and her stomach quivering, she glanced up and met his intense midnight blue gaze.

As she had suspected earlier when she'd glimpsed him through her bedroom window, Edward Byron was still the handsomest man she'd ever met. His face appeared as though it had been sculpted by a master's hand, with a smooth forehead, straight nose and elegant cheekbones that tapered down to a strong, square, almost rugged jawline and chin. His lips were nicely angled as well and utterly masculine—the lower one slightly fuller than the top, with a tilt that was devastating when he smiled.

His hair grew thick and dark as rich mahogany wood, while his brows lay like heavy slashes over his penetrating eyes—giving him an appearance that was either fierce or kind depending upon his mood. As for his physique, he was blessed with broad shoulders, a strong chest and long, well-muscled arms and legs.

Yet it was the way he held himself that gave him a distinguished air. It's what came of being a duke, she supposed. Then again, perhaps it was Edward Byron himself, since she knew of no one else who carried himself with such natural grace and confident assurance. A leader by birth and ability, he commanded whatever room he entered. Without even trying, he commanded this one now.

How magnificent he is, she thought. *What a shame that he holds no more genuine regard for me than he does a stranger. But then again, that's what we are, is it not? Strangers.*

Glancing away, she stood, using the momentary distraction to reassert control over her emotions and her expression as well.

Striding forward, the duke stopped and made her an elegant bow. "Lady Claire."

She sank into an answering curtsey. "Your Grace."

He and her mother exchanged pleasantries before Mama launched into several overly effusive remarks about the weather and the graciousness of his call; comments that very nearly bordered on the ridiculous under the circumstances. Finally, her mother ceased speaking and glanced between them with knowing eyes. Making an excuse about needing to talk to the housekeeper, she left the room.

Quiet descended with the closing of the door.

"How have you been?" the duke began after a long moment. "You look quite well. If I may say, you are much grown since last we met. Taller, I believe?"

"Yes, I would imagine by two or three inches. Girls have a way of continuing to grow past the age of sixteen, whether they might wish to do so or not."

A gleam shone for a moment in his eyes. "You are nearly my sister's height. You must make a comparison of the matter when you have an opportunity to meet her. I hope you and Lady Mallory will find each other pleasant company when that day arrives."

"Thank you. I am sure your sister is a most amiable young lady."

A gentle smile curved his mouth. "She is indeed."

He paused, giving her time to take a seat. She did so, sliding into one of the Sheridan chairs rather than returning to her previous place on the sofa. Once she was settled, he followed her lead, lowering his tall frame into a matching chair with an ease that belied his size.

A width of four feet stretched between them. A far wider gulf existed in the atmosphere.

Again, he began first. "As I expect you are aware, I had the occasion to speak with your father only a few minutes ago."

Her fingers tightened in her lap and she gazed at a vase on the mantel—empty this time of year, since there were no flowers in the garden to fill it.

"He has given his consent for us to proceed with the wedding as soon as we wish. I thought you ought to be the one to set the date and choose the location. Would you like to be married here in your home parish, or at Braebourne perhaps? There is a fine chapel on the estate that I imagine you would approve."

She swallowed and said nothing, knowing he expected her answer.

"Or would you rather the ceremony take place in London? St. George's is a most popular choice. My brother Cade had his nuptials there nearly two summers ago."

Again he waited.

Her pulse thudded with a flood of nerves. Finally, she turned her gaze to his. "Actually, Your Grace," she said, forcing herself to speak in a strong, clear voice, "I am afraid that none of them will suit."

One black brow arched upward. "You have another place in mind?"

"No. You see, it's just that I'd really rather not."

"Rather not?" he repeated in clear confusion. "Rather not what?"

"Marry. I do not wish to be wed."

Chapter 2

Edward rarely found himself at a loss for words, but as he stared across at Lady Claire Marsden, with her peaches and cream complexion and her soft golden hair, his mind went absolutely blank for several long seconds.

What had she just said? Something about not wishing to marry? Surely, he decided, *I must not have heard her correctly.*

"Your pardon, Lady Claire," he ventured. "But would you repeat that please?"

Beneath his appraising gaze, she squared her delicate shoulders and lifted her small, attractively rounded chin, her translucent blue gaze very bright in her face. "I said that I do not wish to be m-married."

So I did hear her right!

His eyebrows drew into a scowl. "Your father gave me to understand quite the opposite not half an hour ago. He informed me you had agreed to this union."

Her honey-colored brows furrowed. "Papa has fixed

opinions about a great many things and does not believe in the necessity of inquiring over other people's wishes, particularly if they do not happen to coincide with his own."

Edward took a long moment to consider her statement. "I see. I did not realize you had any objections, especially considering the lengthy duration of our betrothal." He paused again, his eyes narrowing as a new thought occurred. "Is there someone else perhaps? A beau of whom your father does not approve?"

Her lips parted in obvious surprise. "No, Your Grace, there is no one else. We live a very quiet existence here at Marsden Manor. There is the occasional dinner or card party with our neighbors, but rarely do we go to the assemblies. Papa thinks it's a waste of time and expense to attend. My year at the ladies academy in Bath was more than enough costly socializing. He said much the same about giving me a Season in London. An unnecessary expenditure for a girl whose future is already settled."

So that was the reason she'd never come to London. Although he had to admit he hadn't given it much consideration before. Until recently, he'd always thought of her as a child, too young for beaux and parties—or marriage. But she was one-and-twenty now and well past the age when most aristocratic young women had their presentation to Society. He ought to have questioned her situation sooner and wondered over her absence from Town.

"So your objection lies with me, then? You believe we would not suit?"

Her lovely eyes widened before she glanced away, the room growing so quiet of a sudden that he could hear wind tugging at one of the windowpanes.

"I believe, Your Grace," she said, as her eyes lifted again to meet his own, "that we barely know one another. I have not the basis to judge whether or not we shall truly suit."

Abruptly, he relaxed, not realizing until that moment how tense he'd been. "Well, that's a situation which can be remedied easily enough. And we need not set a wedding date right away. Many couples wait several months before they exchange vows, and we may do the same. During the engagement, we'll have plenty of time to get to know each other better." He paused again, studying her expression. "Unless you have taken a dislike to me."

Color washed into her cheeks and she glanced away once more. "I do not dislike you, Your Grace," she murmured in a low tone. "It is simply that I do not wish to . . . m-marry, as I told you before."

"You mean not marry at all?" His eyebrows shot up. "Now that would be a crime against humanity. Besides, a young woman in your position *must* marry, you have to know that."

"I know nothing of the kind. Can you not simply go to Papa and tell him you have changed your mind? That you do not wish to honor our betrothal after all?"

"No, I am afraid I cannot," he said in a serious tone. "I have considered this fully and a marriage between us makes excellent sense. I have my duty to uphold, as well as my lineage, and I believe you will make an admirable duchess. My father thought so and yours does as well." He leaned forward and reached for her hand, noting that her fingers were cold and stiff.

"You will not find me a difficult husband, Claire. I promise to make no untoward demands upon you and you shall always be treated with the utmost respect. I will want an heir or two, I admit, but not until you are ready. You may have as much time as you require to feel at ease in my company."

Which, he thought, *is a great deal more than most young women are given*. In the Ton, it was the rare couple who knew each other well before marriage, since unmarried men and women were permitted little opportunity to be alone together. They might meet a few times at a ball or party, share a walk or ride out in an open carriage, but their interactions were hardly the stuff of great intimacy. For many, that level of interaction came after the vows were said.

Then he recalled her missed Season and their utter lack of a normal courtship. Mayhap it would please her to have her presentation at court, to be a debutante, however briefly, even if the exercise was, in many regards, only for show.

"Why do I not speak with your father again and tell him that you must travel to London for the Season," he said in a gentle tone. "That way, you may have your come-out, after all. Once the summer is over, we will be better acquainted and you may settle then on a wedding date."

Slowly, she pulled her hand from his. "And that is your final decision? That we shall marry regardless of my wishes? Is honoring this betrothal so very important to you then?"

Is it? he considered, remembering again his mother's urging to abandon the old promise and simply walk away. And yet he found he didn't want to. He needed a suitable duchess, and the idea of starting the search afresh left him unbearably weary. He'd seen the crop of eligible ladies, and none of them stirred the least hint of interest within him. And as he'd already reasoned on his journey here, Lady Claire had been bred for the role and would make an excellent helpmeet.

She might believe she didn't want this marriage, but he was confident he could change her mind. Perhaps he didn't have the same wild reputation as his brothers, but he well knew how to woo a woman. He didn't believe it a boast to say that all Byron men were skilled in the art of seduction—a gift that seemed to run in the blood.

As he studied Claire now, he forced himself to see her through a man's eyes—not as the infant he'd once held, but as a woman fully grown. What he saw pleased him, more than he might have imagined.

Her height, as he'd already noted, was slightly above the average, but that was only to the good for a tall man like himself. Her bone structure was delicate, with small hands and wrists. He speculated that her ankles and feet shared similar proportions and wished of a sudden that he could tug up her skirts a few inches to find out. Her figure was slender and pleasingly formed as well, with curves in all the choicest locations.

As for her face, she was lovely, with an almost ethereal kind of beauty. Her oval features were very English, very refined, with luminous blue eyes, a pert nose and lips that were shaped like a bow.

When the time came, making love to her would be no burden, but rather a delight. He knew he would enjoy teaching her that there was pleasure to be found, even in the midst of doing one's duty.

"You are correct," he stated. "My mind is quite firm in this regard. I feel it incumbent upon us both to honor the wishes of our families, no matter the admittedly feudal nature of our alliance. But as I said, we have time. After all, we've been affianced for the past twenty-one years. What's another several months, give or take a few?"

Her bow of a mouth lengthened into a tight line. "Well then, I suppose you leave me little choice. We shall proceed as you suggest, Your Grace."

He smiled. "In a spirit of accord, I would ask that you call me Edward, at least when we are in private. I hope you will grant me leave to call you Claire?"

"If you wish, Your Grace . . . *Edward*."

I cannot do this, Claire thought a few hours later, when she was once again alone in her bedchamber. *I cannot marry the duke.*

Yet circumstances were rapidly leading her down that

path, and if she could not find a way to prevent the nuptials, she would find herself standing with him at the altar taking vows.

Wrapping her shawl more tightly around her shoulders, she paced across the room. At least he hadn't accepted her mother's invitation to remain for dinner, sparing Claire the necessity of acting the happy fiancée in front of everyone. Instead, he'd closeted himself with her father for another brief exchange, then taken his leave, promising to call upon her again soon.

Now here she was, wondering what was to be done.

She paced a few more steps across the hand-loomed, brown woolen carpet, then sank with a tremulous sigh onto her bed. Resting her elbows on her knees, she covered her face with her palms.

The duke's countenance rose instantly before her mind's eye, every crisp feature and well-defined plane, replaced afresh over the earlier memory of him that she'd carried within herself these past five years.

Edward.

The man she was supposed to marry.

The man she loved and wished to God she did not.

For therein lay the problem. Edward Byron might want her for his wife, but he didn't want *her*—Claire Marsden. He didn't love her, and deep in her soul she knew he never would.

The remembered scent of honeysuckle teased her senses for the flicker of an instant, just as it always did when her thoughts turned back to that warm August night so many years ago . . .

Claire floated down the hallway that led to the gardens planted along the east side of the house. Or at least it seemed as though she were floating, since today was one of the most glorious days of her life.

And why should it not be? she mused, when she was sixteen years old and in love with the most wonderful man in all of England. Likely all of Europe too. For that matter, the whole wide world!

She giggled to herself at the notion, feeling half drunk even though she'd been allowed to sip only a single glass of wine at dinner, and watered wine at that.

Edward Byron was a dream and not just because he happened to be an incredibly handsome, immensely wealthy duke. Rather it was because of who he was as a person. Strong, thoughtful and intelligent, he possessed an intensity that made one feel uniquely special. When he set her in his sights, it was as though she'd been singled out to bask in a radiant beam of sunshine.

Or perhaps the munificence of a god.

Not that he was a god; she wasn't so foolish as to believe that. He was simply a man with the same faults and foibles as everyone else—although to date she had yet to glimpse a single flaw. Regardless, she was sure he must have some imperfection hidden away somewhere. Whatever the case, he was an amazing man with a charm and magnetism that had the power to send shivers racing over her skin even now. Her mouth grew dry at the thought, her step slowing as she paused to press a fist against her frantically beating heart.

Two days ago, when he'd first arrived at the house for her parents' weekend country party, she'd been a little afraid to meet him. After all, she hadn't seen him since she was a child, and even then he'd been an adult, being nearly a dozen years her senior. What if he thought her awkward? What if he decided she was plain? Or worse, a bore?

But the instant they'd met again, she'd been enchanted, his every word and gesture setting her completely at her ease. By that first evening, she'd been well and truly smitten. And continually amazed that the man to whom she'd been betrothed from infancy could turn out to be such a perfect match for her.

Of course he made no romantic overtures toward her, seeing that she was far too young yet for such declarations—at least not in front of her parents. But in two more years she would be a grown woman. In two more years she would be ready to take her place as his wife. Their fathers had agreed to the union, and so long as the duke still wished it, she was to be his bride! She could hardly wait, could scarcely catch her breath for the excitement and anticipation of being his to have and to hold forever.

Which was why she'd decided to follow him to the garden. Outside, where there would be an opportunity for them to be alone. Where the balmy darkness might tempt him to see her as a desirable young woman and maybe, if she was very lucky, coax him to steal a kiss.

A fresh rush of longing filled her, goose bumps rising on her bare forearms as she opened the door into the garden and padded through on slippered feet. Following the path most gentlemen took when they wanted to indulge in a cheroot, she hurried into the darkness. Her step slowed when she heard voices.

Immediately, she recognized the low, silvery tones of the duke, identifying the rumbling cadence of his words rather than their exact meaning. Then another person answered, a second voice that was higher and lighter—and distinctly female.

Claire drew to a halt, her movements soundless on the crushed shell path. She waited, hesitant about whether to withdraw. Then she heard her name.

"Pray do not tell me the rumors are true about you and that Marsden chit," the woman said. "Why, the girl isn't even out of the schoolroom. When Paula Syberton told me there is some understanding between you and that child, I was sure she must be having me on. Tell me I'm right so that I may give her a sound thrashing with my handkerchief when next we meet."

Very softly Clybourne cleared his throat. "As it happens, Lady Syberton is correct, at least in so far as the existence of an understanding. It is of very long standing, however, and not of my design. Nothing between the young lady and myself is settled. She is, as you said, scarcely out of leading strings."

Leading strings! Claire thought, her fingers curling into fists at her sides. *He makes me sound the veriest child when I am nearly a woman full-grown!*

"So she is," his companion agreed. "Still, some men like their females young and innocent. Have you no desire to take a bride?"

"A bride, yes, when the time comes, since the continuation of my line demands no less. But an infant? I think not," he retorted with an obvious shudder in his voice. "Don't mistake the matter, she's a nice enough little girl and pretty in her way, but I've no interest in taking her to wife."

"Then if you are not here to renew this old alliance of yours, why did you come for the weekend?"

"Edgewater and I have business, estate matters concerning rights usage of some adjoining lands. I thought it would be simpler to meet in person and resolve the situation amicably rather than get the lawyers involved." He sighed. "Besides, he's been sending invitations my way for ages. I thought it was time I finally accepted one and have done."

Claire hugged her arms around herself, suddenly cold in spite of the balmy evening air.

"Of course, the earl and countess have been pushing Lady Claire in my direction from the moment of my arrival. I've tried to be pleasant to her for her parents' sake, but I'm a grown man. What interest do I have in a sixteen-year-old girl?"

"What indeed?" agreed his companion in a sultry tone. Claire now recognized the voice as belonging to Lady Bettis. Beautiful, raven-haired, Society darling Lady Bettis, who was well-known for the interesting, influential lovers she took. So well-known that even she—sheltered, naïve Claire Marsden—had heard whispers of the woman's exploits.

"You're right that you'd be bored with a girl like her. Only a woman will do for you, darling. An inventive, experienced woman who can satisfy all your needs," Lady Bettis continued.

The duke chuckled softly. "Do I take it you're applying for the position?"

Felicia Bettis's laughter rang through the air like bells. "Oh, I know all sorts of positions. Care to try a few?"

Quiet descended. For a moment, Claire wondered what they were doing.

Oh stars, are they kissing?

She swallowed against the rush of bile that scalded the lining of her throat. She knew she should turn and hurry back to the house, but her legs refused to work, as immobile as one of the shrubs that were concealing her from view.

"So, you won't be marrying her then, not even in the future?" Lady Bettis murmured.

"Why do you care, Felicia, whom I may marry? Particularly since you already have a husband."

"Curiosity. No more. No less." She paused. "Oh, don't be disagreeable. Go on. Do tell."

"There's not much to tell, since I am far from certain of the answer. The only thing I know for sure is that I'm in no hurry to give up my bachelor status. But if I ever do decide to follow through on this betrothal to the Marsden girl, it will be for duty's sake alone. She has the bloodlines to make a proper bride, and luckily love isn't a requirement for the begetting of sons."

And that's when Claire turned and ran, when she could stand to hear no more over the sound of her own shattering heart.

She'd hated him for a long while after, determined to drive him from her mind and emotions. And as time passed, she'd nearly succeeded—hours elapsing during which she scarcely thought of him, then days, weeks and eventually months.

When she turned eighteen and her father decided not to give her a London Season, she'd made no complaint, inwardly relieved that she wouldn't have cause to encounter the duke. And when another year, then two, and three passed without any contact from Clybourne about the betrothal, she'd convinced herself that he'd rejected the idea of a marriage between them for good.

Then two weeks ago she'd received his letter.

And his visit.

The instant she'd watched him stride into her parents' drawing room and heard the rich, rounded tones of his mellifluous voice, she'd known that time had made no difference at all. A part of her might resent him, even hate him, but love lingered as well; the spark was buried deep but still burned improbably strong. All it would take was the faintest whisper to fan the flames back to life.

And that she could not allow.

A silly, girlish crush had nearly broken her. What would be left of her if she married him and fell truly and irrevocably in love? How would she survive knowing he cared nothing for her? That she was simply a duty and a convenience. A wellborn broodmare capable of giving him heirs and serving as his hostess and the chatelaine of his homes.

He might provide her with an easy, pampered existence. He might even be kind to her in his own way. But no amount of material pleasure could replace the one thing she needed the most. The one thing she was certain he would never share.

His love.

Some might argue that she should fight for his attention, his affection. And perhaps she might win. But what if she did not? What if she gave everything, only to lose? She knew enough to realize that the defeat would destroy her. That she would die inside one slow, small piece at a time, until all that remained was a ghost of someone who used to be Claire Marsden.

I cannot take that chance, she thought now, as she lifted her head and gave a sigh. *Not when he speaks of alliances and obligations. Not when he gazes at me with appraisal in his eyes, but no affection.*

No love.

Before she gave herself further opportunity to consider, she sprang to her feet and crossed the room. Marching out into the hall, she took the stairs at the quick clip. Her footsteps slowed, however, when she reached the door to her father's study.

Briefly, she hesitated. Then, straightening her shoulders as though preparing for battle, she raised a hand and knocked.

"Come."

At her father's softly worded command, she entered the room, careful to close the door behind her. She found him seated in an armchair near the fire, reading a newspaper by the light of a single candle. The meager illumination provided scant defense against the night-shrouded interior, leaving the room draped in thick shadows.

As she moved forward, the earl peered at her over the tops of his silver-framed spectacles. "Claire, what are you doing back downstairs?" he asked. "I thought you'd retired for the evening."

"I . . . um . . . I was going to, but I found that I could not sleep." Walking farther into the room, she sank into a nearby chair.

"Too excited, eh?" Her father gave her a wide grin. "And so you should be, now that the engagement is official. Just think, by this time next year, you'll be the Duchess of Clybourne and one of the most esteemed ladies in the land."

"Hmm, yes. That's what I . . . um . . . wanted to discuss. You see—"

"No need to be nervous, the duke will attend to all the particulars. Only look at how extraordinarily generous he has been already. When he mentioned giving you a Season in London, I assured him such an extravagance was entirely unnecessary."

Well used to Papa's parsimony, she gave no outward reaction to that bit of news.

"But Clybourne insisted," the earl continued as he ran a palm over his thinning blond hair, now liberally laced with white. "He insisted as well on bearing the cost of the whole venture! Said he wouldn't hear otherwise and that he must be given the pleasure of indulging you in this way."

In other words, Claire instantly surmised, Papa had balked at paying and the duke had found himself compelled to accept the expense in order to make good on his promise to her—a magnanimous offer on his part, she had to agree. But she wasn't here to think kind thoughts about the duke, but rather to see to her own well-being.

"That is generous indeed—" she said.

"More than generous," her father interrupted. "He's invited your mother as well, did I tell you that? Said you're both to live at Clybourne House in Grosvenor Square for the duration of the fashionable season. Told me he wanted to give you every opportunity to get to know him and his family better before the wedding."

He sent her an approving nod. "I understand the dowager duchess has her own suite of rooms there, and if I heard right, one of the duke's sisters will be in residence along with a pair of his brothers. Don't worry, though, that you'll be crowded for room, since the duke's town house is as big as a palace."

Papa chortled at the notion.

Claire didn't smile. She hadn't imagined the duke would expect her to live with him in his house, even with her mother and his own there to serve as chaperones. But why was she worrying over such matters when there were far more important issues at hand?

"Yes, I am sure the town house is lovely," she murmured, threading her fingers together in her lap as she rallied the nerve to state her case.

But to her frustration, her father interrupted again. "If you think Clybourne House in London is impressive, just wait until you see Braebourne, the duke's principal estate. Now there's a house and grounds that will turn your eyes round with awe. Majestic, it is, and no mistake. Most beautiful home in England to my way of thinking, and as luxurious as any kept by the royals themselves."

He waggled a finger. "Of course such extravagance isn't strictly necessary in order to maintain a well-run establishment, but as its mistress, you'll be able to exercise a measure of prudence here and there. Only consider that Braebourne shall soon be your home. You, my girl, are an immensely lucky young woman."

I don't feel lucky, she thought, as a lump of panic swelled inside her chest. *I feel trapped.*

"I can't do it, Papa," she said in a rush. "I cannot marry the duke."

Her father stared, his blue eyes boring into her for a long moment. Then he tossed back his head and laughed. "Very funny, child. For a second I thought you were serious."

She leaned forward in her chair. "But I am serious. Completely serious. Please know that I am fully sensible of the great honor of His Grace's proposal and what it would mean to be his duchess, but after much consideration, I realize that I cannot marry him. I fear that . . . we will not suit and I do not wish to be his wife."

The earl stared again, only this time his pale brows scrunched together—hard. "*What!*"

She flinched, cringing at the anger in his voice. "I—I know you want this marriage to proceed and that the union is one of long standing—"

"It certainly is of *long standing*, its duration nearly the same number of years as you have been drawing breath on this planet. What maggoty nonsense are you on about? Not marry Clybourne! Of course you'll marry him. You agreed to do so only a few hours ago."

"Yes, but I have since had time to change my mind. Please, Papa, I do not want to wed him. I just want to stay here with you and Mama and go on as we have been. I promise I won't be a burden and shall ask for nothing. You won't have to buy a single new dress for me all of this year or next if you wish. I won't ask for books or bonnets or extravagances of any kind. Just say I may write and refuse him. Please tell me I don't have to be his bride, after all."

"And then what? You're nearly two-and-twenty years of age, a circumstance I haven't found troubling given that you were promised to Clybourne. But if you don't marry him, you'll soon be a spinster and there'll be no one who'll have you."

Her eyelashes swept downward. "I am willing to accept that risk."

"Well, I am not," he told her in an implacable voice. "Neither is there the need to do so, since you have a perfectly good offer of marriage. An excellent offer of marriage from an honorable nobleman of unassailable character, who will always provide for your well-being and happiness."

My well-being, yes, she thought. *But my happiness . . . Why can Papa not see that is exactly what I am trying to protect?*

He drew an audible breath in a clear effort to regain control of his temper. "Cold feet, that's all this is. A few days from now, you'll be thanking me for refusing to let you withdraw. Go to bed and get some sleep. You'll soon enough change your mind."

She met his gaze, her jaw set with determination. "But I will not. Nothing shall sway me from my decision."

Her father fixed her with an assessing look. "And nothing shall sway me from mine. Hear me and heed my words, Claire. You *will* marry Edward Byron. This union is what I want, what your mother wants and what the duke wants. So unless Clybourne decides to act like a bounder and jilt you, the engagement between the two of you stands. Do I make myself clear?"

Claire glanced away again, fearing she might shame herself otherwise. "Yes, Papa. Perfectly clear," she said, swallowing back tears.

The earl huffed out a breath. "Well then, let us say good night so you may seek your rest. If you see your mother, please inform her I shall be up directly, as soon as I finish reading my paper."

She nodded, no longer trusting herself to speak. After a perfunctory curtsey, she let herself from the room.

To her profound relief, she managed to reach her bedchamber without encountering anyone. Trembling, she flung herself across the bed, sure that sleep would be the last thing she found there. She waited for the tears to start as well. Instead her eyes remained dry, thoughts spinning in circles through her mind.

You will marry Edward Byron.

I will not. Nothing shall sway me from my decision.

Unless Clybourne decides to act like a bounder and jilt you, the engagement between the two of you stands.

Unless he jilts you . . . jilts you . . . jilts you.

She sat up in bed, struck by a sudden thought. *What if the duke did jilt me!*

But no, he never would . . . unless she gave him reason?

A slow smile curved her mouth as the notion took hold.

Could she do it?

Did she dare try?

Oh mercy, they shall all be so angry with me. But what will it matter in the end if it allows me to gain my freedom?

Stretching onto her back, she began to plot.

Chapter 3

As he had only a week earlier, Edward drove his curricle up to the front entrance of Marsden Manor. Alighting from the vehicle, he strode through the door held open by the butler, pausing to exchange a few words with the servant as he divested himself of his greatcoat and top hat.

He was escorted to the same formal drawing room to which he'd been shown before, then the servant withdrew to inform Lady Claire and her mother of his arrival. The earl, it seemed, was away for the afternoon on business, a circumstance about which Edward had no complaint, since it was his fiancée he'd come to see.

Fiancée. How odd that word sounded in his mind. But he supposed he would soon enough grow used to the notion of finally and officially being engaged and, when the time arrived, being married as well.

A scowl settled over his brows as he turned to gaze out the window.

Five minutes passed.

Then ten.

The Marsden ladies did not join him.

Withdrawing his engraved gold timepiece from the pocket of his tobacco brown silk waistcoat, he consulted the hour. A quarter past three. Unless he'd mistaken the hour agreed upon for his visit, he'd arrived precisely as scheduled. Tucking the watch back into his pocket, he took a moment to ponder the novelty of being forced to fritter away his time. As a duke, it wasn't often that he found himself required to wait—for anything or anyone. Generally everyone waited for him.

Not that he sought such a reaction from others. In point of fact, he often wished that he had the luxury of being able to fade into the background and be a bit more ordinary than he was. Far too frequently he was subjected to the fawning behavior of those who hoped to earn his interest and approbation. Little did they realize their mistake, since he detested nothing quite as much as an obsequious toad eater scurrying around his heels.

But even among the nobility, he commanded a certain level of deference due to his elevated title. A heightened courtesy that had nothing to do with him as a person, but that was based instead on his position within the peerage. It was only around his family and friends that he could truly relax and be himself. And although the Marsdens would also become his family in a few months' time, he readily acknowledged that they were still on rather formal footing with one another at present.

But apparently not today, he thought with a faintly amused roll of his eyes, wondering how long the ladies planned to keep him waiting.

Another ten minutes passed.

He was wishing he'd had the foresight to bring a book with him when Lady Edgewater hurried into the room.

"Oh, Your Grace," she said in a breathless rush, her puce woolen skirts swinging as she clutched a hand to her heaving bosom. "Pray forgive my tardy arrival. I have been . . . that is, I was quite unavoidably detained. I hope you have not been waiting a dreadfully long while."

"No, not at all," he dissembled in a reassuring tone. "I trust nothing untoward has occurred?"

"Of course not!" Lady Edgewater declared with an audible, high-pitched squeak in her voice. "Everything is splendid! Wh-Why do you not be seated and I shall ring for tea."

He raised a brow at her unusual reaction, but decided not to remark on the subject. "Tea would be most welcome."

Giving an absent nod, Lady Edgewater crossed to the bellpull and gave a sharp tug. As she did, she craned her neck and glanced out into the hall. Her narrow shoulders slumped in obvious disappointment when she didn't discover whatever—or whomever—it was she'd been hoping to see. Turning back, she sent him a bright smile. "Your journey was pleasant, I hope?"

"Quite pleasant," he confirmed, waiting until she had seated herself before he did the same.

"Good, good," she said, shooting another glance toward the doorway. "The weather remains cold, but at least it is sunny."

"Indeed." He paused, casting a look toward the doorway himself this time. "So, will Lady Claire be joining us shortly?"

Judith Marsden flinched, then shot him another smile. "Of course. She'll be along any moment. She is . . . she is . . ." Her words trailed off as she searched for a way to end her sentence.

"Delayed?" he proffered.

"Exactly!" Lady Edgewater said, looking relieved as she

grabbed on to the word. "Claire is *delayed*. You know how girls her age can be. Gowns and hair and such. Never sufficient hours in the day to make oneself pretty enough, especially for one's fiancé."

So Claire is abovestairs fussing over her appearance?

His brows furrowed, not at all sure that he cared for the notion of having such an apparently self-absorbed, narcissistic bride. Then again, her mother was obviously making excuses and hiding some essential bit of information, so what precisely was the truth?

His future mother-in-law was clearly racking her brain for a new conversational gambit to cover the silence when a sound came from the doorway. He and Lady Edgewater both glanced up at the same moment and found Claire standing framed in the entrance.

But instead of the immaculately groomed young lady he'd been expecting, she looked a fright. Her golden hair encircled her head in a frenzied mass of wisps that had clearly escaped their pins, one slender hank straggling down to her left shoulder. Her fair cheeks glowed with a sheen of perspiration, a long, dark smudge decorating one cheek. She wore a plain linen dress of indeterminate color, the garment appearing to have been laundered so many times it was now little more than a shapeless, greyish rag. Her feet were shod in a pair of scuffed shoes with what looked to be a leather patch across one toe.

But the worst eyesore by far was the apron tied over her dress. Old and stiff, it was stained brown with huge smears and patches of some combination of matter whose origin he could only guess. Although based on a more careful inspection, he thought he detected grease, dried blood and bits of animal hair!

For long moments, all he could do was stare.

"You wanted to see me, Mama?" she said. "Nan said

you've been searching all over the house and that I was to come immediately."

Lady Edgewater said nothing, her expression one of utter horror.

Claire's gaze shifted toward him, her mouth rounding in a silent exclamation, as though she had only just realized he was in the room. "Your Grace! What are you doing here?"

He blinked, recovering himself enough to answer. "I am paying you a call. I believe I was expected, Lady Claire."

Her hands went to her cheeks. "Good heavens! Was that today?" Giggling with obvious nerves, she glanced away. "Mercy, forgive me. I completely mistook the date. I hope you haven't been waiting long?"

"A while. Your . . . um . . . mother has been kind enough to keep me company."

"I can only imagine what you must think of all this," she said, waving a hand over her disheveled attire. "I was down in the servants' wing helping with the tallowing, you see."

"The *what*!" her mother exclaimed.

"The tallowing. And pouring candles as well. You know how the servants' stores have grown low of late and that they were in need of replenishing."

"I know nothing of the sort," Lady Edgewater said, shooting Claire a look that could only be described as appalled. "Wh-What are you talking about? You don't make candles with the servants!"

Claire frowned. "Of course I do." Pausing, she darted a glance at Edward, then back at her mother, her gaze widening slightly as though struck with sudden understanding. "It's all right, Mama. We don't have to pretend about these things anymore, not since the duke and I are engaged. Isn't that right, Your Grace . . . I mean Edward. You did ask me to use your given name now that we are to be wed."

A strange choking noise issued from Judith Marsden's throat before the countess sank onto the sofa.

"Oh, look now, here is the tea," Claire observed, as a pair of maidservants entered the room bearing a pair of large silver trays. "How delightful," she continued, "since I am positively famished after all that work."

The servants arranged the tea service along with an array of biscuits, casting Claire a furtive glance or two out of the corners of their eyes before retreating from the room.

Edward watched as his fiancée crossed to the repast and reached for a plate.

"Claire!" her mother admonished in a restrained half whisper. "Surely you are not planning to dine with us until *after* you have refreshed your attire."

"I took care to scrub my hands before I came in. Besides, if I go upstairs now, the tea will be cold by the time I return. Do not worry, Mama. I am sure a big, strong man like Edward won't turn squeamish over a little stain here and there. Will you, Edward?"

She pinned him with a look, her eyes alive with innocence. And yet, as he gazed deeper, he thought he detected something more, an underlying glint of stubborn rebellion and, if he wasn't wrong, mischief. When he looked again, though, the expression had vanished, her gaze pleasant and untroubled.

He cleared his throat. "Whatever you prefer, my lady. I would not wish to curb your pleasure in any manner."

A wide smile curved her lips, lovely despite her untidy appearance.

"Although, if it wouldn't be remiss of me to suggest," he said, "I believe her ladyship would be more comfortable were you to remove your apron. It is rather . . . striking to say the least."

"Of course. Forgive me, Mama. But you know how I lose

track of these things, always elbow-deep into one mess or another."

"*Claire!* What on earth has gotten into you?" her mother said, finally recovering her voice. "You make no sense at all."

Smiling, Claire put a finger to her lips to pantomime silence. "I know. Mustn't let Edward in on our secrets. But I told you, Mama. It's all right. He'll find out everything soon enough."

"But there is nothing to find out!" the countess stated in an exasperated tone. She turned her gaze to meet his. "Your Grace, you must believe me when I say that we have been concealing nothing from you. Nothing at all!"

Claire gave a little shake of her head, then laid her plate aside long enough to remove her apron. Folding it so as to leave the clean side exposed, she draped it over a silk-covered chair. Her mother groaned and looked as if she might swoon.

"Now for some food," Claire stated, as she picked up the plate again.

He watched, bemused, as Claire prepared a plate piled high with little sandwiches and sweetmeats. For a moment he thought she planned to keep the hearty repast for herself. Instead, as if only then remembering her manners, she passed it to him. Murmuring his thanks, he waited while she served herself and her mother. Moments later, Claire took a seat.

Mutely, he bit into a biscuit.

Meanwhile, Lady Edgewater poured and served cups of tea, her hands shaking visibly while she did so.

"I suppose I'm not to tell you about my predilection for gardening either, Your Grace," Claire announced several moments later. "I just love digging in the dirt. Burying bulbs and planting tubers. Why, sometimes my sisters tease me that I grub around just like a little mole."

He stopped chewing, a long moment passing before he was able to safely swallow the last bite of biscuit in his mouth. Thankfully, he'd already set his tea aside. Otherwise he feared he would have inadvertently given himself a rather nasty burn.

"You do not grub around like a mole, Claire Marsden!" Lady Edgewater asserted. "You can't stand dirt of any kind and I do not know why you are saying these things today." With a mortified expression on her face, she turned toward him. "Your Grace, I apologize."

He studied his fiancée, trying to decipher her mood and behavior. Something wasn't right. Of course he didn't really know her all that well, and yet . . . Did she really make tallow candles with the servants and toil in the garden like some common laborer? Or did she only want him to *think* that she did? And if so, to what end?

"No apologies needed, ma'am," he told the countess. "Many young ladies are lured by the beauties of nature and the opportunity to coax plants and flowers from the soil. There is no indignity in tilling the earth. Actually, many would say there is no finer means of expressing the majesty of the Almighty's plan than growing life from His bounty."

Across from him, Claire sank her teeth into a small cake.

"Braebourne has extensive gardens and grounds. Once Lady Claire is installed there as its duchess, she will have leave to do as much gardening as she likes. In fact, now that I know how much she loves to grow things, I shall make a point of having a special plot laid aside where she can dig and till to her heart's content."

He saw a small frown settle between Claire's golden brows.

"I'll inform the gardening staff that no one is to touch the land but you, Lady Claire," he continued. "Why, in no time at all, I am sure you'll have it looking so beautiful it will be fit to rival the work of the great Capability Brown himself. So, how many plants do you imagine you will be wanting? Five hundred or a thousand?"

Claire sputtered, then swallowed in a hard gulp, her wide-eyed gaze flying across to meet his own. Drawing in an audible breath, she quickly recovered her equilibrium. "My abilities are nothing so grand. I'm more of a . . . dabbler in the garden, you see. I p-putter around here and there, but there is nothing serious in my endeavors."

"Ah. Well then," he said, "perhaps I have gotten ahead of myself on the subject."

"Yes, perhaps," she agreed, her eyes sweeping downward in obvious relief.

Not so enthusiastic now, is she?

"As for the tallowing," he continued in a falsely serious tone, "I employ a chandler who makes all the candles for the estate. I prefer to use beeswax tapers in the main house, of course, but maybe you could stop by on occasion to offer him a tip or two."

Her shoulders straightened, her delicate chin lifting in clear awareness of his underlying sarcasm. "I shall make a point of it, Your Grace."

She set her plate aside with a little *thunk*.

Lowering his head, he hid a smile.

A clatter of feet sounded in the hallway moments before Claire's younger sister Nan came rushing into the room. Skidding to a halt, she dipped a quick curtsey in his direction, then turned to her mother.

"Mama, I know you told us to stay upstairs, but something has occurred and you must come at once."

"What is it, child? Why are you not in the schoolroom with Miss Sampson?"

"I was, but Nipper got in and he went after Puff. Miss Sampson tried to intervene, but she ended up getting scratched and bitten. She's bleeding, and meanwhile Nipper has poor Puff cornered on top of one of the bookshelves. I thought I should come find you."

Lady Edgewater closed her eyes for a brief moment. "Saints preserve me, what a day," she muttered under her breath.

"I'll go, Mama," Claire offered, jumping to her feet.

"You'll do nothing of the sort. Stay with His Grace. I shall be back in a trice." Sending him a patently false smile, the countess sailed from the room, her youngest daughter hurrying in her wake.

Claire hesitated for several seconds more, then resumed her seat.

"Dog and cat skirmish, I presume?" he asked.

She nodded. "Nipper is a very naughty dog and Puff is terrified of him, which is why Nipper is not allowed in the schoolroom. Between the two of them, it seems they're always causing some mischief or other." She paused, a fresh glint entering her eyes. "Do you like animals, Your Grace?"

"Edward," he said, correcting her. "And yes, very much. I have a pack of hounds I keep at Braebourne and a couple of dogs who have the run of the house, both in Town and in the country. My youngest sister keeps cats and a flock of other assorted creatures on the estate as well. There are far too many to count."

The glint receded, almost as though she was disappointed to discover he liked pets. *What is her game?* he wondered. It was almost as though she was deliberately trying to put him off. Well, if that was her goal, she would soon learn that he wasn't deterred so easily.

Rebellious child.

Little did she know he had lots and lots of experience dealing with rebellious children. As the eldest of eight, he was long used to antics of all sorts. Although he had to admit she was inventive. And surprisingly amusing as well, he decided as he gazed again at her appalling attire and straggling hair. Once they were married, though, she would mature and put aside such foolish behavior. A subject that reminded him of the main purpose for his visit.

"Actually," he said, "I'm rather glad your mother had reason to leave us, since I was hoping we might have an opportunity to spend a few minutes alone."

Claire grew still. "Oh? Why?"

He quirked a brow, resisting the urge to smile at her candor. "So I can give you this. Somehow, I thought you might prefer not having an audience." Reaching into his coat pocket, he drew out a small square box, then popped open the lid to reveal a glittering diamond. "Your engagement ring," he announced.

She didn't say a word.

"Here, why don't you try it on to see if it fits." Removing the ring from its velvet bed, he held the jewelry between his thumb and forefinger and waited.

She didn't move.

"It's not going to bite, you know," he said with a half-exasperated chuckle.

She sent him a faintly mocking look before slowly extending her right hand.

He grinned. "Other one. An engagement ring is supposed to go on the left. Tradition holds that the veins in the left hand connect directly to the heart."

Her hand trembled slightly. "Then it seems I chose correctly the first time," she murmured, "since this arrangement between us has nothing to do with hearts."

His smile fell away. "Perhaps not," he said as he slid the

ring into place. "But I am convinced we shall fare well together regardless."

"As you say, Your Grace."

"Edward." He gazed into her lovely, clear eyes for a few moments before taking in the whole of her face. "You've a smudge."

"What?"

"On your cheek. Here, let me help."

"I can get it," she stated, reaching up to rub her fingers across her skin.

"Other cheek," he said, as his smile returned. "Please, allow me." Extracting a handkerchief from his pocket, he stroked the silk across her skin.

"Is it gone?" she asked in a tremulous voice.

"Almost." He rubbed in gentle circles until he'd lifted the mark free. "There."

"Thank you, Your Grace."

"Edward," he corrected in a patient tone. "Your hair needs arranging as well."

"My maid can help me."

"Your maid isn't here." Without waiting for permission, he captured the errant tress in his hand. Rather than tucking it into her coiffure, he looped it around his fingers, winding the deliciously soft strand around and around until there was no more hair left to wind. He let it go, watching it unfurl like a sail. But instead of retrieving it again, he stepped closer and cupped his palm against the side of her face. "I just realized there is something important I have yet to do."

"Wh-What is that, Your . . . Edward?" she whispered, her gaze locking with his own.

"This," he said.

And then he bent his head and pressed his lips to hers.

* * *

Claire couldn't move, her breath trapped inside her lungs, her heart slamming so hard in her chest her ribs ached.

She'd waited so long for this moment, her whole life it seemed, to taste her very first kiss. Once, long ago, she'd hoped Edward would be the one to give her that kiss. And then she'd hoped he wouldn't. But now, dangerous as it might be, that original wish was coming true.

She knew she should pull away, but she couldn't, the sensation of his mouth too glorious to resist. His touch was everything she'd ever dreamed of and more. Warm and firm, yet shockingly soft, as his lips moved over hers.

Patient. Infinitely patient.

And sweetly tender as well.

A shivery sigh rippled through her body, making her tingle from head to foot. Her toes arched inside her half boots as she sank deeper beneath his spell, heady delight roaring in her head like a misty, drumming rain.

One touch and he made her melt.

One kiss and the earth ceased to turn on its axis. Just think what might happen if he dared to do more.

And then he did, drawing the velvety tip of his tongue in a slow, hot glide across her lower lip. She gasped, the sound as startling as a clap of thunder in her ears.

He lifted his head, an expression of bemusement in his dark blue eyes. Seconds passed, as though he were trying to decide whether to kiss her again or let her go.

Then the decision was taken away, as footsteps echoed in the hallway outside the drawing room. Edward straightened and stepped away. "I believe your mother may be returning."

Claire stared blindly, first at him, then down at the carpet, as she struggled to shake off the pleasurable lethargy still humming through her veins. Clenching her fists at her sides, she turned and dropped into the safety of her earlier abandoned chair.

"The crisis has been resolved," her mother declared as she moved into the room. "So, how have you two been faring in my absence?" she inquired, glancing between Claire and Edward.

"Quite well, ma'am," he replied in a smooth tone. "We have managed to keep each other reasonably entertained, I believe. Is that not so, Lady Claire?"

Claire fought down a blush, resisting the urge to shoot him an accusing glare as well.

He's so calm, she thought. *How can he act as though we've been sitting here doing nothing more strenuous than talking about the weather?*

And then she realized that even though she'd just experienced the wonder of her very first kiss, their embrace had been far from the first for him. How many women had he known in his three-and-thirty years? How many kisses had he shared?

Hundreds?

Thousands?

Millions!

The last of her hazy delight fell away. She might be his fiancée and now wear his ring on her hand, but nothing essential had changed between them. She was still a convenience needed to secure his lineage. And he was still the man she couldn't afford to let herself love.

"Yes," she said in a clear voice. "His Grace has made sure I was far from bored. Now, if you will excuse me, I believe I shall seek my room for a change of attire."

"Good heavens, yes, child," her mother said. "Go change. We shall be waiting for your return. Your Grace, can you stay to dinner?"

"That sounds delightful. However, I'm afraid I must beg your indulgence once again. I just received a note from my mother and she asks that I return to Braebourne immediately. I leave at first light. My sister-in-law, Meg, is about to be brought to childbed any day and Mama wants me there for the birth."

"Every pardon, Your Grace," the countess said, "but what possible help can you be to your sister-in-law at such a time?"

"None whatsoever," he replied in an agreeable tone. "It's my brother who is in need of support. I'm to make sure he survives the ordeal."

The countess chuckled.

Claire said nothing, wondering at these other members of his family and realizing that she was going to have to become acquainted with them, after all. Today's plan to extricate herself from the engagement had failed dismally; she had this blighted ring on her finger to prove it. Like it or not, she was going to have to think of something else, a new strategy designed to convince Edward Byron that he didn't want her for a wife. But it seemed her plans would have to wait for now.

"Shall we see you next in Town then?" Claire ventured.

He turned her way. "Yes, I rather suspect that will be the case, since I am doubtful I shall be able to make the journey here again before you join us for the Season."

"Well then, London it shall be."

Reaching for her hand, he made her a bow. "Yes. London it is."

Chapter 4

"Welcome to Clybourne House!" greeted a musical feminine voice, as Claire and her mother stepped into the duke's elegantly appointed drawing room six weeks later.

A smile came instantly to Claire's face, as she found herself unable to do anything but return the infectious grin on the mouth of the beautiful, raven-haired young woman who had issued the greeting. Based on the other girl's resemblance to the duke, Claire could only surmise that she must be one of Edward's sisters—and obviously the one who was *out*, since his youngest sister was still a child.

"Lady Mallory?" Claire inquired.

"Yes! And you must be Lady Claire and Lady Edgewater. What a pleasure it is having both of you here, especially since Mama is away at present. My sister-in-law is confined, you see, and Mama has gone to attend the birth. The baby is due any day now."

The countess frowned. "I thought your sister-in-law had the child last month? A boy, I believe?"

"Oh, that is my *other* sister, Meg. Yes, she did have her baby and she's doing splendidly. We're hoping she'll bring little Maximillian for a visit this summer so we can see just how adorable he is. My sister Grace is the one due to give birth any time now."

"Heavens," Lady Edgewater said. "Two births in two months. No wonder your mama has her hands full."

Mallory laughed. "Leave it up to Cade and Jack to have such impossible timing. First the hasty weddings, and now the babies one right after the other!"

Claire watched her mother's eyes widen at that statement and its potentially shocking implications. But Lady Mallory seemed to find nothing at all amiss in the remark, her smile just as bright as before.

"Oh, but forgive me for keeping you standing here," Mallory said. "I am sure you are weary from your journey and longing to relax and refresh yourselves. Let me show you upstairs to your rooms."

Moving out into the hall, Mallory led them across the wide marble-tiled entrance hall to the staircase. "I must say it will be lovely having ladies in residence again," she stated. "With Mama away and Esme traveling with her, it's just me and my brothers. Or at least a few of my brothers—the twins, Leo and Lawrence, and Drake when he feels like dropping by for a visit. Oh, and Ned, of course."

Ned?

She must mean Edward, Claire realized, not aware until now that he went by a diminutive. Privately she thought of him as Edward. She didn't imagine she would ever be able to get used to anything else. Then again, if the name annoyed him, perhaps she could make an exception.

Hiding a little smile at the thought, she trailed after Mallory. Reaching the landing, they turned and walked along a broad, well-appointed hallway.

"I take it His Grace is not home at present?" Lady Edgewater asked.

Mallory shook her head. "He had business across Town, but should return in time for dinner. Gracious, he asked me to convey his regrets at not being here to greet you. I should have done so immediately, but quite obviously I forgot. What a goose you must think me," she finished with a self-deprecating laugh.

Claire shared a smile.

"Here we are, Countess," Mallory announced a few moments later. "You are to have the blue room. I trust you will be comfortable, but should there be anything you need, you have only to say."

Claire peered into the room, then blinked at the beautiful furnishings, the elegant draperies and wall coverings done in soothing shades of cream and blue. She could tell without asking that her mother was delighted and doing her best not to reveal her pleasure at the luxurious accommodations.

"This shall do nicely," her mother said, strolling inside the room.

Leaving the countess to the ministration of her maid, Mallory took Claire down another one of the corridors. As they walked, Claire couldn't help but notice that every inch of the town house conveyed a sense of taste and refinement. From the fine oil paintings on the walls, the Aubusson carpets on the gleaming wood floors, to the clean scents of fresh flowers and beeswax polish, no detail was left unattended. Although Claire had been raised in an atmosphere of wealth and privilege, she had never known anything quite as grand as this. And if Edward's town house was so exquisite, what must Braebourne be like?

Then again, if my plan succeeds, she mused, *I suppose I shall never find out.*

"I really am so very pleased to meet you," Mallory said,

as they strolled onward. "I wish I could say that Edward has told me everything about you, but I'm afraid he has said very little."

"That sounds like His Grace."

Mallory laughed. "I suppose it does at that. He's a very private man. On the other hand, when the mood strikes, his tongue wags as well as the rest of ours and there's scarcely any shutting him up."

The idea of a loquacious Edward sounded unlikely yet intriguing. He was always so formal and precise. Although there'd been nothing formal about their kiss, an experience that had the power to resonate within her even now.

To her sudden relief, she had no more time to contemplate such notions as Mallory stopped and opened a door. "This," the other young woman declared, "is your room. For the time being at least. Once you marry Edward, you will move into the duchess's suite in his section of the house."

"He has a section?"

"Oh yes. Though nothing so large as at Braebourne. He has an entire wing there. But come, tell me what you think."

Gazing around, Claire decided the room was utterly charming. And soothing, done in muted tones of peach and rose with sheer, warm-white curtains and a rectangular rug decorated with tiny, gold Grecian keys. The satinwood furnishings were carved in a light, sophisticated style that harkened back to late in the last century, while the bed was wide and comfortable-looking—a pale rose counterpane spread invitingly over the plump feather tick.

"I think it's simply lovely," Claire murmured, smiling as she walked deeper into the chamber.

Mallory's face lit with a smile. "Traditionally ducal brides-to-be stay in a room at the other end of the house, since it's larger and overlooks the square. But Edward thought you might like this one better. The furnishings here are so airy and you have a gorgeous view of the garden. Plus it's delightfully quiet in case you wish to sleep late once the Season begins."

Edward suggested it? How unexpectedly thoughtful of him. And observant, since obviously he had realized she would like this room. Then again, after their last encounter, perhaps he was trying to placate her, butter her up a bit so she would fall in with his wishes more easily.

"His Grace is most kind," she said.

"Ned is, actually, even if he puts on a stern face sometimes. All of us just hate to disappoint him, though we still do so with depressing frequency," Mallory said, adding a humorous smile at the last.

Yes, well, I plan to disappoint him quite severely if I have my way.

"I should leave you to change and rest," Mallory said. "Let me know if there's anything you need, even if it's only to talk."

Claire's mood softened, finding herself liking Edward's sister a great deal, probably more than she ought. "I look forward to seeing you at dinner, if not before."

Mallory nodded, then turned toward the door. As she did, a flash of light sparkled on her hand, Claire's gaze going straight to the gleaming ring on Mallory's finger. "Oh," Claire said without thinking, "do you have one too?"

"One what?"

"A ring. I didn't realize that you are engaged as well."

Mallory held out her left hand, staring for a moment at the gemstone. "Yes."

"Will the wedding be soon?"

"No, not soon. Michael is away fighting on the Peninsula. I would wed him in a heartbeat, but he wants to wait until things are more settled with the war. He won't hear of me going abroad with him. He says I'll be safer and happier staying here and I suppose he's right. Still . . ."

"Yes?"

"It's very hard to wait, and worry, though I do my best to keep my spirits high. Which is why I'm so vastly glad you've come to stay. The Season will start soon. Before it does we can visit all the shops on Bond Street. Do say you love to shop."

Given her father's frugal ways and edicts, Claire had long ago resorted to finding other methods of entertaining herself, namely ones that did not involve spending money. However, just because she'd trained herself to be frugal didn't mean the spending impulse wasn't still there.

"Of course I do," Claire said. "What woman doesn't love to shop? And I am in need of a new pair of gloves and some handkerchiefs to refurbish my current supply."

Mallory's aquamarine gaze sparkled with a knowing light. "Oh, you're to have a great deal more than that. Have you not heard? Edward has agreed to give you a trousseau. Whatever you like. I heard him say so myself."

Claire stood in astonishment. "No, I was not aware."

Leave it to Papa to convince the duke to pay for my wardrobe.

"I'm to take you in hand," Mallory continued. "With your mama's help, of course. You're to be outfitted from head to foot. I can scarcely wait."

"Neither can I, it would seem."

"Well, I had best leave before I talk your ear all the way off your head. Until later."

"Until later."

Dinner that evening was a quiet family affair. Or at least it would have been quiet had Claire and her mother been residing with anyone other than the Byrons.

Despite the elegant atmosphere and delectable, sophisticated cuisine, Claire soon realized that the Byrons were as talkative and lively as Mallory had told her. Particularly the twins, Lords Leopold and Lawrence, who lounged in their chairs like a pair of sleek young hunting cats, devilment dancing in their warm hazel eyes as they ate their dinner and sipped from their glasses of wine.

Even now, as the entire family made its way to the drawing room for after-dinner tea and brandy, Claire found herself struggling to tell them apart. Identical as two peas, the twins were both tall and leanly broad-shouldered, with heads of thick golden brown hair and faces so handsome she was sure they regularly drew admiring sighs and wistful glances from any number of hopeful ladies. Were it not for the fact that one twin had a slightly greater amount of green in his green and gold eyes, she would have no hope of distinguishing one from the other.

And then there was Lord Drake, who had put aside one of his experiments for the evening so he could meet her. He was tall and dark with the same gorgeous features as the rest of his siblings. And charming, at least when he paid attention long enough to make the effort.

Earlier, Edward had informed her in a proud, serious tone that Lord Drake was a genius who held several advanced degrees from Oxford and Cambridge. His theoretical work was lauded in the scientific and mathematical communities, and if Drake occasionally appeared to drift away, it was merely because he was having one of his *insights*.

She found Drake equally amusing and endearing, with a keen intellect that clearly took him off into worlds of thought that she imagined only a handful of other people on the planet could even attempt to understand.

Watching now from her place on the sofa, she saw him draw a pencil out of his jacket pocket and begin scribbling something on the back of a calling card. A fresh flash of genius, she assumed.

"Tea?" asked a honeyed masculine voice near her left ear.

"Or sherry?" inquired an identical voice from her right.

Quick as a pair of foxes, the twins took up flanking positions on the sofa, pinning her neatly in between. Glancing from one to the other, she laughed. "At the moment, I'm not sure."

The greener-eyed one—Leo, she believed—sent her a dashing smile. "Not to worry, there are plenty of hours left in the evening."

"Exactly," the twin she surmised to be Lord Lawrence agreed.

"I admit I can see why Edward has kept you hidden in the country all these years," Leo continued. "You're quite a beauty."

"He probably worried one of us might try to steal you away." Lawrence leaned a hand on the back of the sofa.

"Most definitely," Leo agreed. "Shall we try to lure you away now?"

The brothers exchanged wicked looks and chuckled in tandem.

"How old did you say the two of you are?" Claire ventured, suddenly feeling out of her element.

"Eighteen," Lawrence said.

"Nineteen, this July," Leo clarified.

Thirty is more like, she thought. She was three years their senior and yet she felt a complete innocent in their midst. "Is this really your first Season?" she asked.

Two dark golden brown heads nodded, while two identical mouths smiled.

"Your first too, I understand," said Leo. "Vastly exciting, ain't it? I can hardly wait for the parties to begin."

"Although we've gone to a few already," Lawrence volunteered. "None to which we could escort a lady, however."

Before she had a chance to reply to that salvo, Edward appeared. "Enough, you two," he said. "I believe you're scaring my fiancée to death."

"No!" denied Leo, his attractive brows drawing close.

"'Course we aren't," protested Lawrence. "Are we, dear Lady Claire?"

"Well, I . . ." she began.

"See," Edward said, "you've thoroughly discomposed her and on her very first evening in Town. The both of you owe Lady Claire an apology."

Before her eyes, their suave bravado fell away. "We didn't mean any disrespect. Truly," Lawrence defended, abruptly sounding his eighteen years.

"Not a bit. We were only teasing and having a little fun," Leo added with equal chagrin.

"You can have fun at someone else's expense." Crossing his arms, Edward fell silent, his disapproval plain.

In unison, the twins sprang off the couch, each one reaching in turn for her hand.

Lawrence went first, bowing low. "I most humbly beg your forgiveness, if my behavior has offended you in any way."

"And I as well," Leo said, sincerity plain in his hazel eyes. "We're thoughtless buffoons sometimes. We know you are to be our sister and are deuced glad of it. Pray say you forgive us so we may begin again."

"There is nothing to forgive," she said, "but you have it nonetheless."

After making her another pair of respectful bows, they strolled across the room and took up places next to the fireplace, dark golden brown heads bent together in consultation.

Edward reached down a hand to draw her to her feet. "Sorry about that."

"Honestly, I wasn't alarmed or offended," she said, as she let him assist her from the sofa. "They just surprised me is all. You need not have been so severe upon them, you know. They are just boys."

"They're a plague, is what they are. A pair of inveterate flirts and scapegraces, who are going to make my life a misery over the next few months. I can only imagine the peccadilloes into which they are sure to land themselves. I probably ought to save myself the trouble and send the both of them packing back to Braebourne."

Without thinking, Claire laid a hand on his sleeve. "I hope you will not. I should hate to be the cause of any discord." At least not the kind that didn't involve her own personal issues with him.

He nodded. "I hope they'll realize and be grateful that they have you to thank for their reprieve."

Her mouth curved into a smile. "You wouldn't really have sent them away, would you, Your Grace?"

A long moment passed before he gave an enigmatic smile. Tucking her hand more tightly against his arm, he drew her into a slow walk. "We haven't had a chance to speak privately since you arrived. How are you finding the house? Is everything to your liking?"

"Yes, very much. You have a beautiful home."

His gaze met and held her own. "I am glad you approve."

For a few seconds she couldn't look away, her skin tingling as she realized precisely how close they were standing together, near enough that she could feel the warmth of his body through his sleeve and catch the clean scents of soap and man hidden in the clothing he wore. She found herself wanting to lean closer. Then called herself ten times a ninny for the impulse.

"My hope over the next few weeks," Edward said, "is that you will begin to think of this as your home. Because it is, you know. Or at least it shall be soon."

Trembling, she lowered her gaze.

"I see that Mallory is making her way to the pianoforte," he observed. "Perhaps you might care to join her for a song? I understand that you have an excellent singing voice."

"It is nothing remarkable, I assure you, Your Grace."

"Edward," he reminded. "And that is not what your mother says. Lady Edgewater informs me that you sing so sweetly you put canaries to shame."

She gave a dismissive shrug. "Despite my mother's praise, I don't believe that canaries have anything to repine over."

"Nevertheless," he said, drawing them to a halt next to the richly polished pianoforte, "I should like to hear you sing. Mallory, what do you say to accompanying Lady Claire in a song?"

Mallory's face brightened. "Of course. Have you any favorites?"

"Your Grace . . . Edward," Claire corrected. "I would really rather not perform tonight."

"But we are all family here," he said. "I would not ask otherwise, and I think you will find us a kind and generous audience."

"Oh, do say we may make a duet together," Mallory urged. "Your pretty voice will conceal any mistakes I may make in my playing."

Claire chuckled and felt herself weaken. "Very well, since you both insist."

Edward smiled, his deep blue gaze warming in a way that made her feel rather warm in return. With a bow, he excused himself and left her to consult with Mallory. From the corner of her eye, she saw him pause to converse with

Lord Drake before he took up a seat at the far end of one of the Hepplewhite sofas.

Paying only partial attention to Mallory as she discussed which song to choose, Claire silently weighed her options. Without his intending to, she realized that Edward had given her an excellent opportunity to shock and displease him once again. Or try to at least.

Her mother was right that she often garnered praise from others for her singing. But what if tonight she sang poorly? What if she sounded like an off-key screech owl, making sounds so horrible they would all be covering their ears?

She smiled inwardly at the notion and were it only Edward in the room, she would definitely have proceeded with the plan. But considering her first failed attempt back home at Marsden Manor, she wasn't necessarily confident of her success. Edward had seen through her ploy then. What if he did again?

Then too, there was the reaction she was sure to draw from her mother. Last time, after having her mother ring a peal over her head, she'd managed to convince Mama that she had only been playing a silly prank on the duke and that he'd found it vastly amusing. But she knew Mama would not condone a repetition of such antics, particularly in front of half of the duke's family.

And then there were Edward's siblings themselves, who had been nothing but kind to her. Somehow it didn't seem fair to torture them in order to extricate herself from their brother.

Should she or shouldn't she?

She was still considering her decision when Mallory took a seat at the pianoforte and played a few practice notes.

"Ready?" Mallory asked, sending her an encouraging smile.

Nodding, Claire waited for the music to begin. Nerves

writhed like a handful of little green snakes in her stomach, her pulse beating faster than normal. The song began, the notes racing quickly upon her as she tried to keep pace with the beat. And then the moment arrived.

Sing or don't sing? Sing well or make a hash of it?

Pulling in a hasty breath, she decided at the last second to sing well.

Instead, the first note croaked from her throat, a cacophonous sound that erupted like a drunken belch that shot high at the end.

Her eyes widened, along with those of everyone else in the room.

Mallory's gaze flashed upward, despite the fact that her fingers continued to move over the keyboard.

Edward's dark brows drew tight, while the twins' faces froze in mirror images of astonishment.

Lord Drake's pencil fell still.

As for her mother, Claire didn't have the nerve to glance in her direction.

"S-Sorry," she called out, waving a hand for Mallory to quit playing. "I . . . um . . . don't know what happened. A case of dry throat, I suppose."

Without asking her permission, one of the twins—Leo, she believed—poured a glass of wine and brought it across to her.

"Thank you," she whispered, giving him a tiny smile.

Eyes twinkling, he winked at her before turning away.

"Shall we try again?" Mallory asked.

Lifting the wine to her lips, Claire took a long drink.

And so here she was with yet another chance to appall Edward. Several more murdered notes and a few remarks afterward about how much she loved to sing and the duke might indeed have second thoughts about saddling himself to a lifetime of potential auditory torture.

But as she gazed around the room at the others, she knew she still couldn't go through with it. Taking another drink, she set the wine aside, then nodded to Mallory. "All right. Let's try."

A hush fell, as everyone waited to hear her next attempt.

This time when she began, her voice rang out clear and strong, each note rounded and sweet. Approval filled the room, along with relieved pleasure, the entire group relaxing to enjoy the music.

From his place on the sofa, Edward watched her, his gaze filled with contemplation and curiosity. And then he smiled, his mouth curving in a slow upward tilt that signaled the depth of his pleasure.

Pride swelled in her chest. Pride and something more, something treacherous that she had no business letting herself feel. Yet there it was nevertheless, an insidious need to earn his approval. To make him like her.

Love her?

Closing her eyes, she fought the weakness as she let her voice soar, intertwining with Mallory's beautiful piano playing.

Seconds after she finished, applause rang out, together with huzzahs from the twins and enthusiastic clapping from Lord Drake. She smiled, a glow of accomplishment spreading through her chest. Then she gazed at Edward and found him not in his seat, but standing halfway across the room.

He was reading a note; the footman, who must have brought it, already exiting the room. Claire watched as Edward perused the missive, then folded the paper in half. She expected him to turn and rejoin the party, to rejoin her. Instead, he tucked the note into his jacket pocket and crossed to murmur some quick aside to Drake. Without so much as a glance in her direction, he strode to the door and out of the room.

Her shoulders sank, every ounce of her previous pride and excitement evaporating. Perhaps the message he'd received was important and his departure could not be helped. But was it so important that he couldn't have spared a single minute to bid her adieu? Or had he forgotten her the moment the note arrived? Was she little more than an afterthought that had instantly slipped his mind?

What a simpleton I am.

Forcing a smile, she gazed at Mallory. "Shall we sing and play another?"

Grinning, Mallory agreed.

Choking down the rest of the wine in her glass, Claire prepared to make merry—even if it killed her.

Chapter 5

"Where is he?" Edward demanded nearly two hours later, as he stepped out of the frosty March night into a room that was scarcely warmer than the outdoors in spite of the coals burning in the grate.

The senior officer on duty snapped to attention, having clearly been expecting his visit. "This way, Your Grace," he said in a moderate tone. "If you'll follow me, I'll take you to the cell."

With a nod, Edward let the other man lead the way. Their booted footsteps rang loudly against the rough stones that paved the interior of the military prison located nearly twenty miles southeast of London. Dark and drafty, the edifice was foreboding to say the least, light from the lantern the officer carried casting eerie shadows against the heavy granite walls. Despite the prison's bleak atmosphere and lack of amenities, Edward knew that it was luxurious compared to the overcrowded squalor and depravity of places like Newgate, where the gaolers preyed upon prisoners and the prisoners on each other.

They walked down a long hallway, past cells housing soldiers incarcerated for a variety of crimes. With a rattling of keys, the officer opened a heavy iron door that led into a separate section of the gaol.

"This is where we keep the special ones," the man said. "Those interned for high crimes and activities against the state. He's just down here." A few yards later, the officer stopped, then used his key again to unlock a thick wooden door.

Swinging it wide, he pointed toward the figure lying on a narrow bed in one corner of the room, a woolen blanket pulled high over the man's form. There wasn't much else in the six-by-eight cell except for a slop bucket and another that held a couple inches of water. An odor of despair and old sweat permeated the space, overlain by a more pungent, almost sweetly metallic scent that signaled something of a far more sinister nature.

Approaching the bed, Edward reached for the blanket and pulled it back. There, lying on his back with his blond hair tangled around his classically featured face, was Lord Everett. Were it not for the knife sticking out of his slender chest and the huge congealing bloodstain that accompanied it, one might have imagined him to be sleeping.

"How long ago did you find him?" Edward asked, studying the body of the man who had been known in espionage circles as Le Renard.

"Just after dinner rounds. When he didn't take his meal, we came in to check and discovered him like this."

"And you presume he was murdered? He couldn't have come into possession of a knife and done this on his own?"

The officer shook his head. "No, Your Grace. We search the cells every few days for contraband and such. Besides, Everett wasn't the sort who would have taken his own life. Too much of a coward, if you ask me. He may have been called a hero once, but he was nothing but a filthy traitor."

A filthy traitor indeed, Edward thought. A liar and a spy for the French, who had once tortured Cade nearly to death. Because of Everett, his brother would endure a limp and other physical scars for the rest of his days. If not for the fierce devotion of Cade's beloved wife, Edward feared Cade might never have been able to get past the emotional scars he'd carried as well. *Thank God for Meg.*

The officer was right, though. Everett had been too much of a coward to have killed himself. So who had done the deed in his stead?

As for why, that much was obvious. Everett had information, secrets the British government had been working hard to pry out of him for over a year now. Only recently had he begun to talk. Apparently whoever had done this hadn't cared for Everett's newly loosened tongue.

"Nonetheless, he was a potentially useful traitor," Edward said in response to the officer's last remark. "One who might have given us further valuable information if he was still alive. So, if the knife wasn't his, then whose is it? Did he have any visitors today?"

"None. Weren't many who came to see him as a rule and no one in the past couple of months. He was completely alone in here, Your Grace."

Edward raised a brow. "Apparently not completely, since at some point today someone entered his cell and stabbed him to death. Someone, I might add, who obviously had access to not only the cell, but the key, if what you say is correct."

The soldier blanched and cast a frowning look at the keys in his hand. "None of my men would do such a thing."

"Perhaps you don't know your men as well as you think. When is the last time Everett was seen alive?"

"This morning, I believe. One of the guards mentioned

that Everett was complaining about not being allowed to have a newspaper to read."

"Then I'll want the name of everyone who's been in and out of this building since this morning. And I do mean *everyone*, from your colonel down to the lowliest raw recruit. Civilians, government officials, even the boy who comes by to empty the slops."

The officer nodded.

"I want to see if they noticed anything out of the ordinary, or anyone coming in and out of this section of the prison. Are the men who were on duty this morning still here?"

"A few, yes."

"Good. Find them, then locate the rest, especially the guard who traded words with Everett this morning. I want to question him and the others personally. I presume you can find a room where I may talk to these men?"

"Of course. Everything shall be done as you ask."

"Good."

Instead of leaving, the officer hesitated. "Um, what shall we do with the body?"

Edward's gaze turned toward Everett. "It's cold enough that I imagine you can leave him right where he is for now. We'll need to inspect his clothes and any possessions he may have accumulated. Once that's done, notify his family. I assume they'll want to give him a decent burial despite his crimes."

"Yes, of course, Your Grace. I shall see to it myself."

"Very good. Now, that room, if you please, and something hot to drink. Order drinks for yourself and the men as well. I expect it's going to be a long night."

The next morning, Claire helped herself to a spoonful of scrambled eggs, a rasher of bacon and a slice of toast from the breakfast buffet laid out on a long sideboard in the family dining room.

Already seated at the table were Mallory and the twins—Lords Leopold and Lawrence—who were digging with obvious gusto into the mountain of food heaped upon their plates. Lord Drake, as Claire knew, would not be joining them, since he had returned last night to the bachelor's quarters he kept across Town. As for the duke, she had no idea where he was. She didn't even know if he was in the house or still out attending to whatever had called him away so precipitously last evening. Claire's mouth tightened briefly before she made her way to the table, the skirts of her cream-colored muslin gown whispering against her legs as she moved.

Moments after she made herself comfortable, Mallory passed her the butter and jams. "The marmalade is quite divine and the strawberry preserves as well. I'd have some of both now, if I were you, before someone else decides their dozen slices of toast haven't been sufficiently anointed with sweets."

The twins kept eating, neither of them rising to their sister's bait. Although Leo paused—at least Claire thought it was Leo—long enough to give her a wink before returning to his meal.

"Thank you for the advice," Claire said, smiling as she took a small spoonful of each. A footman appeared at her elbow and filled her teacup before withdrawing with silent efficiency.

"I was thinking after breakfast that we ladies might go shopping," Mallory said. "The Season is nearly upon us and there is your new wardrobe to be chosen and ordered."

Claire laid down her fork. "Oh, I would love to, but I'm afraid Mama is having one of her megrims and will not be able to accompany us. She is in her room now, taking nothing more than a biscuit and tea."

Mallory's gaze deepened with concern. "Oh, I am most sorry to hear she is unwell. I shall have a lavender compress sent to her right away." With a nod to one of the footmen, she dispatched the servant to see to the matter.

Taking up her fork again, Claire cut her piece of bacon in half. "Mayhap she will feel better tomorrow and we can go then."

"Go where tomorrow and who is feeling ill?" inquired a rich, resonant voice that could belong to only one man in the world.

Glancing up, Claire watched the duke stride into the room. Briefly, she forgot herself, struck by his beauty and the undeniable impact of his presence. In a single instant he dominated the room, invisible energy swirling around him that bespoke of his innate power and pride.

Clearly, he'd just come from the services of his valet. His mahogany hair was brushed neatly back from his handsome face, the ends still faintly damp from his bath. His cheeks were freshly shaven and a crisp white linen cravat was tied around his neck. He'd chosen to wear Prussian blue today, the shade that was nearly a match for his penetrating eyes. Pausing next to the dining table, he turned those eyes upon everyone assembled and waited for an answer to his query.

Claire decided to go first. "My mother is indisposed this morning," she explained, "which means that Mallory and I will have to delay our shopping excursion until later."

"I am sorry to hear of your mother's illness, Lady Claire. Shall I send for the physician to attend her?"

"Oh no, it is only one of her megrims. We have found there is very little to be done except to close the drapes and let her sleep. She will be better anon."

He nodded. "Should you change your mind, you have only to say."

"Thank you, Your Grace."

His dark brows drew together.

"Edward," she corrected in a soft voice.

An approving smile curved his mouth. "Good morning, by the way. I hope you slept well."

"Quite well."

After a moment, he gave a nod, then crossed to the buffet.

"You didn't ask how I slept," Lawrence called out in a teasing singsong.

Edward paused in the act of serving himself. "No," he replied without turning around, "I did not. But if it was anything per your usual, then you slept like the dead while sawing several cords of wood."

"I don't snore!" Lawrence defended. "At least not unless I'm in my cups."

His twin choked out a laugh and slapped his sibling on the back. With a shrug, Lawrence grinned, then once again applied himself to his meal.

Edward, his plate filled with a hearty, yet more moderate portion than his brothers, slipped into the chair at the head of the table, Claire on his right.

One of the footmen immediately appeared to fill his cup. He also placed a silver salver containing a neatly ironed copy of the *Morning Post* not far from the duke's elbow. "About this shopping expedition," Edward said, "where were you planning to go?"

"To the linen draper and the mantua maker," Mallory said. "For Claire's trousseau."

He swallowed a mouthful of eggs and ham, then patted his lips with his napkin. "Ah yes, the trousseau." His gaze moved to Claire. "I assume Mallory told you that you are to select whatever you require."

"She did, yes," Claire replied. "It is most generous of you, Your Grace."

He ate another bite of breakfast, his expression thoughtful. "I can see no reason why Lady Edgewater must accompany you," he continued. "Unless you expressly require her opinion."

"I value Mama's opinion, of course," Claire said, "but I have been choosing my own wardrobe for quite some while now."

"Then you and Mallory must go as planned. One of the twins can accompany you. I'm sure they'll prove useful carrying bandboxes and such."

Two golden brown heads jerked up at the same moment.

"Go *dress* shopping?" Leo complained.

"*Carry bandboxes?*" Lawrence said, the set of his rigid shoulders mirroring those of his twin.

"You know, Ned," stated Leo, "we do have plans of our own."

"Cancel them." Edward took another leisurely drink of his coffee. "I'm sure there'll be another boxing mill in a day or two."

Lawrence laid down his fork. "Not like this one. Hammer Hollands is fighting and I have five guineas on the outcome."

"And I've laid down ten," Leo added.

"One of your cronies can collect your winnings, assuming you didn't back the wrong man. Of course only one of you is required to escort Mallory and Lady Claire. The other can still go to the match."

Both young men crossed their arms over their chests.

"Wouldn't seem right for one of us to go without the other," Leo said.

"We'll both give the ladies our assistance," Lawrence agreed.

"Good, that's settled then," Edward said, cutting into a kipper this time. He glanced over at Claire. "I would accompany you myself," he said, "but I am afraid I have pressing matters that cannot wait."

"Of course," she murmured. "I understand."

Briefly, their gazes met.

The duke frowned.

"However, I would be pleased to accompany you to the theater this evening," he said. "If you would enjoy the outing?"

Claire frowned this time.

"*Hamlet* is being performed, I believe."

Hamlet, she thought. How apropos, with the tragic Ophelia dying from her unrequited love. *But it's not as if I'm in any danger of drowning myself in the Thames, is it?*

"Yes, Your Grace," she replied in a soft tone. "An evening at the theater sounds like a most excellent plan."

"Here are the newest pattern books arrived only this morning, ladies," Madame Morelle, London's most fashionable mantua maker, said later that day as she handed them the volumes. "I expect you shall find several selections to tempt you. And of course we can make any alterations you wish, so that each dress is unique and exclusively your own."

"Thank you, Madame," Mallory said from where she sat next to Claire on a very comfortable rose velvet divan. "You are always most kind. As I told you, we are here today to shop for Lady Claire's trousseau. She is in need of nearly everything, so please don't hesitate to offer suggestions."

"Not everything," Claire corrected in a hushed tone. "I have several attractive gowns that I brought with me from home."

"Of course your gowns are lovely," Mallory agreed with quiet sincerity. "But even you must admit they're not in the first stare of fashion. As Edward's affianced, you'll be expected to be on the cusp of the latest styles."

Madame Morelle agreed with a sage nod. "And I feel sure if Her Grace, the dowager duchess, were here, she would advise the same."

Would she? Claire mused. *Perhaps I ought to refuse the new wardrobe and shame Edward by wearing my shabby, out-of-date gowns?* But then she remembered her own mother and knew such a ploy would never succeed. Her shoulders slumped.

"Why don't I give you ladies a few minutes to look over those sketches," Madame Morelle said, "then I shall return so we can consult."

As she turned, the older woman's gaze moved across the room, her eyes narrowing slightly. "I see your two younger brothers have accompanied you today, Lady Mallory."

"Yes. They're acting as our escorts, since Lady Claire's mother was indisposed," Mallory told her.

"Your family members are always most welcome and I shall see they are kept replete with refreshments." Chin up, she sailed across the room. As she did, a girlish laugh floated in the air. Only then did Claire notice that one of the shop's young assistants was talking to the twins, the girl's cheeks flushed and her eyes bright from whatever flirtatious remarks were being showered upon her.

Madame made a *tsk*ing noise. "Sally, there are ladies in need of your attention. I shall see to their lordships now. You may go."

Pinking again, this time with alarm, the girl bobbed a curtsey and hurried away. Moments after she did, Lords Leo and Lawrence turned their combined charms on Madame and soon had her cheeks glowing girlishly and her eyes twinkling as well.

Irrepressible, Claire thought.

Returning her attention to the matter at hand, she began looking at the fashions. Every page held a new delight, each design more beautiful than the next. "They're all so pretty," she confessed. "I don't know how I'll ever choose. Which one are you getting?"

Mallory shot her a rueful glance. "Me? Oh, I'd love to get several, but I fear I exceeded my quota after I first arrived in Town. When Edward got the bill for this Season's dresses, steam practically rolled out of his ears. I thought little horns would sprout on his head he was so cross. He told me I was forbidden to buy another frock until my next allowance or he'd confiscate every dress and pack me off home."

Pausing, Mallory gave her a confidential little smile. "Of course Ned wouldn't really make good on his threat. But then again, you never know, so it's best not to push. Besides, my new allowance comes due mid-month, which means I've only a couple weeks left before I can buy more." She tapped a finger against one cheek. "Perhaps I should order something today and ask Madame to delay the delivery until after the fifteenth! Oh, you are brilliant, Claire!"

"I didn't say anything."

But Mallory had, Claire realized, abruptly struck by the other girl's remark.

So Edward had been angry at his sister's excessive spending? Furious, from the sound of it. And if he was anything like her father, then she could well imagine the scene, since Papa hated nothing quite so much as spending money. Edward had given her leave to purchase anything she required. But how many gowns did that mean? Obviously there must be a limit. What if she exceeded it? What if she bought so immense an order she made him furious? Might he call off the engagement for fear of being saddled with a spendthrift wife, then pack *her* off home?

With flutters dancing in her breast, she studied the pattern book with renewed enthusiasm. "You know, Mallory, mayhap I won't be able to choose only a few. I may just have to buy them all!"

Chapter 6

The hum of conversation wound like smoke through the Drury Lane Theater that evening as Edward assisted Lady Edgewater to her seat inside his private box. Earlier that evening, she'd declared her headache much improved and expressed an eagerness to attend tonight's entertainment. Mallory sat next to her, leaving him to take his place beside Claire in one of the chairs arranged on the opposite side of the small aisle.

Only the four of them were present, since Leo and Lawrence had begged out of the performance. The twins had asserted a dire need to engage in "manly" activities after spending the day loitering in linen drapers, dress shops and millinery stores. As an obvious precaution against being waylaid again, they'd left Clybourne House well before dinner, no doubt planning to meet up with their friends for a night of carousing and card play.

Glancing over, Edward studied Claire as she watched the theatergoers in the other boxes and the mass of commoners jostling one another for the best spots in the three-shilling seats below. Quite often he found the activities of the patrons far more entertaining than the performance itself. But he wasn't watching the crowd tonight. He was watching Claire.

She looked especially lovely tonight dressed in a gown of ecru silk with short, straight sleeves that hugged her slender arms. Matching silk ribbons were threaded into her honey blond tresses, a few strands left to dangle in tiny curls along the nape of her neck.

He imagined himself reaching out to play with one of those curls, slipping his finger inside so that he could stroke the circular strand and the delicate pale skin that lay beneath. Ever so slowly, he would lean over and kiss the spot, running his mouth across her satiny flesh while he breathed in the lush feminine perfume of her skin.

Would she quiver with pleasure for me? he wondered. *Would she sigh aloud and catch her bottom lip between her teeth in anticipation of more?*

With such things in mind, he couldn't help but recall the kiss they'd shared back at Marsden Manor. Even now, he remembered the sweet warmth and endearing vulnerability of her touch. How she'd trembled at first before her hesitation fell away, her fledgling responses revealing a depth of passion that left him wanting more.

She'd surprised him with that kiss. He'd surprised himself. He'd kissed her, intending to stake his claim as her duty-bound betrothed. Instead, he'd found himself wanting her simply as a woman.

For despite her youthful demeanor and impetuous willfulness, no one could dispute that she was a woman and not a girl. He had only to gaze at the ripe swell of her breasts and the tantalizing glimpse of bare flesh revealed by the low-cut bodice of her evening gown to be reminded of that fact.

As though to prove the point, Claire drew in a quick

breath and leaned forward in her seat, causing the tops of her breasts to jiggle ever so slightly. He wondered how much they'd bounce if he pulled her onto his lap and claimed her lips.

Shifting in his seat, he forced the image away, aware that he couldn't so much as hold her hand in a public setting such as this one. If he had any sense, he would put aside all such notions until after they were wed.

I shouldn't have given up my mistress so soon, he thought. *God knows, I could do with the physical release.* But considering the fact that Claire was living at the town house, he hadn't wanted there to be any possibility that she might overhear rumors of him visiting a demirep. Not that he'd promised fidelity to Claire, but still it didn't seem right to carry on an affair during their engagement.

Given that he enjoyed sex as much as the next man and had a healthy carnal appetite, the next several weeks weren't going to be easy. But as a rational, thinking individual, he had control over his instincts and knew he could do without libidinous pleasures for the time being.

Besides, she would be his soon enough. And once she was, he would do a great deal more than just think about toying with her hair and bouncing her on his lap.

"How was the shopping excursion?" he asked her abruptly, his words sounding throaty even to his own ears. "Were you and Mallory able to find everything you need?"

Turning, she met his gaze, her irises very blue. As he watched, her eyes seemed to twinkle with a curious, almost mischievous light.

But what mischief could there be in clothes shopping?

"The outing was delightful," she said. "Mallory and I found everything and more. Tomorrow we're going shoe and glove shopping."

He gave a faint laugh. "My little sister will be in heaven

then. She loves shoes even more than she does clothes. And if I am not mistaken, she already owns enough gloves to match every color in the rainbow."

Claire's eyebrow arched. "Well, as they say, no ensemble is complete without the right pair of shoes and gloves to accompany it."

"Is that what they say?" he asked, his mouth turning up at the corners. "Or is that what Mallory says?"

She paused. "Oh, both, I believe."

He laughed, enjoying the answering sparkle in her eyes. Before he had time to continue their conversation, various lights around the theater were dimmed, while the curtains on stage were drawn back to reveal a painted panorama that depicted the Danish castle of Elsinore. Calls for quiet erupted from the pit as the actors took their places.

Leaning back in his chair, Edward listened to the familiar opening lines.

Claire's skin tingled along the back of her neck and shoulders as she did her best to watch the action unfolding below. She'd never attended a performance of this caliber before, having seen only the pantomimes and the traveling Punch and Judy shows at the occasional county fair. A troupe of Shakespearean actors had played near Marsden Manor a time or two over the years, but she hadn't been allowed to attend, the nighttime crowd deemed too rough for a lady of her delicate sensibilities.

But she was in London now where plays were performed each and every day. When Edward suggested tonight's outing, she'd been excited by the prospect of attending her first London theatrical, despite her display of outward calm at the time. But now that she was here, she couldn't seem to concentrate on the play.

And it was all Edward's fault.

He was too close. His large masculine frame seated barely inches away from her, one of his big gloved hands near enough to touch. Not to mention the powerful thigh on which it rested, his muscular legs outlined to perfection in a pair of snug black silk evening breeches.

Every so often, a delicious shiver of awareness traced over her flesh as though he were looking at her. But whenever she glanced sideways to check, she always found his gaze directed toward the action unfolding on stage. Her own inner musings must be causing her to react this way, she decided, making her feel things that weren't really there.

Angling another glance at him through the low light, she surreptitiously studied his profile—tracing the clean lines of his forehead and brow, and the bold shape of his patrician nose before roaming over the close-shaven plane of his cheeks to his strong, square-cut jaw and chin. And then there were his lips. His gorgeous, sensuous, elegantly sculpted lips that she had reason to know were incredibly soft and indescribably seductive.

Just thinking about those lips made her remember their kiss—*The Kiss*—that, try as she might, she could not seem to forget. That one and only embrace haunted her dreams and memories with a sweet longing she knew she shouldn't let herself feel. And yet still she did.

Luckily for her, Edward had made no further efforts to test her willpower on that score. Living as they were in the same house with her mother and his own family, there was little occasion for privacy, and even less chance for intimacy. Still, if he'd wanted to kiss her again, he could surely have managed the matter. But maybe a single kiss had been enough for him, sufficient to satisfy whatever curiosity had led him to take that first—and only—one.

Not that she wanted him to kiss her again, Claire assured herself. Not at all. She wanted to be rid of him, needed to be free, and if her newest salvo proved effective, she would soon have her wish. Particularly since Madame Morelle had promised to rush the order for Claire's new wardrobe—for an extra, astonishingly extravagant fee, of course!

She swallowed at the thought and the anticipated reaction. Fingers curling in her lap, she cast another glance at Edward and froze.

His gaze, so blue as to be nearly black in the dim light, was locked on her own—not imagined this time, but real. A fresh shiver traced over her skin, her lips parting on an involuntary inhalation.

"How are you enjoying the performance?" he asked in a hushed voice.

What performance? She'd scarcely listened to a word that had been said. "It's wonderful," she whispered, lying with false cheer.

"Yes, wonderful," he repeated. His brows drew together for a moment before he gave her a slight smile, then turned his attention back to the play.

With a sigh, she forced herself to do the same.

The next week passed quickly for Claire. Her days were filled with additional shopping excursions while her evenings were occupied by at-home dinners, family entertainments and the occasional excursion out on the Town.

Edward didn't always accompany the ladies. Sometimes Drake or the twins stepped in to serve as escorts when pressing business prevented the duke from fulfilling the role. Edward never deigned to explain just what his "pressing business" might be, informing her, her mother and Mallory only that he would not be able to accompany them to a particular event. At those times he would stop by the drawing room for a few minutes to wish them an enjoyable evening before he bid them adieu and withdrew with a bow.

Claire couldn't help but wonder where Edward went and what he was doing. He didn't seem the type to indulge in gambling and she'd observed his habits long enough to know he was no more than a moderate drinker. A woman, then? Was he visiting his mistress in another part of the city? After all, a man like Edward must have physical needs that required appeasement.

Of course a sheltered young lady like herself wasn't supposed to know about such things, but one heard servants' chatter on the most interesting of subjects sometimes. And so, what if Edward were carrying on with a lightskirt . . . ? Well, that was his "business," and despite the queasy churning such thoughts gave her, she vowed to dwell on them no more.

Instead, there was her new trousseau to consider and what would happen once all of it arrived. Four of her new dresses had been delivered yesterday, but only four. The vast majority of her order was still being created—along with the bill.

Seated now in the family drawing room, she skimmed a hand over the skirt of her new green-and-white striped merino crepe day dress and tried to concentrate on her mother's conversation with Mallory. The two of them were discussing the art of decorative table painting—a topic Claire had never been able to abide.

"Which do you like better, Claire?" her mother asked. "Oranges or apples?"

She frowned. "I'm sorry. What?"

"Oranges or apples?" her mother repeated with a measure of exasperation. "Which one makes the better visual tableau? Or have you not been attending, child?"

"Your pardon, Mama. I am afraid you have caught me out. But since you have asked my opinion, then apples, I believe."

Her mother heaved a sigh. "I prefer oranges. So much more colorful to my way of thinking."

Over her mother's shoulder, Claire met Mallory's twinkling gaze, her new friend lifting her teacup to her lips to conceal a smile.

"And I have a decided preference for roses," her mother continued. "None of those woodland flowers that are so popular with some. As I told our neighbor Jessica—"

A sharp knock came at the door, interrupting Lady Edgewater in mid-sentence.

"Ever so sorry to intrude," one of the maids said. "But this letter just come by special messenger for her ladyship."

"For me! Who could be writing in such haste?" Claire's mother extended a hand to receive the missive, absently nodding her thanks as the servant bobbed a curtsey and departed from the room. Without hesitating, Lady Edgewater tore open the wax seal on the letter, a scowl descending across her brow as she read. "Oh dear. Oh good heavens!"

Claire leaned forward. "What is it, Mama? What has occurred?"

"It's Nan," her mother said, the parchment crackling faintly beneath her fingers. "She has fallen out of a tree and injured herself."

"Oh, Mama, no!" Claire clutched a hand to her chest.

"She has broken her leg and is confined to bed. The doctor has attended her and apparently she is faring well enough under the circumstances, but your father writes beseeching me to come home at once. He says he hasn't the faintest notion of how to care for a sick child, and as we all know, he does not. Of course I must go and without delay."

"What dreadful news," Mallory said. "Poor little girl. Let me call for my brother and apprise him of the matter, so that you may be quickly on your way. Edward will know precisely what is to be done. Then I shall ring for the maids to help you with your packing."

Lady Edgewater rose to her feet, reaching out a grateful hand. "Lady Mallory, you are such a dear girl. So kind and good. But oh, what is to be done about a chaperone for Claire, since the dowager duchess is not yet in residence? Your family is highly respectable and above reproach, but still some might disapprove of Claire unwed and living here with only you other young people for company."

Claire stood. "But I must come with you, Mama. Nan will be utterly miserable and in need of all the aid and comfort we can give her. I can't possibly remain behind."

Her mother's mouth firmed. "Of course you can. I am sure something may be worked out. Lady Mallory, you must have some female relation who could come to stay until your mama returns?"

Mallory nodded. "Yes, ma'am, I have any number of cousins and quite a few in Town. I expect one would be willing to relocate to the town house for a short while."

"There, you see, Claire. Everything is settled."

"But Mama—"

"No buts. The Season starts in only two more weeks and I will not have you miss an instant of it."

"I have missed the Season before," Claire said in a patient tone. "It won't be so very great a loss."

"Of course it will be!" Lady Edgewater said with a disbelieving flip of her hand. "This is your one and only opportunity to enjoy the social Season before you become a bride. It shan't be the same at all once you wed, and I will not have you miss it simply because your sister is so foolish as to have broken her leg."

"But Nan will be so unhappy—"

"And so she should," her mother declared. "How many times have I told her not to climb those trees around the house, and for this very reason too. She is headstrong and disobedient and should be thankful she hasn't suffered a worse injury than a broken leg. You are right that she'll be miserable, but she will recover."

Reaching out, she patted Claire's shoulder. "In the meantime, her distress should not be your own nor keep you from enjoying your time here in Town. Just because I have to return home doesn't mean you must suffer as well."

But I wouldn't be suffering, Claire thought. *I want to go home.*

But she couldn't very well tell her mother that. Her mother, who would neither approve nor understand. Mama was delighted by her engagement to the duke. If Claire ever expressed her real feelings and fears, her mother would only shake her head in confusion and ask if Claire had taken leave of her senses.

Not want to marry the duke? What nonsense! her mother would say.

If Mama had any idea what she was plotting, her mother would be aghast.

And when Edward jilts me, she thought, *Mama will be far angrier with me than she is now with Nan.* But she was counting on her mother and father getting over their displeasure and disappointment with her, just as they would with Nan.

Eventually.

Poor Nan. Claire sympathized with her sister, knowing she climbed trees because it made her feel alive. But now that Nan had injured herself, she would find her freedom sorely curtailed. Claire wished she could go to her, but mayhap it was better if she remained here in London for now, since if all went as planned, she would be joining her shortly.

Claire frowned. "You are sure, Mama? I would accompany you in an instant."

"I know you would," her mother said in a solemn voice. "But we shall manage at home without you. Ella will help me with your sister and we shall muddle along just fine. If it would relieve your mind, why do you not go now and write letters to them both? If you are quick about it, there should be time while I pack and the coach is made ready. Lady Mallory, perhaps you would see me to my room?"

"Of course, ma'am. And not to worry, a servant has been dispatched for my brother. He should be here anytime."

Claire curved her arms close around her body as she watched Mallory lead Lady Edgewater from the room. After giving herself a little inward shake, she went to find pen and paper.

Two hours later, amid hugs and a few tears, Claire watched her mother climb into the duke's fastest coach. With a thunk of the door and a snap of a whip, the vehicle set off, bowling along Grosvenor Square before disappearing into the crush of afternoon traffic.

As Claire turned to go inside, she found Edward at her side. His handsome features were steady and reassuring.

"She'll be fine," he told her. "Broken limbs can be very serious if not attended to properly, but you are not to worry. I have asked our family physician to see to Nan."

She tipped her head back to meet his gaze. " 'See to her'? What do you mean?"

"Dr. Cole is one of the finest doctors in the country. At my request, he is traveling to Nottinghamshire to examine your sister and make sure she is receiving the very best of care. With his aid, she'll be well again in no time at all, you shall see."

Her lips parted with surprise. "Your Grace, I do not know what to say. How extraordinarily thoughtful. Thank you."

He waved off her expression of gratitude as the two of

them ascended the front steps and re-entered the town house. "No thanks are needed. It is no more than I would do for any other member of my family and since Nan is to be my sister, then it seems only right she receive the same care I would give one of my own siblings."

Crossing the wide entrance hall, she walked beside him toward the main staircase. "Still, it is most generous of you," she said. "I find I am in your debt."

In his debt . . . which was the very last thing she wished to be. Why did he have to be so kind? And why did she have to like him, despite her best intentions not to? Hating him would make everything so much easier, would let her draw the battle lines in crisp hues of black and white, instead of muddied shades of indeterminate grey.

But wasn't that the heart of the problem? If she were indifferent, perhaps the thought of this marriage would not trouble her so. If it were merely a matter of convenience and duty, as it was for him, maybe she could make do, even be content. Was she wrong to feel this way when everyone else wanted them to wed? Was she being a fool for wanting to toss aside a life of comfort and luxury, with an admittedly good and honorable man, just because he didn't—couldn't—love her?

She turned toward him, unsure of her next words, when a reedy, bespectacled young man in a precisely tailored coat and trousers hurried up to the duke.

"Your Grace," his secretary said, "If I might intrude, perhaps you could spare a few minutes. There are several matters of a rather urgent nature still requiring resolution. I had hoped we would be able to finish them this afternoon in time to catch the last post."

Edward's brows drew together. "Yes, of course, I shall be along in a moment, Hughes." Pausing, he gazed back at Claire. "Is there anything else you require at present? I have sent word 'round to my cousin Wilhelmina, asking her to attend you while your mother is away. She has agreed and should arrive no later than dinnertime. In the meanwhile, will you be all right?"

Claire's shoulders straightened, chilled by Edward's abrupt formality. "I shall be quite well. Pray do not trouble yourself further on my behalf."

With another frown, he gave an absent nod. Turning, he fell into conversation with his secretary and strode away, the younger man walking quickly at his side, business matters pouring from his lips.

Forgotten already, she thought. *I suppose I am no more important than any other item in his very long list of things to which he must attend.*

For a moment, she watched Edward move away down the hall, then she swung around and took the stairs with a determined stride.

Chapter 7

Inside his study three days later, Edward finished reading a letter from Jack, smiling as he folded the missive and set it aside.

It would seem he was an uncle twice over now, his sister-in-law Grace having given birth a week ago to a baby girl. They'd decided to name her Nicola, and Jack declared she was the most beautiful child he'd ever beheld—and not just because she was his daughter. Grace and the baby were doing splendidly, especially with Jack and Edward's mother, Ava, there to offer advice and support. Jack wrote that he and Grace hoped to come to Town this summer once Grace was recovered and the baby old enough to travel. From what Edward understood, Cade and Meg planned to journey to London this summer as well to show off their new son. Undoubtedly, it would be quite a reunion.

Edward suspected, however, that the two couples might have postponed their visits a while longer were it not for their rather poorly concealed curiosity about Claire. He had to admit that he'd taken everyone unawares with his sudden decision to go through with the betrothal, particularly since the entire family had long ago assumed he'd decided not to honor the old arrangement made by their father and Claire's. But circumstances changed and so had his view of the betrothal.

To his relief, it seemed as though Claire had acclimated herself to the idea of their engagement as well, her initial resistance having apparently faded once she'd arrived in Town. Claire seemed content enough, she and Mallory getting on like bosom friends from the very first. He would give her the next several weeks to enjoy the Season and then they would proceed with the wedding.

Meanwhile, he was still working on solving the puzzle of who had killed Everett, as well as identifying the man Everett had named a few days before his death.

Wolf.

The name could be real or an alias. He and his contacts at the War Office still didn't know which, despite extensive attempts to locate someone answering to that surname. The man could be nearly anyone, if it was indeed an assumed name. Although if he was the same shadowy figure Meg had glimpsed meeting with Everett that night two Seasons ago, then it narrowed the field somewhat. They had her description of the man, even if it was vague.

Then as now, Edward had been secretly working to uncover the identity of a spy buried deep in the system—a mole who had access to information at the highest levels of the government. After Everett's initial capture, the mole had disappeared. At first, they'd wondered if Everett himself was the man, and if by catching him, they'd ended the leak. But last fall, with Everett firmly in custody, information had begun going astray once more. The mole, they quickly realized, was still free and clear and operating with impunity.

Was the mole this Wolf, or someone else entirely?

And was Wolf Everett's killer or not? Edward's only lead was a pair of corroborating reports from a couple of the soldiers who remembered seeing a new man in the vicinity of Everett's cell block around noontime on the day of his murder. The man had been dressed in a lieutenant's uniform and none of the soldiers had thought to question his presence, assuming he'd come over from another regiment. He'd left no name, nor had he been seen since.

Taking out a sheath of notes and reports, Edward began to read them again, hoping for some clue he might have missed. He was deep into the stack when he became aware of a frenzy of activity going on in the front of the house. From the sound of it, the house was being invaded, there were so many footsteps going to and fro. Curious, he tucked the papers back inside the leather folio in which they were kept, then locked them inside a drawer in his desk.

Standing, he walked out of his study and down the hall. Near the front entrance he stopped, struck by the sight of a virtual army of deliverymen making their way up and down the main staircase. Even his own footmen had been enlisted in the effort.

"Croft," Edward called, signaling his butler. "What in the world is all this?"

The usually unflappable older man glanced over, his expression faintly dismayed. "A delivery, Your Grace. From the mantua maker, I am given to understand."

As Edward watched, another three servants came through the open front door, their arms stacked high with boxes. Angling their heads to see around their burdens, each man carefully negotiated the stairs in a small but impressive procession. As they did, more servants returned downstairs and back out the door, apparently intending to retrieve more from the wagon parked outside.

Edward raised a single eyebrow at the spectacle. The

second brow joined its mate when he heard high-pitched feminine squeals echoing from one of the bedchambers upstairs. Obviously boxes were being opened and garments revealed, much to the ladies' great delight.

He was trying to decide how to react to all the commotion when Croft appeared at his elbow, a silver salver containing a letter held in the servant's hand. "This arrived with the delivery, Your Grace. Shall I give it to Mr. Hughes for his attention?"

Edward turned an eye toward the missive, which was clearly a bill of sale from Madame Morelle. He'd seen enough of them over the years to recognize her business stationery. "No, I'll take it," he said, curious to see exactly how many gowns were being delivered and at what cost.

Reaching out, he picked up the correspondence and broke the wax seal, revealing a full dozen pages. On each were rows of notations with descriptions of individual items and the accompanying price, all penned in fine black ink. As he scanned one page after the other, his brows shot high on his forehead. Flipping to the final page, he searched for the grand total and felt his eyes strain wide, his jaw dropping as he read the figure written at the bottom.

That can't be right! he thought. Not even a royal princess would spend this much on her wardrobe. Doing another quick review, he began to count gowns, wishing Drake were here to confirm his hasty math. If he was right—and he had the sinking suspicion that he was—there were over one hundred and fifty gowns on the invoice.

One hundred and fifty!

Surely there had to be a mistake, since all these clothes couldn't possibly be for Claire alone.

Mallory! he thought, his head coming up again. *Mallory must have defied me and gone shopping too.*

Well, he'd see about this and see about it now.

Paying no attention to the last of the deliverymen as they made their way out the door, Edward took the stairs two at a time. The thick paper invoice crinkled inside his grasp, his emerald signet ring tapping against the polished handrail with each of his steps. Turning at the landing, he made his way down the long corridor.

Feminine talk and murmurs of admiration floated from one of the guest bedchambers, growing louder and more distinct the closer he got. He hadn't been to this room since Claire had taken up residence, knowing it was hers. The lilting cadence of her voice floated like sunbeams on the air. Stopping in front of the partially open door, he rapped on the panel.

A maidservant soon appeared at the door, her eyes growing large when she saw him standing there.

"Is my sister within?" he asked.

"Yes, Your Grace," the girl told him, dipping a curtsey.

"Who is it, Penny?" he heard Mallory call. The girl withdrew, a quick hush of conversation following. "Edward's here? You mean right outside the door?" Mallory said.

"That's right," he retorted in a voice loud enough to carry. "And I want to speak with you. Now, if you would be so good."

Mallory arrived at the door moments later. "Oh, hallo, Ned. What do you want? I'm helping Claire try on her new gowns. We're having a bit of a fashion exhibition at the moment."

"Yes, I'm sure you are," he said in a wry tone. "That's what I'm here to discuss."

Mallory gave him a look of surprise, the one she used when she had been caught at something she knew she oughtn't to have done.

He scowled. "So how many of these gowns have *you* been trying on?"

She scowled back. "None. Well, one. All right, *two*," she corrected, "but those two are quite within bounds, since my new allowance just became available."

"Come now, how many of those gowns are really yours? And don't try to cozen me. We've been through this more times than I can count and I thought I had your pledge."

She crossed her arms, her lips firming. "You do have my pledge and I have honored it."

"So you're telling me that all of these gowns"—he lifted the stack of bills in his grasp—"were ordered for Lady Claire?"

Mallory opened her mouth to reply, but before she could, the door opened wider and there stood Claire.

She looked flushed and lovely, a few wayward tendrils of golden hair curled against her cheeks in a most becoming fashion. Blue as a summer sky, her eyes shone with vivid brightness against her creamy skin, her cheeks stained the same lush pink as her lips.

Claire met his gaze with a direct look of her own. "That's exactly what she is saying, Your Grace. The gowns *are* all mine. Lady Mallory was very circumspect in her purchases, so pray do not be cross with her for something in which she took no part."

"Actually, I did take part," Mallory amended in a conspiratorial aside to Claire. "In the shopping, that is, and the selection of the garments."

"Yes, well, I fear your brother is displeased with the wrong person whatever the circumstances," Claire said.

"I fail to see why he should be," Mallory interjected, turning her attention back to her brother. "Claire may have shopped with an admittedly liberal hand, but she bought nothing she did not need for her entrance into Society. Do you not want her looking her best?"

His jaw tightened this time. "Of course I do. But—"

"She couldn't very well buy second-rate goods and patronize an inferior seamstress, who might charge pennies rather than pounds but provide slipshod work."

"I never expected her to do so, and that isn't the point."

"Madame Morelle does not come cheap, you know, nor should she for the quality she provides."

"I have never complained about Madame Morelle or your patronage of her shop."

"Well then, why are you all beetle-browed?"

"Beetle-browed!" he shot back. "I am nothing of the kind."

Mallory gave a delicate snort. "Tell that to your eyebrows."

He paused, then blew out a breath. "Sometimes, Mallory, you try my patience beyond measure. If you weren't my sister I would—"

"What?" she dared, undaunted by his words. "What would you do?"

Briefly, Edward closed his eyes, clearly striving for that patience he'd mentioned. When he opened them again, his expression was calm, despite the faintly militant gleam that lingered in his gaze.

Concerned that her scheme was having unintended consequences, Claire decided it was time to intercede. "Please, do not quarrel," she implored. "Certainly not over me. I appreciate your defense, Mallory, but I believe this is an issue that needs to be resolved between your brother and myself. Is that not right, Your Grace?"

He met her gaze for a long moment. "If you prefer."

"I know you mentioned your eagerness to try on the pair of gowns you purchased," Claire said to Mallory. "Why do you not take them now and go to your room? Penny can accompany you to help. And I'm sure Cousin Wilhelmina would be happy to proffer an opinion, assuming she has awakened from her nap by now."

Mallory hesitated. "Are you sure? I don't mind staying in the least."

"I shall be fine."

Mallory looked between them, clearly weighing the situation. "Well, if you are certain. But remember that I am only just down the hall."

"I'm not likely to murder her," Edward remarked in a half-exasperated tone. "If that were the case, you'd have been dead years ago. Now take your dresses—the *two* that are most definitely coming out of your pin money, I might add—and go to your room. I shall see you tonight at dinner."

After another considering glance between her and Edward, Mallory departed, the maid trailing behind with a large bandbox in hand.

Standing back, Claire silently invited Edward into her room despite the impropriety of the act. "Surely the servants have heard more than enough already," she explained.

"My staff is extremely discreet," he told her, then strode inside.

Drawing another breath, Claire pushed the door inward, leaving it open by a scant inch. She wanted privacy, but she wasn't lost to all sense of discretion. With her pulse beating at a rapid gallop, she took a moment to compose herself, then turned.

She found Edward standing with a fist on one hip as he surveyed the ocean of clothing spread over every piece of furniture in the room, along with another small mountain of boxes that had yet to be unpacked.

"Merciful heavens, did you buy every yard of fabric in the city?" he remarked.

She ignored his sarcasm, well aware of her extravagance. After all, that had been the point. Determined to proceed with her plan, she'd ended up having Madame Morelle recreate nearly all the fashion plates she'd admired that day at the mantua maker's shop. Additionally she and Mallory had included several designs from *La Belle Assemblée* and had a few more made up from the fashion babies on display. They'd taken Madame's shop by storm, as the seamstress herself had declared, even her jaded eyes growing a bit round at the enormity of the order.

Now the moment of truth had arrived.

Just how angry is he? she wondered. *Enough to blister me with a tirade that would do my father proud? Sufficiently furious to toss me out of the house and end our engagement?* She waited, nearly rubbing her hands together in anticipation.

However, unlike her father when his ire was roused, the duke seemed composed, almost cool, despite his earlier heated remarks. He said nothing as he continued gazing at the array of garments, pausing every so often to peruse the bill in his hand.

"Is there something in particular you are looking for, Your Grace?"

"No, simply curious. For instance, there is a notation about several gowns with . . . let me see what it was called again . . ." Pausing, he thumbed through the pages he held. "Ah yes, the rose-point lace that costs a mere forty pounds a yard."

Well now, she thought, *that's more like it.* As a rule, men were notorious for disdaining feminine trimmings and fripperies, particularly expensive ones. Perhaps a detailed description of her purchase would really set him on edge.

"That lace is handmade by Belgian nuns and takes hundreds of hours to create," she informed him in an enthusiastic voice. "Madame assured me it is the finest lace in existence and well worth the extra expense of importing it from abroad. Wartime tariffs, you see, make the price extremely dear."

Abroad! her father would have complained. *Aren't there any cloistered spinsters here in England who can tat a bit of thread? And for a fraction of this outrageous price!*

But the duke remained calm. "Yes, the tariffs are quite steep for most imported goods these days. Lace included."

"Thus all the smuggling that's so popular," she said. "But Madame doesn't deal in contraband lace, so that wasn't an option. Not that you would approve such goings-on. I'm sure you would never have cause to find yourself on the wrong side of the excise man," she added, hoping he got her allusion to the French wine they'd drunk at dinner the other evening.

From the wry look he gave her, he did. "No, certainly not."

Studying the garments, she crossed to a pale pink silk evening gown. "This one has the rose-point lace. Exquisite, is it not?" Taking up the dress, she held it out for his inspection.

His gaze roamed over the lace. "Indeed. Those nuns definitely know their stitchery."

He sounded serious enough, she decided, and yet as she studied him, she thought she detected the faintest hint of a twinkle in his eyes.

Is he teasing me?

Frowning, she suddenly worried that her plan might not be working as expected. He was supposed to be angry, not amused.

"What else, Your Grace?" she pressed. "What other portions of the bill have you curious?"

At the reminder, he gazed again at the invoice. "Well, the sheer number of gowns for one. By my count there are over one hundred and fifty. Did you have any idea that you'd ordered quite so many?"

Her eyes widened, surprised in spite of herself. At the

time, she'd known that she was buying an enormous number of gowns, but even she hadn't realized it was that many! *Gracious, Papa would be red-faced with an apoplexy if he were the one holding the bill. So why isn't the duke?*

"No, Your Grace," she admitted, "though as Mallory said, I only ordered what I needed."

He raised a brow.

"As I recall, you did say I was to buy whatever I required." She paused with apparent innocence. "It would seem I required a very great deal."

But rather than glowering as she expected, he barked out a laugh. "That's the understatement of the century. And what of this one gown I saw that cost five hundred pounds? I believe there was some mention of diamonds in the description."

Oh goody, she thought. *He noticed that one!*

She'd realized when she ordered the dress that it was the most outrageously extravagant, utterly decadent thing she'd ever done in her life. In several lifetimes. Even Mallory had hesitated over the purchase, biting one of her fingernails with indecision, while Claire forged ahead and gave her approval of the purchase.

"Oh, that one is for a very special occasion, although I haven't decided which one yet. The dress is made of a magnificent cream sarcenet. Tiny diamonds are encrusted in the bodice, with an array of leaves and flowers across the skirt that are sewn with a thread made of real gold. The effect is quite dazzling. Oh, and I ordered shoes to match! Those haven't arrived yet, I'm afraid. The boot maker is still fashioning my footwear. And I have orders with three different milliners and two glove makers as well."

Her heart pounded in her chest, nerves trembling as she waited again for the explosion.

Instead, the corners of his mouth turned up. "No one will

be able to say you aren't dressed as befitting my duchess. Although I'll probably be forced to raise the rents on my tenants to pay for all this," he added with a sweep of his arm.

Her jaw dropped, aghast. "Surely not!" Good heavens! She'd never thought of such a thing. How awful! She would return everything at once, if that was the case.

He tossed back his head and laughed. "Not to worry. I have more than sufficient funds to pay for your spree. Who knows, however, what shall happen if you continue in this vein after we are married."

Married.

Her shoulders sank. So he was still set on the engagement. Wasn't he the least bit perturbed? Wasn't he going to fume and fuss and yell at her at all?

"Then you aren't angry?" she asked.

He gave her a contemplative look before calmly folding the invoice he held in neat thirds and tucking it inside his coat pocket. "Were you expecting me to be?"

"I . . . I . . . well, perhaps."

"Did you think I'd disapprove of the expense? Ah, I can see that you did." He paused, meeting her gaze. "I'll admit I was taken aback at first by the rather substantial size of your purchase. But this is your trousseau, so I suppose a bit of excess is to be expected."

She stared. Why was he being so reasonable? Why wasn't he outraged?

He gave her a reassuring smile. "I know you're used to dealing with your father, but you'll have to remember that I have different attitudes about spending money. Not that you shouldn't exercise a measure of prudence in future, but it takes a great deal more than one lavish shopping excursion to ruffle my feathers."

Breath rushed from her lungs as she realized how thoroughly she had misjudged him, and worse, that all her efforts had once again been for naught. *Damn and blast*, she cursed silently, resisting the urge to beat her fists against her sides. *He might not be vexed, but I certainly am!*

"You don't look pleased," he said. "Nor should I say relieved."

"Oh, I—I am," she dissembled. "It is just that I am surprised, especially after your squabble with Mallory."

"Yes, well, Mallory is another matter entirely, since every time she shops, it's with a lavish hand. It's a good thing Hargreaves has deep pockets or else I fear there might be discord over household expenses once they're wed. But enough talk of my sister. Is that gown you are wearing one of your new purchases?"

Absently, she brushed her fingers over the skirt of her lilac spotted muslin day dress. "As it happens, it is."

His gaze swept over her. "Very becoming."

"I'm so glad you approve, Your Grace."

"I do," he said with sincerity, leaving her unsure whether he hadn't heard the hint of sarcasm in her voice or he'd just chosen to ignore it.

"But there it is again. *Your Grace*," he said. "I thought we had dispensed with such formality, at least in private. Considering the amount of money I've just spent on your wardrobe, I would think you could muster up an 'Edward' or two."

"In that case, I'm so glad you approve—*Edward*."

He laughed, his midnight blue eyes gleaming in a way she ought not find attractive. She shouldn't find the rest of him so attractive either, especially not when she was annoyed and disappointed that her latest attempt to free herself from their engagement had met with such disaster. But happy, sad or vexed, nothing changed the fact that Edward Byron was one undeniably gorgeous man. Particularly when he smiled as he was doing now, tiny lines fanning near his eyes, the seductive hint of a dimple creasing his cheek in a way that begged to be touched. Or kissed.

Her fingers curled against the fabric of her skirt.

Still smiling, he raised his hand and waggled a pair of fingers in a circular motion. "Let's see it all."

"All what?"

"The dress. Spin around so I can take in the full effect."

"Your Grace!"

He raised a brow.

"*Edward*," she amended. "That is a highly improper suggestion."

"It's equally improper that we're alone in your bedchamber, as you already pointed out. Come along, let's see what Madame has created."

She shot him a mutinous look, but his expression didn't change not by so much as a flicker of an eyelash. Her nerve endings prickled, flutters dancing in her stomach at the idea of displaying herself to him. Swallowing with a self-consciousness she rarely felt, she turned around as rapidly as her feet would take her.

"That was much too fast." He crossed his arms. "Do it again."

"Again!"

"Only slower this time so I can appreciate the view. Of the gown, of course."

"Oh, of course."

And that's when she realized that he was having a tiny bit of revenge after all. He might not bluster and bully like her father. Instead, he found other, far more insidious ways to wring a penance out of his victims. She was surprised his siblings didn't live in more abject fear of him than they did. But as she'd witnessed firsthand, they all seemed to adore him.

As do I, she thought, *much to my supreme regret.*

Exhaling in silent resignation, she held her arms out at her sides, then turned in a steady circle, one slow step at a time. After a full revolution, she stopped, facing him. "There," she said. "Satisfied?"

A light flickered deep in his eyes, one she wasn't quite certain how to interpret. "Madame's work is lovely," he said in a low tone. "As is the wearer of her design. You shall do me proud, Claire. Every man in Town will be throwing himself at your feet this Season."

Every man but you.

Glancing away, she lowered her arms to her sides. "Yes, well, if that is all, Your Gr— Edward, I believe I should ring for one of the maids so they can set the room aright. As you've already noted, there are a great many gowns to be unpacked and hung in the armoires."

"So there are," he agreed. "But first there is one more detail you appear to have overlooked."

Her brows drew tight on her forehead. "What detail?"

"I'm sure it has simply slipped your mind, but you have yet to thank me. I believe the purchase of more than a hundred and fifty gowns deserves some show of gratitude."

She laid a hand on her chest. "Oh, stars, you're right! How remiss of me not to have said anything earlier. Amid all the talk, thanking you *did* slip my mind. Pray forgive me for not conveying my sincere appreciation from the very start."

"That's quite all right," he said with a negligent shrug. "Although if you wish to make it up to me, there is something you could do."

"Yes, of course, you have only to ask."

"Do I?" he mused aloud, crossing the distance between them so that he stood barely inches away. "I am glad to hear it. You won't mind expressing your gratitude with a kiss then, will you?"

Her heart leapt, crashing so hard inside her chest that she

felt the thump under her hand. Only in that instant did she understand the trap into which she'd fallen and recognize the bait he'd laid out like sweetmeats arranged on a tray.

Oh, he's sly. And dangerous. Very, very dangerous.

Neatly caught, she knew there was no way around it, short of ordering him from her room. And given the circumstances, she didn't think he would simply obey. He was a duke, after all, and used to giving commands, not taking them. If only there was some way she could push him out, she might have tried, but he outweighed her by half a dozen stone at least. Moving him would be like trying to dislodge a tree. And he knew it. She could see it on his face.

Drawing a breath, she linked her hands together. "Very well. You may kiss me."

His mouth curved in an amused little smile. "Oh, I didn't say I wanted to kiss you. I want *you* to kiss *me*. You are expressing your thanks, after all."

Her jaw dropped, nerves bouncing like tiny springs in her stomach.

He isn't just dangerous, she thought, *he is wicked too.*

"I'm waiting," he said, bending his head slightly to compensate for the difference in their heights.

Without giving herself more time to consider, she lifted up on her toes and touched her mouth to his cheek with a hasty brush of her lips. "There," she declared. "Your kiss."

He turned a derisive eye upon her. "That wasn't a kiss. That was a dry-as-dust peck, the sort I might expect from one of my elderly aunts arrived for a holiday visit. Come now, you can do better than that." Moving even closer, he took her hands and laid them on his chest. "Go on, Claire," he encouraged in a husky voice. "Give it another try. After all, it's only a kiss."

Only a kiss.

Maybe for him, but to her it was so much more. And yet

Chapter 8

Edward didn't know why he'd started this lunacy of playing kissing games with Claire. But considering her antics over her trousseau, he hadn't been able to resist teasing and tormenting her just the tiniest bit, barely able to contain his amusement as she'd grown round-eyed at his suggested method of thanking him.

He had to admit she looked adorable in her pretty lavender dress, as bright and fresh as a new spring day and every bit as lovely. Despite knowing he should bid her adieu and return to work in his study, he'd found himself lingering, unwilling to let her off the hook without at least a token measure of retribution.

Not that he really minded the expense, since to be blunt, he was rich and could well afford the extravagance. As he'd told her, he had far more liberally minded views on spending money than her father. And yet he sensed there was a great deal more to this excessive dress-buying business than met the eye. Particularly since her father was such a nip cheese and she'd obviously been anticipating an explosive reaction on his own part.

What he wanted to know was why? It was almost as if she'd wanted him to be angry, as though she'd deliberately purchased an outrageous number of dresses just to irritate him.

He'd nearly questioned her on the subject, but decided that he would let the matter go for now. She was still settling in here in London, still getting used to her new situation and status as his fiancée. Perhaps she was simply testing her boundaries and stretching her new wings, as she boldly explored what she could and could not do as his duchess-to-be.

Then again, perhaps she'd simply wanted to get his attention, since he had to admit he had been distracted of late with this Everett matter and hadn't devoted as much time to her as he'd originally promised.

Well, if gaining my attention is her goal, he thought, as he clasped her little palms against his chest, *she has it now!*

The question was, would she take his dare or refuse? Would she give him a real kiss and not another sexless peck on the cheek? He supposed he was asking a lot of Claire given her innocence. *But a man could hope*, he decided, his senses alert and ready for whatever she decided to do.

Without any further warning on her part, she arched up on her toes again and touched her mouth to his. Satiny soft and tender as rose petals, her lips pressed against his own with a guileless determination that made him want to smile. He remained still, giving her time to explore, despite the fact that her efforts were tentative and unsure. Trembling, she pressed harder, sliding her closed mouth over his in a way that was decidedly pleasurable, yet uninspiring all the same.

On a small gasp, she drew away, her sweet breath stealing over his senses with a fragrant warmth that made him want to pull her back. Instead, he remained motionless.

"Was that better?" she asked on a near whisper.

He smiled. "Better, yes, but you could do with a little more practice. Why do you not try again."

Her eyelashes fluttered, her gaze growing faintly lambent. "Again?"

"Exactly," he confirmed, careful to keep her hands trapped beneath his own. "And relax this time. Let your lips and jaw loosen up a bit. After all, it's a kiss not a competition."

Her gaze locked with his, her hesitation plain, as though she were battling some inner demon. For a moment, he thought she was going to retreat, but then she gave a small sigh and leaned toward him again. "All right," she murmured, "but only one more."

"Only one," he repeated. "If that is what you wish."

Seemingly relieved by his response, she leaned up, then joined her mouth with his. Her eyelids slid closed, concentrating as though she were determined to prove herself this time.

He could have taken control of the embrace. Could have kissed her back with an intensity that would have moved things along quite nicely. But he decided to wait a little more, wanting to know what she would do and how far she might be willing to push the embrace.

Having obviously taken his instructions to heart, she parted her lips and moved them against his with a gentle caressing action that set his senses abuzz. Tipping her head one way, then the other, she deepened the kiss, testing each angle as though searching for exactly the right fit.

And suddenly she found it, using the most sublime combination of friction and finesse to send his senses winging skyward. His pulse raced faster, his thoughts growing lazy and slow as she drew him deeper into her spell.

Throwing off the yoke of restraint he'd kept around himself, he drew her hands upward and looped them around his neck. As soon as her fingers curved against the back of his cravat, he slid his arms down and around to clasp her body snugly to his.

She shivered and kissed him harder, finding the honeyed spot again that made him groan with pleasure. She whimpered in response, opening her mouth a little wider as she increased the range of her exploration.

Then, without so much as a hint of her intentions, she drew the warm, wet tip of her tongue against his bottom lip. He shuddered and pulled away, staring into her bemused gaze.

"Where did you learn to do that?" he asked on a husky demand.

She blinked, eyelashes fluttering as though he'd asked her to solve a rather perplexing riddle. Her fair brows drew together with concentration. "Fr-From you. Last time." Pausing, she met his gaze. "D-Didn't you like it?"

His arms tightened around her waist. "Of course I liked it. Do it again and don't be shy."

With an agreeable nod, she slid her fingers into the hair at the back of his head, then claimed his mouth again. Her kiss was long and slow and utterly delicious. He was beginning to wonder if she'd let nerves talk her out of making a second attempt at the rest, when her tongue eased out and trailed like hot velvet across his lower lip once again.

He shivered and intensified the kiss, mirroring her last move with a slow, gliding lick of his own. Her mouth parted on a pleasured gasp, granting him the opportunity to press his advantage. Unable to resist her unwitting invitation, he eased his tongue inside, reveling in the sweet suction as he began teaching her an entirely new set of skills.

To his gratification, she caught on quickly, following his lead as their kisses grew more ardent and intimate, wilder and increasingly more perilous as the passion spiked higher between them.

He couldn't help but think about the fact that her bed stood only a few feet distant. A couple of strategic steps and he could have her off her feet and on her back before she even realized what he was doing. He could tumble her amid her trousseau, stripping off her pretty new gown while he played with her among the silks and satins.

But I can't, he thought on a near groan. Not only would he be taking unfair advantage of her inexperience, he would be stealing her innocence at the same time. She was a virgin and his bride-to-be. She deserved a proper wedding night, not a hasty, impromptu fling on the guestroom bed.

Besides, he'd promised her time. Time to settle into her new life. Time to get used to the idea of marrying him. Time for the two of them to learn more about each other and find common interests, and even friendship, if they were lucky.

And here he was on the verge of tupping her like some doxy.

Good Lord, now that a few drops of blood were leaking back into his brain, he remembered that her door wasn't even closed. Meaning that anyone could walk in—her maidservant, even Mallory. The thought hit him like a bucketful of cold water, desire falling away as quickly as it had come.

Breaking their kiss, he reached up to unlock her arms from around his neck. She swayed, her eyelids opening with obvious confusion. Rather than let her fall, he caught her, but kept his embrace loose and impersonal.

"Edward?" she murmured. "Wh-What is it? What's wrong?"

"Nothing is wrong," he told her in as even a tone as he could manage. "It's just time that we stopped."

"Oh, I see." But it was obvious that she didn't see, too caught up in their kisses to even realize how fast matters had been progressing between them.

Reminded again of her innocence, he knew he'd been

right to stop, even if his body was still complaining about the matter.

"I had best be going," he said. "Hughes is probably pacing a hole in my office carpet right now, wondering where I've disappeared to."

"O-Of course." She clutched his arms for a moment to steady herself, then straightened and stepped away. "Don't let me keep you. I'm sure I have taken up a great deal more of your time today than you ever envisioned."

"Not at all. Our encounter has been quite enlightening. Thank you for the . . ." He paused, searching for the right words, but finding none that came easily to mind. "Well, thank you for the thank-you. It was most enjoyable."

Color crept like a budding sunrise into her cheeks. "And thank you for the new wardrobe, Your . . . Edward. It was most generous of you to provide."

Her remark ought to have pleased him. Instead, he found himself disturbed by the tenor of the conversation. Suddenly it was as though they were discussing a business transaction instead of a gift between bridegroom and bride. It was as if she'd kissed him not for pleasure, but as payment. And considering everything that had passed between them, perhaps she had. Their engagement was based on convenience and duty. Was her passion as much about obligation as it was about real desire?

He scowled, not liking the thought at all. "I shall leave you now so that you may ring for your maid."

She hesitated as though she might say something more, then inclined her head instead.

Executing a neat bow, he turned and left the room.

Claire waited until she couldn't hear Edward's footsteps anymore before she crossed the room and closed the door.

Shutting her eyes, she leaned back against the door's

thick, polished wood surface and wondered how everything had gone so topsy-turvy. Not only had her plan failed—again—but she'd found herself lured for a second time into Edward's devastating embrace.

She trembled, remembering their heated kisses, her lips throbbing even now to recall the delirious pleasure of joining her mouth with his. When he'd asked her to thank him with a kiss, she'd been startled, but intrigued, tempted beyond her ability to resist. Unsure at first, she hadn't known exactly how to proceed. But then he'd coaxed her into trying it again and zounds, what bliss! What delight!

Curling a fist against the flutters in her stomach, she pushed away from the door and went across to her bed. Finding a spot that wasn't covered in her new gowns, she sank down with a sigh.

As wonderful as Edward's touch was, giving in to the impulse to kiss him had been a dreadful mistake. He'd had only to crook his little finger and she'd turned as gooey as a dish of warm toffee, melting against him as she practically begged for his regard. Her behavior was so pitiable she nearly disgusted herself, she was so weak-willed and compliant.

Was she so desperate for his attention that she was willing to cast aside her resolve in order to partake of a few crumbs? Was she so pathetic that she was ready to turn into that silly, stupid girl who'd once hung on his every word and worshipped the very ground on which he walked? If she wasn't careful, she could see herself turning back into the wretched creature of five years before, willing to do anything for even a hint of his affection.

Not that she was deluded enough to imagine that what had passed between her and Edward had anything to do with affection. After all, he'd invited her kisses out of a kind of teasing retribution. Who knew why he'd decided to continue the embrace.

Curiosity?

Simple contrariness?

Lust?

She might like to flatter herself that he desired her, but she suspected any impulses in that direction were no stronger than those he might feel for any reasonably attractive woman. She'd been convenient and he'd been in the mood to play games.

Well, she didn't want to be trifled with again. She couldn't afford the risk involved, since every emotion she'd experienced in his arms only made her wish for more.

As for her ultimate goal? She would simply have to try again. What other choice did she have, since she refused to ever let herself become that pitiable girl again.

Stretching out on her side, she pressed her cheek against the satin counterpane, her gaze roaming absently over the ribbons and lace and silk of the gowns that were lying in her near vision.

She ought to get up and ring for her maid, she supposed. Instead, she snuggled deeper and let her mind take her where it would.

Chapter 9

Claire strolled into the family dining room the next morning, dressed in one of her new frocks—a gown of pale peach silk with half sleeves and a ringed flounce trimmed in sleek bronze satin.

For a moment she stopped short, her gaze riveted on the room's sole occupant. Given the hour, she'd expected Mallory and the twins to be here already. Instead, only Edward sat in his accustomed place at the head of the table, a newspaper folded open at his elbow, while he dined on a plate of eggs, toast, sausage and kippers.

She nearly retreated, but knew it was already too late. Even if Edward hadn't seen her yet, he would surely notice her turning around to effect a hasty withdrawal. Inhaling low, she drew back her shoulders and continued inside.

Maybe the others had just overslept and would be joining her and Edward soon, she told herself. Until then, she would have to deal with him alone.

Some of the confidence slid out of her spine at the thought.

He glanced up then and gave her a slight smile before he turned a page of his newspaper. "Good morning, Claire."

"Good morning," she answered, not pausing as she moved past him to the buffet.

The room grew quiet while she took up a plate and made her selections. Once she'd taken her seat at the table on Edward's right, one of the footmen came forward to pour her tea. He refreshed the duke's coffee as well before withdrawing from the room.

"So, how was your night?" Edward asked. "Did you sleep well?"

No, she mused, remembering the way she'd tossed and turned, dreams and thoughts of Edward and his kisses plaguing her through the long, dark hours.

"Splendidly," she declared with false cheer. "And you?"

He drank some coffee. "Quite well."

Of course, she thought. *How else would he sleep? Likely nothing ever disturbs Edward's rest.*

"Mallory and the twins are obviously late," she commented, as she spread butter onto a crumpet. "Perhaps their night was not so easy as yours and mine."

"Actually, Leo and Lawrence are off on some sporting jaunt for the day. While Mallory sent word along just a few minutes ago that she has decided to take breakfast in her room. Apparently there were a couple of letters from Hargreaves in this morning's post and she can't be torn away."

"No, of course she can't," Claire agreed. In order to cover her dismay at finding herself deserted, she bit into her crumpet.

Edward continued his breakfast as well, polishing off the last of his sausage and eggs before wiping his mouth clean with his napkin. Taking up his coffee, he leaned back in his chair. "Is that another of your new gowns?"

She nodded, glad her mouth was too full to answer.

"It's even more becoming than the other one. The color suits you well," he said. "Lovely."

She swallowed, warmth inching up her neck at the reminder of a very similar conversation they'd had yesterday and everything that had happened afterward. Gathering her fork and knife, she stabbed the slice of ham on her plate and cut off a piece. Instead of eating it, though, she slid it around with the tines of her fork.

"Unless you are otherwise engaged," Edward said, "I wondered if you might care to take a drive with me this afternoon?"

She stopped fidgeting and looked up. "A drive?"

"In the park, if you would enjoy it. It occurred to me that we haven't been able to spend a great deal of time together since your arrival in Town. I thought this might be a good opportunity to do so."

Spend time together? Why? The question nearly shot out of her mouth, but she recalled it just in time.

Her brows furrowed as she thought over his invitation. On the surface, the excursion sounded pleasant, and despite her present misgivings, being with Edward was never a hardship. Then again, the duke was a busy man and not the sort to idle his days away with drives through the park. And it wasn't as though they were courting, seeing that they were already engaged. So what was he really up to?

Then suddenly she knew. *He's doing his duty again. Getting to know me better as he once had promised.* It wasn't that he *really* wanted to go driving with her; it was only that he thought he ought to. Her mouth tightened at the realization. *Well, if he wants to get to know me better, perhaps I ought to let him.*

With that decision made, she relaxed and laid her silverware onto her plate. "The park would be enjoyable, I'm sure.

Although from what Mallory tells me, the crowds can make it a rather plodding exercise, given the necessity of stopping every half minute to converse with some acquaintance or other."

He regarded her over his cup. "True enough, though I had envisioned us going before the afternoon crush when there wouldn't be quite so many people. But if you would enjoy something other than a carriage ride, you have only to say."

"It's not the carriage ride, it is just . . ." She hesitated, waiting to see if he would give her further encouragement.

"Just what?" he asked.

"Only that instead of taking me for a drive, I would much rather you showed me how to drive."

His eyes widened. "Teach you, you mean?"

"Exactly!" she said with genuine excitement. "I have always wanted to learn to drive a carriage, but Papa wouldn't hear of such a thing. In his opinion, it's a useless skill for a woman, since he says that ladies may always rely on a gentleman to escort them wherever they wish to go."

She paused to gauge his reaction. When he didn't instantly agree, she continued, "But I have always supposed it a worthwhile ability for either sex. In my estimation, women would benefit from being far less dependent upon the men in their lives, at least for small things such as going about Town. Besides, driving just looks fun. It is, is it not?"

As she watched, he cocked his head slightly and peered at her again over the rim of his coffee cup. His eyes were very blue and filled with curiosity, as if he didn't quite recognize her after her small outburst.

But she didn't mind. She was glad she'd said what she had, no matter his reaction. And who knew, if he took exception, maybe that would be the key to placing a wedge between them.

He set his cup into its saucer. "Driving is most enjoyable, particularly with a reliable team. So, you want to learn, do you?"

She tipped up her chin. "I do. Yes."

"Well then, why don't we change our outing from a drive in the park to a driving lesson? Finish your breakfast, then go find your maid, so you can change into a suitable gown for the occasion."

"You mean now? This morning?"

"Yes, this morning. The earlier the better, in fact, since the streets will only get busier as the day goes on."

A wide smile broke over her face and she leapt up from her chair.

"What about your breakfast?" he asked.

"I'm not hungry. Besides, I'm too excited to eat another bite."

And she was, giddy with an almost childlike delight she hadn't felt in years. Without thinking, she took a step in his direction, then checked herself when she realized she'd been about to throw her arms around him for a hug. Instead, she sent him another smile.

He smiled back, his dimples disappearing in a way that made her pulse stutter. "Go on, then," he said. "I'll meet you downstairs in an hour, shall we say?"

"Forty-five minutes. I am sure I can be ready by then."

"Three quarters of an hour it is." Edward laughed, then took up his coffee cup again.

Grinning in spite of herself, she turned and sprinted from the room.

Seated beside Edward in his glossy black curricle a little over an hour later, Claire listened attentively as he explained the rudiments of carriage driving. So far, they hadn't moved so much as an inch, the horses standing at the ready, end-lessly patient except for the occasional betraying swish of a tail or the shifting of a hoof.

Still, in spite of the delay, Claire was rather glad they hadn't gone anywhere yet, considering all the information Edward was imparting. As she had quickly discovered, there was a great deal more to this learning-to-drive business than she had ever imagined.

Abruptly, Edward's lecture came to an end. "That should more than cover it," he said. "Shall we go?"

She met his gaze. "Go?"

"If you're ready. Give the ribbons a gentle flick and take us up the street. I thought we'd drive around the square a time or two, then proceed from there."

"Oh, I . . . all right." Her stomach quivered with a combination of nerves and excitement. She had only to give the command and the horses would be off.

"Don't worry," he said reassuringly. "You'll be safe. I promise not to let you crash into anything."

"I certainly hope not!"

He chuckled. "You'll do fine. Signal the team like I told you and we'll be on our way."

Marshalling her determination, she sat up straighter, then gathered the reins again. After glancing over her shoulder to make sure there was no traffic approaching, she gave a soft click of her tongue and flicked her wrists with a gentle but decisive snap. Equine ears perked up, the pair of matched bays tossing their heads with enthusiasm as they eased into a walk.

Elation swelled inside Claire's chest, a smile spreading over her mouth as the curricle rolled forward. One yard, and two, then three . . . *Why, this isn't so hard.* In fact, it seemed downright simple. What had she been worried about? And why had Edward insisted on so many instructions when a baby could drive this rig? Relaxing into an easy rhythm, she let the horses guide them forward as she settled back to enjoy the ride.

"Get ready now to ease off as you prepare to make your turn ahead," Edward said, low and calm.

Turn? What turn?

Her eyes widened as she realized he was right. The first left turn in the square was coming up in only a few more yards. And she hadn't the vaguest idea how to manage it. As though sensing her quandary, the horses took advantage and increased their gait. A knot formed in her throat and she pulled back sharply on the reins. The lead horse whinnied out a protest.

"Not so hard," Edward told her in a patient voice. "Gentle and easy is always best. Here, let me show you."

Before she knew what he intended, he slid an arm around her waist, then covered both of her hands with his. Using almost imperceptible pressure, he coaxed the team into a controlled walk, while at the same time lining up the curricle to make the approaching turn. With the easy confidence of long practice, he slowed them a faint bit more, then made the turn—all the while clasping her hands securely inside his own.

"Feel the shift in the ribbons and how little effort is required to communicate with the team," he said.

Yes, she thought, her breath hitching in her chest. She could most definitely feel the reins, the horses—and the man! With Edward's strong arms wrapped around her and his hands holding hers so securely, it was as though they were embracing. Even their hips and thighs were touching where they sat nestled together on the seat. The sensations were enough that, for a moment, she forgot all about the driving. Luckily, Edward managed to keep his head and prevent them from veering off course.

"A light pressure is often all that's required for the horses to understand exactly what you want," he observed, as they safely completed the next turn and moved slowly along the street.

"After that," he continued, "it's simply a matter of letting them do their job. Animals, you will find, are far more intelligent than people give them credit for being, especially horses. Be good to your team, show them respect, and they will be good to you in return."

Swallowing, she nodded.

"Ready to try it alone again?" he asked.

She hesitated, then reminded herself that she wanted to learn to drive. This lesson had been her idea, after all, and she had more pluck than to let a mild case of nerves keep her from achieving her goal. "Yes," she stated with determination. "At least I think so."

Laughing again, he released her hands and returned full control of the team to her. She expected him to slide his arm free as well. Instead, he left it curved around her waist, his gloved palm resting on the seat next to her hip.

Her skin tingled everywhere he touched, and places where he didn't as well, her body growing warm beneath her corded lilac muslin carriage dress. With the horses on a straight stretch, she took a moment to dart a glance at Edward from beneath the narrow brim of her white chipstraw bonnet.

And found his gaze on her—his eyes vividly blue in the sunshine of the crisp spring day.

Her heart squeezed out an extra beat, then another when a slow smile curved his mouth in a move that displayed his beautiful white teeth.

Good heavens. He really shouldn't be allowed to do that, she thought, her pulse hammering. *And I should have more sense than to let it scramble every logical thought in my head!*

"The next turn is approaching," he murmured, his gaze never leaving hers. "You may want to get ready."

Giving herself a stern mental shake, and a scold as well, she turned her gaze forward again. The horses' ears twitched as if anticipating her next command. Adjusting the reins, she prepared herself to give it.

"Need help?" Edward offered.

She refused to glance at him. "No. I can do it."

She wasn't sure, but she was nearly positive that he smiled again.

Displaying more confidence than she felt, she took the turn, pleased when the team—and the curricle—rounded the corner with an easy grace. Edward's hand touched hers only once, making a slight adjustment as she maneuvered past a coach standing idle in front of a stately town house.

And then they were proceeding up the street, picking up speed as they went. Only she was controlling the pace now and not the team.

"How was that?" she asked, daring to shoot him a grin.

"Splendid. Now keep going."

Nodding, she maintained her concentration, her initial concerns falling away. When the next corner approached, she was ready, positioning the team in just the right way. She made the turn smoothly, the yards sliding past with no difficulty.

Glancing ahead, she was surprised to find Clybourne House rising with grandeur on the horizon.

"Go around another time or two," Edward remarked. "We've already given our neighbors plenty of fodder for their afternoon calls, why not add a bit more."

"What do you mean?" Keeping a steady grip on the reins, she maneuvered around a delivery wagon, then slowed to let a nursery maid and her young charges walk across the street. Edward covered her hands to direct her well out of harm's way before returning control to her again.

"Surely no one is paying us any mind?" she remarked, as she signaled the team to continue on.

"Of course they are," he said. "I expect half the draperies on the square have been drawn back by now to witness our excursion."

"I certainly hope you jest. I don't much care for the notion of being spied upon."

"Unfortunately, you'll find that one is under almost constant surveillance here in Town. After all, gossip is the lifeblood of the Ton, and the buzz will do nothing but increase as more and more families arrive for the Season. As it is, Mallory and I have been fending off calls for the past two weeks in order to let you settle in. Soon, though, there'll be no stopping them, particularly once the Season is officially under way."

Fending off calls? She'd had no idea. But she supposed it was only natural that people would be curious about the Duke of Clybourne's fiancée, even if she would much rather they weren't.

Frowning, she shot a glance at the windows of the nearest town house to see if any of the curtains were moving.

"Don't let it bother you," Edward said, having obviously caught the direction of her gaze. "Besides, you must be used to a certain level of scrutiny, even in the country."

"Yes, but old Mrs. Roddy isn't quite the same as having an entire city full of tattlers."

"Oh, it's not so bad as all that. Well, maybe it is," he corrected with a laugh. "But you'll find it easiest to just ignore their inquiring gazes and go on about your affairs as if they weren't there at all. Besides, any talk about our outing today will only be of the complimentary sort, since you're doing brilliantly."

"Am I?" she asked, unable to keep the hopeful note out of her voice.

"Yes," he confirmed. "If you aren't careful, I shall have to suggest that the Four-in-Hand Club change their rules about admitting women. We're around the square again. Shall we venture farther afield or have you had enough driving for today?"

"Farther afield, please. Perhaps there is somewhere we could go that would allow us to take the horses above a fast walk."

"There might be a place or two," he drawled with amusement, "if we venture out of the city a bit."

"I'm game, if you are. Or have you duties to which you must attend this afternoon?" she added. "Perhaps your prolonged absence will cause Mr. Hughes to wear more holes in your office carpet should you fail to return apace."

Their gazes met, his brow arching with clear awareness of her thinly veiled sarcasm. "Oh, I expect I can be spared for a few hours at least."

"Good. You work too much anyway."

"Do I?" he said in a surprised tone before pointing toward the street ahead. "Take Upper Brook Street over to Park Lane. We'll go up to Tyburn Turnpike, then north of the city. There are some farms up there that should provide a few reasonable roads on which you can let the horses have their heads."

Guiding the curricle, she followed his directions.

"Actually," he continued, "you should probably let me drive for now. The traffic is bound to be heavy until we're out of the city." He laid his hands over hers to take the reins.

Instead of relinquishing them, however, she tightened her grip. "I'm fine. For now at least. If the traffic is heavy and I become uncomfortable, I will let you drive."

His hands tightened fractionally over hers, sending a fresh round of quivers through her. Then he let go. Leaning back, he relaxed. But he left his arm looped behind her with his palm on the seat near her hip, exactly where it had been before. "I had no idea you could be so stubborn."

"There are a great many things you don't know about me, Your Grace."

"So it would seem. And it's Edward, remember?" he said, his words silky and warm.

Yes, I remember, she thought with a wistful inner sigh.

"So tell me more," he encouraged.

She tossed him a glance. "About what?"

"About you, of course."

"Me? Oh, there's nothing to tell."

He quirked a brow. "That's not what you said a moment ago."

"Nothing interesting, that is." Slowing the curricle to let a coach-and-four roll past, she used the distraction to change the subject. "Why do you not tell me about yourself instead? For instance, what do you like to do, when you aren't working, that is?"

"Hmm, when I'm not working—which according to you is rarely—I like to do any number of things. I enjoy reading and music and collecting art. I like to fence at Angelo's when I'm in Town, and I love to ride. We must ride out together one morning. I have several gentle mares in the stable. I am sure we could find a suitable mount for you."

"If that is the case," she replied without governing her response, "then I hope you will choose an animal with a bit more spirit than merely gentle. I am not so accomplished a horsewoman that I ride to hounds, but neither am I shy in the saddle."

"No," he said in a considering tone. "I am beginning to realize that you would not be—in the saddle or anywhere else."

Wishing suddenly that she'd kept her mouth closed, she focused on her driving. Having turned onto the more well-traveled Park Lane, she realized that Edward had been right about the traffic. It was heavier and a great deal more difficult to negotiate. Still, she was determined to try.

"What else then?" she asked, taking up a position behind a rather slow-moving dray. "What else do you particularly enjoy doing?"

"Oh no," he countered. "I believe it's your turn now."

"But there is—"

"Nothing interesting to tell. Yes, I know. Pray enlighten me nevertheless about all the tedious things which give you pleasure. Other than gardening, of course," he added.

Claire shot him a look, but if he was teasing, she couldn't tell. Composing herself, she forged on. "At home, I occupy myself with the usual feminine endeavors. Stitchery and the occasional sad attempt at watercolor painting. Flower arranging when the blossoms are in season, and flower pressing if there is an especially lovely specimen. I trim hats, take long walks and pick berries off the wild brambles in the hottest days of summer."

"Those are all things you do, but you haven't really answered my question. What do you like?"

"I like those things," she defended. "Except for the painting. I'm really dreadful with a brush and would be better off painting a fence than a canvas."

"I shall remember not to accept any invitations to painting parties on your behalf. What else?"

"Reading. I like books, although I rather doubt we share the same interests when it comes to subject matter. I love romances and mystery stories. The more lurid, the better."

"Mallory loves those too."

"Yes, I know. She has loaned me several already. She possesses quite an impressive collection of Minerva Press novels."

"What more?"

"Oh, I don't know. Nothing in particular."

He cocked his head and gave her an inquiring look. "But there is something more. What?"

"Your turn again."

"After you answer," he insisted. "What else?"

Pausing, she watched as the dray pulled over and stopped, forcing her to go around and continue ahead without its reassuring bulk.

Why, she wondered, *did I say anything to him?* She wished now that she'd never started this line of questioning. If she'd had any sense she would have spent the entire time making up a series of ridiculous inventions in hopes that a few of them might displease him.

Instead, she'd been hopelessly candid when she ought to have guarded her thoughts and feelings. But it was too late now and couldn't be helped. And truly, what difference did it make what she'd told him? He was only being polite with his inquiries. He was only doing his duty with this whole outing. And with any luck, mayhap he wouldn't like the real her at all.

"Puzzles," she declared. "I like puzzles and games, the sort that give most people a headache. But I find them fascinating and frustrating and immensely satisfying to solve. I'm always looking for new ones to try."

She expected him to greet her comment with boredom or disapproval, as her family always did. Instead, Edward had a peculiar look on his face, his eyes gleaming with an enigmatic light she couldn't quite read.

"As it happens, I like puzzles too," he said. "Love them, in fact. There's nothing more interesting than solving something deemed unsolvable, is there?"

"No, there isn't."

He leaned slightly closer, looking for a moment as if he might say more. Instead, he glanced up and nodded toward the cross street ahead. "You'll need to turn left for the turnpike. If you won't take it amiss, why do you not let me drive this last portion?"

In the past minutes, the traffic had grown steadily thicker and more difficult to manage. Her pride had kept her going, but she had to confess she wouldn't mind his assistance. Hiding her relief, she nodded. "Very well. But I want to drive again when we reach the countryside."

"Of course. I promise."

She handed over the reins, more sorry than she wished when he slid his arm out from around her. Relaxing back, she lifted her face to the sun, determined to enjoy the rest of the outing.

Chapter 10

Edward strode into his study later that afternoon to find Drake lounging in one of the wide brown leather armchairs positioned near the fireplace. Drake's eyes were closed, his fingers linked across his flat stomach, his long legs stretched out before him. Anyone looking at him would assume he was asleep, but Edward knew better, the pose one of his brother's favorites when he wanted to think something through.

Of course, sometimes he really was just sleeping.

"Where have you been then?" Drake said without opening his eyes, proving Edward's initial assumption to be correct. "I've been waiting here over an hour. Croft said something about you taking a drive with Lady Claire."

"Croft obviously keeps you well informed."

Drake smiled. "He guards your important secrets, don't worry."

Edward gave a mild snort, then crossed to the liquor cabinet. "Care for a drink?"

"Only if you have some of that Madeira you served the other evening. Otherwise, I'll pass."

Reaching for the vintage in question, Edward poured them each a glass, returning the crystal stopper to the decanter with a near silent click. Taking up the goblets, he walked over and handed one to his brother, who opened his eyes just in time to accept it.

"My thanks," Drake said before taking a long swallow. "Delicious."

Edward lowered himself into the chair opposite, moving Drake's feet out of the way with a good-natured shove.

Grinning, Drake sat up in his chair. "So, you took Lady Claire out driving, did you?"

Pausing, Edward sipped from his glass, enjoying the dry, slightly fruity notes of the wine. "Actually, she took me. We had our first driving lesson today."

"Driving lesson? How did that come about?"

Edward shrugged. "This morning at breakfast she expressed an interest in learning. So I offered to teach her."

"How'd she do?"

"In truth? Phenomenally well. Don't tell her I said this, but she could drive solo after just the one lesson. Handled the reins like she was born to it. Of course I'd never let her explore the city on her own, but so long as she has a proper escort, I can't see any harm in letting her take a team out on occasion."

Drake shot him a look of surprise. "Next I suppose I'll hear that you've bought her a phaeton or some such. Painted in her favorite color, of course, with specially upholstered kidskin seats and fittings made of real gold."

"How ridiculous. Don't be absurd."

"Then again, I'm not sure she's the type who'd fancy an ostentatious rig," Drake speculated aloud. "Simple black with plain leather seats and not so much as a crest on the door might be more in keeping with her tastes."

Edward frowned, realizing he didn't know what Claire

would prefer; he didn't even know her favorite color. He thought about the twitching curtains of their neighbors and her reaction to the idea of being watched. A showy color that drew every eye would only make her uncomfortable, he decided, whereas the black . . . not that he was buying her a phaeton. He'd already bought her a fortune in clothes.

Not that he minded.

Not really.

Maybe not at all.

Frowning again, he drank more wine.

"It's interesting, but she isn't what I expected," Drake remarked.

"Oh?" Edward drawled, spinning his glass slowly between his fingers. "How so?"

"I'm not sure. I suppose I thought she might be haughty and vain, having grown up knowing she was going to be a duchess one day. But she's not. She's . . . sweet and interesting and amusingly unpredictable. I like Lady Claire. It may have been nothing more than fool's luck and Papa's obstinacy that brought you two together, but you've made a good choice. I can see why you decided to go through with the match."

But he hadn't decided to go through with the match because of Claire. He'd done it for the sake of duty, honor and, yes, expediency. Yet Drake was right. Claire was sweet and interesting and amusingly unpredictable. She was also a puzzle. A very intricate, very complicated and as yet unsolved conundrum that he was still in the process of figuring out.

But I like puzzles and I like her too, Edward thought, surprised by the truth of the realization. He hadn't really considered it before, since liking Claire wasn't a requirement for their marriage, but he found that he did indeed like her.

Their drive today, for one, had been remarkably entertaining, and not because of the lesson, but because of Claire herself. She was a lively and enjoyable companion and yet she didn't preen and wheedle as so many ladies of the Ton were wont to do. Nor did she insist on constant conversation, although she was very easy to converse with. Claire was amiable and desirable, and his brother was right that she would make him a good wife—and because of far more than her excellent bloodlines.

Downing another mouthful of Madeira, he swirled the remaining inch of pale gold liquor in his glass, then returned his attention to Drake. "So did you just drop by to chat about my fiancée and drink my wine or was there something else you wanted?"

Drake barked out a quick laugh. "Something *you* want, you mean. As good as your wine cellar may be, I did come by with another purpose in mind. I've been studying that newspaper clipping you gave me."

"Oh?" Edward said, his interest immediately piqued. "And?"

"And I'm certain it contains a code, just as you suspected."

"I knew it." Edward tapped a fist against the arm of his chair. "Why else would Everett have folded it up and hidden it inside that false heel of his shoe? If the bloody thing hadn't shaken loose while I was searching his belongings, we'd never have known. Brazen bastard."

"Brazen is right and not just about Everett. His contacts, whoever they may be, are trading messages in plain sight and using the newspapers to do it. I'm working on breaking the cipher and I will. It's more sophisticated than I initially expected. If you could find me another example or two, it would speed matters along."

"We're looking, now that we know *to* look. Everett's guard at the prison mentioned that he'd been complaining about not receiving his morning newspaper the day he was killed. Considered in this new light, his outburst takes on a completely different significance."

"Clearly," Drake agreed. "But was he still receiving new messages or was he only hoping to find something he might be able to use as leverage to gain his freedom? I wonder if he knew he'd been slated for death?"

"Maybe so," Edward mused aloud. "Perhaps that's why he'd started talking recently, hoping he could make a deal with us once he'd been abandoned by them. Of course, if that were the case, why wouldn't he have simply offered us an exchange rather than wait?"

"Perhaps he still thought he could work both sides."

"Unfortunately, it's all speculation at this point." Edward spun his glass in another slow circle, then tossed back the last of his wine. "When you break that cipher, let me know."

Drake smiled, his gaze alight with undisguised anticipation. "You'll be the first."

"In the meantime, I shall be busy escorting Claire to one entertainment or another. Easter arrives next week and with it the start of the Season. There'll be no getting out of the myriad invitations that are pouring in already, especially not with Mama still away."

"Better you than me. Can't stand all the hullabaloo that goes on this time of year."

"I thought you enjoyed the parties."

"The parties, yes. The frenzied jockeying to snare a husband . . . now, that I can do without, even if I am left mainly out of the fray. Being fourth in line will do that for a fellow, thank God."

Edward laughed. "Just think of the trouble you'd be put to if Cade, Jack and I were all killed in some freak accident. Oh, and little Maximillian too. I guess our new nephew bumps you down to number five in the succession."

"Good, I'm glad of it. You, Cade and Jack are welcome to have as many sons as the three of you like. But for heaven's sake, Ned, don't even joke about a thing like all of you dying. In addition to grieving over such a dreadful loss, the idea of being duke gives me the shudders. Frankly, I don't know how you stand it."

Edward hid a smile. "Oh, it's not so very dreadful. Most days at least."

"Luckily, the odds of such an occurrence aren't all that good," Drake continued, obviously running calculations in his head. "Somewhere around two million, seven hundred ninety-three thousand, nine hundred and seventy-six to one, assuming the four of you aren't all riding in the same coach or sailing on the same ship, to say nothing of contracting the same disease, then the odds increase to . . ." He paused, a fierce scowl settling over his dark brows before they shot high. "None of you are allowed to be together at the same time ever again!"

"That's what I love about you," Edward said, grinning as he got to his feet. "Ever the optimist."

Drake shot him a look. "You'd be a pessimist too, if you were more serious about math."

"Then it's a good thing I'm rather indifferent on that score. Now, enough of such maudlin talk. Are you planning to stay for dinner this evening?"

"Oh, I hadn't considered it. I suppose I could, depending on the menu."

"Beef medallions and a potato cheese tart, I believe."

"Well, in that case, I shall."

"Let me get you some tea, dear," Wilhelmina Byron said only moments after Claire took a seat next to Mallory on one of the sofas in the family drawing room.

The older woman smiled as she prepared the beverage,

her dark eyes kind in her pleasant, slightly doughy, face. Her shape was slightly doughy as well, her hips and bosom ample beneath her dark aubergine crepe gown. When her husband had died several years before, she'd never quite come out of mourning, preferring to remain in somber colors, a lace widow's cap tied over her greying brunette hair.

Nonetheless, Claire found her a cheerful companion without a hint of malice. She always had a ready smile and never uttered a critical word. If anything she was perhaps a bit too amiable and trusting, giving Claire and Mallory far more latitude than most chaperones normally would. Not that Claire had any complaints, far from it. Nor Mallory, who had confided to Claire that she reveled in the unexpected freedom, especially here in Town. With Cousin Wilhelmina here, Mallory had commented that she could "get away with murder" if she wanted, so long as Edward didn't find out.

Claire hid a smile at the recollection, as she accepted the cup Cousin Wilhelmina passed her, the steaming tea prepared with one sugar and extra milk, just the way Claire liked it.

"I certainly hope you had a good time on your outing," Cousin Wilhelmina said, returning the Meissen teapot to the silver tray. "Did Edward take you to the park?"

"Actually, we went north. And I drove for much of the way. He's giving me lessons, you see."

"Carriage-driving lessons!" Mallory exclaimed. "You didn't say you were having lessons. How diverting. What was it like?"

Accepting a plate with lemon biscuits and a small poppy seed cake from Cousin Wilhelmina, Claire regaled her and Mallory with the highlights. She decided to say nothing of the fact that Edward had agreed to the excursion only because he was fulfilling his promise to get to know her better, rather than because he'd genuinely wanted to spend time with her.

Although he had seemed to enjoy himself. At least she thought he had, though maybe he was simply too polite to let on otherwise. But even if he had truly had fun, it meant nothing. He was still marrying her for duty's sake, and she was still determined not to let him.

After finishing her tale a couple of minutes later, she sipped her tea and nibbled on one of the biscuits.

"Oh, dear heavens," Cousin Wilhelmina exclaimed, setting down her own cup and plate before reaching for something inside her pocket. "Pray forgive me, Claire dear, but I quite forgot. I can be such a chucklehead sometimes. This letter came for you while you were out. I promised most faithfully that I would deliver it into your hands and I suppose I have . . . finally." She giggled at the last, looking embarrassed and younger than her years.

Claire accepted the missive with a grateful smile. Breaking open the seal, she scanned the contents. "It's from Mama. And there are notes enclosed from Nan and Ella as well. Everyone is as well as can be expected. The doctor Edward sent proved highly knowledgeable and greatly reassuring. To everyone's relief, he says Nan should recover full use of her leg."

She paused to read on, leafing through the pages. "Nan is recovering slowly but is frightfully bored and miserable confined to her bed, just as I knew she would be. They all miss me and send their love. There are more details from home but I shan't bore you with those. Although Mama says that she wants a full accounting of all the balls and parties she is being forced to miss, since she couldn't stay to enjoy the Season as planned."

"And so she should," Cousin Wilhelmina said. "I would be delighted to provide my own account of goings-on, if you think she would appreciate my meager renditions."

"How kind of you to offer, Mrs. Byron. I am sure Mama would be most obliged were you to share your observations about life here in Town with her. My sisters as well, who are always eager for news about Society. They would all be thrilled to receive your letters, which would be of the most excellent kind."

The older woman's cheeks pinked with pleasure. "Then I shall do my best to write. And speaking of the Season, His Grace has asked me to consult with both of you about which invitations to accept. The duke has narrowed them down to a manageable number, but is leaving the final selection up to us ladies. What do you think? Shall I go get the stack of cards now, so we may decide?"

Claire shared a look with Mallory, who gave an agreeable nod. "Yes, most definitely. Let us begin."

Chapter 11

"Five balls in six days. I think I may collapse," Claire said, as she joined Mallory on the side of the ballroom two weeks later. Finding a pair of empty chairs, they sank into them, Claire's feet tingling with relief from having danced the last three sets. As she watched, Mallory opened her painted silk and ivory fan and waved it in front of her face, her cheeks rosy from her own dancing.

"Oh, this is nothing," Mallory remarked. "There have been times when I've gone to five different balls in one evening. Though only on rare occasions when several important hostesses all decided to hold their entertainments on the same night. Most inconvenient of them, I've always thought."

Claire felt her eyes widen, relieved they hadn't encountered a similar situation so far, although it was still very early yet in the Season. Even so, there was never a paucity of invitations, as she had learned that first afternoon when she, Cousin Wilhelmina and Mallory culled through their first batch of cards. A constant flood of new invitations had been arriving ever since, each group requiring careful attention and consideration, lest they slight someone who dare not be slighted.

As for her own initial foray into Society, it had proven alternately enlightening, daunting and exciting, requiring every ounce of her composure during those times when she found all eyes upon her.

She'd known being Edward's fiancée came with a certain amount of notoriety. Even so, she hadn't expected the intense level of scrutiny she faced, especially when she met someone for the first time. Almost uniformly, they stared for a split second longer than normal and smiled just a touch too brightly, silently taking her measure while they strove to impress her with their own. Not that there weren't any number of genuinely warm, pleasant people—there were; it was simply a matter of being able to distinguish one from the other and acquiring the knowledge to do so.

Mallory proved invaluable on that score, since she knew nearly everyone. And Edward as well, when he went to the trouble of commenting. Mostly he seemed to think she knew how to handle herself, letting her deal with various situations on her own.

Not that he wasn't always readily at hand, since he escorted her to all the evening entertainments. But often after a single dance, he would excuse himself, reappearing at her side only when it was time to return home. She understood that such behavior was the accepted standard for most Society couples.

Nevertheless, it rankled.

It also served to remind her of her ultimate objective, even if she'd done nothing recently to encourage the plan. She'd been busy trying to find her balance among the Ton and hadn't been able to take further steps toward securing her freedom.

But plenty of time still remained, she assured herself. If only there wouldn't be such a very great scandal when he ended their engagement. She shivered at the idea, realizing more than ever the enormity of such an event.

But it was what she wanted.

Wasn't it?

Or at least what she knew she must do in order to retain some measure of self-respect when all this was done. Despite her deepening acquaintance with Edward, it was plain he was no more in love with her than ever. If he were, everything would be different. If he loved her, this would be the happiest time of her life. But as she'd learned many years ago, wishing for a thing didn't make it so. And pinning false hopes on faerie stories only led to disillusionment and regret.

She had only to consider her own parents to know that much. For as long as she could remember, she'd watched her mother do everything in her power to win a greater share of her father's affection. He cared for his wife in his way, but there was an intensity of feeling she craved that he seemed incapable of returning. The simple truth was she loved him and he didn't love her back. And even though Mama hid it well and never said a word, Claire knew the toll such knowledge had taken on her mother. And took still, day by day.

I refuse to let that be me. I deserve better. And so does Edward. Everyone, she thought, *has a right to be loved.*

Suppressing a sigh, she forced a smile and returned her attention to her friend.

"I'll be glad when midnight supper is served," Mallory said in a quiet confession. "I'm famished in spite of the dinner we ate before we left home. All that dancing, I assume."

"Very likely," Claire agreed. "Have you already promised the supper dance to someone?"

Mallory shook her head. "Not yet, no. It's silly of me, I realize, but I always think of Michael during that particular set, since he was so very clever about making sure he got to claim that dance from me. Now I find myself reluctant to pledge it, as though he might somehow walk through the door, in spite of the fact that I know he's hundreds of miles away in Spain. Still . . ."

Reaching out, Claire patted her hand. "It sounds only natural to me. You miss him, that's all. Just know that he'll be home soon. Didn't he just write to say that he's planning to take leave in a few more weeks?"

Mallory's aquamarine gaze brightened at the reminder. "Yes. And stay two months entire once he arrives. I am quite beside myself with anticipation."

"So should you be. Until then, you will have to allow some other gentlemen to share supper with you and not feel guilty about doing so. I am sure Major Hargreaves wouldn't begrudge you the meal or the company."

Mallory met her gaze, then smiled. "You're right. As I said at the outset, I am only being silly. Now whom should I pick?" Her spirits much revived, Mallory began scanning the ballroom for a likely prospect.

Smiling back, Claire followed her lead. "What about Lord Longsworth? He seems a pleasant enough fellow."

"Oh, he is, and an excellent dancer as well. It is only that he's rather enthusiastic about the outdoors, and for some reason, whenever we are in each other's company, he invariably starts telling me the details of his latest hunting expedition. His stories would quite put me off my food, if you know what I mean."

"I can see that they would. Hmm, so who else?"

Perusing the room together, they considered and discarded another half-dozen prospects. "What about that gentleman?" Claire said, studying an elegantly built man with tawny hair and deep-set grey eyes. "He seems rather interesting."

Mallory turned her head to study the man in question, her brows sliding downward. "That is Lord Islington and although he may indeed be as interesting as you say, he is also one of London's most disreputable rakehells. He's not the sort with whom young ladies generally associate."

"Why not? What has he done?"

"I don't know the details, but he has a most unsavory reputation."

"If it is so dreadful, then what is he doing here tonight?"

"He has position and money and no one dares cut him. But neither do mamas put their young daughters in his path for fear he might take advantage without doing the honorable thing. Edward warned me against him most strenuously during my first Season and I have heard nothing since to dissuade me from taking his advice. Stay away from that one, Claire. He is a very bad man."

"Did I hear mention made of a bad man?" asked a male voice in tones that were as rich and smooth as a dram of aged dark rum. "Then I assume you ladies must be talking about me."

Claire glanced up, then up some more, pausing at the sight of an extremely handsome, extremely tall gentleman with the warmest brown eyes she'd ever seen. They twinkled, those eyes, his gaze fixed on Mallory with a friendly regard that spoke of long familiarity.

Her supposition proved correct as Mallory laughed and wagged a finger at the man. "Adam! Where did you come from?" she declared, leaping to her feet.

Claire stood as well.

"Purgatory, of course," he replied with a naughty grin. "Where else would a devil like me take refuge when he's not in Town?" Catching hold of Mallory's hand, he bowed low.

Ignoring the usual bounds of decorum, Mallory threw her arms around him for a quick but exuberant hug that Adam—whoever he might be—didn't seem to mind in the least.

Off to one side, a pair of matrons clicked their tongues, then turned away. Adam and Mallory didn't appear to take any notice of their disapproval, or else they simply didn't care.

"Did you just come up from Gresham Park?" Mallory asked. "You ought to have sent word ahead so we could have known to expect you."

"My plans weren't fixed and I wasn't sure when I might arrive. Besides, this way, I was able to surprise you. And we both know how you like surprises."

"Very true, but still you might have at least given a hint, my lord." Mallory sent him a mock glare before her expression softened again into a pleased smile. "It's so good to see you."

"Yes. It has been far too long."

"Christmas, if I remember correctly," Mallory said, "when we were all gathered at Braebourne. What a happy time that was."

"Yes, very happy indeed." He inclined his head, but not in time to completely conceal the slight shadow that flickered over his gaze. When he straightened again, however, the expression was gone, leaving Claire to wonder if it had merely been some trick of the candlelight. Apparently so, since he looked in the best of spirits.

"But we have kept to ourselves far too long," he said. "Pray introduce me to your friend, since I have not yet had the pleasure of making her acquaintance."

"Of course. Forgive me. I am always so lax about the formalities." Sliding her arm through Adam's, she turned so they were both facing Claire. "Adam, allow me to make you known to Lady Claire Marsden. Claire, this devilish gentleman, as he falsely claims to be, is Lord Gresham, a very old and dear friend of the family."

"A pleasure, Lady Claire," he said, executing another elegant bow, his teeth white against his swarthy complexion.

Claire curtseyed, spreading the skirts of her ivory silk evening gown out to the sides. "The pleasure is mine as well, my lord."

"And there is nothing the least bit false in my claims," he continued in a casual tone. "I know what I am and take no pains to conceal it. Although I must take umbrage at your description of me as a very 'old' friend, Lady Mallory. There is nothing old about a gentleman, who is scarcely a year into his third decade. Ask any of your older brothers and they will tell you the same. We are in the prime of our lives."

"Indisputably," Mallory said. "Though should you find yourself in need of an ear trumpet, shout very loudly and I shall procure one for you," she added in a teasing voice.

Gresham gave a laugh, his dark eyes twinkling again. "Minx. That kind of sass should not be tolerated. I see I shall have to take you in hand."

Mallory grinned, her sea-colored gaze alight with clear inspiration. "In that case, you must ask me to dance. I have been trying to decide on someone to partner me for the supper dance and you are the perfect choice."

"I find it hard to believe you have trouble locating partners, but I would be most happy to oblige. Lady Mallory, may I have the supper dance with you this evening?"

"Of course, my lord. I would be absolutely delighted." Mallory shared a contented look with him.

Before she had time to say more, another gentleman arrived, his fair cheeks sporting ruddy flags of color, as he stopped to bow to them all.

"How d'ye do." Pausing, he cleared his throat as though his cravat was a fraction too tight. "Th-The next set is about to form, Lady Mallory. I believe we are engaged for this dance."

Claire watched as Mallory gave the young man a gracious

smile that had the immediate effect of easing his nervousness. "And so we are, Mr. Molleson. I was but waiting for your arrival."

With a grin that displayed a great many crooked teeth, he offered his arm to Mallory, which she accepted with aplomb. "If you will excuse me, Lady Claire, Lord Gresham."

Claire and Gresham traded smiles with Mallory, watching together for a moment as she made her way toward the dance floor.

Gresham turned, his gaze full of affable warmth. "Lady Claire, would you care to take a turn as well? Unless you are already promised."

"I have no such commitment, so yes, that would be lovely."

Laying her hand on his sleeve, he led her toward the others assembling for the set.

"So how long have you and Lady Mallory been acquainted?" she ventured.

"Literally ages, just as she said. I roomed with her brother Jack my first term at university, and he and I have been friends ever since. He invited me to Braebourne that first summer and that's where I met Mallory. She was just a child then, nine or ten, I believe, and spent her time trailing after us." He chuckled at the memory. "She made quite a nuisance of herself, as I recall. Ended up with a pair of skinned knees and a stained frock after she tumbled down a grassy hillock and landed nearly at our feet. She'd been spying on us, you see, and lost her balance."

His gaze strayed to where Mallory stood, his eyes softening. "You wouldn't know to look at her now, but she was quite the tomboy in her youth. I suppose it's what comes of having six brothers, most of whom are older."

"She sounds like my little sister Nan, although Nan hasn't the excuse of brothers. She broke her leg this spring climbing a tree."

His gaze returned to Claire. "Did she indeed? I hope she is recovering well."

"Most admirably. If one doesn't count boredom and grumpiness. Do you have siblings, my lord?" Claire inquired as they took their places for the set.

"No, none," he said, his expression sobering. "I had a sister but she died quite young."

"I am sorry."

He waved aside her regret. "No need. Many years have passed since then." He paused before redirecting the conversation. "Forgive me for not conveying my good wishes to you sooner, but I understand that you and Edward are to be wed."

She nodded. "That's right, though we have yet to make the announcement official. No date has been set or plans arranged for the . . . for the wedding."

He raised a brow. "Many couples have long engagements. There is nothing unusual in that. Although, if you will forgive me once more, I hear that yours is of an especially long duration. You were promised to each other as children, I believe?"

"We were."

"Then the rumors are true? Leave it to the duke to say nothing about the particulars."

"Has he not?" she asked, unable to hide her surprise. She'd assumed everyone knew the circumstances of her engagement to Edward, but apparently he'd decided to leave the origin of their union a secret—or at least publicly unacknowledged.

The music began then, and with it the start of the set. Moving to the familiar rhythms of a country dance, she and Gresham threaded their way in and around the other couples, continuing their conversation as the movements of the dance allowed.

She turned to reform the line, when out of the corner of her eye she noticed Edward. As she did, she couldn't help but see the woman standing at his side as well. Breath whooshed from her lungs in a sudden, dizzying gust.

Five years fell away as she stared. Five years rushed upon her as she recognized Felicia, Lady Bettis, who was just as beautiful now as she had been while a guest during her parents' country house party all those years ago.

Gresham caught her hand as Claire swayed. "Are you all right?" he asked.

Taking a deep breath, she steadied herself, managing somehow to take the steps required by the dance. "F-Fine. The warmth of the room was too much for a moment, but I am better now."

"You look a bit pale. Are you sure we shouldn't withdraw and find you a seat?"

"No. I am quite well. Let us continue."

Before he could question her further, the dance separated them once again.

She tried not to look when Edward and Lady Bettis came into view again. But she couldn't help it, her gaze locking on them with a kind of helpless fascination.

What were they doing together?

Was it just a matter of them both being in London for the Season or was it more?

Surely they weren't still involved after all this time?

Surely she wasn't still his mistress?

Nausea churned in her stomach, willpower alone the only thing that kept her moving to the music.

And then suddenly, gratefully, it was over. Ignoring Lord Gresham's looks and murmurs of concern, she strode from the dance floor, wanting to put as much distance as possible between herself, and Edward and his mistress.

Stomach roiling again, she continued toward the far corner of the ballroom.

Lord Gresham followed. "Take a seat and let me get you a cool refreshment. You look most unwell."

"I am fine."

"Shall I find Mrs. Byron or Edward instead? Perhaps you should go home."

"No!" she said in a fierce voice. "Not Edward."

Gresham stared.

"There is no need to trouble him," she dissembled in a far more modulated tone. "He will only worry, and for naught. Truly, it is only the warmth of the room. I am feeling recovered already."

Gresham frowned, appearing unconvinced. "If you are sure—"

"Very sure. Though, as you so generously offered, a cool glass of punch would not go amiss."

Pausing, he took a moment to consider. "Stay here and rest. I will be back presently with your refreshment."

"Thank you. You are most kind."

Casting her a last concerned look, he bowed and departed.

She slumped in her chair seconds after he left. As she did, her gaze fell on a man standing only a few feet distant. It was Lord Islington, she realized, and he was watching her, as he leaned in a negligent pose against a tall marble pillar.

Without considering the ramifications of her actions, she stared back, meeting his gaze.

He smiled and lifted an inquiring brow.

She knew she should lower her eyes, even turn around in her chair to dismiss him. Instead, she kept gazing at him, thinking as she did how much Edward would disapprove. But why did she care what Edward thought? Didn't she want to earn his displeasure? He'd certainly earned hers by being with Lady Bettis. Her hands tightening into fists in her lap, she continued to study Lord Islington.

Should I or shouldn't I? she wondered. *Do I dare?*

Abruptly, she tossed aside her caution and smiled.

Chapter 12

Claire wondered precisely what she'd gotten herself into as she watched Lord Islington straighten away from the pillar and saunter toward her.

A shiver raced along her spine, but not the delicious sort she always felt around Edward. This one was forbidding, almost menacing, as though she'd beckoned a cobra and it had decided to accept her invitation. But then he stopped in front of her and bowed, his manner both polished and easy. His smile was pleasant, his grey eyes alive with curiosity and a barely concealed amusement that seemed to belie her initial reaction.

He most definitely did not look harmless, she decided, but neither did he alarm her. She was only letting Mallory's earlier warnings against him color her opinion. And even Mallory had admitted that she really didn't know the man, only what Edward had said of him. Islington had a bad reputation. Well, most men had something about their pasts they wished to conceal. Anyway, how bad could he really be?

"Good evening," he said. "I couldn't help but notice you

sitting here alone. It doesn't seem right to leave such a beautiful woman to her own devices."

"Lord Gresham is procuring a glass of punch for me and will return momentarily."

"Parched from all your dancing, are you? I must confess that I noticed you out on the floor. You're very graceful."

"You flatter me, sir."

"Not at all," he said, his gaze shining warmly. "I am Islington, by the way. Forgive my lack of decorum in introducing myself, but such formalities have always struck me as rather antiquated in our modern age. Particularly since you need not tell me your name."

"Do I not?"

He shook his head. "Talk of Lady Claire Marsden is on everyone's lips these days."

"Oh?" she asked in an arch voice. "And what is it they are saying?"

"That you are either the luckiest young woman in the Ton or the cleverest to have wrung an engagement band out of the elusive Duke of Clybourne. Personally, I think it's neither and you just haven't had enough time to think the matter through."

She laughed, fully aware that he was being deliberately provocative. He was practically inviting her to rebel. "Perhaps I shall mention your opinion to His Grace when next I see him?"

"If you were wise, you wouldn't mention me to him at all. He doesn't exactly approve of me, you see."

"Really? And why is that, my lord?"

He shrugged. "An unfortunate misunderstanding is all, one for which he refuses to let me provide a proper explanation. I have tried, but his opinions tend to be rather rigidly held once they have been formed. What of your own, Lady Claire? Do you prefer to judge people on their merits or merely prejudge them based on the talk of others?"

"I am of an independent mind. Were I not, I wouldn't be conversing with you at all."

"Touché." Smiling more widely, he dipped his head in approval.

Casting a quick glance across the ballroom, she scanned the room for Lord Gresham. She didn't see him yet, but knew her time must be growing short.

"I . . . um . . . I believe the next set is about to form. Do you dance, my lord?"

"I have been known to on occasion."

"Then perhaps you should make this one of them. I have yet to promise this set."

He paused, his gaze taking on a speculative gleam. "And you would like me to ask you? I must caution that you would be playing with fire to accept."

She cast another glance across the ballroom, locating Edward—and Lady Bettis, who was still standing at his side. She drew back her shoulders. "I like fire. I find it keeps things warm and lively."

He looked in the duke's direction. "Hoping to spark a reaction, are you?"

"Why no," she denied. "I just want to dance."

Tossing back his head, Islington laughed and reached down a hand. "Lady Claire, may I have this next dance?"

"You may." Stomach somersaulting, she got to her feet.

Seconds later, Lord Gresham returned, a glass of pink punch held in his gloved hand, a scowl on his face. "Lady Claire, how are you feeling?"

"Much improved." Reaching out, she accepted the beverage, grateful for the cool, sweet slide of the drink as she swallowed. She hadn't realized how dry her mouth had become, or how much in need she was of the small distraction. "Delicious. My thanks," she declared, handing the cup back to Gresham.

He took it, then held out his arm. As he did, he tossed a look of ill-concealed disdain at Islington. "Allow me to return you to Mrs. Byron."

So, Lord Gresham doesn't approve of Islington either, she realized.

Trepidation swam in her system, but she pushed it aside. After all, even if Islington was a bounder, he couldn't do anything to her inside a crowded ballroom, other than cause a bit of scandal—and wasn't that precisely what she wanted?

"Thank you again, my lord," she told Gresham, "but there is no need. Lord Islington has asked me to stand up with him for the next set, which, from the sound the musicians are making, is about to begin."

"Lady Claire, I really don't think—" Gresham began.

"Don't concern yourself, Gresham. I'll see she's properly returned," Islington drawled, offering his own arm to Claire.

Drawing a resolute breath, she laid her hand on Islington's black sleeve, not daring to glance at Lord Gresham for fear of what he might glimpse in her eyes.

Then she and Islington were strolling across the ballroom, gazes turning their way as they went.

Edward fought off a yawn, as Lady Bettis launched into yet another round of flirtatious chatter. He didn't smile as he knew she was hoping, or laugh, weary of her poorly concealed attempts to amuse and beguile him.

Years ago, they'd had a brief affair, one he'd ended without a moment of regret. She'd been less sanguine about the breakup, confiding that he was the best lover she'd ever had. Some men might have preened at the remark, since it was well-known even then that Felicia Bettis had had a great many lovers indeed. But Edward had merely wanted out of the relationship, sorry she desired him when he didn't feel the same about her.

Their encounters since had been friendly enough—at least on the surface. But she made it plain that her offer was still open and that he was free to return to her bed any time he wished. To her regret, he didn't, enduring her occasional attempts to rekindle something between them with stoic patience.

But tonight, she was not only boring him, she was irritating him as well. Before he could elude her, she'd snared him for a private coze. At first he'd thought she merely wanted to gossip. Soon he realized her true intentions, questions pouring off her lips about his engagement to that "Marsden chit" and her astonishment that he was going through with the marriage after all.

But he didn't want to talk to her about Claire. His rationale for the marriage, his feelings for Claire and hers for him were private and had nothing to do with the Felicia Bettises of the world. Claire wasn't a topic for conjecture or discussion, and he revealed as little to Lady Bettis as possible.

Yes, he was marrying Lady Claire.

No, they hadn't set a wedding date.

No, he didn't find her too much of a child anymore. In fact, she'd turned into a lovely, charming young woman whom any man would be pleased to wed.

Felicia didn't like that last at all, her mouth screwing tight with obvious displeasure. But then her expression suddenly cleared like the sun coming out from behind a bank of clouds. That was when she began to flirt, trying to put him in a better mood. Unfortunately for her, all she succeeded in doing was boring him to death.

While she was chattering away, he scanned the room for Claire, wondering if she might like to join him for supper. He'd caught a glimpse of her dancing with Adam Gresham, but when he'd looked again, she was gone, lost somewhere in the milling crowd.

Having had more than enough, he finally decided to extricate himself from Lady Bettis's attentions.

"Yes, how amusing," he said in response to her latest remark. "But now, if you will excuse me, I must be going."

"Must you?" she replied with a pout that was undoubtedly meant to be alluring. "I was rather hoping you might ask me to dance."

"My apologies, but I cannot." He refused to say more, or to make further excuses that both of them would know for lies.

"Until later then," she said on an audible sigh, her shoulders slumping in resignation and defeat.

With a practiced bow, he departed, threading his way through the squeeze of guests in hopes of locating Claire. He hadn't gone twenty feet, however, before another woman he could have done without seeing this evening stepped into his path.

"Your Grace, what a pleasant surprise running into you tonight," said Philipa, Lady Stockton, her blue eyes shrewd in her winsome face, her lips rouged as red and ripe as cherries.

He inclined his head. "My lady."

"I must say, it's been ages since we last met," she continued with a faint toss of her brunette head. "How is dear Jack these days?"

At one time, she had been his brother Jack's mistress, although Edward had never fully understood the attraction, in spite of her outward beauty.

"Still married," he said.

A laugh rippled from her throat. "Yes, so I hear. And a father now too."

"Yes. A daughter, on whom he dotes already. The baby and Lady John are doing exceptionally well and the three of them remain very happy together in the country."

Her smile faded ever so slightly. "Well, I am glad to hear it. I would ask you to send my best regards to dear Jack in your next letter, but I suppose you would find it frightfully inappropriate."

Silence supplied his answer.

"Speaking of things one hears, I understand congratulations are in order, Your Grace. Allow me to wish you happiness on your coming nuptials."

He paused. "Thank you."

How civil of her, he thought. *Surprisingly so.* In his experience, however, Lady Stockton wasn't the sort who did things out of mere politeness. Generally there was some underlying motivation behind her actions. Did she want something? Or was he misjudging her and she really was simply extending her well-wishes?

"Oh, you're quite welcome," she continued in a friendly tone. "Your fiancée is lovely, I must say, with that beautiful blond hair and rosy complexion. The two of you make quite a striking couple. Light and dark are always complementary."

He said nothing, silently twisting his signet ring on his little finger as he waited for her to continue.

"She is certain to do you credit as your duchess."

"Yes, I am sure she shall," he stated, wondering how soon he might be able to slip away without appearing impolite.

"Although I cannot help but note that she is young and obviously new to Town. There may be a few small pointers you wish to share with her about how to go on in Society. Clearly, she doesn't realize her misstep, but I suppose all of us are entitled to one or two at first."

His brows lowered. "What do you mean? What misstep?"

An expression of surprise rounded her features. "I assumed you knew."

"Knew what?"

"Why, that she's dancing with Lord Islington. They just started a second set together moments ago and I must say, they are drawing comment. Good girls, even engaged ones, don't generally dance with such a roué."

Islington!

Edward's hands turned to fists at his side, the emerald in his ring cutting tightly against the inside of his palm. *Why, that bounder.* How dare Islington ask Claire to dance when he knew exactly what sort of attention it would draw.

Flipping his ring around to its correct position, he executed a clipped bow. "If you will excuse me, Lady Stockton, I find I am needed elsewhere."

She managed not to smirk, but couldn't quite conceal the delight glittering in her eyes. "Of course, Your Grace. So good chatting with you."

Suppressing the growl that rose in his chest, he turned away and strode through the crowd. People parted for him as he passed, stepping aside like wheat sheaves laid flat by a scythe.

Soon he found himself on the perimeter of the dance floor, couples moving to and fro with practiced movements. And there in the center of the action was Claire, her steps lively as she glided in time to the music with her partner, Gregory, Lord Islington, exactly as Philipa Stockton had claimed.

Edward forced himself not to stalk forward and wrest Claire out of Islington's arms. The pair of them were causing enough comment without him creating a scene that would be the talk of every drawing room and dining table in London come tomorrow morning. Instead, he decided he would wait, calmly and with an apparent lack of concern. Once the set concluded, he would arrive at Claire's side and lead her safely away.

No harm. No fuss.

Well, maybe a small amount of fuss, but once he had

Claire back where she belonged, the situation would seem altogether ordinary, a raindrop in an ocean that was quickly absorbed and forgotten.

What he wanted to know, however, was how she had come to be acquainted with Islington in the first place. Who had introduced them? Clearly not Cousin Wilhelmina, who might be a bit silly at times, but who knew enough to keep her young charges well away from scoundrels like Islington. He remembered seeing Claire in Gresham's company, but despite Adam's own wild reputation, Edward knew Gresham wouldn't put an innocent like Claire in Islington's path.

So how had they met? he wondered again, struggling not to glower and glare like an enraged bull as he watched the two of them dance.

Generally, Islington confined himself to experienced widows and bored wives, who didn't mind kicking up a cloud of scandal and gossip while they conducted an illicit liaison with him. Debutantes and unmarried young women were on his do-not-touch list, though, and after "the incident" three years ago, everyone knew why and were careful to keep their marriageable daughters away.

Although to be fair, Edward was certain Claire didn't realize what Islington was or that she ought to have steered well clear of him and refused his offer to take a turn on the floor. But the dance would conclude shortly, and once he had Claire by his side, all would be well.

While he stood waiting, a few people were brave enough to make whispered asides. But for the most part no one in his vicinity said a word, nor was anyone daring enough to meet his gaze. Not that he was looking, his eyes directed toward the line of dancers, and two individuals in particular.

Finally, the music ceased, the set done.

Gentlemen and ladies broke into pairs, including Gresham and Mallory, who had been dancing as well and now glanced his way. They started toward him, but he gave a nearly imperceptible shake of his head that stopped them both. Apparently understanding his wish to handle the situation on his own, Adam nodded and took Mallory's arm to lead her away, which she agreed to with a little frown of worry on her forehead.

Meanwhile, Islington offered his arm to Claire. As he did, Edward strode forward, his patience officially at an end. He met Claire and Islington at the halfway point, forcing them to halt as he stopped directly in their path. He didn't spare Islington so much as a glance.

"I have come to see you into supper," he said, giving Claire a deliberate smile. "Let us go and procure a comfortable seat." He extended his arm for her to take.

Claire, however, made no effort to accept. "I'm sorry, but I am afraid I must decline."

For a moment, he thought he hadn't heard her correctly. "What?"

"I didn't realize you planned to take me into supper tonight, so I accepted Lord Islington's invitation. The dance that just concluded was the supper dance, in case you were unaware."

Actually, he hadn't been aware, but it hardly mattered what dance it was. She wasn't eating supper with Islington!

He ground his teeth together. "Yes, well, there's obviously been a misunderstanding. I'm sure Islington here won't mind if you have supper with me, seeing that I am your fiancé."

And that, he thought, *was that.*

Before Islington could comment, Claire stepped in again. "That may be true, Edward, but I did give my promise and I don't feel right breaking it. I'm sure you'll find another very pleasant lady who will be only too happy to join you for the midnight buffet. As for me, I am promised to Lord Islington tonight."

Edward felt his eyes strain inside their sockets, ire pumping through his bloodstream. The sensation only increased when he caught sight of the smirk on Islington's face. His hands clenched at his sides, muscle and bone aching for the chance to land a punch that would wipe the smug look off the other man's face.

"Claire," he said on a low rumble, "I don't think you fully understand what is involved here—"

"And I don't think you are aware, Your Grace, that we are starting to attract attention with our tête-à-tête. Now, I am dining with his lordship and that is the end of the discussion. I shall see you later on this evening."

"*Claire*—" he warned.

"Oh, Edward, don't be such a grouchy Gus."

Grouchy Gus!

"Come, your lordship," she said, tightening her grip on Islington's arm. "If we do not move along, all the good seats will be taken."

"Far be it from me to deny pleasure to a lady," Islington said.

Edward stood as though riveted in place, astonished all the way to his depths. He couldn't believe she had outmaneuvered him, and so adroitly too. But she was right that everyone was watching, ears strained to catch each possible word. She'd truly backed him into a corner, since short of physically separating her from Islington, there was nothing he could do to stop her.

For a second, he actually considered yanking her away from the other man—scandal be damned. But he stopped himself. Claire and Islington were going into the supper room where they would be surrounded by dozens of other guests. Edward would be there as well, and he would make certain he found a seat with an excellent and unobstructed view. Nothing would happen that he didn't know about, and once supper concluded, so would Claire's association with Islington.

Chapter 13

"Good heavens, what do you think you're doing?" Mallory whispered as she perched on a dining room chair next to Claire. "I thought I told you to stay away from Lord Islington."

As for Islington, once he'd located a table for himself and Claire, he'd made his excuses and left to procure selections from the buffet spread out in glorious excess across the room. The moment he'd departed, Mallory had hurried over and dropped down into his empty seat.

Claire sent her friend a look of deliberate unconcern. "I know you did, but then I met him and he asked me to dance. I couldn't very well refuse."

"Of course you could. You ought to have given him the cut direct and refused to speak with him at all."

"Why? Despite your admonitions, he seems an amiable sort of person, quite intelligent and interesting. I can't understand what's so very dreadful about him. You said yourself you don't even know what it is he is supposed to have done wrong."

"No," Mallory agreed, her expression troubled. "But

Edward wouldn't have warned me off without good cause." Pausing, she cast a glance toward her brother where he sat at a table a few yards distant. "By the way, Ned looks positively glacial. I really don't think it was wise to have insisted on supper with Islington."

Claire gave a derisive sniff. "Then he ought to have thought to ask me to share supper with him before the supper dance was concluded."

Mallory gave her a thoughtful look. "Is that what this is about? Teaching Ned a lesson?"

"In a manner of speaking. Look now, Lord Islington appears to be returning, so if you don't want to make conversation with him, you'd best run along. I'm sure Lord Gresham is wondering where you are anyway."

"Oh, he knows." Mallory shot her a smile. "Just be careful, all right?"

"It's not as if Islington's going to murder me here in front of everyone."

"No, but from the expression on Ned's face, my brother might do the job for him."

"Very funny," Claire replied with a sarcastic smile. Mallory grinned, then hurried away.

Lord Islington arrived a few moments later, two laden plates in hand. He set one in front of her before doing so for himself, then taking a seat. "Still here, then? I couldn't help but notice Lady Malloy talking with you and figured she would have led you away by now."

"Of course I am still here. I have agreed to share supper with you, and share supper I shall."

"Even if it lands you in a tub of very hot water?"

She paused, trying her best to ignore Edward where he sat gazing—or should she say *glaring*—at her from across the room, the lady he had ended up escorting in to supper chatting aimlessly at his side.

"Yes, even then," she told him in a low voice. "I may be small, blond and female, but you will find I have a will of iron when my mind is set upon a particular path."

He arched a tawny brow. "That I can well believe. I must warn you, however, that this path of yours may have unintended consequences. Clybourne isn't the sort to be trifled with."

She sent him a haughty look. "Neither, my lord, am I."

Surprise lit his face, then he laughed, a hearty outburst that drew an even greater number of gazes. "You're going to make a fine duchess, Lady Claire."

I certainly hope not, she thought, wondering just how far she was going to have to take this battle of wills between her and Edward. But he'd brought this on himself by insisting on their engagement when she had asked to be released from it from the very start. Regardless of the repercussions, she wasn't backing down, even if it meant dancing, flirting and sharing a meal with a man of questionable character.

"Well then, my lord," she said in a carefree tone as she regarded her plate. "What delicacies have you brought me? Lobster patties, I hope, since they are my favorite."

"I believe there are one or two hidden among the rest," he said with an indulgent chuckle. "And I understand ices are to be served later."

"Ices! Then I'm in heaven already."

Hell and damnation! Edward thought over an hour later as he strode into the ballroom in search of Claire.

He'd assumed it would be a simple matter to retrieve Claire once supper was concluded. But somehow, without quite knowing how she managed, he'd ended up watching her sail out of the dining room on Islington's arm before he had a chance to reach them. And with his own dinner partner to be seen to, far more time had passed than he liked before he was free to resume the pursuit.

A new set was already forming inside the ballroom when he entered, people arranging themselves in couples on the dance floor, while the quartet of musicians played a few rounds of practice notes.

Scanning the assembled guests, he looked for Claire. By now, he expected to find her either in the company of Cousin Wilhelmina or with Mallory or another of her female friends. But in spite of locating his cousin and his sister, he couldn't find Claire.

Then the new set began, music filling the room with a lively harmony. As it did, he heard the rumble of hushed murmurs and felt the power of pointed stares, directed both at him and toward the dance floor. Only then did he catch sight of Claire's lovely blond head and with her a tall, tawny-haired one that made his mouth drop open.

Claire was dancing with Islington again.

For the third time!

Without further consideration, Edward stalked across the room.

For Hades' sake, what is she thinking? He might be able to excuse her earlier dances with Islington as a case of ignorance, but this was another matter entirely. Every girl of good breeding knew that standing up for more than two dances with any one gentleman in a single evening was tantamount to announcing her engagement to that gentleman.

Obviously she's lost her mind, considering she's already engaged to me!

Marching along the line of dancers until he located the guilty couple, he stopped and reached out with a hard hand to tap Islington on the shoulder. "This dance is mine," he stated in an implacable growl.

Islington and Claire both shot him looks—Islington's one of amusement while Claire's appeared startled yet oddly defiant.

"Edward," she exclaimed.

"Not a word from you," he ground out.

Without waiting for further assent, Edward removed Claire's hand from Islington's and secured it inside his own. For Islington's part, he stepped aside, clearly aware that he'd just been officially dismissed.

Edward swung Claire into the steps of the dance as though they had been partnered the entire time. One minute passed, then two, the music playing as their feet traveled across the floor.

"Have you nothing to say?" he asked as the dance brought them together.

"As I recall, you told me not to speak."

And so I did, he realized, a heavy frown creasing his forehead. His gaze narrowed. "You haven't paid attention to anything else I've told you to do tonight, so I presumed that remark would have no more effect than any of the rest."

Her blue eyes flashed as the movements of the dance drew them apart.

He didn't attempt to engage her in conversation again for the rest of the set. There seemed little use, considering the fact that everything he had to say needed to be said in private. And so he danced for what seemed an endless span of time until, finally, the musicians played their last notes and the couples around them came to a final halt.

The instant the dance ended, Edward caught Claire's hand tightly inside his own. Past caring what anyone else might think, he drew her along next to him, compelling her to keep pace as he strode toward the French doors that led to the garden beyond.

Into the night they went, cool air surrounding them, the noise of the ballroom fading to a dull hum. Onward he proceeded, tugging her with him until even the hum was gone, leaving only the sound of their dress shoes beating against the terrace flagstones and the sibilant respiration of Claire's breath as she hurried to keep up.

Finally, he stopped, not far from one of the garden lanterns that emitted a mellow golden glow. For a moment, he fought to steady his temper. The effort, however, proved worthless. "Just what in the blazes was all that about?" he demanded, low and harsh.

Pulling away, she crossed her arms over her chest. "I will thank you not to curse at me, Your Grace."

"That wasn't cursing. Asking you what in the *bloody blazes* you thought you were doing, now that is cursing."

She sent him a reproving stare.

"Well?" he pressed when she gave no further response.

"I believe it is called dancing," she said. "Or rather a cotillion, if you wish to be specific."

A muscle flexed in his jaw. "Don't trifle with me, since you know precisely what I mean. What were you doing dancing with Islington again?"

With a slight shrug, she lowered her gaze. "He asked and I agreed."

"Even though it was the third dance?"

Her pale eyebrows arched high in feigned innocence. "Was it? I must have lost count."

He wrapped his hand around her arm and gave her a harmless shake. "You didn't lose count and neither did anyone else in that ballroom. Everyone is talking and they'll be doing little else for days to come. By morning, the Society columns will be full of tonight's escapade, not to mention that it'll be on the tongues of every tattlemonger in London. I know Islington doesn't give a fig about his reputation, since his is already painted as black as tar. But what about you, Claire? Have you no concern for yourself and what this may do to you?"

"Don't you mean what it will do to *your* reputation, Your

Grace? I suspect you are far more outraged over how my behavior will reflect upon you and your honor than about any possible damage to me. After all, your primary concern must always be to the Byron name and your title as the Duke of Clybourne, is that not so?"

He grew abruptly still, a deeper hush falling over the already quiet night. "Is that what you believe?" His tone was hauntingly soft.

"Of course. As for me, I care little for the opinions of strangers. My true friends shall always like me in spite of a . . . bit of talk."

"That is a noble sentiment indeed. However, as I recall, you once told me you dislike being the focus of speculation, and nothing brings on speculation quite so forcefully as flouting Society's rules."

She drew a steadying breath. "Sometimes rules must be broken and sacrifices made in order to achieve one's aims."

What is she on about? he wondered, puzzling over her bold statement. Was there more to her dancing and dining with Islington tonight than careless abandon and a bit of youthful rebellion? He'd been incensed to think that she might be attracted to Islington, even casually. But now he wondered if there was something else at work.

Taking hold of her other arm, he forced her to retreat a few steps until her back was nearly touching the smooth, cool stone façade of the town house. "What game are you playing, Claire? What is it you want?"

When she said nothing, he pressed her further, as a new thought occurred. "You aren't deliberately courting scandal, are you?" Gazing into her eyes, he read the truth. "By God, you are! To what end?"

Beneath his hands, he felt a fine tremor chase over her skin, yet her expression remained defiant. "For my own ends and it's no game," she said. "I told you from the outset that

I do not wish to be wed and I have not changed my mind. You ought to have listened to me rather than insisting on this engagement."

Edward felt his eyes widen. "Good Lord! I knew you hoped to dissuade me at first, but I thought you'd accepted the inevitability of our union. I see now that you have not. So your plan is to, what, anger and embarrass me to the point where I'll decide to call off the wedding?"

She angled her chin at a proud tilt. "If that is what it takes."

He stared for several long seconds and then he began to laugh.

Her mouth tightened, then trembled, her blue eyes glittering as though lit by a fire. "Why are you laughing?"

"Because you obviously don't know me very well if you think such tactics are going to dissuade me. My siblings embarrass me with regular frequency and in spite of what you may believe about the supposed dignity of my family, we Byrons spend our lives stirring up one pot of scandal broth after another."

He paused, chuckling wryly. "You've nothing on them, in fact. Jack nearly fled to Italy three years ago for dueling in Green Park. He'd been caught in bed with an earl's wife, you see, and the earl didn't much like it. Then two Seasons ago, Cade tried to choke a nobleman to death in the middle of a ball."

Her lips parted. "He *what*?"

"Of course, the man was a traitor, which Cade knew, but Society cared nothing for the truth at the time."

"Good heavens."

"Precisely. So you see the futility of your plan?"

She stiffened beneath his hands. "You speak of futility and inevitability, but I see nothing of the sort. And if you are so inured to scandal, then why are you upset tonight? What does it matter to you how many times I dance with someone else, if you aren't concerned about your reputation?"

His humor fell away. "Not someone else. Islington. He's a cad and you are to stay away from him."

"And if I don't? I'm not a child, you know. I may do as I please."

"No, you're not a child, at least not chronologically. But you're acting like one with these silly games of yours. They're not going to work, so you might as well give up."

"That's what you'd like, wouldn't you? If you knew *me* better, though, you'd realize I'm not a quitter."

"Shall I rename you *Doña* Quixote, then, since you apparently enjoy tilting at windmills?"

"Very droll, Your Grace, but since we're being so forthright this evening, I might as well warn you that this isn't over. Unless you care to release me from our engagement, that is?"

In the flickering shadows, he studied her face. Should he let Claire have her way and end their engagement? If she truly didn't want to marry him, then perhaps he ought to release her from her pledge. But as he considered the idea, something inside him rebelled—and not simply for reasons of familial obligation and practicality.

Until now, part of him had thought of their engagement in terms of fate, a destiny that had been chosen for each of them when they were too young to refuse. As much as he'd once chafed against the arrangement, he'd come to accept the idea of taking Claire as his wife. But suddenly, as he looked at her now, he realized those reasons were no longer of primary concern to him. It wasn't any longer a case of *having* to marry Claire—he *wanted* to marry Claire. Or maybe the more honest answer was that he desired her and he wasn't about to let her go—not when she was very nearly his.

Yet she said she wished to be free, so much so that she was willing to force his hand in front of the entire Ton. He hadn't realized before what an idealist she was, or what a romantic. He supposed she wanted love, or the fantasy of it, not some reasonable, rational arrangement that made sense in every practicable way. He also knew that her father must have made it impossible for her to cry off herself, so she needed him to do the deed for her.

But he couldn't jilt her. If he did, she would be disgraced, conceivably to the point where no other man of good character would have her. What's more, he had serious doubts that her parents would receive her back with open arms, despite her having obviously convinced herself otherwise. Considering how desperately the earl wanted this marriage to take place, Edward worried that Edgewater might become so angry he would cast Claire out, and then what would become of her?

No, he thought, *Claire Marsden is mine now, whether she wants to be or not.*

Yet to his credit, he knew she wasn't indifferent to him, in spite of her protestations against their marriage. He'd felt her desire the times he'd held her in his arms. He just needed to encourage that desire and give her a further taste of the pleasure she would find once she came to his bed.

"Well?" she ventured in a voice made hopeful by his silence. "Will you cry off, Your Grace?"

He met her gaze, her eyes a pure, bright blue even in the tenebrous light. "No," he stated in a gruff tone. "And it's Edward. How many times must I remind you?"

Then his mouth was on hers, silencing her protest, stealing whatever objections she might claim to have. And it was in this that he knew again he was right, her attraction to him impossible for her to conceal, as she melted instantly beneath his touch. She might decry the notion of marriage, but she clearly approved of his kisses, curling into his embrace with a ready need that made him smile.

Dancing her backward a couple more steps, he slid his arms around her and deepened their kiss, leaning her against the stone town house so he could plunder her mouth at his leisure.

Suddenly she broke their kiss and turned her head away. "St-Stop," she panted.

"Why?" Undeterred, he glided his lips over the soft skin of her temple and cheek before delving lower to caress the graceful length of her throat.

"B-Because you are just tr-trying to distract me."

"Am I?" Moving downward, he punctuated each new touch with a kiss.

"And it won't s-serve."

Reaching her nape, he swirled his tongue across her skin in a sleek circle.

"*Ohhhhhh.*" Quivering, she shifted against him with restless limbs. "I—I shall not be dissuaded from my course."

"Are you sure?" he murmured, blowing gently against her neck in a way that made her eyelids fall to half mast.

"V-Very sure," she declared, forcing her eyes open again. "There is nothing you can do to stop me."

Pausing, he raised his head. "So, it's to be a battle then, is it?"

Her breasts rose on a bracing inhalation. "I-If necessary, yes."

He met her gaze, their eyes locking in a silent duel. "If you insist," he said, "then let the games begin."

Claire started to reply, but before she could utter even a single syllable, Edward captured her mouth, taking her with a dark hunger that she was helpless to resist. His tongue tangled with her own before roving across the smooth flesh of her inner cheeks in a way that made her gasp with pleasure. Blood thrummed in crazy beats between her temples, her senses spinning in dizzying circles as her mind grew slow and hazy. The garden, the house, even the ballroom full of people faded from her thoughts.

Only Edward remained.

Only Edward's kisses and caresses held any meaning—the intoxicating flavor of his mouth, the heady scent of his skin, the pure heaven of his touch, her sole connection with reality.

Curving her arms around his neck, she held him tighter, moaning as he intensified their kiss. Needing more, she threaded her fingers into his hair, delighting in the way his thick, silky locks curled against her skin with a tensile grip. Angling her mouth, she kissed him back, striving to match his seductive forays with passionate ones of her own.

He seemed to approve, his touch growing bolder, his kisses becoming longer, deeper and even more intense. She was floating in a warm sea of bliss when the world suddenly turned hot, his hands gliding over her back and hips before roving farther afield.

Down went one wide, masculine palm to gently knead the pliant curves of her bottom, while up slid the other to cup one of her breasts, massaging her sensitive flesh with a bold, blatant possession that made her cry out in need.

Luckily, he was still kissing her, her exaltation muffled inside his open mouth so that she made no more than a small whimper. But inside her head, her response sounded like a shout, her pleasure so strong her skin burned, as though he'd set her ablaze.

An ache settled between her legs, desire awakening with a strength that left her shaking and needy, all her brave intentions scattered like sere leaves in an autumn wind. He had only to touch her and she turned malleable as clay. He had but to kiss her and she was lost.

She was even more lost when he unfastened the buttons on her bodice and loosened her stays enough to free the breast he'd been fondling. A brief draft of cool air came as a shock against her bare flesh. Then she was instantly hot again, his palm setting her once more on fire. She couldn't think at all, as his thumb began circling, his fingers finessing her nipple with a tantalizing stroke that turned her knees weak as wax.

If not for the grip of his strong arm at her back, she would surely have tumbled to the ground. Instead, he pulled her tighter, fitting their bodies close as he continued his caresses.

Suddenly he broke their kiss, leaving her bereft. But she had barely a moment to repine, since rather than deserting her, he merely transferred his attentions elsewhere. She gasped as he lowered his head to her breast and replaced his fingers with his mouth.

The wet warmth of his lips and tongue sent shudders pouring through her, her hand clutching fast in his hair. Rather than trying to push him away, she pulled him closer, instinctively arching her back so he could take more. He smiled against her breast and opened his mouth wider before lapping at her taut nipple with wicked little flicks of his tongue.

She groaned, her eyes falling closed in ecstasy. Another helpless moan warbled from her throat seconds later when he reached under her skirt to find bare flesh. With agonizing slowness, his fingers trailed up the back of her knee, playing there for long, long moments before roving higher. Along her thigh and around her garter he went, until his hand slid up over the rounded edge of her bottom. Flattening his palm there, he gave a gentle squeeze.

She startled, then sighed, making him chuckle against her naked breast before he angled his head to suckle even more fiercely upon her. Enthralled, she gave herself completely into his keeping, biting her lip to hold back the moans of pleasure that rose inside her throat.

Her bodice and stays slid lower as he transferred his attention to her other breast, lavishing her willing flesh with licks and kisses that made her writhe inside his arms. Half insensible, she could do nothing more than cling, her fingers stroking his hair and the back of his neck, silently urging him to do anything he wished as he brought her the most exquisite delight.

Slowly, he left her breasts, trailing kisses up over her chest and collarbone, along her neck and chin and cheeks. Straightening, he fit her closer against him and plundered her mouth, taking her with another round of long, deep, drugging kisses that once again robbed her of coherent thought.

Her eyes popped wide, though, when he edged her legs apart with the hand that had been fondling her bottom and slid a single finger deep inside her. She bucked at the novel sensation, her femininity astonishingly wet and aching as he touched her in ways she'd never expected.

Smothering her cries with voracious kisses, he mimicked the movements of his finger with those of his tongue, both gliding in and out in rhythmic tempos that threatened to undo her completely.

Just when she thought she'd reached the pinnacle of delight, he began stroking another particularly sensitive area of flesh with his thumb. Blood throbbed in her veins, her heart thundering in her chest as she labored for breath. Hunger engulfed her as a yearning need spiraled higher and faster within her.

Up, up she went until suddenly she was flying, the world spinning wildly as she wailed out her bliss against his mouth. He drank down her cries, holding her safe in his arms as rapture filled her from head to toe. Limp, she sagged against him, her body shaking from the force of her release—the first she'd ever had.

Dazed and astonished, she broke their kiss and leaned her cheek against his neck cloth. Eyes closed, she fought to recover, breathing in the faint scents of fine-milled soap, lemon water and man—Edward's skin warm, musky and delicious.

Only then did she notice the state of his body and the thick bulge pressed against her stomach.

Is that his erection? Of course it must be, she realized, quivering as she waited to see how much further he might take matters.

Stroking her a last couple of times, he gently withdrew, caressing the back of her bare thigh before letting her skirts fall back into place. She lifted her face and he kissed her again, slowly and tenderly.

"We'd better stop," he said, releasing an audible sigh before taking a step back. His hands went to her sagging stays and bodice to slide the garments up over her exposed breasts and bare shoulders. He had her laced and buttoned before she had time to completely gather her thoughts, leaving her to wonder at his level of composure in the face of their overwhelming passion.

Or was it only *her* passion—his need no greater than he might have felt for any woman? Did he truly want her or had he only been dallying with her in order to win an early victory in their battle of wills?

Quite obviously, he'd stopped before he was satisfied; his erection was proof of that. Was he planning to slake his needs with another woman later tonight? With Felicia Bettis perhaps? Had they already arranged an assignation, and once he'd delivered Claire back to the town house, he would sneak out again to meet his mistress?

Her stomach gave an oily lurch at the thought, her hot skin cooling instantly. "I—I should go back," she said, wanting suddenly to be away from him.

"It isn't necessary, you know. It's late. I can call for the carriage."

"Everyone will be wondering," she whispered.

"Let them wonder." Drawing her into the lantern's gleam, Edward studied her face. "Let's go home, Claire, to our home, where you belong."

She paused for a long moment before raising her eyes to his. "But I don't belong and this . . . interlude . . . we just shared changes nothing. You may be able to seduce me, but it doesn't mean I'm any more willing to be your wife."

His jaw tightened, his eyes flashing blue fire. "Oh, you'll be my wife, mark my words on that. Personally, I prefer making love, but if it's war you really want, then be my guest. Just know that, despite my gentlemanly exterior, I fight dirty. You can rebel all you want, but it will make no difference in the end. You're mine and you're not getting away."

I'm his, am I?

His possession, he means. His chattel, she thought, her heart sinking, even as it hardened again with silent resolve. For no matter how much she adored him or how deeply he'd pleasured her tonight, she wouldn't be used and maneuvered like a pawn on a chessboard. He'd called this a game, and to him it was. But to her it meant her whole life.

Her chest tightened at the prospect of returning to the ball and pretending everything was fine, but she refused to be cowed. She would not bend—either to Society dictates or to Edward's.

Stepping away from him, she smoothed a hand over her hair to check for stray wisps. "How do I look?" she asked with a determined tilt of her chin.

Edward swept her with an assessing gaze. "Beautiful. Although given the color in your cheeks and lips, everyone will have a rather good idea what it is we've been doing out here."

Her fingers fisted at her sides. "So long as they only suspect, then there's no harm done."

He smiled before turning serious again. "Surely you're not returning to the dancing?"

"That's exactly what I'm doing. Now, if you'll excuse me, Your Grace, I shall be on my way."

Reaching out, he took hold of her arm. "Not without me, you won't. And not before I have your promise that you shall have no further contact with Islington. If I see you anywhere near him, you're going home immediately."

Slowly, she withdrew her arm from his grasp. "His lordship may have already departed for all I know. However, I give you my word that I shall see no more of him this evening."

As for other occasions in the future, she mused, *I cannot say.* Holding her breath, she waited to see if Edward would make further stipulations regarding her association with Lord Islington.

Instead, he gave a nod and took her hand in his, laying her palm onto his sleeve. "We shall return to the ballroom together."

Briefly, she considered refusing. "As you wish, Your Grace."

"*Edward*," he growled. "One of these days, I'm going to make sure you say nothing else."

Meeting his gaze, she gave him a wide, unrepentant smile.

Moments later, they returned to the ball.

Chapter 14

"Ha ha, I won!" Claire laughed as she pulled the curricle to a halt with a little spray of Green Park gravel. The painted wooden cherries on her stylish chip-straw bonnet swayed gently, their color an excellent foil for her pink-and-cream striped carriage dress and matching, long-sleeved sarcenet spencer.

Lord Blevins—the loser—drew his own rig up beside hers nearly half a minute later.

Glancing over, Claire saw the expression of surprise and begrudging respect on his face. Clearly, he hadn't expected to be soundly beaten by a novice driver and a woman to boot. Not just any woman, though, since he'd been bested by *Claire the Dare*, as Society had taken to calling her.

Over the past month, the Ton had arrived at the conclusion that Lady Claire Marsden was wildly out of control. *Which I am*, Claire conceded with a secret smile, recalling the myriad scandals she'd kicked up in her efforts to free herself from Edward.

To date, she'd shot pistols with a trio of Corinthians, who'd smuggled her into Manton's; smoked cigars with Lord Oxnard and Mr. Carstairs behind a row of rose bushes at the Pettigrews' garden party; and thrown dice in the company of a quartet of rather tipsy young men at a masked ball. Luckily, she'd gotten away before they'd decided to turn their attention to anything more than gambling—and most importantly, before Edward had managed to locate her after she'd slipped away from his watchful eye.

And only four days ago, she'd engaged in a rowboat race across the Serpentine with the infamous Loreena Lovechild, one of London's most beautiful and notorious Cyprians. With poor Cousin Wilhelmina and Mallory looking on in helpless astonishment, Claire and Miss Lovechild had each selected a gentleman champion to row them across the lake, seating themselves in the bow while they urged their chosen man on with encouragement and cheers. To her delight, Claire had won. In celebration, she'd given her champion a kiss on the cheek, her wild actions bringing on swoons from a pair of fainthearted young ladies who stood watching on the opposite shore.

As for Edward, she kept expecting him to explode and send her packing, each new escapade the one she was certain would drive him beyond his limit. Instead, he maintained a seemingly stoic countenance, never displaying more upset than a mild furrowing of his brow—at least not in public.

As for their private encounters, he was far less forbearing, clearly infuriated by her continued defiance. He threatened to lock her in her room, but they both knew he wouldn't. Not only would it be useless, it would simply cause more scandal. *The duke's ungovernable fiancée is imprisoned in his house*, everyone would whisper. Why, the story would be delicious enough that it might tempt Mrs. Radcliffe to use it as inspiration for one of her upcoming gothic romances.

No, in that regard, Edward's hands were tied.

However, he had other rather diabolical ways of exacting retribution. She shivered now, squirming a bit on the curricle seat, as she remembered another particularly intense, intimate encounter during which he'd had her literally begging for release. She might still be a virgin, but she blushed nonetheless to recall the things they'd done together.

Shaking off the memory, she turned a cheerful smile on Lord Blevins. "I believe our wager was for ten pounds, my lord. If you haven't sufficient cash on your person, you may, of course, send it 'round to me at Clybourne House. Just be sure to put my name on the missive and not the duke's."

Blevins gave her a wry smile, reaching into his coat for his purse. "I had best settle up with you now. Somehow I suspect Clybourne will take offense if I have one of my footmen knocking at his door to pay off vowels I owe you." Opening his purse, he extracted a ten-pound note and handed it across the space separating them. "*You* may have no compunction about provoking Clybourne's ire, but I cannot say the same."

Leaning forward, she accepted her winnings with a gracious smile. "Then I'm surprised you agreed to race me this morning, my lord. Particularly since there were witnesses to our competition."

A few of whom were even now regarding her and Blevins with undisguised interest. Meeting the gaze of a pair of middle-aged gentlemen on horseback—who she knew to be every inch as gossipy as any woman—she sent them a jaunty, unrepentant wave of her gloved hand. Plainly startled to have been caught staring, they tipped their hats, then rode on.

She smirked inwardly, no longer sensitive about being the focus of Society's omnipresent gaze. After all, her current goal was to draw attention to herself and her outrageous schemes. Once she succeeded and was no longer affianced to Edward, she could go back to being plain Lady Claire again.

At least I hope I can, she thought with a hint of a frown. *Once a person becomes notorious, can they ever go back to being just their ordinary self again?*

"As to my reasons for racing you, Lady Claire," Blevins said in response to her comment, "my only defense is that you have a way about you that is utterly impossible to resist. Once you challenged me, I was powerless to say no."

She laughed again.

Blevins joined her, a bit of ruddy color spreading into his cheeks. Moments later, his smile vanished, as he looked ahead along the lane. "Um . . . unless I am mistaken, I believe Clybourne is riding this way."

Her hands tightened reflexively against the reins, as she glanced up and caught sight of the approaching horse and rider. "Ah, and so he is," she remarked on a breezy tone. "Someone at the house must have told His Grace where I'd gone. One of the servants, no doubt."

Blevins hunched forward a bit, as though bracing himself for the approaching encounter.

"If you'd like to take your leave, my lord, pray feel free to do so. I won't mind in the slightest."

He hesitated. "Are you certain? I can't help thinking that I would be deserting you."

"No, no, not at all. Clybourne is my fiancé. I am eminently safe in his hands."

Lord Blevins didn't look wholly convinced by that statement, but obviously his sense of self-preservation was better developed than his gallantry. "Well, if you are sure," he said, darting another glance toward Edward, who was now only a few yards distant. "I . . . um . . . do have an early nuncheon engagement today."

"By all means then, you ought not delay. Go on, and I shall see you again one of these times soon."

With a nod, he gathered his reins. "A pleasure, Lady Claire. Please send my best regards to Lady Mallory and her cousin when next you see them."

"You may count upon it."

With a seemingly cheerful smile, she sent him on his way, the wheels of his curricle revolving fast as he drove away.

Coward, she thought, watching him exchange passing greetings with Edward as the two men rode by each other. Then Blevins was gone and Edward arrived, drawing his great roan stallion to a halt at her side.

The large, deep-chested steed pawed the ground and tossed his head to establish his dominance in front of Claire and her carriage horses, both of whom were mares. Edward didn't need to put on a show, his innate dominance always on display, together with his unassailable masculine good looks. Attired in a coat of Spanish blue superfine with fawn trousers and black Hessians polished to a near-blinding gleam, he would have drawn any woman's eye.

And, in fact, he already had, a trio of ladies in an open barouche sending him admiring looks as their coach rolled past.

However, he paid them no heed whatsoever, his interest focused squarely on Claire. Leaning slightly forward in his saddle, he met her gaze. "I thought we had an understanding that you were forbidden to drive out without me to escort you?"

"Well, good day to you too, Your Grace," she said in pleasant reproof. "I see you left your manners at home this morning. And your good humor as well."

His jaw flexed. "Actually, my humor was in excellent form until I learned you had taken the curricle *and* left your maid behind as well."

She'd known both would irritate him, since a proper lady never went anywhere unaccompanied. Increasingly, she was having to push her actions farther and farther past the bounds of acceptable decorum in hopes of breaking his resolve.

So far, he'd held fast to his pledge that nothing she did could make him repudiate her and break off their engagement. But just because he hadn't tossed her out yet didn't mean he wasn't angry over her escapades—blisteringly so at times.

Gauging his level of irritation by the intensity of his midnight blue eyes, she gave a negligent shrug. "Penny wasn't feeling well," she said in reference to her lack of a maid.

"And Mallory?" he intoned, low and deep.

"Mallory was still abed. You know as well as I that we didn't get home from last night's ball until nearly four this morning. I couldn't possibly have made her come out with me."

"What of you? Are you not tired from all your dancing?"

"Not in the slightest. I need very little rest, rather like yourself, Your Grace. I can't help but notice that you're an early riser as well."

His mouth tightened, but he made no effort to respond to her observations or admonish her for not using his given name, aware now exactly why she insisted on maintaining the formality. Releasing a breath, he glanced back along the lane. "So what did Blevins want? Did he merely stop to pay his respects? Or to express his concern over finding you here alone?"

"He did seem mildly surprised when I arrived without at least Penny in tow. But no, actually his lordship and I were engaged in a race."

Edward's eyes darkened to the shade of thunderclouds. "What kind of race?"

"With our carriages, of course. I won ten pounds from

him." Reaching into her pocket, she withdrew the folded Bank of England note and gave it a little waggle. "I haven't decided yet how to spend it."

Before she could react, Edward reached out and snatched it from her hand. "And you won't either. This money will be returned to him today. I'll see that a messenger is sent over along with an accompanying note asking him to forget this morning's caper ever happened."

Her mouth opened. "You'll do no such thing. I won that money fair and square. I beat him by two full lengths, I'll have you know, so give me back my winnings."

Instead, he tucked the cash into his coat pocket. "You shouldn't have beaten him at all, since ladies do not race. Nor do they gamble."

"Pish-tosh, of course they gamble. I see ladies playing cards every single evening, even the old women."

"Not for significant stakes. Penny wagers are the standard fare."

"I know what is standard. I also know that you can send 'round all the notes you like and it won't expunge my race with Lord Blevins, even if he should come down with a case of gentlemanly amnesia. There were lots of people in the park. They all saw my triumph." Smiling, she showed her teeth.

He showed his teeth as well, though with far less humor. "Which reminds me of another infraction," he said. "As I recall, you were expressly told to stay out of the park after that benighted spectacle you staged last week, rowing across the Serpentine against that courtesan."

"Miss Lovechild was delightful and an excellent sport. She confided in me afterward that she hopes to marry a duke someday too." A laugh rippled from her throat at his nonplussed expression. "As for your draconian edict concerning the park, you only said I couldn't go to *Hyde* Park again. You didn't say anything about Green."

Growling low in his throat, he walked his horse back a few paces, then dismounted.

The smile fell from Claire's face. "What are you doing?"

"Seeing to it you go home."

Taking the reins in hand, he led his mount around to the rear of the curricle and with a murmur to the animal and a pat on his neck, secured him to the vehicle. The horse tossed his proud equine head and stamped his hooves before he settled down to the notion of being made to walk behind the carriage.

Edward strode forward. "Scoot over. I'm driving."

Her shoulders drew tight, her hands fixed on the ribbons. "I am perfectly capable of driving myself."

In answer, he made a shooing motion with one hand, then leapt up onto the curricle rim. With him looming above her, she had little choice but to do as he demanded. Dropping into the now vacated spot, he settled himself beside her, then reached out to take the reins.

"This is completely unnecessary," she said, as she was forced to surrender the ribbons, the team shifting slightly in recognition of the change of driver.

Edward's eyes glinted as he sent her a look. "Not given the circumstances. From this time forward, my lady, your driving days are done."

"What!"

"That's right," he told her, giving the reins a light flick that set the horses into a moderate walk. "You are hereby banned from driving this, or any other vehicle, without my express permission, which I can safely assure will not be forthcoming."

"But Edward—"

"Oh, so I'm Edward now, am I? Not Your Grace? Or Duke?"

Composing herself, she swallowed the retort that rose to her lips. "But *Edward*, I am a very good driver. You have said so yourself."

"Your ability is not in question. It's your judgment that is lacking, and since I cannot trust that there will be no further races in the park, or other untoward vehicular excursions, the simplest solution would appear to be to take away your wheels, as it were."

Her hands turned to fists in her lap, her teeth clenched so hard they grated together. "That is grossly unfair."

"I don't think it's unfair at all. Considering all of your antics of late, I believe I've been amazingly forbearing up until now. I didn't say a word about your pistol shooting at Manton's or your dice play with those drunken imbeciles that night at the masque. As for Carstairs and Oxnard letting you smoke a cigar at that garden party, well, I thought the aftereffects of that were punishment enough. You looked positively green for hours after, so I doubt you'll be trying *that* again."

He was right. She wouldn't be smoking again considering how ill she'd been. Not only had inhaling made her cough hard enough to expel a lung, it had also made her nauseous. Plus she'd never thought she'd get the disgusting taste out of her mouth no matter how much tooth powder and lemon water she'd used.

"But this predilection for racing that you've developed has to stop. And in case you're already busy thinking up ways to get around my decision to end your driving, I would advise against it."

She crossed her arms over her muslin-covered breasts. "Oh? And what are you going to do about it, if I don't obey?"

"Nothing to *you*. As for the servants, if any of them help you defy me on this point, they will be sacked on the spot."

Her lips parted. "But th-that's horrible. The servants shouldn't be bartered in this fashion. That's their livelihood. You can't turn them out in such a summary fashion."

"I won't turn any of them out, so long as you don't persuade them to disobey my instructions. If anyone loses his or her position, their dismissal will be on your head."

"Oh!" She huffed out a breath.

That he would even threaten such a thing was monstrous. Then again, perhaps he was only bluffing in hopes of assuring her compliance on this point. *Devil*, she thought. Clearly, he was counting on her being too tenderhearted to test his resolve and find out whether he was serious. He was right though. Her differences were with him alone, and she wouldn't risk hurting someone else, not even to achieve her freedom.

"I never realized it before, Your Grace, but you are a bully."

Glancing over, he met her gaze. "If I am, it's because you have made me one." His chest rose, then fell again on a sigh. "End this futile campaign of yours, Claire. You've more than lived up to your rebellious promise, but it's not succeeding, nor is it going to. I am not going to jilt you, and all you're doing is giving yourself a reputation for wildness. Even my irrepressible brother Jack would be awestruck by your audacity, but enough is enough."

She swallowed, wishing that she *could* end it. What a relief it would be to stop all the games and schemes and be just like any other young woman. But if she gave up now she would have achieved nothing. She would have lost in every conceivable way that mattered.

Her head began shaking before the words had even formed on her tongue. "No, not unless you release me. The choice is up to you."

Glancing ahead, she realized that their journey was

nearly over, Clybourne House rising before them in imposing splendor. Drawing up in front of the residence, Edward stopped the curricle, then turned toward her on the seat.

He met her gaze. "My answer has not changed. It remains no."

For a long moment, she studied him, considering his utter inflexibility. *Why*, she raged inwardly, *can't he just let me go? Why does he care, other than his stubborn pride and his endless sense of honor?* If only he felt something deeper for her. If only it wasn't all just an empty game.

Unable to bear another minute of their latest dispute, she jumped to the ground, not waiting for him to help her alight. Hurrying around the carriage, she took the front stairs in a rustling swirl of skirts, barely acknowledging Croft's friendly greeting, as the butler opened the door.

Stepping down from the curricle, Edward watched her disappear inside, his jaw stiff as he went to untie his mount from the back of the vehicle. One of the grooms could have handled the matter, but right now he felt like doing it himself. Taking Jupiter's reins in hand, he patted the horse's muscled neck and began leading him toward the mews. A groom came to see to the carriage and its team, all of them creating a minor procession of sorts.

Inside the neat, brick-paved stable yard, Edward exchanged hellos with more of the lads, then led his mount toward the stable. Clean and well-tended, the building held nearly two dozen equine occupants. The earthy scents of hay and horseflesh greeted him as he led Jupiter toward his stall. Other horses ambled forward to lean their heads over their stall doors, a few pawing or puffing out sounds of welcome.

The head groom came forward, a smile on his long, middle-aged face. "Here now, Your Grace, I'll see to him."

"No need. I shall do it."

If the other man was surprised, he showed no sign. "As

you wish. Let me know if you 'ave need o' anything, Your Grace. Meanwhile, I'll send a boy 'round with fresh water. Feed bucket's already inside."

"Actually, there is something I want to discuss, but it can wait until after Jupiter is settled."

Nodding in understanding, the servant gave a smile, then walked away with a loose-limbed gait.

Leading the stallion into his stall, Edward began unsaddling him with a calm, easy familiarity he'd learned as a youth. Tack removed, he took up a currycomb and began to brush, careful to let the horse know what he was doing so the animal wouldn't spook. Soon the two of them fell into a rhythm.

So she thinks I'm a bully, does she? he mused, his mouth drawing into a severe line. *If that were true, I'd have done a great deal worse than giving her a scold and forbidding her to drive the curricle again.*

Considering her behavior these past four weeks, she'd provided him with ample cause for irritation. More than irritation actually, since most men would have put a harsh and immediate end to her antics. From the talk going 'round, his response was considered extraordinarily tolerant, the betting books rife with wagers about Claire and what outrageous imbroglio she would land herself in next—and how he would react.

Despite her warning to him that night at the ball, he'd had no idea just how far she would be willing to take matters. She'd created more scandal and mayhem than any one small woman ought to be capable of stirring up. But short of locking her in her room or packing her off to the country, there wasn't a great deal he could do to stop her.

Besides, he'd wanted to give her enough latitude that she would be able to see just how useless her efforts really were. He'd assumed she would make one or two meager attempts, then admit defeat. But there was nothing meager in either her attempts or her resolve, Claire taking both him and the Ton by storm.

She was a clever minx, he'd give her that. And astonishingly bold to boot. How he'd ever gotten the impression that she was demure and biddable, he couldn't imagine. The woman had a spine of steel and nerves brazen enough to clash with a king.

As fortune would have it, poor mad King George was indisposed at present and the new Prince Regent was too busy planning his gala fête being held at Carlton House next month to pay much heed to Claire. Without question, however, Edward was sure Prinny had heard about "Clybourne's wild bride-to-be" and no doubt found such stories highly amusing. Edward just hoped the prince didn't take it into his head to seek Claire out at a ball, or who knew what trouble might unravel from the meeting.

He rolled his eyes at the possibilities, then straightened and reached for another brush. Jupiter shifted, the horse's muscles rippling with pleasure as Edward resumed the grooming routine.

She'll concede the fight soon, Edward told himself, *despite her continued show of defiance this morning.* He'd cut her off from the parks and now her driving. With her movements so restricted, she would have far less opportunity to wage her campaign. But he wished she would relent and accept their engagement, since it was the only prudent course for either of them to take. He didn't like being at odds with her. He didn't care for this war with Claire, even if he was confident of coming out the victor.

Blister it, but she's turning me into a rule-bound prig. Worse, she's driving me mad. Half the time he didn't know whether to paddle her or kiss her, and given that he didn't hold with administering corporal punishment to women and children, that left the kissing.

Not that he minded—not a bit, he thought, recalling their last heated encounter. Each time he touched her, he wanted her more, desire urging him to cast aside the bounds of propriety and take her.

Restraining himself was becoming increasingly difficult, each passionate encounter going farther and becoming more intimate than the one before. How easy it would be to let matters progress to their full and natural conclusion. She wouldn't deny him, he knew that much from the way her body turned pliant and needy at his faintest touch. He could have her naked and moaning beneath him with only a few kisses and caresses.

And once he took her, there would be no more talk of ending their engagement, no further outrageous attempts to force him to jilt her. They would marry and that would be that.

But despite all the havoc she was currently wreaking, he didn't want to trick her into the marriage, didn't want to steal her innocence and leave her with no choice but to obey. She would hate him for that, and he couldn't say he would blame her.

No, he would have to be patient awhile longer and let her work this rebellion out of her system. Once she gave up and accepted him, they would wed. That's when he would begin showing her how groundless her fears had been, how pleasant and pleasurable life would be as his wife—despite having married for duty and convenience.

Until then, he would have to restrain his desire for her, at least as far as claiming her virginity. As he'd already shown her, there were other ways they could enjoy each other. He wasn't above indulging himself and Claire in that regard, but only as far as his willpower would allow.

He groaned softly at the thought, his loins heavy and aching from his musings. Closing his eyes for a moment, he fought the need, struggling against the urge to go find Claire inside the house, carry her to his bedroom, and ignore every one of his noble intentions.

Instead, he laid the brush aside and reached for the hoof pick, a task that would require his complete attention. Jupiter was an excellent horse, but he was a stallion and his temper needed watching. Even at the best of times, an inattentive man could end up with a kick to the chest or head if he wasn't careful. What better way to shake off his desire than scraping pebbles and filth out of horse hooves?

Leaning into the task, Edward did just that, using the labor to drive Claire out of his head—for a few minutes at least.

Upstairs in her bedchamber, Claire stood as her maid assisted her into a fresh gown, a short-sleeved day dress of pale yellow silk with an overskirt of translucent white dotted swiss.

Fastening a last row of buttons, the servant stepped back to regard her. "You look a right picture, my lady, if I do say so meself," she declared with one of her toothy grins.

If only I felt that way, Claire thought, as she smiled her thanks.

Nearly an hour had passed and she was still stewing over her confrontation with Edward. Not only had he curtailed her right to drive and a great many other freedoms along with it, but it would seem that her efforts still weren't achieving the desired effect.

Confound it, what do I have to do to make him relent? More worrisome, what if he was right and there really was nothing she could do to force his hand? But there must be something, and despite any setbacks, she would discover what it was.

Claire was contemplating ways around his edicts, and potential new transgressions she might attempt, when a knock came at the door.

Penny went to answer it, greeting Mallory as she entered the room. Excusing herself, the servant departed, leaving the two of them alone.

"I came to find out if you are ready for our picnic nuncheon," Mallory said, looking lovely in a gown of light blue sarcenet, a color that made her eyes gleam like jewels.

"I am, as you can see."

Mallory paused for a moment before continuing. "I also had to find out if the servant gossip is true. Did you really take the curricle out on your own this morning?"

Claire nodded. "I did."

"And Ned went after you?"

"You certainly are well-informed," she replied with wry amusement.

Mallory grinned. "You know the staff tell me everything. So, what happened?"

Crossing toward the window, Claire sank into a nearby chair. "The condensed version is that I am officially forbidden to drive anymore."

Mallory took a seat opposite. "Just for leaving your maid behind?"

"In part, but mostly because I raced Lord Blevins. And won, I'll have you know." Leaning back, she crossed her arms. "Edward confiscated my winnings and is returning them to his lordship today, for all the difference that shall make. I am sure if you know the story, half of London will soon as well."

"*Zounds!* I know you're trying to get Ned's attention, but are you still sure this is the best way to go about it?

You astonish even me with your bravado, and I was born a Byron!"

Claire smiled, recalling Edward's remarks about the family penchant for landing themselves in the suds. As for Mallory's belief that Claire was engaging in various eyebrow-raising peccadilloes in order to draw Edward's attention . . . well, the half-truth had seemed the easiest way to explain the situation when Mallory had first quizzed her about her outlandish exploits.

It wasn't that she didn't trust Mallory—she did—but still, Edward was Mallory's brother, and she didn't want to put her in the position of having to take sides. Even more, if Claire admitted her real goal, Mallory would have been astute enough to demand to know why. Perhaps it was prideful, but Claire couldn't bring herself to admit what was truly in her heart. So rather than confide her actual plan, Claire let Mallory believe a modified version of the truth.

"I thought your strategy was half insane from the start," Mallory told her, not for the first time, "but I must admit that I've never seen anyone shake Ned up the way you do. He's always so coolly reasonable and rational, even when you know he's furious. But not with you. Around you he acts first and thinks about it afterward. I rather like seeing that collected calm of his rattled up a bit."

"Do you?" Claire asked with a slight smile.

"Oh, definitely. It's about time my brother fell in love. And with such a wonderful woman too."

Claire's brows drew tight. *Love? He doesn't love me.*

If Mallory had heard Edward dressing her down today in the park, she wouldn't be crediting him with any such tender emotions. But Mallory was a romantic who saw love behind every glance and sigh. Because of her own personal happiness, she assumed everyone was happy. But Mallory's comments about her brother were nothing more than wishful thinking, and Claire couldn't afford to let herself believe otherwise. Nor could she let herself forget for an instant what it was she must do. As she had told him today, their battle was far from finished.

"Yes, well," Claire said, glancing briefly away, "we shall see what sort of expressions of affection he evinces at today's nuncheon party. Will it be growls or glowers, I wonder?"

Mallory laughed, the sound drawing a smile from Claire. "In the meantime," Claire said, "you must advise me on which bonnet to wear. I have narrowed it down to my top three favorites, but I just can't decide."

"Show them to me at once," Mallory agreed with enthusiasm. "You know I love nothing so much as perfecting an ensemble. Let us see which one will turn you out at your stylish best."

Chapter 15

"Would you care for anything further?" Edward inquired later that same afternoon.

Seated beside him on a surprisingly comfortable blue-and-white checked lawn blanket, Claire sent him a glance from beneath the short straw brim of her basket bonnet, its lemon silk ribbons left long to dangle becomingly over her bodice.

She and Mallory had decided on the hat because the light color and airy construction seemed in keeping with the event. Based on the warm late spring air, they had chosen well.

"Thank you, no, I've had more than sufficient," she stated, laying her plate aside. "You oughtn't to have encouraged me to try the strawberry tart at all. It was too delicious by half."

"The first berries of the year are never to be missed, or the fresh clotted cream. I can ask one of the footmen if there are any more."

"Don't you dare. As it is, I fear I shall be overcome and need a nap at any moment."

A dark gleam shone in his eyes. "Everyone is resting. I am sure no one would mind if you shut your eyes for a few minutes. Here," he said, leaning back against the tree under which they were sitting, "pray feel at your leisure to use me as a pillow." Gently, he patted his thigh.

She stared. First at him and then surreptitiously at his heavily muscled thigh, unable to help but imagine how it would feel to lay her head in his lap. Her skin grew warm in ways that had nothing to do with the mild May temperature and plentiful sunshine.

And he accuses me of being scandalous.

But he was right that the lawn party had quieted down to a number of small lazy groups and gently murmuring couples, a few of the older ladies and gentlemen already stretched out and quite unashamedly asleep.

As for Edward's mood, she couldn't entirely fathom it. She'd expected him to be polite, but curt, still showing his displeasure over this morning's curricle race. But when he'd met her and Mallory earlier in the entrance hall, he'd greeted them with a pleasant smile. And later, in the coach, he'd laughed with good humor at Leo and Lawrence's round of stories, as the five of them traveled across Town.

She'd also assumed Edward would keep a close watch on her today, sticking by her side like a gaoler so that she didn't attempt some new scandalous peccadillo. But although he had been attentive, she hadn't felt smothered or unduly watched, his actions no more or less what could be expected from one's fiancé.

Yet that was exactly the trouble. Their relationship wasn't typical and they'd never enjoyed a traditional courtship where he would have wooed her with flattering words and showy displays of attention, however false such attentions might ultimately have proven to be.

Surely that isn't what he's doing now?

Surely he wasn't trying to woo her in order to win their war?

Of course she was probably mistaken and he was only teasing her. Or maybe he was merely in a generous mood after having banned her from driving his curricle and he wanted to make a few small amends.

Raising an encouraging eyebrow, he patted his thigh again, inviting her to give in to temptation.

Suppressing a delicious shiver, she shook her head. "I believe I would fare better with a walk rather than a nap. If you prefer to remain here, however, I can see if Mallory might like to join me."

As if sensing that she was being spoken about, Mallory glanced up from where she sat several feet distant, sharing nuncheon on another blanket with Adam Gresham. Mallory smiled and waved.

Claire waved back.

"I shall take you," Edward said. "A walk would do me good as well."

Standing, Edward helped her to her feet, then offered his arm. Taking it, she let him lead her across the grassy lawn.

"Determined to keep me out of trouble, Your Grace?" she remarked.

He met her gaze and smiled. "Always. But let's not get into that at the moment. It's a beautiful day, far too pleasant to quarrel. I won't even correct you about my name."

"Ah. How very forbearing of you," she said in a guileless tone.

A laugh rolled from his throat. "You are irrepressible, aren't you?"

"When it suits me."

"Well, believe it or not, it suits me too." He tucked her hand closer against his arm. "So long as you aren't demonstrating that particular trait for broad public consumption, that is."

"I thought we weren't going to—how did you put it?—'get into that' at the moment."

A gleam sparkled in his vibrant blue eyes. "Quite right, and so I did. What other topics might we discuss then, do you think?"

"There are all the usual ones, of course," she stated. "The weather, although I believe you already voiced your opinion on that, and I agree, it is lovely today. We could talk about the party, making mention of all the couples in attendance and what a delightful event it has been. Or we might each venture a comment or two regarding the excellent health and beneficent nature of our hostess. Lady Harold does cut a fine figure today in her Spitalfields silk gown. Puce quite becomes her, do you not agree?"

He threw up a hand on a laugh. "Enough."

"Oh, so you'd rather converse on loftier subjects then?" she said with mock seriousness. "Art, music or literature perhaps? What about history or politics? Although, as a woman, I am to pretend a polite ignorance on such topics and act as though my mind is too frail to absorb the elements of difficult, manly debate."

Slowing his pace, he shifted to meet her gaze. "There is nothing in the least frail about your mind, my lady. And you are never to pretend ignorance on any subject, not with me. You may always say exactly what you wish while in my company."

She paused, her lips parting on a soft inhalation. "Even if we disagree and my remarks make you cross?"

A faint smile played over his mouth. "Yes, even then. And so far I haven't noticed you caviling at the prospect of making me cross. You do it with astonishing frequency."

"Do I? You rarely seem out of countenance."

"Oh, believe me, I am. It's just that I was trained from an early age not to wear my emotions on my sleeve. A peer is always in control of both his thoughts and feelings, no matter the provocation."

His remark reminded her of Mallory's earlier comment about Claire shaking him out of his usual reserve. *Does he hide himself?* she wondered. *Are there layers below the surface that he never reveals, not even to his intimates, his family?*

Certainly he didn't show them to her, and if her plan succeeded, he never would, he wouldn't have the chance. Yet even were she willing to give him that chance, such things required time and familiarity. Even more, they took a willingness of spirit from both parties, since bonds of trust could not be formed by one person alone. Like love, such feelings must be given and returned, mutually nurtured, or else they would wither and eventually cease to exist at all. It would seem, then, that whatever secrets each of them kept, they were destined to remain their own.

"Well, you are always at liberty to express your anger with me," she told him in a carefree tone.

Having reached the neatly manicured perimeter of Lady Harold's rose garden, he drew them to a halt. "That's very good of you. What about others?"

She cocked her head. "Other what?"

"Emotions?" he said in a deep rumble. "Have I your leave to express those as well?"

Suddenly she couldn't quite catch her breath. "Of course. We must always be ourselves in each other's company."

An enigmatic expression came into his eyes. "Yes. I rather think we must."

He leaned toward her.

Is he going to kiss me? she wondered. Her heart hammered in anticipation, eyelids growing heavy. He drew nearer still, his gaze on her lips. But then he stopped and straightened, as if remembering they were not alone, dozens of other guests strolling around the property as well.

She expected him to escort her back. Instead, he reached into his coat pocket. "I have something for you."

"Oh?"

"I've been meaning to give it to you for days, but something always seemed to interfere. What that might have been, I can't imagine," he teased, as he handed her a small parcel wrapped in plain brown paper.

After barely a second's hestitation, she pulled off the ribbon and tore open the wrapping. Inside lay a cube of wood, which had been cut and smoothed into a series of interlocking pieces.

"It's a Chinese wood knot," Edward supplied. "You take the pieces apart, then try to fit them back in order. You did say you like puzzles, as I recall."

"Oh, I do!" She turned the polished cube over in her hand. "I'm half afraid of trying it though. What if I can never make it whole again?"

"You will. It kept me guessing for a while, but eventually I figured out the trick. You shall as well."

She smiled. "Wherever did you get it? No wait, don't tell me. Lord Drake."

His eyes twinkled. "Correct on the first guess. Drake is always looking for interesting bits and pieces from around the world, so when he gave this to me, I immediately thought of you and had him procure another. I hope it brings you pleasure."

"It will, I am sure. Thank you, Your—" Stopping, she started again. "Thank you, Edward."

His mouth curved into a broad smile. "You are most welcome. And had I known a mere trifle was all it would take to convince you to use my given name, I would have presented you with one ages ago."

She couldn't help but laugh. "Well, do not get too used to it. You may yet be 'Your Grace' again. Unless you have more presents hiding somewhere on your person, that is," she teased.

But instead of joining in her humor, he sent her a serious, inquiring look. "Would that make a difference, if I did? I am pleased to give you whatever you like, you know. You have only to ask and I shall do my utmost to see that it is yours."

The smile fell from her mouth, her breath caught almost painfully inside her chest. She stared at the puzzle block with which she had been so delighted. Now it felt hard and cold, lifeless like her heart.

Unable to look at it anymore, she squeezed the puzzle tightly inside her palm. "Generous as your offer may be, I am not one to be swayed by the acquisition of physical things. What I find most important are those intangibles, which can neither be bought nor wrapped with ribbon and paper. But apparently you know me even less than I had imagined."

"Claire, you've misconstrued—"

"I believe I should like to go back now, if you would be so good as to escort me."

The muscle grew taut in his jaw. "You know I did not mean—"

"Very well then," she declared, gazing away from him across the lawn. "I shall go on my own." She'd taken three steps before he caught her.

"You'll do no such thing," he said. "As for this other matter, we shall talk of it later."

But there was nothing about which to talk, she realized with a weary sigh. Did he really imagine he could shower her with gifts and the strife between them would be over? Did he honestly believe her reasons for wanting to be free of this engagement were so thoughtless and superficial that *possessions* would change her mind? Well, if her initial pleasure in his company had put any chinks in her wall of resolve, he'd just neatly plastered them up again.

They spoke not a word as he led her back to the center of the festivities. By now, everyone had finished their meals and their naps, and were once again engaged in a variety of amusements.

She and Edward had been back for less than a minute when their hostess approached, her purplish-brown skirts swaying around her plump ankles.

"Your Grace, Lady Claire," the older woman said, "I do hope you are enjoying yourselves this afternoon. I couldn't help but notice the two of you walking near my rose garden."

Claire used the distraction to slip her hand off Edward's arm.

"Yes, your grounds are exquisite, as are your flowers," Edward replied, giving no indication that he noticed Claire's desertion, although Claire was sure he had.

Lady Harold preened, her landscape a well-known pride and joy. "Thank you, Your Grace." She hesitated for a brief moment, then continued on. "There is a group of us discussing great architects and I understand that your beautiful grounds at Braebourne were designed by Capability Brown himself."

"In part. My father had many of the gardens expanded in his time as duke."

"Oh, we would love to hear. Would you mind terribly joining our little conversation? And Lady Claire, I promise I shall borrow him only for the veriest little while, then have him right back to you. If His Grace is in accord, that is?"

"Of course you must go, Edward," Claire said, sending Lady Harold a beatific smile. "Pray do not worry about me. I am sure I shall find some other means of entertaining myself during your absence."

His brows drew sharp and he shot Claire a look, but as they both knew, there was nothing he could do to escape their hostess's request. Not without appearing impolite, that is. "I should be honored, Lady Harold," he said. "Please lead the way."

With the older woman tittering at his side, Claire watched her squire Edward off across the lawn. He sent Claire one last glance over his shoulder, his warning to stay out of trouble clear in his gaze. Smiling, she waggled her fingers, then turned away.

Let him stew, she thought. *It's no more than he deserves.*

Once he was out of sight, she let her shoulders droop, sighing softly under her breath as she studied the puzzle again. Running her thumb over the polished wood, she considered striding across the way to throw it into Lady Harold's decorative fishpond.

She imagined doing just that, watching the block sink to the bottom and nestle unseen among the reeds. But such an act would be childish. Even more, she knew that her impulsiveness would only wound her that much more deeply. For in spite of Edward's thoughtless words, she wanted his gift, stupid as such feelings might be.

"And what, dear lady, has put such a serious expression on your face?" asked a low masculine voice from just over her shoulder.

Glancing up, she met a pair of handsome grey eyes. "Lord Islington. Heavens, you startled me."

"My apologies. I should not have intruded on your private contemplation."

"No, no, it is entirely all right. I didn't realize you were in attendance today or I should have greeted you earlier."

He smiled, both of them aware that she would have done no such thing, not with Edward close at hand.

In fact, she had barely seen Islington since that night of the ball when they had shocked everyone with their dancing. The couple of times she had encountered him afterward had been from a distance, their only contact an exchange of formal nods.

Truthfully, she'd been somewhat relieved by his absence, not only because of her promise to Edward, but because Lord Islington made her the tiniest bit nervous—and not in a good way.

But she was only letting Edward's warning influence her, she was sure. Even now, she had yet to hear anyone give an accurate accounting of Lord Islington's disgrace. Why, he was probably no worse a scoundrel than she was herself with her newly minted "wild" reputation.

"I arrived but a short while ago," he explained in response to her inquiry. "Unavoidable business kept me away from the earlier festivities. I had promised Lady Harold, however, that I would stop by if I could possibly manage. She is a distant cousin of mine and puts great store in such familial bonds."

"I am sure she does. It is good of you to attend, although you might perhaps wish to wait to say your hellos, since she is with the duke and several others at present. I am given to understand that they are discussing estate landscaping."

His eyes sparkled with unconcealed amusement. "Then I thank you most sincerely for the advice."

She returned the smile, turning the puzzle cube around inside her hand.

"What have you there?"

"Nothing of note," she told him, slipping the Chinese wood knot into her pocket. "The weather is quite lovely today, do you not think?"

"Most definitely," he agreed, allowing her to change the subject. "Although it is by no means so lovely as you. You are as radiant as a newly blossomed rose in your pretty yellow finery. I am surprised hummingbirds aren't fluttering around you in search of nectar. I know I would be, were I a bird."

She didn't know whether to be flattered or amused by his remark. It struck her in that moment that Edward never said such things. He didn't fawn or cajole, didn't employ clever turns of phrase to coax a smile or make her feminine pulse beat faster. Then again, one never had to wonder if his words were exaggerations. He was scrupulously honest and forthright, and when he did offer a compliment, there was no doubt that it was genuinely and sincerely meant. Comparing the styles of the two men, she decided she much preferred Edward's way of doing things.

Besides, Edward was far too serious to spout flowery phrases and syrupy metaphors. He would sound utterly ridiculous in the attempt. And while it was true that he shared his surname with a famous poet, she knew it was the only thing the two men had in common.

"You are very quiet, Lady Claire. Surely I have not discomfited you?" Islington said, drawing her back from her musings. "Given the stories I have been hearing of late, I had rather thought you would be full of verve. Your daring has becoming legendary."

Her shoulders went back. "Legendary? No, nothing of the sort. Unexpected in an entertaining kind of way—to that I might admit—but not legendary."

Islington laughed, an appreciative grin on his face. "What do you say to a stroll? It's sure to create ruffled feathers on more than the ducks in my cousin's pond."

Claire was debating how best to answer, when Leo and Lawrence appeared, taking up positions on either side of her.

"Lady Claire," Leo said, taking her hand to kiss.

"Dearest sister-to-be," Lawrence followed, repeating his brother's action in an exaggerated way that made her guffaw.

"We were only just looking for you," Leo continued, "wondering where you had got, when suddenly there you were." Maintaining his hold, he threaded her hand over his arm. On her other side, Lawrence did the same.

"Oh, hallo, your lordship," Leo remarked, as if he only then realized that Islington was present. "Capital day, is it not? You won't mind if we spirit Lady Claire away for a while. Family matters, you understand."

Islington scowled, looking as if he did indeed want to object. But before he could say so much as a word, the twins were trundling her off. Glancing back, she called a laughing good-bye to Islington. He nodded, scowling harder.

Claire let the twins march her several yards away, waiting to speak until they were out of Islington's earshot. "That was rather badly done of you both, you know. You bordered on rudeness."

"I thought it was very well done," Leo declared with an unrepentant grin on his mouth. "Wouldn't you agree, Lawrence, old man?"

"Unquestionably," his brother concurred. "We got in and out with a minimum of fuss, neatly liberating you from that libertine."

"How do you know he's a libertine? Or that I wanted liberating?" she charged.

"Well, of course you did," Leo stated, drawing the three of them to a halt. "We could see it on your face."

"Indeed we could," Lawrence asserted, defending his brother's assertion.

She gave a delicate snort to let them both know what she thought of that. "I suspect there is another reason entirely."

"Oh? And what might that be?" both twins said in unison as they sent her direct stares, plainly hoping she would believe them if they put up a united front.

She didn't. "And how do you know Lord Islington is a libertine?" she repeated. "That's what Edward told you, I suppose."

Leo grew serious. "He did, but I've also heard other talk."

"What sort of talk? What is he supposed to have done?"

"Had to do with a girl, although I'm not sure about the particulars," Lawrence said. "Still and all, he's a bad sort and we knew you were in need of rescue."

"I am perfectly capable of looking after myself and had no need of rescue," she stated in a reproving tone that belied her relief that they'd hurried her away. "I am sure, however, that you have only my best interests at heart."

They both looked mollified by her statement. "'Course we do," Leo said.

"Exactly," Lawrence agreed.

"Why do I suspect, however, that there is more to your intervention than you are letting on?"

"Don't know what you mean," Leo bristled.

"Not a bit," Lawrence declared.

She turned a gimlet eye on them, watching as they began to shuffle their feet and cross their arms. "So Edward had no part in this?"

Leo kicked at a tuft of grass. "No, not specifically. He might have asked us to keep an eye on you."

"But that was earlier before we even left the house," Lawrence said.

"And getting you away from Islington was our idea," Leo continued. "Ned was busy and we knew he would approve."

Claire cleared her throat. "Yes, I daresay he would." Linking her arms once again with theirs, she encouraged them to resume their stroll. "So, gentlemen. Your eldest brother wants you to keep an eye on me, does he?"

They both nodded, but remained quiet.

"Well then, what would you say to being able to keep an even closer eye on me? I have an idea and it requires your particular assistance."

Knowing she'd sparked their interest, she explained further while the three of them walked on.

Chapter 16

"What else, Mr. Hughes?" Edward asked nearly a week later, as he sat behind his desk at Clybourne House. Laying down his pen, he held out the correspondence he'd just finished signing.

His secretary took the letters in hand. "There is only the issue of appointing a new steward at Rexhill Lodge. Have I your permission to begin interviewing likely candidates for your consideration?"

He and Mr. Hughes had previously discussed the need to replace the elderly steward of Edward's Norfolk estate. Once the loyal old retainer had agreed to take a generous pension and retire, the way had been paved to search for his replacement. "Yes, of course, see to it with all due haste. Is that everything for today, then?"

"It is, Your Grace." Bowing, the young man withdrew, off to work at his own desk located in a room two doors down the hall.

Once he'd departed, Edward leaned back in his chair,

his thoughts drifting to the place, or rather the person, with whom they seemed constantly occupied these days.

Claire.

After barely touching her breakfast this morning, she'd complained that she wasn't feeling well and had asked to be excused from that afternoon's engagements. Immediately concerned, Mallory and Cousin Wilhelmina said she must of course stay home, and Edward agreed. She'd urged the ladies to go on without her, saying she would only be in bed sleeping, so there was no point in them remaining behind and missing out on their planned entertainment.

Not long after his sister and cousin left the house, he'd checked on Claire and was informed by her maid that she was resting comfortably and had asked not to be disturbed. Honoring her wishes, he'd gone downstairs to his study to work.

A check of the mantel clock showed that nearly three hours had passed since then. Perhaps she was awake now and would enjoy some company? Although likely not his, since she'd maintained a rather cool reserve toward him ever since that disastrous episode at Lady Harold's nuncheon party.

He was still kicking himself over his imbecilic remark, wondering even now what had possessed him to say such a thing. They'd been enjoying themselves, her gaze alive with pleasure over his gift, when out came the words. Immediately he'd known he was making a mistake. But by then it was too late to stop, his comment impossible to recall.

She'd been miffed with him ever since, speaking only when she had no other choice. He'd expected her to continue her small rebellions, but she had not—her actions quiet, even circumspect, these last several days.

He was surprised and, yes, a bit suspicious, but perhaps she'd finally realized that her pranks weren't working and she'd decided to cede the battle to him, after all.

And if he wished very hard, horses might sprout wings and begin to fly.

Once again, he considered checking on her, then dismissed the idea. *Let her sleep. The extra rest can only do her good.*

In the meantime, perhaps he would go to his club and spend a couple of hours perusing periodicals and newspapers in hopes of spotting something that might be of use in the Everett matter.

A few days ago, Drake had given him the excellent news that he'd broken the cipher that was being used by the spies with whom Everett had associated. Now able to decipher Everett's note, they'd found that it revealed the address of a town house located in a squalid part of London's East End. Unfortunately, it was a property that had recently come to their attention by other means, a house that was apparently no longer being used as a rendezvous or hiding place. In the interest of prudence, however, Edward had ordered a man posted in the area to keep watch in case it became an active site again in the future.

Otherwise, they'd had no luck finding or identifying Everett's murderer or locating the man he'd named before his death—the elusive Wolf. As for the mole, the fellow was buried deep. But Edward was determined to find him, and one of these days he would.

For now, however, he and his small group of trusted men at the War Office would continue studying the newspapers in hopes of retrieving a new, active message or two. And although he subscribed to most of the widely read newspapers and periodicals, he didn't receive them all, nor did he get many of the smaller publications. But Brooks's Club did. The club received them all.

With his afternoon satisfactorily planned, Edward went to the bellpull and rang for his carriage. As he did, he found himself hoping that by the time he returned, Claire would be feeling like herself again.

"You're certain you want to go through with this?"

From her place inside the coach, Claire stared across at the twins, her heart beating quickly inside her chest.

A half hour ago, with Edward still safely occupied inside his study, Leo and Lawrence had helped her sneak out of Clybourne House and into a coach for the ride across Town. Before their departure, she'd wondered how they were going to leave without being noticed. To her astonished delight, she'd learned there was a system of hidden passageways that led through the entire residence. The twins weren't supposed to know it existed, but they'd discovered the secret as young boys when they'd seen their brother Jack slip in and out one night.

Their knowledge proved invaluable, since they knew just which passageway to take in order to find the rear servants' staircase and the exit that led to a quiet corner of the mews. From there it had been an easy thing for the three of them to make their way to the coach waiting one block over.

Now they were here at their final destination, mere footsteps away from putting her latest plan into action. Her pulse sped again at the idea, at the sheer audacity of the scheme.

"It's not too late to change your mind," Lawrence counseled, giving her an understanding smile.

Leo nodded. "We won't think anything less of you if you want to return home."

"Well, I'll think less of me. God knows, I didn't do *this* to myself in order to turn craven now."

This, as it happened, referred to her hair.

Reaching up, she touched the end of one shorn lock, remembering her initial horror at seeing the blond strands of her waist-length hair fall to her bedroom floor, as she'd ruthlessly cut them off with a scissors. After trimming the ends as best she could to even them up, she'd bundled the cut hair into a bag and stuffed it inside her sewing basket where her maid would never look.

Soon after, the twins had arrived with her attire—a set of Leo's old clothes cut down and tailored to the measurements she'd provided them earlier that week. At first, they'd stared when they'd seen her cropped tresses, their mouths agape in mirror images of astonishment. For a moment, she wondered just how shocking she looked. But it was only hair, she'd assured herself, and would grow back—eventually at least.

She gave them credit for recovering quickly, however, and again for helping her arrange her cropped hair and tie her cravat once she'd changed into the masculine garb required for her masquerade.

"Surely you two aren't turning coward, are you?" she asked, knowing the challenge would be exactly what was needed to reinvigorate their support.

Both young men bristled as one.

"Not a bit!" Lawrence cried.

"If I didn't know you were a woman inside those trousers, I'd challenge you here and now." Leo crossed his arms over his chest.

"Now, now, don't ruffle up. I didn't mean anything and you know it. I appreciate you both being gallant enough to offer to let me renege, but there's no need." Swallowing down her nerves, she smiled. "Just think what a lark this is going to be and what splendid fun we'll have!"

The twins' gazes met for a moment before a pair of identical grins spread across their mouths.

"Wicked fun!" Leo proclaimed.

"Brilliant entertainment," Lawrence concurred.

"Well then, gentlemen, shall we embark?" she asked.

"Whenever you're ready," Lawrence stated.

Yet Claire hesitated, her hands going again to her short, brushed-back hair. "One last check. How do I look?"

Two sets of male eyes appraised her.

Leo tapped a finger against his chin. "Pretty."

"And young," Lawrence added with a sigh.

"And slight," Leo said. "Wish we could have found some way to give you a few whiskers, but there's just no managing it."

"Luckily you're blond," Lawrence remarked, "and blonds never show much beard anyway."

Leo nodded. "You'll do. Just keep your hat low when we go in and no one will suspect."

"After all," Lawrence reasoned, "they won't be expecting a girl, so it'll never occur to them that's what you are."

"Even if you are effeminate-looking," Leo mused. "Worst they'll think is that you're a Miss Molly."

She cocked her head. "Miss Molly? Who's that? I thought women weren't allowed inside."

"They aren't," Leo said, looking distinctly uncomfortable of a sudden.

"Then what do you mean?" she persisted.

The twins exchanged a glance, snickering softly under their breaths as they rolled their eyes at each other.

"Never mind," Lawrence said.

"Not important," Leo seconded.

"So? Are you ready?" they asked together.

Deciding to let the matter drop, she drew an invigorating breath, then nodded. "I am."

Letting the twins step down first, she followed, glad of the stylish cane they'd lent her since neither offered her the assistance of a hand.

Men didn't hand each other down, she reminded herself. She would have to remember that fact and a dozen others, if she wanted to make this work. Otherwise, she risked not even getting past the butler at the entrance.

Adopting the same arrogant swagger as the twins—or at least what she hoped passed for an arrogant swagger—she strode beside them toward the entrance of the exclusive all-male domain. The door swung open at their approach, a regal-looking servant inclining his head in greeting.

"Gentlemen," the butler said. "Welcome to Brooks's Club."

Over an hour later, Edward laid yet another periodical atop the growing pile of those he'd already inspected, then reached for a new one. So far, his search of the club's collection of newspapers and periodicals had revealed nothing of import and he was beginning to suspect that, for today at least, such would continue to be the case.

After arriving, he'd gone directly to the library, taking a seat in one of the comfortable leather chairs and accepting a glass of very decent Burgundy from a solicitous waiter. Settling into the peaceful quiet, he'd begun his search. But now that his efforts were proving fruitless, he wondered if he ought to stop and return home. Once there, he could ask after Claire's health and, if she was feeling well enough, maybe coax her into sharing a small afternoon repast.

He'd made up his mind to depart when the library's calm was disturbed by the sound of excited exclamations drifting in from the gaming room beyond.

The waiter approached again. "Another libation, Your Grace?"

"No, thank you. I'm wondering, however, about the commotion coming from next door. Is there a particularly exciting game afoot?"

"There is indeed. Some rather heavy play, from what I hear, that's caught the attention of several of the members. I believe a number of side bets are being wagered on the outcome even now. Would you like me to place one for you, Your Grace?"

"Not without seeing the table first. Who's playing?"

"Some young gentlemen, I believe. And Lord Moregrave."

Moregrave? The man had a reputation for ruthlessness. He was known as well for his love of drink and also for his enjoyment in taking advantage of wet-behind-the-ears whelps who didn't know enough to steer clear of his lures.

What surprised Edward, however, was the other members' interest in the game. Generally, if the young rubes couldn't be convinced early on not to seat themselves at Moregrave's table, the others turned a resigned eye—and sometimes literally their backs—to the sight of the skinning to come. Many said the drubbing those pups received at Moregrave's hand was a lesson well-learned. Yet now, according to the servant, wagers were being cast on the outcome of one of those games—a game whose outcome had always been considered a foregone conclusion, at least until today. Could it be that the young gentlemen were actually holding their own? Was it possible that Moregrave might lose?

Intrigued, Edward rose from his chair.

The noise grew in volume as he left the library and approached the gambling salon. Entering, he found a sizeable number of gentlemen arrayed throughout the large chamber, with a great many standing in a circle around a table near the center.

The waiter had been right that wagers were being placed on the play at hand. Judging by the calls going back and forth, most of the men were backing Moregrave. But a few brave, or perhaps foolhardy, souls were championing his opponents.

Surrounded as the players were, Edward still couldn't see who sat at the table. As he made his way forward though, a strange hush began to descend; men would glance up, only to fall silent and step aside to let him pass. He was pondering their peculiar reaction when he reached the inner circle and gained an unimpeded view of the card table and its collection of players.

Abruptly, the reason for the men's reactions became apparent, Edward's brows drawing close as he recognized Leo and Lawrence. The twins looked like identical bookends seated across from each other, Leo's back toward Edward. Lord Moregrave, with his distinctive shock of black and white hair and pugnacious jowl, sat on Leo's right. His eyes were flat and black, cold as his name as he studied his cards.

The last player was angled in his chair so that only a portion of the side of his face showed. From what little Edward could glimpse, the slight-set blond youth didn't look old enough to be out of leading strings. His cheek was as smooth as a baby's rump, his chin equally soft. Only his hands holding his cards were fully visible—small, white hands with long, delicate fingers and well-trimmed nails. A tingle unlike any Edward had ever felt before traced over his spine as he gazed at those hands, together with a strange familiarity that made no sense at all. But then why should it? he thought, shaking off the sensation. He'd never seen this boy before in his life.

As for his brothers . . . He fixed each of them with an implacable stare, wondering if the other young man was a friend of theirs from school. No wonder Moregrave had been so eager to wager against these three. The sight of them must have set him salivating like a ravenous wolf who'd happened upon three lost lambs.

"I'm out," Lawrence announced, tossing down his cards in clear defeat.

Edward watched his brother reach for the glass at his elbow and raise the red wine to his lips. Lawrence glanced up and as he did, their gazes met. Lawrence froze, nearly gagging as his gold-green eyes bulged halfway out of his head.

Meanwhile, Lord Moregrave slid a tall stack of coins into the pile already amassed in the center of the table.

"What's the matter, Lawrence?" Leo asked. "You look deuced queer of a sudden. Wine go down wrong or something?"

But Lawrence didn't speak, making bobbing gestures with his chin and upward, darting motions with his eyes.

"What on earth?" Leo continued. "You look as though you've developed a palsy."

Lawrence sighed and bowed his head, shaking it in clear exasperation. As though suddenly understanding that he was to look behind him, Leo swung his head around.

Edward met his brother's gaze. Leo's cheeks went white.

"Are you wagering, your lordship?" Moregrave demanded in an impatient tone.

"I . . . um . . . I—" Breaking off, Leo turned back and stared at his cards. Long moments slid past before he tossed them down. "No, bother it. I'm out too."

And then it was the stripling's turn.

Moregrave regarded his final opponent, a sneer on his belligerent face. "What about you then, Mr. . . . Densmar, was it not? Will you challenge me further or concede defeat like your friends?"

The stripling held still, in no way revealing his thoughts or emotions while he calmly studied his cards. Slowly, as though there wasn't a small fortune at risk, he fanned his hand closed, cupping the cards inside his small palm.

"Well?" Moregrave hissed. "What is it then? In or out? I haven't got the whole damned day."

"Pray have patience. You won't need all day, only a few moments more," the boy said in an oddly husky voice. "I'm in." Reaching for a large stack of gold coins, he slid all of them into the pot.

Exclamations went up from the crowd, as another flurry of wild betting commenced.

But Edward was scarcely aware of the commotion around him. A visceral shiver flowed through his veins, his skin prickling, as the boy's voice echoed in his mind. He'd heard that voice before. Only it had been different somehow, and higher. He'd heard the words as well, but they'd been lilting, carefree and feminine, as they'd drifted to his ears.

Pray have patience. I'll only be a few moments more.

Striding forward suddenly, Edward laid a hand on the boy's shoulder. Instinctively, the youth looked up. His eyes were a pure robin's-egg blue that could belong to only one person in the world.

Edward's chest grew tight. *Claire!*

He nearly blurted out her name, but caught himself at the last instant, mute as he took in the sight of her dressed and coiffed like a man. She looked bizarre and yet herself. How could everyone else not see? And God's nightgown, what had she done to her hair? If he didn't mistake the matter, she'd cut it. How could she have committed such a barbarism, cutting all that glorious flowing gold? His hand curved harder around her shoulder and she let out a faint squeak.

No wonder the twins looked as though they'd both eaten a side of rancid beef. By the time he got through with them, they'd have a great deal more reason to feel green around the gills.

"Here now, Clybourne, what do you think you're doing?" Moregrave complained. "There's a game to finish and I'll thank you not to interfere."

"These young . . . *men*," he said with his gaze locked on Claire, "are here without permission and they are leaving forthwith."

"Well, that one ain't," Moregrave said, pointing a finger at Claire, "not until the play is concluded. He has my money and I don't intend to leave here without it."

"*My* money, don't you mean?" Claire challenged in a

proud, "masculine" tone. "What makes you so sure I haven't won?"

Moregrave's face creased into a nasty sneer, as a round of collective muttering went around the room.

"Let the boy play, Clybourne," someone called.

"Most irregular not to see things out," said another.

"Besides, he and Moregrave aren't the only ones with a bit of blunt riding on the outcome," remarked a third.

"Be that as it may," Edward said, tugging Claire to her feet, "these three young gentlemen are leaving."

"So it's a forfeit then, is it?" Moregrave drawled. "Fine by me." Without waiting, he began to reach for the mass of coins in the center of the table.

"No!" Claire shouted, stopping all the action. "I have *not* forfeited. The game is still active. We have only to turn over our cards to determine the winner." Gazing up, she met Edward's eyes. "Just a flip of the cards, Your Grace. Once that is done, I will gladly do as you wish."

He stared at her for a long moment, then released his hold. "Finish it." His voice lowered so only she could hear. "Then you and I shall deal with each other at home."

He felt her shiver before she straightened her shoulders, drawing herself up with aplomb. Returning to her chair, she faced her opponent. "My Lord Moregrave, I believe the turn was yours."

His upper lip curled, arrogant confidence in his calculating visage. "And so it was." Smiling, he turned over his hand. Groans and gasps rose at the sight of his cards, which were all in the trump suit. Chuckling, he reached again for the winnings' pool.

"Hold there, my lord, if you would," Claire remarked in her deliberately low voice. "I haven't shown you *my* cards yet." Nonchalantly, she flipped them over to reveal not only trumps, but the jack of clubs.

"By Jove, the lad's got Pam," one of the gentlemen watching exclaimed. "Imagine him having the one card in the deck that beats them all."

A loud cheer erupted inside the gaming salon, along with several groans from Moregrave's backers. Leo and Lawrence let out whoops and grins, slapping their hands on the table in jubilation. Automatically, the corners of Edward's lips began to turn up. Then he cast a fresh glance at Claire and felt the urge vanish, as he caught sight of her shorn hair and masculine attire.

Across the table, Moregrave's cheeks were flushed red, his eyes black and angry as a pair of enraged beetles. Edward could tell that the other man wanted to protest his loss, but the game had been fair—or at least as fair as any game played with Moregrave. Nevertheless, Moregrave reached again toward the stakes to take his portion of the last trick, as was often permitted in games of loo.

But Claire stopped him. "Per our amendment to the rules, my lord, which we all agreed to at the start of the game, this was a winner-take-all contest. No dividing the pool."

He drew back as if stung, his hand shaking for a moment before he tossed down the coins with a disdainful flip of his wrist. Two gold guineas bounced across the baize and onto the floor.

"And that sort of behavior shows a marked lack of good sportsmanship," Claire reprimanded in a cool tone. "You may carry a nobleman's title, but you are no gentleman, sir."

A sudden hush fell over the room. Instinctively, Edward moved closer to Claire, wondering if she had any idea the magnitude of the insult she'd just issued. Then again, judging by her actions of late, she likely did.

Moregrave's cheeks grew even more mottled. "I'll have your liver, man! Name your seconds," he bellowed. "I demand satisfaction!"

"Satisfaction?" Claire retorted. "If anyone is entitled to satisfaction, I should think it's myself and my friends for putting up with your insolent manner. However, I shall forgive the entire matter, if you will but go away." Giving him a dismissive stare, she began gathering her winnings as though nothing at all had occurred.

Moregrave sputtered, his eyes rolling in his head as if he were contemplating murder. Edward moved to intercede. Before he could, however, Claire spoke again.

"Besides," she said, glancing up as she scooped the coins into a leather pouch. "It is utterly impossible for me to meet you on the field of honor. Not only is dueling illegal by order of the Prince Regent himself, but you see, I am a—"

"Don't!" Edward ordered, realizing exactly what was about to come out of her mouth.

"—woman," she finished, an impudent gleam twinkling in her eyes.

Moregrave stared, along with everyone else, as a new hush fell. The twins groaned in unison, while Edward clenched his hands at his sides to keep from strangling her himself.

"A *what*!" Moregrave demanded.

"You heard me," she said. "I am a lady."

"By damn you are."

"I'll thank you not to swear."

"*Hah!*" Moregrave shot back. "I'll swear if I want, especially in front of a brazen piece like you."

"Watch what you say, Moregrave," Edward bit out between clenched teeth. "Or else you'll be facing me come dawn."

Some of the color drained out of Moregrave's cheeks at Edward's threat. Generally Edward didn't hold with dueling, but he'd met a couple of men on the field of honor in his time. He'd bested both—one at swords, the other at pistols—leaving each man so badly wounded he'd had to be carried off the green. His opponents had each lived to tell the tale, and since then, men didn't challenge him—not unless they were prepared to face injury, or death.

"Good Lord," someone called. "It's Lady Claire."

"Claire the Dare, you mean?" asked another.

Murmurs rose in the air.

"By Jove, you're right," interjected a third man. "And what did you call yourself, my lady? Mr. Densmar? Thought it a deuced odd name, but now I see how clever it is. Densmar, Marsden! Must say Clybourne, you've taken a firecracker in hand with Lady Claire."

All eyes turned toward Edward, waiting to see how he was going to react. But Edward had himself firmly in control now and wasn't about to let on how he actually felt.

He smiled. "Indeed, she is a firecracker and a lighted one at that. Or are you a loaded pistol, my dear?" he added, slipping his hand around her arm again.

Gentlemen laughed and shook their heads, tension easing from the room. There would be plenty of time later, Edward knew, for all of them to act shocked and disapproving. For now, however, they were highly entertained.

Everyone, that is, except Moregrave.

As the excitement died down, gentlemen began to move away. As they did, Moregrave met Edward's gaze. "I shall be speaking to the membership committee about this, Clybourne. Bringing a woman into the club is an explicit violation. I'm going to ask them to have you removed."

"You can try," Edward replied with silky menace. "If you do, however, I will, of course, be forced to mention your penchant for predatory gaming. I don't believe that's permitted in the rules either."

Moregrave bristled with unconcealed fury. "You may be safe, since you own half the country." Flinging out a hand, he gestured toward the twins. "But these two aren't, especially since they're the ones who smuggled her in here. Their lordships are merely guests and they won't be setting foot over the club's doorstep again if I have any say in the matter."

Leo and Lawrence opened their mouths to protest, but Edward shut them up with a look. Then he turned back to Moregrave. "I shall deal with my brothers in my own way, my lord. If I were you, however, I would think twice about what you say and to whom. Opening Pandora's box can be a dangerous thing, you know. Speaking out on this particular subject is an act you may come to regret." Edward's tone left it clear that he would make sure Moregrave did exactly that.

Knowing himself outmaneuvered, Moregrave shot Edward another seething glare, then turned on his heel and stalked from the room.

"Of all the deuced rotters—" Leo began, once the other man had gone.

"Not a word out of you," Edward stated, cutting him off. "Not from any of you. Gather up your belongings, we're leaving."

The twins gave doleful nods.

Claire, on the other hand, leaned toward the table. "The rest of my winnings," she explained, tugging against his grip.

"Leave them," he growled.

"I am *not* leaving them. That's my money—and the twins'."

His gaze met and locked with hers. "Fine. Retrieve it, then we're going home."

Looking suddenly less defiant, she nodded and did as she was told.

Chapter 17

The silence inside the coach on the drive home was how Claire imagined the inside of a coffin must sound—oppressive and all but impenetrable. And the atmosphere between her and the Byron men wasn't a whole lot better.

Rather than sit next to Edward, Claire had opted to squeeze in between the twins. But now that the coach was under way, she realized that they offered scant protection, since they were in just as much trouble as she. Angled in opposite corners, Leo and Lawrence sat with their arms crossed and shoulders hunched. As for Edward, he'd arranged himself in the middle of the seat opposite, so that whenever she happened to glance up, she was forced to encounter his flinty-eyed glare.

Which was why she did the only reasonable thing she could and stared at her clasped hands and the toes of her black leather shoes. Thankfully, the journey wasn't a long one. Then again, once they arrived at Clybourne House, she fully expected Edward's self-imposed restraint to disappear. Despite his seemingly relaxed posture, she could tell he was seething inside. His jaw was set, his lips compressed into a hard line that she'd never seen him wear before. Of all her transgressions, this one appeared to have made a real impact.

Maybe *the* impact?

Would he blister her with a tirade, then order her home? Her heart beat madly at the idea, as she contemplated the confrontation to come.

She couldn't claim to regret her actions. Still, she was heartily sorry that she'd ended up involving the twins, even if their help had been essential to her plan. When she'd thought up the idea of sneaking into Brooks's Club, she hadn't really considered what a damaging impact the escapade might have on Leo and Lawrence. After all, who could have predicted that the three of them would end up playing cards with the despicable Lord Moregrave? Or that he would challenge her, then threaten them and Edward afterward?

An apology rose to her lips, but she held back, knowing this wasn't the moment to ask the twins' pardon. Later when they could be in private, and Edward wasn't sitting two feet away, she would tell them how sorry she was for getting them in trouble.

Soon the coach pulled to a stop and the door was opened by a waiting footman. The servant gave her a long stare, eyes wide as he watched her descend from the vehicle. As for Croft, he greeted them all with his usual composed aplomb as they filed past into the house. Although Claire felt certain he recognized her in her male garb, he gave no outward indication. Nor did he make mention of the fact that until a few moments ago, the entire staff had assumed she was asleep in her bedchamber. What a great bushel of gossip they would have to share in the servants' hall tonight!

As soon as all of them were inside, Edward rounded on the twins. "You two, upstairs to your rooms," he ordered. "I shall deal with you later. And you are not to go out, not even if your trousers catch fire and the only water is in a bucket across the square. Do I make myself clear?"

The pair of them grumbled.

"What was that? I didn't quite hear?" Edward demanded.

"Yes, Ned. Quite clear, Ned," each of them answered in respectful tones. Clearly downcast, they made their way up the staircase and along the corridor to their bedrooms, neither one of them saying a word. Claire moved to follow.

"And just where do you think you're going?" Edward asked, low and clipped.

"Upstairs. To change."

His eyes narrowed, his gaze sweeping over her. "You can change later. Or don't you enjoy playing dress-up anymore, *Mr. Densmar*?"

Forcing down the urge to gulp, she drew a deep breath and straightened her shoulders.

A muscle contracted in his jaw at her silent defiance. Fixing her with a hard stare, he gestured along the hallway. "My study. Now!"

Marching before him, she led the way.

Once inside, she half expected him to slam the door closed behind them, but he shut it with a quiet click that was all the more intimidating for its level of control. But then Edward was always in control, even when he was angry—just as Mallory had once pointed out.

And he was angry, his eyes glittering with a frosty blue tint that reminded her of the icy sheen on a frozen winter lake. But she was prepared for his displeasure, she told herself. Let him do his worst. After all, that was what she was counting on.

Striding across to his wide desk, he leaned a hip against the edge and crossed his arms over his broad chest. "Well? What have you to say for yourself, Lady Claire?"

After a pause, she shrugged. "Very little actually. I believe the day speaks for itself."

He glowered. "Quite right. It does. Beginning with your very convincing performance this morning at the breakfast table. I had no notion what a consummate actress you could be. But then I don't suppose it bothers you to have lied with such bald-faced ease to Cousin Wilhelmina and Mallory, not to mention myself."

She thrust her hands into the pockets of her borrowed trousers. "Of course it does and I owe them both a huge apology, and you as well, Your Grace. I never like to deceive people. But under the circumstances, it could not be helped."

"Oh, could it not? Of all the incredible stunts to have pulled, this is without question the most egregious. Have you any idea the extent of the scandal you've caused? Every tongue in London will be wagging come nightfall, and likely across half of England by tomorrow!"

"I thought you didn't mind scandal," she said. "What was it you said? That I'd have to do a great deal better than a few extra dances to make you take notice."

He growled under his breath. "Oh, you've definitely got my attention. In case *you* didn't notice, you've had it these past few weeks while you've flitted from one peccadillo to another. But this time you've gone too far."

"Why? Because I dressed up like a man and went to your club?"

"No, because you involved others in your scheme, and worse, you've made an enemy of a very ugly-tempered man. By God, what were you thinking playing cards with a brute like Moregrave?"

"He sat down at our table and there was nothing we could do to prevent him. Besides, I had no idea what sort of villain he is, nor did the twins. At least not until the game began and then it was too late to withdraw."

"It's never too late to withdraw and you should have made your excuses."

"But he was into us for five hundred pounds by then. I wasn't about to give him the satisfaction of walking away with all that money."

"That's exactly what you should have done. Stood up and left. And the pot I saw had a great deal more than five hundred pounds in it, closer to five thousand."

"Actually, I believe the pool was more in the realm of ten to fifteen thousand pounds during that final hand, since I'd put in a rather hefty IOU."

His eyebrows shot high. "You gave him vowels! And what on earth would you have done if you'd lost? How would you have paid him?"

She lifted her gaze to the ceiling, noticing what lovely molding and cornice work had been done in the room, before looking back. "I rather imagined you could pay."

"*Me!*" His eyes narrowed in clear speculation. "Well, of course. I'm sure that was part of your plan to provoke me. So what went wrong? Or did you just get lucky at the wrong time?"

"Getting that high card was pure luck, but otherwise, I was in complete control of the game. Believe me, when you grow up in the country, you learn to play cards or else die of boredom. My sisters and I spent countless evenings playing whist and loo, and I'm quite skilled at both. Obviously we never played for stakes, but the principles are the same."

"So why didn't you lose to Moregrave?"

She hesitated before admitting the truth. "Because he is utterly contemptible and I couldn't bring myself to let him win, not even so much as a penny. Besides, the twins would have been devastated, since most of the original stake was theirs. I didn't think it was right to lose their money."

"Oh, you didn't, did you? But it was fine to lose mine?"

"Well, yes, considering how rich you are."

He stared, then barked out a harsh laugh. "By God, you're an outrageous baggage, do you know that?"

And too outrageous to be a duchess, she waited for him to say. Too outrageous to be *his* duchess.

Instead, a heavy silence lengthened between them.

"Do you know," he mused aloud in an abrupt change of subject, "I've decided what I'm going to do with the twins. They'll be sent home to Braebourne first thing tomorrow, where they're to remain until their next term begins at university."

"No! You can't," she protested. "They love London and the Season. Leo and Lawrence only went along with this scheme because I dared them into it. It wasn't their idea, so don't lay the blame at their doorstep. This was my doing."

"And they are old enough to know better. If they didn't want to take their lumps, they shouldn't have jumped into the fray."

"But—"

"As for *you* now, that is the more difficult quandary," he continued, resuming his speculation. "The Ton is already well-used to your ungoverned antics, so perhaps this Brooks's debacle shall pass over as nothing more than a nine-day wonder. Then again, repercussions of the scandal could carry on throughout the remainder of the Season. A few hostesses may withdraw their patronage, and I rather doubt you'll be welcome at Almack's, at least not for the rest of this year."

He tilted his head, studying her with an expression that made her shift her feet like some naughty schoolgirl, despite her current masculine mode of dress. "I know that most men would pack you off somewhere too," he continued. "Or else ignore their duty and send you back to your parents. But that isn't possible. I gave my word, and I am nothing if not a man of my word. You may have these fanciful notions that we can break off this engagement and that everything will go back to the way it was before. But that choice ended the day you accepted my offer.

"You may not realize it yet," he said, "but we're as good as married already in the eyes of Society. Has it never occurred to you why you've been given so much freedom and why the Ton is so willing to cast a benign eye on your escapades rather than condemn you? It's because you are The Clybourne Bride, *my* bride, whether you wear a wedding ring yet or not."

"No," she retorted, air rushing from her lungs.

"And as such, you are my responsibility."

"I don't want to be your responsibility—"

"And it's up to me to see to your welfare and to regulate your conduct."

Her chest grew tight. "You don't own me, not yet, Your Grace."

The gaze he turned on her was penetrating and implacable. "But I do, Claire. You just need to accept that fact and stop all this nonsense."

Temper burned like fire in her veins. "Never!"

He arched a warning brow. "I would be careful about using absolutes, if I were you. Such statements often have a way of coming back to haunt their issuers."

"Well, that's one 'never' that won't haunt me, since I mean what I say. You are absolutely unreasonable, rigid and controlling, without so much as a spark of spontaneity. Your entire existence is dictated by duty and convention and doing everything that is expected of you."

"Unlike yourself, who does whatever you please, whenever you please, and devil take the hindmost."

Her hands turned to fists at her sides. "That's unfair and you know it."

"As are your accusations against me," he countered. "Just because I see to my responsibilities doesn't make me rigid. If I were, you certainly wouldn't have been allowed to get away with half the things you've perpetrated these last few weeks."

Pausing, he drew a breath. "I suppose you're right, however, that I take my duties seriously. But then I must, since my actions have a direct impact on a great many people's lives. People who look to me for their livelihoods and welfare, even the shelter over their heads. It's true that I could shirk my responsibilities and be some self-absorbed, irresponsible ne'er-do-well, as far too many of my brethren are. I could indulge my vices and laze away my days while my tenants and pensioners are left to fend for themselves as best they may. But I happen to care about my legacy and my lands, and most of all, my people. If that makes me rule-bound and inflexible, then so be it."

She lowered her gaze. "I never meant to imply that you shouldn't see to your people or your lands. Of course you must, and I would think very ill of you if you did not."

"Well then, that complaint appears resolved. As for your charge that I lack spontaneity, I believe you will find that I can be as unpredictable as the next man. Consider those clothes you're wearing, for instance. You might imagine I don't care for them, but you'd be wrong. I especially like the trousers and the way they hug your bottom when you move."

Her lips parted on a gasp.

"And although I don't much care for the coat, since it covers up the lovely shape of your breasts," he went on, "the idea of removing the cravat offers several interesting possibilities. But I suppose I'll have to keep those to myself for the time being."

She could only speculate about what he meant by that last

remark, but her heart sped up nevertheless, her pulse throbbing in her neck and wrists.

"Come here, Claire," he commanded.

"Why?"

"Just come here."

When she didn't move, he straightened away from the desk and strode toward her. "Fine then, I shall come to you." Reaching out, he took her by the shoulders. "You're the most contrary female I've ever met, do you know that? You drive me so mad that half the time I'm not sure whether I'd rather paddle you or kiss you."

Refusing to be cowed, she met his gaze. "I'd prefer the paddling, if you don't mind," she taunted.

His eyes narrowed. "That can be arranged." Catching hold of her wrist, he pulled her after him.

"What are you doing?"

He dragged her forward.

"Surely you aren't going to . . . no, I didn't mean it," she called as she fathomed his intent.

"Did you not?" he tossed out in a gruff voice. "Has no one ever told you that you shouldn't say things you don't mean?"

Clearing aside a space on one side of his desk, he whirled her around and bent her over its wide wooden expanse so that she lay on her stomach. She tried to squirm away, but he wouldn't let her, his hold as strong as a steel clamp. Yet he wasn't hurting her, she realized, careful to control her movements without inflicting any pain.

"So you want a paddling, do you?" he goaded with dark satisfaction.

"No! I told you to stop. Let me go."

"Not until you've learned your lesson. Perhaps this is what's been missing from our earlier confrontations."

"Edward Byron, *don't you dare!*" She squirmed again

for good measure, but it made no difference, her body firmly under his control.

"Oh, so I'm Edward again, am I? As for not daring, I believe you'll find that I'm capable of daring a very great deal. Most especially when I'm provoked."

She lay there helpless and trembling, waiting to see what he would do next. But surely he was only trying to scare her. Surely he wouldn't actually make good on this threat. Then he struck her bottom with the flat of his hand and showed her that he was indeed a man of his word. She wiggled, her bottom stinging as his palm made contact. The blow wasn't painful, so much as it was humiliating.

"Stop!" she beseeched.

"Say please," he said mockingly.

Her spine grew rigid and she bucked against his hold again, trying futilely to free herself.

"You know," he remarked aloud, "I don't believe I'll ever be able to look at a pair of trousers the same way again after this. Maybe I should have a couple extra pair made up for you to wear when we're alone."

"*Ohhhh*," she raged, heat scalding her face.

Then he struck her again twice more, sending another kind of heat flowing fast over her stinging buttocks and thighs. She lay tense, preparing herself for the next blow, when suddenly he stopped, his wide palm coming to rest on her bottom, but not with force this time.

He stroked her, slowly, gently, as if trying to massage away the discomfort. She twisted again, but for an entirely different reason, no longer eager to get away. His movements slowed even more, turning into something that very definitely resembled a caress—and more. Closing her eyes, she gave herself over to the helpless shudder that racked her frame. Her nipples drew into taut, aching peaks, moisture pooling between her thighs in a way that left her shocked.

How could she desire him now? Like this, when she was lying completely at his mercy? But to her shame, she did.

Quite deeply.

He shifted, leaning up and over her back. A whimper escaped her as he pressed his mouth to her ear. "Forgive me, Claire. I should not have done that. I've never struck a woman before in my life. I have no excuse. None at all."

"And I should not have goaded you," she whispered, honest enough to admit her part in their skirmish. "It was just as much me as you." To her horror, a single tear leaked from her eye.

"Oh God," he whispered, "don't cry. Have I hurt you?"

"No."

"Then what?"

But she couldn't tell him. How could she when she herself barely understood all the feelings welling up inside her, threatening to overflow, warning of emotions best left unexplored.

Brushing away her tear with his thumb, he kissed her damp cheek, soothing her as he silently begged her pardon.

One kiss.

Then another.

Light and tender, gliding and gossamer as butterfly wings.

Her lips parted on a shivery inhalation, her body flashing hot, then cold, then hot all over again. He kissed her, taking her mouth with a sweet suction that made the world melt away and her senses along with it.

Her toes curled inside her shoes, her muscles aching to stretch and curve, needing to reach out and wrap around him like twining vines. Shifting, she tried to roll over, but couldn't quite manage, accepting his aid once he realized what it was she wanted. She shimmied and scooted, inadvertently pushing something off his desk that dropped to the carpet with a muffled thump. Fleetingly, she found herself hoping it hadn't been fragile or worse—ink.

Then there was no more time to worry as he parted her trouser-clad legs and stepped between. Leaning fully over her, he left her in no doubt of his own desire, his erection pressing thick and hard against her belly, despite the barrier of their clothes.

Claiming her mouth, he slipped his tongue inside, tangling against her own with warm dips and seductive glides that drove her half wild. Reaching up, she wrapped her arms around him, caressing his shoulders and neck with languid strokes that incited his own answering shudder. Her senses spun, his every touch as intoxicating as wine—rich and sweet and supple. Drunk on him, she craved more, wanting him more forcefully than she did her next breath. Spearing her fingers into his hair, she kissed him back, matching his possession with a dark, heady longing of her own.

Her breathing quickened, turning shallow and ragged. She discovered that Edward was in a similar state when he broke away to kiss her jaw and throat.

Suddenly he growled, his movements plainly hampered by the cravat tied around her neck. "Of all the strange things, this is the strangest," he murmured, tugging at the material without untying it. "I've never kissed anyone before who was wearing a neck cloth. It's a pure nuisance."

"Oh, it's not so bad," she said, reaching up to run a pair of fingers under the edge of his own cravat. He groaned and paused long enough to give her a hard, dizzying kiss before returning to his inspection of her attire.

"At least this waistcoat is dispensed with easily enough," he observed, gliding his hands over the gold buttons. Nimble as a tailor, he had them open with a few quick twists. Spreading apart the sides, he revealed a shirt made of fine white lawn, her nipples jutting visibly upward beneath the thin cloth.

His hands moved to cover her breasts, her rib cage angling up on a quick breath at his touch. "My God, are you bare under there?" he said.

She nodded. "I couldn't wear my stays, and a binding didn't seem necessary, not with my coat and waistcoat to provide protection."

"I'm glad I didn't realize that earlier," he said, flexing his fingers gently over her aching flesh, "or I wouldn't have been capable of thinking about anything else."

He squeezed her breasts again, letting them completely fill his palms before circling the peaks with his thumbs. She moaned, arching into his touch with unconcealed pleasure. Hunger pounded through her, leaving her wanton and restless. Her body turned to fire when he leaned low and drew one taut peak into his mouth. Suckling through the cloth, he did things that made her mind whirl, her nerve endings turn to embers.

Then, without her quite realizing that he'd managed to yank the shirt free of her trousers, he suckled on her again. Only this time her breasts were naked, the shirt bunched up just below her neck. His hands stayed busy too, playing with her other breast using clever, devastating moves that sent her flying, before his fingers roved lower to trace over the sleek, flat length of her belly and back.

She was utterly dazed, blood thrumming in dizzying beats and heady pulses through her system by the time he left her breasts to trail a line of kisses across her stomach. Somehow, the buttons on her trousers had come free, his big hands reaching inside.

"No drawers either?" he murmured in half-amazed, half-appreciative tones, his fingers stroking over her hipbones and around to her bare bottom.

"N-No. Too big for me."

He kissed her just above her triangle of pale blond curls,

her stomach drawing in tight, while a fist of aching need lodged between her thighs.

Then he was pulling down her trousers, stripping them to her knees before yanking one leg completely free, a shoe tumbling to the floor along with it. She didn't have time to say a word, or even think, before he dropped to his knees and kissed her again—in the last place she'd ever thought to be kissed!

Arching upward onto her elbows, she tried to reach forward, tried to tell him to stop. But in the next second, her body bucked against his mouth as he did the most incredibly wicked thing with his tongue. Suddenly she didn't want him to stop at all, knew it would have killed her if he did. Or she would have killed him, the ache throbbing like a heartbeat deep in her core, begging to be assuaged.

Sliding down again onto her back, she lay there atop the desk and let him take her with his mouth, whimpering and moaning with each new sensation. His palms slid under her buttocks, spreading her wider, angling her so she was totally at his mercy.

In those moments, she felt as if her very breath, her life, was completely dependent on his next move. He lapped longer, deeper, apparently relishing how wet she'd become, enjoying her every groan and quiver, as though he were dining on some succulent dessert.

She wasn't sure how much more she could stand, how far he could take her before she went mad. Her fingernails slid against the smooth wood surface of the desk, searching for purchase and finding none. She nearly roared with frustration.

"Please," she moaned. "Oh, please."

He paused for a moment, leaving her in even worse agony than before, especially when he slid a finger inside her and began to stroke. "Please what?" he asked in a deep devil's voice.

"Y-You know."

"Know what?" he teased, stroking her deeper.

"Don't be horrid," she panted on a moan.

He laughed. "But it's so much fun." Then he grew serious again, easing two fingers inside her so that her flesh pulsed around him. "Beg me, Claire. I want to hear you say my name while I drive you wild. Say it while I make you come."

She gasped, but couldn't stop herself. "Pl-Please, Edward. Please."

Smiling, he went back to his ministrations, sliding his fingers free again as he drew upon her with even more intensity than before. He swept her high, then higher still, his name on her lips often as he truly did drive her wild. Quaking in his grasp, she was nearly incoherent by the time he brought her closer. Opening his mouth over her, he raked her with his teeth in a way that sent her plunging hard over the edge.

Bliss shook her, her body trembling, rapture soaring through her as though she'd taken flight. A keening cry sang from her throat. "Edward!"

Then she couldn't speak, limp and lax and satiated.

Standing, he glided his palms over her body, caressing her with bold, possessive strokes that were a claiming of their own. Leaning over her, he took her mouth in another long, rapacious kiss that drew a fresh moan from her. He straightened and reached for the buttons on his falls, his erection straining visibly against the cloth.

A knock sounded at the door. "Your Grace, are you there?"

She and Edward both froze, his head whipping around as the doorknob began to turn.

"No!" he ordered loudly, his voice harsh and strained. "I mean, do not come in!" Turning in a protective move, Edward placed himself so that his body blocked as much of hers from view as possible.

The door opened the faintest crack, but not enough to see

inside. "I am sorry to interrupt, but I have additional correspondence to be signed. I can come back later."

This time she recognized the voice. It was Mr. Hughes, Edward's secretary.

Her passion vanished. Suddenly cold and violently aware of her state of undress, she sat up and began tugging her clothes into place.

Edward took a few steps toward the door. "Yes, come back later. I am . . . busy at present."

"Oh, of course, Your Grace. So sorry to have disturbed you."

Hughes shut the door, his footfalls retreating in the direction of his office. Crossing the room, Edward reached for the key and turned it in the lock.

She'd just fastened her trousers and was searching for her shoe when he returned.

Without a word, he leaned down and picked up a small black leather men's dress pump. "Looking for this?"

"Y-Yes," she said, doing her best not to notice the very obvious erection still tenting his trousers. Accepting the shoe from him, she fit her stockinged foot into it.

"Your waistcoat is misbuttoned."

Her gaze flew to his. "What?"

"Your waistcoat," he said. "You've buttoned it wrong."

Automatically, her fingers moved to the garment, searching for the mistake.

"Here," he said in a gentle voice, brushing aside her hands. "Allow me."

Rather than argue, she lowered her arms to her sides. "How can you be so calm?" she murmured after a moment, unable to meet his gaze.

"My rigid control, remember?"

Of course, that's not the only thing that was rigid about him at the moment. She suppressed a blush at the thought.

As for his remark, she knew he was teasing, but she couldn't laugh. Another minute and he would have taken her. Another minute and she would have let him, and gladly. And then where would her plan have been?

Mr. Hughes, quite ironically, had saved the day. Or her virginity at least. So why wasn't she happier about it? Or at least relieved?

But I am. Of course I am, she told herself.

"Claire."

She forced her gaze up to meet his. "Yes?"

"Everything will be fine. You're not to worry. Not about anything." Finishing with her waistcoat, he drew her coat closed and buttoned it too, giving the hem a quick, sharp tug to set it to rights.

"There. No one will suspect. Except for your hair." Reaching out, he combed his fingers through her locks—what little there was left of them. "I wish you hadn't cut it," he mused, rubbing the end of one short strand. "Your hair was so beautiful."

"It'll grow back."

"And so it shall." With a sigh, he lowered his hand. "I think you should set a date."

"Excuse me?"

"For our wedding. I want you to decide on the day, and likely sooner rather than later. If you prefer, we can wait long enough to arrange a formal church ceremony. It's what Society will expect, I am sure. Let's limit the guest list to no more than five hundred though. Anything additional will start to take on the trappings of an army encampment."

"But—" she said.

"And the talk will die down much sooner if we make the announcement now," he continued in a matter-of-fact tone. "Better to have this new scandal over with quickly and out of the way."

Like our wedding, she thought. *Another duty fulfilled, another responsibility to check off the list.*

Her heart sank to her stomach, realizing that he was just as adamant as ever about proceeding with their marriage. Perhaps doubly so because of the intimacy they'd just shared, and had shared in the past as well. But as intense as their passion, it didn't change any of the essentials between them.

She still did not want to be wed out of obligation.

And he still did not love her.

So even if her heart was shredding to pieces inside her chest, her decision about their union remained the same.

For a moment, she almost wished he would lie. That he would take her in his arms right now and spin some faerie story to convince her what it was she wanted to hear. She was vulnerable enough right now that she might let herself believe him, even if his words were nothing but falsehoods and deceits.

But he didn't take her in his arms.

And he spoke no words of love.

Because Edward Byron did not lie.

Thank goodness, he hadn't a clue how she really felt about him. Nor did she plan to enlighten him.

A deep weariness passed through her, along with a chill that made her think of January rather than the presently warm days of May. "I believe I'll go upstairs and change. I need to return to skirts, I believe."

"Cousin Wilhelmina would be aghast if she saw you in your current attire, so yes, go change before she and Mallory get home. Your hair is going to take enough explaining as it is."

He paused as if he might say something further about the wedding date. To her relief, he did not. "I shall see you at dinner then. I think it might be wise to stay at home tonight."

She opened her mouth to disagree, but realized that she wouldn't mind a quiet evening tonight. Along with a measure of time to consider exactly what she should do next. "Yes. All right."

Catching hold of her hand, he pressed a kiss against her palm, then released her. Escorting her to the door, he unlocked it and sent her on her way.

As soon as Claire was gone, Edward closed the door again, crossed to the nearest chair and sat down. Shutting his eyes, he fought for composure, willing the fierce arousal that still plagued him to subside. If not for Hughes's inconvenient interruption, Edward knew he would have taken Claire right there on the desk, despite the fact that she was a virgin. Truly, she drove him mad, scattering his senses to the point where all he'd been able to think about was having her, regardless of the location or the propriety or the consequences.

Lucifer's tail, what a place for a consummation—or rather a near consummation.

Any other girl would have slapped him, but not Claire. Then again, no other young woman of his acquaintance would have dressed in men's clothes, snuck into Brooks's Club, won at cards against a bounder, then come home to battle toe-to-toe with her fiancé.

Despite his earlier fury, he couldn't help but admire her panache. She possessed the most indomitable spirit he'd ever encountered, almost fearless at times—proud, beautiful and determined. She would make him a magnificent duchess once she settled down—and once he got her to the altar.

He hoped she would do as he asked and set a wedding date. And one that wasn't too many months in the future, since he didn't know how much longer he could manage to keep his hands off her. Not that he'd done terribly well on that score today. Even now, he wanted to go upstairs to her room, strip her to the skin and continue what they'd started here in his study. Wouldn't she be surprised if he barged in. Maybe he'd even find her in her bath. His erection throbbed with renewed strength, reminding him exactly how unsatisfied he was and how long he'd been without a woman.

But he didn't just want a woman. He wanted Claire.

What was it she'd said about him being too controlled? With her, he wasn't nearly controlled enough. Just a touch of her sweet lips, the brush of her delicate hand, and all he could think about was losing himself inside her. He would never have expected it, but she had a way of stripping him of his civilized veneer and leaving only the man behind. An incautious man who'd been on the verge of tupping his fiancée on top of his desk.

Blister it, why had Hughes had to interrupt? And why do I have to act the gentleman now rather than going upstairs to do as I so badly wish to do?

But he wouldn't.

It might half kill him, but he would be patient awhile more. In the end, Claire would be his. Once she was, there would be no more talk about wanting her freedom. She wouldn't have the time or the need, not with him keeping her satisfied—first as his wife and later as the mother of their children.

Groaning at heated thoughts of exactly how they would make those children, he shut his eyes again and stared counting backward from a thousand. He'd reached the mid–six hundreds before he decided he was steady enough to resume his usual activities.

Standing, he walked to his desk and realized he probably ought to set the surface back to rights rather than leave it to raise speculation among the staff. As he rounded the corner, he caught sight of an object lying on the carpet. Bending, he picked it up.

It was a small golden frame decorated with ivy leaves. Inside was a painted miniature of Braebourne, the stately house's honey gold stone gleaming in the sunlight. He'd had the picture on his desk for years, a reminder of his home in the Gloucestershire countryside. It had always been one of his favorites. Claire must have knocked it to the floor during their lovemaking. Smiling at the recollection, he went to put it back where he'd always kept it. Suddenly he stopped, rubbing his thumb over the gold as he thought again of Claire. That was when he remembered the miniature he had of her.

Years ago, her father had sent him a likeness of Claire to reacquaint him with his betrothed. At the time, he'd had scant intention of going through with the marriage and had tucked the small painting away in a drawer.

In this very desk, if he wasn't mistaken.

Setting down the Braebourne miniature, he began opening drawers in search of Claire's likeness. He was on his third one when he found it, hidden in the back. Untying the strings of a black velvet pouch, he let the miniature drop into his palm.

And there was Claire, smiling and lovely and looking so very young. She couldn't have been more than fifteen at the time, he realized. Still just a child. No wonder he'd run from the arrangement. No wonder he'd dismissed her and buried this portrait away where he wouldn't need to be reminded of his then-unwanted obligation.

But she wasn't a child any longer and he wasn't running from their betrothal now.

Ironically, she was the one doing the running this time. But he was catching up and would soon have her firmly in hand with her vows spoken and his ring on her finger.

I shall have a new miniature painted, he decided. *This one of Claire in all her womanly glory.*

As his duchess, there would be official portraits of her

commissioned to hang in the family galleries, both here and at Braebourne. As for the miniature, however, that he would keep for himself. And he would place it right here on his desk. Or inside his pocket, were he of a mind.

Gazing again at the painting of young Claire, he was about to slip it back inside its pouch, when he stopped. Leaning forward instead, he propped the portrait next to the rendering of Braebourne, pleased by the result.

Once again surveying the mess he and Claire had created, he returned to his straightening up.

Chapter 18

Over the next two weeks, Claire and Edward settled into an unspoken truce of sorts. For her part, Claire didn't engage in any new acts of rebellion. As for Edward, he refrained from pressing her further on the topic of a wedding date.

That first morning following her visit to Brooks's Club had been an unhappy one as she'd pleaded unsuccessfully again with Edward to let his brothers remain in Town. But despite her entreaties, and those of Mallory and the twins themselves, Edward had remained unmoved. And so, at exactly ten o'clock, a coach containing Lords Leo and Lawrence and their baggage had rolled away, leaving London far behind.

Claire found herself wondering when, or if, she would see them again, her conscience weighing heavy over the fact that she had gotten them banished. But then she had no time for further reflection about that particular transgression, since she had her own to explain. Beginning with her hair.

The moment Cousin Wilhelmina saw, she'd called for her

smelling salts and fainted dead away into a nearby chair. Mallory, on the other hand, pressed her fingers to her mouth for a long moment and stared. Walking forward, she'd smiled at Claire, then leaned near. "It's just adorable," she'd whispered. "I only wish I had the nerve."

But over the next few days, Claire realized that Mallory was lucky she didn't, in fact, have so much nerve, since flouting social convention could elicit uncomfortable results.

For in spite of Edward's visible show of support, Claire found herself disinvited to several entertainments. Everywhere she went, people stared and whispered, and not in the sort of lighthearted way she'd experienced in the past. Not only was the Ton scandalized, many were openly disapproving; a few sticklers even gave her the cut direct.

Additionally, Edward's warning about Almack's proved true, when the patronesses withdrew her vouchers. With apparent gracious condescension—or so Claire was informed in the letter she received—the great ladies had decided to allow Mallory to retain her own vouchers, since she had done nothing untoward. Mallory, however, refused to use them, declaring that she would not attend the Wednesday evening dance, if Claire could not also attend. But at least Mallory was not being punished, since Claire couldn't have stood knowing she'd hurt her friend.

At first, she'd hoped the furor would unsettle Edward enough that he would change his mind and cast her out after all. But as always, he was unflappable, going on as if nothing out of the ordinary had ever occurred.

"Keep your chin up," he advised her on the evening of their first public appearance, "and it will all blow past quickly enough."

As the first week moved into the next, she discovered that he was right. In fact, among the younger, ultra-fashionable set, she was considered something of a cause célèbre, spoken of in reverential tones and given awe-struck glances. A few bold young women even cropped their own hair, dubbing their short new style *la Marsden*.

Then there was the gaming, people constantly inviting her to play cards in order for her to demonstrate her amazing skill. But despite her reputation, she wasn't a lady gamester and had no interest in proving herself as such.

As for her share of the winnings from her game with Lord Moregrave, Edward had taken the money in hand to invest for her. She'd won what many might consider a substantial nest egg and she had been rather grateful for his assistance, especially when he assured her the funds would be held in her name alone.

Most men would have kept the money for themselves. As their excuse, they would have cited the laws which stipulated that a woman's property belonged to her husband, or her father, and arranged for the funds to be included in her dowry. But not Edward. Instead, he'd established an account for her, suggesting that if she didn't spend it herself, she might want to consider leaving it to the children he hoped they would have one day.

But there would be no children, she thought with a wistful sigh, because there would be no marriage. For in spite of everything, she was still set on proceeding with her original plan.

Standing now inside Hatchard's on the second Tuesday of June, Claire idly browsed the stacks, Mallory and Cousin Wilhelmina busy doing the same in another section of the store. Holding open a book, Claire stared at the pages. But the words blurred before her gaze, her thoughts centered instead on Edward and her future with—or rather without—him.

Their passionate interlude in his study two weeks ago had quite literally shaken her to her toes. More than ever, she understood how deeply vulnerable she was to him, since all he had to do was touch her and she was lost. Just think what it would be like if she relented and married him. Only imagine how it would be if she lay in his bed, in his arms, each night.

Wonderful on the one hand, she thought with a dreamy sigh. Terrifying on the other, since she could easily see herself becoming his devoted supplicant—hanging on his every word, longing for each new touch, his next smile, his next laugh. How simple it would be to let herself believe there was more to his caresses than simple passion.

But what if that's all it was, lust?

Worse, what if his current interest came not from true desire, but was driven instead by their battle of wills, and his natural need to win? Once the war was over, what then? And if he won, would his interest in her die? After all, he would have what he wanted then, would he not?

She couldn't help but notice that he hadn't tried to touch her again since that afternoon, not even to steal a kiss. She told herself it was because he didn't trust himself not to take things too far, remembering how very close he'd come to claiming her virginity. But what if it was something else entirely? What if it really was all just a game?

Oh, heavens, I don't know anymore what to think or what to do.

He wanted her to set a wedding date, but she couldn't.

He wanted her to give in, but she was still afraid that she might be making the biggest mistake of her life if she did. Not without some declaration of affection on his part. Not without some assurance that he wanted to marry her for more than reasons of duty. For more than the necessity of assuring his line and producing the next Clybourne heir.

Snapping the book closed, she shoved it back onto its shelf.

"Not to your liking, I take it," said a voice in a smooth drawl. "Is it the subject matter or the author who has given offense?"

Turning on a sharp inhalation, Claire gazed up. "Lord Islington," she said, laying a hand against her chest, "you startled me."

"How thoughtless. Pray forgive me, since I fear that I am now the one who has given offense." Taking a step back, he made her an elegant bow.

"No, of course you have not," she rushed to assure him, shaking off her initial fright. "What brings you here this afternoon?"

A faint smile curved his mouth. "The same thing that has led you here today, I would imagine. I have been known to read on occasion, you know."

"I am sure you do and I have never imagined otherwise." Pausing, she drew a breath. "How have you been, my lord? Some while has passed since last we met. Have you been away?"

He nodded. "Indeed. Personal business called me into the country, but now I am returned. I hope you will not take it amiss if I tell you that I hear your name mentioned everywhere. I understand you've earned something of a reputation. Brooks's Club, was it not?"

She lifted her chin. "It was. But then you should know all about reputations, my lord."

He laughed. "Quite correct. It would appear you and I share something in common now."

"Well, I wouldn't go that far, particularly since I still do not know what it is that you are supposed to have done." She paused the moment the words were out, amazed at her boldness. "Forgive me, I had no right to inquire. Please forget I asked."

"No, it's quite all right," he said, dismissing her concern. "The matter involved a young lady and a rather unfortunate incident with a storm. We had gone out riding, just us two, and were some miles from her home when a severe thunderstorm struck. We took shelter in a nearby cottage, but by the time the rain and lightning passed sufficiently for us to return, evening had fallen. Her father claimed she was ruined. I thought otherwise and refused to do what some might deem the honorable thing. Nothing untoward had occurred and I couldn't see the point of forcing her into a loveless marriage, nor myself for that matter."

He sighed, his features reserved. "Since then, the story has been greatly embellished, casting me in the role of heartless debaucher. I assure you, Lady Claire, that I never touched that young lady and did only as I thought best for us both. It is unfortunate that so many in Society choose to see evil where only innocence exists."

Claire was silent, struck by the fact that she and Lord Islington did have more in common than she might ever have imagined. He too knew what it was like to be compelled to accept a marriage not of one's own choosing. He too knew what it was to refuse such a match, even in the face of immense disapproval. He'd only wanted his own happiness, as she did herself, yet he was condemned. Unfairly now, she could see.

"But enough of that," he said with a cheerful look, "especially since I haven't had the opportunity to compliment you on your hair. It is exquisite, worthy of being dubbed *la Marsden.* A pity there is a war, since the French would adore you. They love saucy *jeune fille*, unlike their stuffy English counterparts." Taking a moment, he tugged at the cuff of one glove. "So how is Clybourne these days?"

Claire forced her lips not to twitch. "His Grace is quite well."

"Frankly, I am surprised to see you here. I half expected you to be confined to your residence."

"Not at all. And I am out with Lady Mallory and her cousin Mrs. Byron for the day."

"Well, I am glad we had a chance to speak," he said.

She smiled. "As am I."

"A shame I cannot ask you to walk with me in the park one afternoon. Or to take a carriage ride. I've a brand new phaeton I should love you to try."

A carriage ride with Lord Islington?

Imagine the outcry.

Imagine how furious Edward would be.

And suddenly she knew precisely how to separate herself from Edward. Assuming she had the fortitude to go that far. Were she to do what she was thinking, Edward would not only break things off, he would likely never speak to her again. Was that what she wanted? Did she dare take such a drastic step? One she knew would be utterly irrevocable?

Suddenly she realized it was her only option, her very last chance.

"I would enjoy that too, my lord," she said, her heart beating painfully inside her chest. "Do you ever drive out into the countryside? London can become so close in the summer."

He lifted a brow, a curious light gleaming in his gaze. "It can indeed."

"But I suppose we couldn't go during the day," she mused. "Perhaps some evening during a ball, just for a lark. What would you say to that?"

"I would say that you like to court scandal. Then again, so do I. Tell me more."

Swallowing against the knot in her throat, she did just that.

* * *

Five evenings later, Edward stood aside as Claire was led onto the dance floor by her latest partner. Looking beautiful in a gown of creamy lemon silk, she glided across the room like a sunbeam whose radiance put the candlelight completely to shame. Her cropped golden curls bounced around her head with a lively impudence, her blue eyes gleaming with magic and mystery as she worked her charms on the young man with whom she'd agreed to dance.

The amazing thing was that Claire wasn't even aware of her power over the opposite sex. All she had to do was smile and men fell over their feet trying to please her. Lately he found himself fighting the urge to send the whole lot of them scurrying away, so he could keep her all to himself. But Claire had drummed up enough raised eyebrows and disapproving stares all on her own without him creating an entirely new stir.

At least she seemed to have finally accepted the reality of their engagement.

Or so he hoped.

Since their encounter in his study, she'd been a model of propriety. She never went anywhere without an appropriate chaperone, her behavior as circumspect as the most demure of maidens. Initially, he'd been suspicious, alert for any sign that she was up to her old tricks. But as the days passed without incident, his worry eased, leaving him to wonder if she had truly given up waging her campaign to convince him to let her go.

So unassuming was she, in fact, that he'd even overheard one of the patronesses remark that perhaps they'd been too harsh with Claire and should rethink their decision to revoke her Almack's vouchers. Of course, their change of heart might also stem from the fact that Claire was more popular than ever.

Rather than Claire becoming a social pariah, as was generally the case after expulsion from the Ton's most exclusive gathering place, her absence was apparently thinning numbers inside the hallowed assembly rooms on dance night. Many of the younger set, it seemed, were opting to attend whatever ball Claire decided to visit rather than spend their Wednesday evening on King Street.

Apparently Claire was de rigueur even in disgrace.

Edward would have found it all rather amusing were it not for one thing—she still hadn't set a wedding date.

He considered pushing the issue, and pushing it forcefully, but decided that perhaps she needed just a little more time to adjust. His patience was dwindling rapidly, however, and if she didn't choose soon, he would choose for her.

Since he had no interest in dancing, at least not with any lady other than Claire, he turned and made his way into the nearby library. There he found a group of gentlemen engaged in an enthusiastic debate about the war. Accepting a glass of port, he leaned against the fireplace mantel and listened.

Inside the ballroom, the dance drew to an end. After curtseying to her partner, Claire allowed him to escort her from the floor. They were halfway across when she faltered, weaving slightly as she came to a sudden halt.

"Oh, good heavens," she declared. "I think I've stepped on my hem." Glancing down, she inspected her skirt, while the man at her side stood by with an expression of bemusement on his face.

"I'm afraid I've torn my gown," she told him after a minute. "Forgive my clumsiness, but I am going to have to excuse myself to effect a repair."

Releasing her, he stepped aside. "Of course. Do you require assistance?"

She shook her head. "I'm sure there will be a maid in the ladies' withdrawing room who can help me. I shall be fine."

With a bow, he accepted her word and stepped aside.

The instant he was gone, Claire whirled around and hurried toward the doorway. There was nothing wrong with her gown, of course, but she'd needed some plausible excuse in order to get away. She was late, the clock having struck ten some minutes ago, the time she was supposed to have met Lord Islington for their planned evening ride. They'd agreed they would rendezvous outside and then be on their way.

Her tardiness was Edward's fault. She'd thought he would never leave the ballroom and she'd had no choice but to accept another dance, even though the appointed hour was already upon her. Then, finally, she'd looked up and Edward was gone. She knew if she wanted to proceed with her plan that this was the moment.

The only moment.

Her heart pounded beneath her breasts, nerves jangling, as she moved into the corridor leading to a side exit that Islington had suggested might aid her departure. Reaching the garden door, she took hold of the curved brass handle, then paused.

Do I really want to do this?

Do I honestly want to keep an assignation with Lord Islington that will ruin me utterly and completely in the eyes of Society?

More importantly, one that will damage me forever in Edward's estimation?

Of course she had no intention of making her ruin an actual fact, since she wasn't about to let Gregory Islington touch her. But if Edward believed he had, if he thought she'd given her innocence to another man, all his talk of duty and responsibility would cease. For what man would abide a sullied bride? What duke would want a duchess who had been unfaithful to him even before the vows had been said?

Her hand trembled on the doorknob. It wasn't too late to

change her mind. All she need do was return to the ballroom and no one would realize what she'd been contemplating. A queasy swell crested in her stomach, knowing that once she set foot outside this house, her path was fixed. Then again, her path was fixed if she turned back. She would marry Edward. The battle between them would be done.

A murmur of voices sounded in the distance and she knew it was now or never. Stay or go, the choice was hers to make.

Five seconds passed, then ten.

Drawing a sharp breath, she opened the door and stepped outside.

Edward tossed back a draught of port, then set his glass aside. He'd listened to the conversation and had gleaned nothing of particular import. Most of the men gathered liked to puff around as though they were privy to all sorts of vital secrets. Edward knew for a fact that they were not.

The only man in the group with any real connections was Lord Lymehurst and he was a close-lipped sort. Actually, he rarely spoke freely about any subject unless it had to do with horses or women; he was always available for a conversation about those. The last Edward heard, Lymehurst had been dallying with Jack's old flame, Philipa Stockton. But then Lady Stockton dallied with a great many men. If rumors were to be believed, she'd taken several lovers since Jack had ended things with her, as though she was trying to erase his memory.

Maybe his brother really had broken her heart—assuming she had a heart to break, that is.

Edward was shrugging off that train of thought and considering whether to return to the ballroom and Claire when Adam Gresham strode into the room.

Moving with purpose, Gresham crossed to his side. "Hallo,

Clybourne," he said in a low voice. "Sorry to interrupt, but I wonder if I might have a word?"

Edward lifted a brow, but didn't hesitate. "Yes, of course." Keeping his curiosity to himself, he made his excuses to the other men, then followed Gresham. But Gresham didn't stop on the other side of the room, as Edward had expected. Instead, he led him out of the room and into an empty study, where there was no possibility of being overheard.

"What's this all about?" Edward asked the moment they arrived, the other man closing the door.

"Lady Claire," Gresham explained without preamble.

Edward's mouth tightened. "What about Lady Claire? What has she done now?"

"Left, that's what. I was outside in the garden smoking a cigar not five minutes ago, when I saw her traipse across the side lawn."

"And?" Edward encouraged in a glowering tone.

"And she got into a carriage." Gresham paused, as though reluctant to continue. "I think she's with Islington."

Edward froze, his body ceasing to function for a full count of five.

Islington!

What in Hades was she thinking? Was this another one of her ridiculous escapades? Or had she actually run off with him? Surely not? Either way, though, she'd gone much too far this time. Whatever her reasons, she'd put herself at far greater risk than she could conceive. Fury and fear twisted like slippery serpents in his gut, as he considered all the possibilities.

Edward met Gresham's gaze. "Did you see which direction they took?"

Gresham nodded. "I thought of following them myself, but sent a groom instead. He's to trail them, then come back. I told him if it was very late that he was to go straight to Clybourne House with the news."

"Thank you."

A brief silence fell.

"We'll hope Islington's only taken her out for an evening drive around Mayfair," Gresham volunteered. "With luck, they'll be back within the hour."

"Yes. Let us hope."

But Edward knew they wouldn't be back, since he was certain Islington had no intention of returning Claire anytime soon. Meanwhile, there was little he could do. The pair of them could be anywhere in the city by now. Or anywhere out of it as well.

"I know I can count on your discretion," Edward said, relieved Gresham was the one who'd seen Claire leave. If it had been anyone else, there would be no hope of recovering her without her reputation ending up in irreparable shreds. As it stood, the chances weren't terribly good anyway.

Suddenly Edward realized what she'd done and why.

Good God, she's deliberately trying to ruin herself. She's going to truly force my hand.

Edward raked his fingers through his hair. "If she doesn't return within the hour, we'll put about that she's taken ill and has gone home for the evening."

"I'll keep Lady Mallory and your cousin occupied in the meantime," Adam said. "I'll escort them home as well. Try not to worry. We'll get her back." Again, he paused. "Assuming you want her back."

Something fierce clenched inside Edward's chest. "Oh, I want her back."

And he did.

He wanted her. And he would have her, at any cost.

God help Claire, though, when he caught up to her. For once he did, she would have a reckoning in store.

Chapter 19

"Mayhap we should turn around now," Claire suggested from where she sat in the phaeton next to Lord Islington. "We've been gone for well over an hour now."

Time enough, she thought, for people to have started noticing her absence. She caught her lower lip between her teeth, hoping that Mallory and Cousin Wilhelmina weren't too alarmed by her disappearance. She'd considered leaving them a note, but had decided against it, not knowing precisely what to say under the circumstances.

As for Edward . . . she didn't want to think about his reaction, or about him. She assumed he would be livid. Or perhaps he would only be mortified instead. And once his initial outrage faded, she suspected he might be relieved. He would be free of her and of his obligation.

Given the seriousness of her indiscretion, he would have the absolute right to wash his hands of her without suffering the least injury to his conscience. Society would expect him to walk away, to turn his back and never wish to gaze upon her again.

The only thing she knew for certain was that he would hate her. From this day forward, she would be as good as dead to Edward Byron.

An ache formed as though a hole had been sliced in her chest. But better a sharp stab now than a lifetime of heartache married to a man who'd wed her for convenience rather than love. Eyes stinging, she bent her head against the light summer breeze that rushed into the open carriage.

She and Islington had traveled into the countryside that surrounded London, far enough now that night creatures could be heard singing in the fields. The air smelled sweeter here than in the city, damp and grassy. The night sky was dark, only the low-hanging half moon providing any illumination to light their way on the quiet country road.

She wished now she'd taken the time to retrieve her pelisse. She would have liked its comfort, even if she didn't require its warmth. "At the next opportunity," she said again. "I really think we should turn around."

Islington shifted the reins in his hands and turned his head to give her a smile. "There's a very nice inn up ahead. I thought we might stop and enjoy a meal. We've both missed supper and I'm sure they'll have something delicious to satisfy our palates."

"Oh, I don't know . . ." she began, never having considered the idea of stopping at an inn.

But now that she did, she supposed the detour would only bolster the notion of her being ruined. Once she'd taken supper alone at an inn with a gentleman, there would be no retrieving her reputation.

"Come now, Lady Claire," he said. "I thought you were up for a lark?"

"Oh, always. You know that, my lord."

"Well then, what's an hour to take refreshments? Besides,

who's to know but us? A cup of tea, a biscuit, and we'll be back on the road."

She hesitated, wondering if she ought. "I suppose a light repast would not go amiss. Just tea, however," she stated in a firm voice.

"Of course. Just tea," he agreed.

As the horses continued along the road, she wondered if she was doing the right thing agreeing to his suggestion. But the inn was sure to be full of people and Lord Islington was only stopping because he was hungry. Once he'd eaten, they would be back on the road to London—back to explain exactly where it was she'd been these last few hours.

Anyway, she was safe enough with his lordship. In all the time she'd known him, he'd never attempted to so much as hold her hand. He wasn't interested in taking liberties. Even on the slight chance that he was, she could manage him. He was only rebelling against Society's rules, just as he assumed she was doing herself. They were both just having an adventure and nothing more.

Then it was too late for second thoughts as the inn appeared on the road ahead. As soon as Islington pulled to a stop, a sleepy-looking hostler trudged forward to tend to the horses. Leaping to the ground, Islington came around the phaeton to help her down. Threading her hand over his arm, he escorted her inside.

The inn was crowded, just as she'd expected, especially the common room where men were gathered to drink, smoke and carouse. For that reason, she didn't balk when Lord Islington requested a private parlor, silently relieved to be away from the drunken, ogling stares being sent in her direction.

The innkeeper was genial and polite, leading them to a pleasant room on the second floor, well away from the noisy crowd. If he thought it odd for her to be wearing an elegant ball gown rather than a carriage dress, he made no remark.

Accepting a seat at the round wooden table spread with a clean white linen cloth, she prepared to take tea. What arrived only minutes later, however, left her dismayed, as dish after dish was served in what turned out to be a full supper.

Nearly two hours later, a dessert of fruit and cheese was laid on the table, the innkeeper withdrawing with a bow before closing the door behind him.

"More wine, my dear?" Lord Islington inquired, picking up the half-empty decanter of Burgundy.

"No." She laid a hand over the rim of her glass and refused to let him pour. Despite his urgings, she'd barely touched the wine he'd ordered rather than the promised tea. He'd drunk the vintage largely on his own, keeping up a robust conversation while they ate—or rather while *he* ate.

She'd scarcely touched her meal, picking at her food while offering the requisite remarks and observations. Initially, she tried to be cheerful, even witty, but as the first hour elapsed and moved into the second with no apparent willingness on his part to restart their journey back to Town, she became increasingly irritated.

And increasingly worried.

By now, her plan had obviously succeeded. She was well and thoroughly ruined, and by the time she returned to London, everyone would know she'd left the party and gone night driving with Lord Islington. What worried her, though, was when Lord Islington was going to take her back to the city. Or if he was going to do so at all.

As though aware of her thoughts, he gave a slow smile. "Dear me, it's grown rather late, has it not?"

"Yes, it most certainly has, as I believe I have previously pointed out. If you are quite finished now, my lord, I should like to depart."

Rather than making ready, however, he relaxed back in his chair and swirled the wine inside his glass. For some reason it reminded her of blood, especially when the rivulets flowed downward in crimson streaks. She shuddered as he downed a leisurely swallow, then set the glass aside.

"Actually," he mused aloud, "it's a long drive back and the roads aren't terribly safe at this time of evening. Perhaps we should stay here tonight."

She stared, her muscles growing taut. Pushing back her chair, she stood, then tossed her napkin down onto her uneaten dessert. "Perhaps we should *not*. I wish to return to the city right now."

"Don't carry on so," he replied smoothly. "There's no need to be coy, you know."

Coy? What on earth is he talking about?

"We both know why we're here," he continued, as he took up his glass again and drained the contents. "So why continue the pretense? In fact, I've already made arrangements with the innkeeper for his best accommodations. He assures me the sheets are clean and that the mattress is very soft."

Mattress!

Her stomach lurched. "Clearly, you misunderstand, my lord. Drive me back now, or I shall find someone else who will."

He chuckled. "You won't find anyone willing to drive you to London at this time of night."

With a lowering sensation, she realized he was right. Then again, if she could secure a carriage she could drive herself back. Reassured by the thought, she held her ground.

"I must say you're talented enough to tread the boards," he said. "Your maidenly sensibilities do you every credit. If it will make you feel better, I promise to let you cry no at all the appropriate intervals tonight. You girls always like to say no, don't you, when what you really mean is yes?"

Dear heavens, was that what he thought? That she was

putting on a show in order to invite his attentions? That she'd made this assignation tonight in order to climb into his bed? Her stomach flipped over again, making her glad she'd eaten so little.

Sliding his chair back, he patted his thigh. "Come here then, and let's have a sample of that fine resistance of yours."

"How dare you!"

He laughed. "No, I dare you. *Claire the Dare*, you delicious little hoyden."

"Lord Islington, you are quite mistaken about my intentions or my desires. I have no interest in you, at least not in an . . . amorous sense. Nor do I wish to stay the night with you here in an accommodation. I want to return to London, *now*! And when I say no, I assure you that *no* is exactly what I mean."

His eyes narrowed, the smile falling from his lips. "This had best be more of your game, dear girl, or I warn you that I shall be very displeased."

Head held high, she forced herself not to tremble. "Then I am afraid you must be displeased, my lord. I am leaving."

His eyes turned viciously dark. "Why you little tease. You think you can lure me here, then refuse to put out? I don't think so."

Her lips parted on a silent gasp. "I did not *lure* you anywhere. I merely agreed to go driving with you and that is all."

"At night! No lady goes driving with a man at night unless she expects to be taken, and for far more than a simple drive. Well, I provided the first ride and now I want the second." Springing to his feet, he strode toward her, reaching out fast to catch hold of her arm.

Leaping away, she eluded him. Moving in the only direction available, she put the dining table between them. "Stay away, my lord. Leave me alone."

He tried for her again, but she escaped him once more.

Abruptly, a thought occurred, making her cringe. "That

girl, the one you were trapped with in the storm. You really did ruin her, didn't you?"

His mouth curved into a smile, one that froze her to the bone. "Of course I ruined her. But then she wanted it, same as you. And just like then, I was no more inclined to marry that little tart than I am to marry you. But I forget that you already have a fiancé. I wonder what Clybourne will do? Do you think he'll take you back once I've had a chance to sample your wares?"

Breath hitched in her lungs, her chest squeezing tight. Why hadn't she listened? Edward had told her what Islington was, he'd warned her to stay away. If only she hadn't been so stupidly naïve, if only she hadn't been so prideful and arrogant. But she wasn't giving up. She would never stop fighting.

"You won't be *sampling* anything of mine, my lord. Go away and I'll say nothing," she told him. "Leave now and we shall act as if this evening never happened."

"Leave, shall I?" He tossed his head back on a laugh. "You are amusing, dear girl. Why should I leave, especially when the fun part is just starting."

She darted a glance toward the door, knowing she'd never get it open before he caught her. And even if she did, even if she made it all the way downstairs, she didn't imagine the men she'd find below would offer her much protection. No, she would have to protect herself. Reaching forward, she grabbed a knife off the table and held it straight out.

Islington laughed again. "And what's that for?"

"Defense. Now, stay away."

"Or what? You're going to stab me with a fruit knife? Deadly for sure." Stalking forward in a quick rush, he lunged at her.

Jumping back, she slashed at him with the knife, silently horrified when she saw she'd drawn blood.

He hissed and drew back his injured hand. "So you want to play rough, do you?" Pausing, he took a moment to wipe the blood on a discarded napkin before flinging it aside. "I like it rough."

She held the knife more tightly, trying to find some means of holding him at bay while she made it past him to the door. Pointing the sharpest side of the weapon, she gestured with as much menace as she could muster. "I'll cut you again. I'm warning you."

"Oh, I'm scared," he taunted. "Trembling, in fact." His lips thinned, his eyes cold and vicious. "Come here, you little bitch," he demanded, "before I really have to hurt you."

Suddenly the door slammed against the wall. And there stood Edward, magnificent as an avenging angel. He filled the doorway, tall and broad-shouldered and more wonderful than any sight she could have imagined.

Claire nearly cried out, wanting to run to him. But she held herself back, not trusting what Islington might do. She didn't completely trust Edward's reception either, not sure how to interpret the barely banked fury smoldering deep in his gaze.

Edward's attention was fixed on Islington. "Perhaps you'd like to try hurting me," he said to the other man. "I'm more your size, after all. Or do you only have the courage to assault defenseless young women?"

"Defenseless, hah!" Islington tossed back his head on a nasty laugh. "She's about as defenseless as a cat with a full set of claws."

"Then you'd best clear out before she scratches you again," Edward remarked. "I see you're bleeding already."

Islington cursed beneath his breath, glancing between her and Edward, as though he were weighing his options. "Fine then, take her. Though you're a fool if you keep her, since she's naught but a tease and a trollop. Hardly the sort worthy of the title duchess despite her excellent lineage."

Claire gasped at the insult, nearly dropping the knife still clutched in her hand. But she refused to let down her guard with Islington so near. She waited, expecting him to leave, praying that he would just go away.

But before he could, Edward was across the room, springing into action so quickly she hardly had time to register his movements. He was on Islington, shoving the man backward across the room and slamming him hard against the wall. He rammed a fist into Islington's face—once, twice, drawing a howl of agony before his fingers wrapped around the other man's throat.

Islington fought, twisting against Edward's grip and throwing a few punches of his own. But they had little effect, Edward sloughing off the blows as he tightened his grip on the other man's jugular until Islington's face turned a ghastly red.

"Can't breathe!" Islington wheezed. "Stop!"

"Not until I hear you apologize."

Islington grimaced, clearly struggling against being compelled to do so. But Edward's relentless grip soon convinced him otherwise. "S-Sorry," he rasped.

"Don't say it to me. Say it to the lady. Apologize to Lady Claire!" Transferring his punishing hold to the back of Islington's neck, he whirled him around so he faced her.

She'd rather Edward hadn't, though, since she didn't care about Islington's apology. But she could tell there was no gainsaying Edward. In the past, she'd never seen him look anything but calmly controlled and urbane. But there was something half wild, almost ferocious about him tonight. It was a quality that made her wonder, with an inconsequential turn of mind, if this was how one of his ancestors might have looked centuries ago, when they'd sacked castles, conquered enemy lands and fought at the side of kings.

Then all such musings went out of her head as Edward

shook Islington with merciless force. "Go on, you good-for-nothing scoundrel," he ordered. "Make your excuses."

Islington stared at the floor, refusing to meet her gaze. "My pardon, Lady Claire, for any offense I may have caused."

With a growl of disgust, Edward dragged Islington to the door, then gave him a shove. "I ought to kill you. Or at the very least beat you to a bloody pulp. But frankly, you aren't worth the exercise."

Islington laid a hand on the door frame, resting against it as he caught his breath and his balance.

"I want you out of London immediately," Edward told him. "Don't even return to pack your clothes. You can send for them once you reach whatever distant place you plan to settle in. The farther away the better."

Reaching up, Islington rubbed a hand over his abused neck, his voice raw. "I could go to Timbuktu and everyone will still know she was here with me tonight."

"They don't know anything and they won't, not unless you tell them. And I'd strongly advise that you don't. If I hear so much as a whisper in connection with this evening, I'll make sure you're sorry. Extremely sorry. If you give me cause, I'll be administering more than a beating."

Color drained out of Islington's cheeks, making the bruises forming on his neck and jaw stand out even more. Shooting them both venomous glances, he wheeled around and stalked from the room.

Only when the pounding of his boot heels on the stairs faded away did Claire relax. Only then did she finally let down her guard. Shuddering, she let go of the knife, the wooden handle clattering against the floorboards. Across the room, she met Edward's bright gaze.

"Are you all right?" he asked. "How badly did he hurt you, Claire?"

Chapter 20

Edward stood, muscles knotted with strain, as he waited for her answer.

When he'd reached the inn scant minutes ago and flung himself off his lathered mount, he'd still been in a race against time. After questioning the innkeeper, he'd bolted up the stairs only to hear Islington's vicious threats coming through the thick wooden door. He hadn't known what sight might greet him on the other side, but he'd prepared himself for the worst.

And yet, there'd been Claire, glorious in her defiance, fierce and brave, even in the face of imminent danger. It was a scene he couldn't possibly have imagined, nor one he would ever forget. Leave it to Claire to defend herself in such a creative, resourceful manner—and using no more than a fruit knife!

Even so, now that Islington had been sent on his way and she was safe, he could see the lingering terror in her eyes, her pupils so wide and dark only a tiny sliver of blue iris remained.

"Well," he demanded again. "Are you hurt?"

She shook her head.

"He didn't touch you?"

"No," she said, folding her arms around herself. "At least not in the way you mean."

He scowled and slammed the door closed. She flinched at the noise. Swinging around, he noticed her regarding him with those same wide, frightened eyes.

Well, she ought to be frightened, considering the jeopardy she put herself in. A fresh surge of anger coursed through him, as he imagined everything that could have gone wrong.

"Do you have any idea what he might have done to you?" he asked, deep and harsh. "Do you realize how close you came to being violated? Or was that the chance you were willing to take in order to let yourself be ruined tonight?"

Her lips trembled. "It wasn't like that."

"Was it not?" he challenged. "Isn't that why you went with him tonight? To test me again? To push me to the point where I really would cry off for good this time? How far were you willing to go, Claire? Were you planning to let him bed you, but changed your mind when the time came?"

"No!" The fright went out of her face, replaced by shock and affront. "How can you think such a thing?"

"I don't know what to think, not when you run off in the middle of a ball without a word to anyone. Not when you put yourself at the mercy of a man, who hasn't so much as a scrap of honor or conscience."

"He said we were going for a drive in his carriage," she defended. "He told me we would go no farther than the countryside just outside of London, then turn back. But he kept driving and brought me here instead."

Edward made a sound of disgust. "And you got out of the carriage with him?"

"He told me he was hungry. He said he wanted tea." She stared at the floor, obviously realizing how naïve she'd been to believe such patent lies. "I thought I could handle him."

"Humph. Well, we both see how you handled him." Stalking forward, he bent and picked the knife up from the floor. "I believe *this* might have held him off another two or three minutes at best. What do you think?"

Rather than cowering, her head came up again, her gaze locking with his. "That I was an idiot, is that what you want to hear? I misjudged him, badly, and were it not for your timely intervention, Your Grace, I would likely now be in the bedchamber for which he'd arranged, my chastity quite beyond reclaiming."

A vein throbbed in his forehead. "He reserved a room?"

"Apparently. Though it certainly wasn't with my knowledge or consent."

Pacing a few steps, he stopped and stabbed the knife deep into the wooden fruit and cheese board that sat in the center of the table. The blade stood straight up, vibrating from the force of his thrust.

Claire shivered, but made no comment.

"Then it is a good thing that I arrived when I did."

"H-How did you come to arrive?" she asked. "How did you even know I was here?"

"Gresham saw you. He was in the garden when you left the ball."

"Oh."

"He came looking for me immediately afterward, but had the forethought first to send a servant to track your movements. Otherwise . . ."

He stopped, unable to keep from imagining again all the horrible things that would have transpired. He fisted his hands and willed himself to drive away the thoughts.

"It seems then," she said in a soft voice, "that I have Lord

Gresham to thank as well. I shall do so at my earliest convenience." She shivered again.

"Are you cold?" he asked, suddenly taking in the fact that she stood in the same thin, yellow silk ball gown he'd admired so many hours ago.

A lifetime now, or so it seemed.

She shook her head. "Merely tired. It is quite late."

And so it was. Nearly two in the morning, if he had to guess. It would be a long, dark, wearying trip back to London. He had no desire to make the journey, though, at least not until the situation was resolved between him and Claire.

Yet could it be resolved? Considering her actions, especially tonight, he was actually beginning to have his doubts.

Before he could stop himself, the words came tumbling out. "Is it so bad between us then, Claire?" he asked. "Is the idea of marrying me so repugnant that you would rather run off with a cad than become my bride?"

Her skin paled, her lips opened, but no sound emerged.

"You can tell me." Crossing to her, he reached out and clasped her shoulders between his hands. "There need be no restraint between us, no secrets. Be frank and don't spare any concern for my feelings. I shall not condemn you for speaking the truth. If you hate me, just say it. Be plain and let's have done with this."

Her eyes filled with pain. "I do not hate you."

"Just the idea of marrying me, then? Why? Why do you refuse to be my duchess time and again? What is it you want? Make me understand."

She shook her head, refusing to answer.

"You've made it plain you don't want to be married for the sake of honor and obligation, but there's more, isn't there?" Emotion boiled inside him, threatening to spill over.

He gave her a little shake. "Tell me, Claire. Tell me what it is you really want."

For a moment, he didn't think she was going to respond. But suddenly her eyes flashed, tears overflowing. "I want *you*!" she cried. "I love you and I want you to love me back."

His hands fell from her shoulders, his mind fighting to wrap around her unexpected revelation.

"But you don't love me," she said in anguish. "And I can't abide the thought of being married to you knowing you're taking me as your wife because of some pledge our fathers made before either of us were old enough to refuse. You only asked for my hand because it was expected and convenient and because you require an heir. Well, I don't want to be your broodmare, bought and paid for because I happen to possess the right bloodlines. I want to be wanted for myself. I want to be loved for me."

Turning her back, she walked away from him, her arms hugged close, her voice almost too low to be heard. "I'd rather be ruined and alone than spend my life knowing that I'm just another possession you've acquired. Like some trinket you purchased that's entertaining and pretty to look at on occasion, but easy to dismiss, simple to forget."

Slowly, he crossed to her. "You greatly underestimate your worth, if you imagine I could ever dismiss or forget you."

"Why not? You've done it before."

"Before? When was that?"

She shook her head. "It doesn't signify."

"Clearly, it does." With a gentle hand on her shoulder, he compelled her to face him. "When did I supposedly forget you?"

"When have you not, Your Grace? I am two-and-twenty years of age and in all that time you have never once remembered that my birthday is in March, not even this year after we reaffirmed our engagement. And until you decided it was time for us to marry, I recall seeing you precisely twice in my life. When I was ten and you dropped by with your mother for a visit, then again when I was sixteen. It seemed on that occasion as though you couldn't wait to get away. And once you did, you had no trouble forgetting I even existed, not until it suited you again to remember."

He looked into her shuttered face, astonished by the knowledge that he had hurt her at a time when he hadn't even imagined he had the power to do so.

And she was correct.

He had forgotten her through most of those long years. He'd wanted to forget her then, avoiding anything that might remind him of their betrothal. He supposed he'd even resented her, though he'd had no right. She'd been just as much a pawn in their fathers' schemes as he, perhaps more so since she'd been only an infant when the agreement had been made. They hadn't given her a choice, and neither had he.

"I am sorry," he said. "It was thoughtless of me and wrong, but you were a child then and I never imagined your feelings might be injured. I did not mean to hurt you, that was not my intention."

"I am sure it wasn't." Her lips tightened, her gaze rising to meet his own. "But you may keep your pity, Your Grace. I have no need of it."

"You certainly do not," he agreed. "Any woman as spirited and resourceful as yourself has no need of anyone's pity, least of all mine. As for being forgotten or dismissed, I am as likely to do that now as I am to disremember my next breath. You are quite memorable, Claire. Even more so after tonight."

A wisp of color came into her cheeks. "Ah, yes, tonight. I am quite ruined, you know. There'll be no showing my face in London again."

"You may show your face in London whenever you like. We put the word 'round that you went home ill. The Ton thinks you're tucked up tight in bed at Clybourne House. You heard what I said to Islington. He's not going to dispute our story, not if he knows what's good for him."

"Oh." She lowered her gaze, a tiny frown puckering her fair brows.

"Are you disappointed?" he asked. "I suppose you would rather I'd let everyone think the worst."

"It doesn't matter. Not anymore."

"Do you really want to end things between us?"

"Don't you?" she asked, her eyes rimmed with surprise.

"No. Despite everything you've put me through, I want you, Claire. In my bed. In my life. As my bride."

"But—"

"No buts. Hear me out, then you can decide. You're right that we came together for reasons of convenience and obligation. But over the past few months, things have changed between us. I've come to know you in ways I never imagined I would. You infuriate me at times—far more often than I might wish—but you also please me greatly. Marrying you is no longer only about duty and honor and responsibility. I want to marry you, and not simply because we were promised to each other as children."

He moved a step closer. "The plain truth is that I desire you. I'm not sure you realize how much. It's all I can do not to come to your room at night and make love to you until neither one of us can think clearly. But I've been forcing myself to stay away, assuming you needed time and distance in order to acclimate to the idea of our marriage."

His lips curved into a deprecating smile. "I begin to think now I should have done away with the gallantry and made those midnight visits instead."

New color rushed over her cheeks, her eyes gleaming with a wealth of emotions.

Reaching out, he took her hand. "As for your assumptions about being required to produce an heir, I want it understood that you are under no obligation to do so."

She opened her mouth to speak, but he forestalled her.

"I want children," he explained, "and I hope we shall have several. But as for their gender, either sex shall do. If we have nothing but daughters, I shall count myself blessed."

"But how can you say that?" she declared. "You need a son to carry on the title. You want an heir."

He shook his head. "I have an heir, my brother Cade, who could step easily into my shoes and would make an excellent duke. And he has a son already, so the line is assured. Besides Cade, I have four other brothers, who are all Byrons as fully as me. Any one of them would do admirably in my stead. So even if you were to give me no children at all, it would not be the end of the world or of the Clybourne legacy."

"Yes, but even so—"

"Even so," he murmured, "I would still want you. I've become quite fixed on the idea of having you for my wife, resistant as you may be to the idea."

"Edward," she whispered, a tear sliding from one eye.

He brushed it away with his thumb. "Am I Edward again, then?"

A second tear slid over her cheek.

"Shh, don't cry," he hushed. "Have I made you unhappy again? Don't be sad, Claire." He sighed, resignation sliding over him. "It's all right. If you'd rather go back to your father, then I'll find some way to convince him to take you back with no shame coming to bear upon you. I'll take all the blame and he can rail at me for the rest of his life. It's what you've been wanting, is it not? To be free of me. Is it still your wish?"

Claire could hardly breathe for the pressure in her chest, her thoughts scattered, her emotions in turmoil.

He was letting her go.

He was giving her exactly what she'd struggled to achieve these long weeks past.

Yet nothing he'd said tonight had been what she'd expected. She could barely take in all the passionate things he'd said. She didn't know what to think or what to do. While it was true that he hadn't actually said he loved her, he must have feelings for her. Mustn't he? He wanted her and clearly he was not indifferent to her. Not any longer. But was desire enough to sustain a marriage? Was liking on one side and love on the other enough to last a lifetime? Quite likely, he would still break her heart.

But wasn't it broken already?

A serious expression darkened Edward's gaze. "What is it to be then? Shall I send you back home?"

Her mouth trembled, more tears dampening her eyes. Suddenly she shook her head and flung her arms around him. "No! No, don't send me away. I thought I could leave, but I can't. Not anymore. Not ever."

Then before she could draw her next breath, his mouth was on hers, taking her with a savage kiss that staked his claim upon her in a way that left no doubt of his intentions or his desire.

Wrapping her arms around him as tightly as they would go, Claire kissed him back.

Chapter 21

Fifteen minutes later, Claire was still in Edward's arms and still being kissed. But the two of them weren't in the private parlor any longer. Instead, they'd made their way down the hall to the room Islington had originally reserved.

For an extra handful of coins, the sleepy innkeeper had been only too happy to give them the accommodation. And for another handful, he'd agreed to forget that Claire had arrived with a gentleman other than Edward.

Now she and Edward were alone inside the chamber. A wide wooden bed dominated the clean but homely room, the coverlet and sheets turned back with drowsy invitation. There was a dresser, a washstand, and a small table on top of which stood a single branch of candles. The small amount of light helped dispel the heavy nighttime darkness, with more illumination provided by the glow from the warm fire crackling in the grate.

But the fire wasn't the only thing emitting heat—Claire was as well. Her senses sizzled, hungry need burning through her with such ferocity, she wondered if she might be consumed by the flames. Slanting her mouth against Edward's, she shared another deep, rapacious kiss, glorying in the flood of dark pleasure and dizzying delight.

She quivered as his wide, capable palms stroked over her back, sliding low, then lower still to fondle the pliant curves of her hips and bottom. Anchoring her arms around his neck, she stretched higher, powerfully aware of the hard jut of his erection as it pressed insistently against her stomach.

He claimed her lips in another long, drugging kiss that stole the air from her lungs and the strength from her muscles. But she had no fear of falling.

Not with Edward there to hold her.

Not with Edward there to keep her safe.

And yet, when his fingers began unfastening the buttons on the back of her gown, she couldn't help but experience one last twinge of uncertainty. After tonight, there would be no changing her mind, no going back ever again. Once she gave herself to Edward, she would be his unconditionally and forever.

But I am his already, she thought with a kind of finality. *Maybe I have been from the very day I was born.*

And if he never comes to love me?

Ruthlessly, she pushed the thought away, determined not to let herself have regrets, or to in any way spoil this magical night.

Edward wanted her.

She wanted him.

So let the night unfold as it would. Let her revel in the joy of being with the one man she was absolutely helpless to resist.

The one and only man she knew she would ever love.

Then she had no more time for speculation or doubt as he

gently lowered her arms from around his neck and slipped her silk gown from her body.

Her nipples tightened instantaneously as he stripped away the dress, then tossed it onto a nearby chair. She trembled, resisting the urge to cover herself with her arms, glad for the warmth of the room.

Silly, she thought, considering that he'd already seen her naked once before; memories returning of that day in his study when she'd been spread across his desk like a succulent confection. So why a bout of modesty should befall her now, when she was still dressed in her shift and stays, she couldn't imagine.

Yet Edward seemed to instinctively understand, skimming his warm hands over her cool bare arms before leaning down to take her lips in a sweet, leisurely kiss. Her qualms floated away on a haze of delight, her body knowing what it craved and not averse to taking it.

Away came her stays, laces parting before she knew he had them undone. Tossing the undergarment after her gown, he cupped his hands around her breasts and finessed her aching flesh through the final barrier of her sheer lawn shift. Leaning into him, she let him boldly caress her, quavering as he tugged the ribbon open on her bodice and exposed her breasts to his appreciative eyes and hands.

For even in the room's low light, there was no mistaking the fact that he approved of what he saw, his eyelids growing heavy, his arousal even more pronounced as it strained against his already snug black evening breeches. So much so that it was a wonder the buttons didn't pop straight off.

But Edward apparently had other concerns as he hooked the delicate straps of her bodice between his fingertips and drew the garment down her shoulders. Within seconds, she was bared from the waist up.

Bending, he feathered a line of kisses over the skin he'd

revealed, beginning with a particularly sensitive spot just behind her ear. Working his way down, he drove her half mad with his roving touches. Trembling and on edge, she was never quite sure where he would kiss her next.

Her breath was coming in pants by the time he reached her breasts, the centers peaked and aching, practically begging for his attention. She shuddered when he took one into his mouth, gripping his arms as he opened his lips wider to suckle before flicking her with his tongue. He moved over her breasts, one then the other, kissing and laving her until his ministrations took on the guise of near torment.

Exquisite torment, but torment all the same.

With a groan, she dug her fingers into the fine wool of his coat, only then realizing that he was still fully dressed.

Ineffectually, she plucked at the material. "Aren't you going to take something off too?" she asked, not stopping to question her sudden bravado. "It hardly seems fair that I'm always the one disrobed, while you never take off a stitch."

He stopped, his head coming up to meet her gaze. And then he laughed. "You're quite right, sweetheart. You are leagues ahead of me, while I'm woefully overdressed. Lie down and I'll take care of the problem immediately."

But in spite of her weakened knees and the aching desire that throbbed inside her like a beating fist, she reached toward him instead. "Maybe I can help," she said, her hands going to his neck cloth. "You did the same for me, after all. Why don't I valet for you tonight?"

He met her gaze, hot blue flashing deep in his eyes.

Her hands fell still. "Unless you'd rather I didn't," she amended.

Before she could pull away, he caught her palms and placed them back on his cravat. "No," he told her in a thick rasp. "Undress me. Please."

"You don't think I'm a wanton, do you?" she blurted out, unexpectedly worried he might think she was fast.

He arched a brow, his smile serious and devastatingly seductive. "No. But even if you were, you'd be *my* wanton. When we are alone, Claire, you may do anything that brings you pleasure. Anything at all. I want there to be no barriers or reservations between us—most especially in bed."

A bone-deep shiver raced through her at his words.

Anything, he'd said.

She had no idea what that really meant but she supposed he would show her. Her body throbbed violently at the idea.

Drawing a shivery breath, she reached up and tugged at the strip of linen tied around his throat, slowly easing it loose. When the knot was free, she unwound the length of cloth until it came away in her hand. Blindly, she tossed it after her own garments, hoping it landed where it was supposed to go.

Next came his coat, then the short placket of shirt buttons at his throat. His waistcoat took more time, her fingers fumbling slightly against the long row of gold buttons that fastened down its silken length. Somehow, she worked them all open, parting the cloth to draw it off. But when it came time to remove his shirt, she hesitated.

Obviously aware of her sudden reticence, Edward did it himself, peeling the fine linen over his head in a quick burst of energy. Lowering his bare arms to his sides, he stood quiet for her appraisal.

Her eyes rounded at the sight of him, pulse thrumming faster as she drank in her first glimpse of his bare chest. And what a chest it was, her mouth pooling with moisture at his undeniable appeal.

He was beautiful, all firm musculature and long sinewy planes. Dark hair grew in a rugged swath across his pectorals before thinning into a narrow line that trailed down his lean stomach. It disappeared beneath the waistband of his breeches, inviting an exploration she wasn't yet bold enough to attempt.

Yet she had to touch him, gliding her palms over his shoulders and arms, then across his hard chest. His skin was toasty warm and clearly sensitive, his muscles rippling beneath her inquisitive touch. Threading her fingers into his chest hair, she indulged herself by investigating all the contrasting textures—soft and crisp, supple but firm. Inadvertently, she grazed one of his flat male nipples and heard him catch his breath on a sharp inhale. Curious, she stroked him again and watched his flesh pucker tightly.

Does he like that? she wondered. *Does it give him the same exquisite pleasure I feel when he touches me that way?*

Leaning forward, she put her mouth on his other nipple and gave a tentative lick. His arousal jerked against her belly, one of his palms coming up to cup the back of her head and draw her nearer. Closing her eyes, she swirled her tongue against him, using little flicks and circles. Then, letting instinct guide her, she gave him a light nip with her teeth.

He jerked again and shuddered, groaning as he took hold of her arms and pulled her away. His eyes were dark and hungry, and glittering with unconcealed need. "I can see you're going to be good at this." He reached for the ties at her waist. "And I'm going to enjoy being the man with whom you learn to perfect your talent."

Before she could reply, he stripped off her petticoat and shift, then swept her naked into his arms. Carrying her a few short steps, he laid her against the cool cotton sheets, then began removing the rest of his clothes with quick, efficient movements.

Blood beat in thick, hot strokes, as she watched him undress, her breath growing increasingly shallow with each successive inch of flesh he revealed.

He was everything she'd dreamed of and more. His body bold and majestic, spectacular where he stood silhouetted in the dim light. She couldn't help the pleasured gasp that came to her lips as she caught her first glimpse of him completely nude.

Grecian art couldn't begin to compare with the grandeur that was Edward. Narrow hips, long thighs heavily muscled from riding, tapering calves and elegant ankles and feet, he made her mouth water. And yet it was his ample erection that drew and held her gaze, a knot of excitement and trepidation lodging in her throat.

Then he eased into the bed beside her, sliding close to take her in his arms. Her bare skin slid against his own like warm silk, as he crushed his mouth to hers with possessive demand. She met it and more, returning his kisses with a frantic, fiery ardor of her own.

The burning need blazed higher, consuming her, emboldening her, leaving her aching and breathless. His hands were everywhere, driving her wild, each touch lifting her to new heights of pleasure and passion.

She touched him as well, tentatively at first, beginning only with his arms and shoulders. He murmured words of approval and encouragement, and her confidence grew. Widening her range, she delved lower, her palms wandering wherever they would in a roaming path that brought her great delight.

Edward clearly approved as well, deepening their kiss, as he claimed her mouth in a torrid mating that left her thoroughly intoxicated. Her hands continued their downward slide, gliding over the interesting dip at the base of his spine before continuing across his leanly muscled buttocks. He groaned at her daring foray, his kiss turning even more savage.

His hands went to her breasts, caressing them until the

tips were hardened to aching peaks. His mouth followed, closing over one nipple to draw upon her, while his fingers roved below.

Trails of fire spread wherever he touched, her skin awash with overlapping waves of intensity and need. Over her stomach he roamed, across her hips and down her thighs, his every touch turning her molten and moist. Parting her legs, he slipped a finger inside, her wet flesh clinging eagerly to his gentle questing.

She tossed her head and moaned, eyelids floating closed at the sweet sensations racking her body. Her senses spun as though she were caught in a gale, pleasure building in breathless beats, each intimate stroke better than the last.

Her pulse leapt, inner flesh stretching almost to the point of pain as he added another finger and pressed deeper. In and out he went, his thumb finessing an ultra-sensitive bit of flesh that made her writhe.

He suckled her breasts until they ached, each pull of his mouth mirroring the soft, rhythmic thrust of his fingers. Blood pounded between her temples, a red haze flickering behind her closed eyes.

Then suddenly she was sailing, floating high and light somewhere, as a brilliant bliss spread through her, its radiance shimmering all the way to her hands and toes.

A smile curved her mouth and she tangled her fingers into his thick satiny hair, cradling his head against her breast as he tongued her in the most delightful of ways.

Easing upward on one elbow, he took her mouth in another devastating kiss, his fingers continuing to stroke her flesh a few more delicious, devastating times. Parting her legs wider, he settled himself between her spread thighs.

Her eyes came open, mouth parting on a trembling breath, as he withdrew his fingers to guide himself into her instead. He pressed on slowly, her inner muscles shifting to accommodate his length. She bit her lip to stifle a gasp of pain.

"You're tight," he murmured, kissing her softly, almost apologetically. "It can't be helped this first time."

He pressed into her again, barely gaining an inch, her body resisting his penetration.

Biting her lip again, she squeezed her eyes tight and prepared to endure whatever followed.

Abruptly, he stopped, chest heaving for breath and restraint. She opened her eyes again, noticing the damp on his forehead, the strain in his jaw, neck and shoulders, his muscles held tautly in a clear battle for control.

"G-Go on," she whispered, only then realizing how much he was holding back, how much he must want her. "I love you, Edward. It will be fine."

Heaving out a breath, he rolled onto his back.

She lay there, half stunned, half devastated by his abandonment.

Was it over? When he'd barely even claimed her?

But then he reached for her wrist, tugging her to him. "Come here. Let's try a different approach."

Different?

She had no idea what he meant, but she would do whatever he wished.

"Straddle me," he told her.

"What?"

"Climb on top and take me inside you. I'm hoping it will be easier. Here, let me show you what I mean."

Lifting her, he settled her over him, her breasts bouncing as he angled her so that the tip of his shaft was pressing against the entrance to her slick folds. Holding her hips, he lowered her just far enough to claim that first inch he'd taken before.

"Your turn now," he said, his voice gruff with strain and

suppressed desire. "Take as much of me as you can bear, as slowly as you need."

"Edward," she gasped. "I don't know if I can."

"You can." One of his hands went to her breasts again, playing over her with purpose, pausing to give one nipple a light pinch that made her groan. His other hand went between her thighs and began to stroke her in a way that roused her hunger.

Aching with want, she rose up then forced herself down on him, biting her lip again against the discomfort as she impaled herself upon his length.

Up, then down she went, bouncing and stopping in ways that left her a bit crazed. Yet she was beginning to take him in, each try gaining him a little more access. Bracing her palms on his chest, she rose up, then down, but it wasn't enough. Her gaze met his in frustration, her skin glistening with perspiration from her efforts.

"Once more," he rasped.

When she rose up this time, his hands settled on her hips. She came down, and without her realizing his intention, he thrust upward, using his strength to lodge her fully onto him.

A sharp pain slashed through her and she cried out. But he was in, his shaft buried deep. For a long moment they rested, silent and unmoving.

Then, with his hands still on her hips, he began to move, thrusting slowly into her.

To her surprise, the discomfort began to recede, her body growing needy as he built her desire again. Reaching up, he cupped the back of her head and brought her down for a fervid kiss, their tongues tangling in a wet, wild slide that made her feel as wanton as she'd earlier feared she might become.

Tossing all restraint aside, she met each of his strokes

with ones of her own, shimmying her hips to take as much of him as she could manage. Air grew thin in her lungs, her muscles quivering beneath the unfamiliar movements.

In a quick flip, she found herself beneath him, Edward keeping them together as he rolled her onto her back. Reaching down, he coaxed her legs high around his waist in a move that sent him even deeper. She gasped and shivered, wrapping her arms around his shoulders to hold on as he began thrusting harder and faster inside her. He kissed her again, crushing her mouth to his as though he couldn't get enough.

And perhaps he couldn't.

Her own thoughts were hazy, her blood racing at a fevered pitch until she wondered if she might melt right then and there. But the need was too great, hunger clutching her in a fierce grip that drove her on. Dark madness hovered on the edges of her consciousness, a yawning desire that demanded to be satisfied and assuaged.

Suddenly she was flying again, senses scattering in a whirlwind of rapture and completion. Bliss poured through her, spreading like sweet, hot honey into her muscles and deep into her bones. She clung, feeling lax and lazy and divine.

Edward claimed his own satisfaction within moments, quaking inside her arms as he called out his pleasure.

Together they collapsed, recovering their breaths and their senses in a heated tangle of limbs. Rolling over again so she lay on top of him, he cradled her close.

She floated, drowsy and replete. "Well goodness," she said. "That was . . . that was wonderful."

Edward smiled. "It most certainly was."

Chapter 22

Claire came gradually awake the next morning, memories of the night past sweeping over her like a dream. She reached for Edward, but found nothing except an expanse of cool, empty sheet where he ought to have been.

Her eyes snapped open and for the briefest moment, she wondered if she had imagined it all. Then she caught sight of a pair of polished brown leather Hessians—Edward's Hessians—and knew that every second of it had been real.

Her gaze flashed up and met his where he sat fully dressed in one of the room's cane-backed chairs. He was watching her, a warm but curiously enigmatic expression on his face.

"Good morning," he said, low and smooth.

"Good morning," she whispered.

Somehow she kept from blushing as another round of memories returned, including one that had taken place not long past dawn. She'd awakened in a welter of feverish need to find him kissing and caressing her, one of his hands stroking between her thighs. Trembling on the edge, neither of them needed to speak as he'd slid into her from behind, taking her in a sweet, slow rhythm that had proven her complete undoing.

She was still rather undone now at finding herself so closely observed. How long had he been sitting there, watching her sleep?

When had he gotten out of the bed and dressed?

And how could she not have noticed?

A tiny frown puckered her forehead as she stared again at the clothes he was wearing. Rather than last night's formal black cutaway coat, knee breeches and snowy white linen, he had on a dark blue jacket, tan waistcoat, and fawn trousers.

Before she could ask where he'd come by a fresh change of clothing, he stood and walked to her. Leaning over, he placed his hands on either side of her head and gave her a long, warm, intimate kiss that made her wish he would crawl back into bed with her.

She raised her arms to pull him closer, but he eased away. "I'll send the maid in to help you bathe and dress. Breakfast will be waiting for us in the parlor whenever you're ready."

A sigh of unconcealed disappointment puffed from her lips.

He gave a soft chuckle, his expression rueful. "Believe me, I'd like nothing better than to join you again. I could spend the whole day in that bed and only let you up for necessities. But I suspect you're rather sore and could use a measure of time to yourself."

She shifted against the sheets, chagrined to realize he was right. She was sore, and not only between her thighs, but in other spots as well. Last night, she'd used muscles she'd never used in her life and they were all letting her know it.

Smiling, he bent low for another kiss, then stepped back and left the room.

She heard the door shut and his footsteps recede. The moment they did, she wanted to call him back, realizing that she didn't have anything suitable to wear. She'd traveled here in her yellow silk ball gown last night, and although it would certainly keep her adequately covered, the dress was completely inappropriate for daytime wear. She cringed to imagine the looks her garment would elicit. Then again, considering the fact that she'd spent the night in this room with Edward, she supposed her mode of dress was the least of her indiscretions.

But she needn't have worried, she quickly discovered.

The maid arrived on a knock, a kind country girl with a cheerful smile and a chattering tongue. After waiting for Claire's permission to enter, the girl breezed in with one of Claire's own day dresses pressed and ready in her hand.

Claire soon learned that Edward had been busy while she'd slumbered the morning away. Having awakened early, he'd sent word to Clybourne House, ordering a change of clothing for them both. A small valise had also been sent that contained a wealth of toiletries—toothbrush and tooth powder, her comb and hairbrush, soap, lotion, pins and more.

Relaxing in a warm hip bath, she let the water's soothing heat relieve most of her soreness. The fine-milled soap smelled lightly of roses, washing away evidence of the night past, including the smear of virgin's blood dried on the inside of her thighs. She'd found more on the sheets when she'd climbed from the bed, and was glad the maid had enough discretion not to make some remark on the subject in spite of her open manner.

After drying off with a plush linen towel that had also been sent from home, she allowed the maid to help her into the day dress of dotted violet muslin and to style her bobbed hair.

Emerging from the bedchamber nearly an hour later, she made her way down the hall to the parlor.

Edward gazed out the upstairs parlor window, observing the action going on in the inn yard with desultory interest. His mind was on more important matters, his thoughts full of Claire and the night they'd just spent in each other's arms.

Taking Claire to bed before their nuptials hadn't been traditional, but then matters between the two of them seldom seemed to be. And yet, in the most basic of ways, last night had been their wedding night. Perhaps they hadn't exchanged vows, but she was his wife now all the same. At this point, the ceremony was merely a formality—one he didn't plan to put off any longer.

He knew she assumed they would be returning to London today. Instead, he planned to take her to a small estate of his in Oxfordshire. He was acquainted with the parish priest there—he'd given the man the living, after all—and knew the clergyman would be only too happy to conduct a quiet ceremony to join him and Claire.

Not sure when or where she might agree to wed him, Edward had taken the precaution of obtaining a special license a few weeks ago. This morning, he'd sent word to Hughes to have the document delivered to him here at the inn. He'd also made arrangements to have the Oxfordshire house opened and all preparations made for his and Claire's arrival. For despite her declaration last night, he worried that she might still change her mind.

Once back in London with months of wedding details ahead, Claire might turn doubtful again. He could even imagine her calling off the ceremony at the last minute. Well, he wasn't going to give her the chance. Instead, he planned to race her to the altar as fast as they could proceed.

He wanted her bound to him in every possible way. He'd

taken her body last night. Now he planned to have her vow, even if it meant a hasty wedding without a single family member from either side in attendance.

Moreover, after spending the night in her bed, he had no intention of being denied it, or her, ever again. He wasn't about to return to Clybourne House and be forced to skulk around in secret, indulging in clandestine midnight rendezvous until the wedding. Now that he'd claimed her, he was going to keep on claiming her, since he wanted her too much to stay away.

She was his, and would be his, tonight and every night from this day forward.

His body hardened at the thought, aching to return to her now, to lift her wet and naked out of her bath, and take her until they both collapsed shuddering from the pleasure. But physically, she needed time, since she'd been a virgin. And he needed to get a wedding ring on her finger, and make her his bride.

My Clybourne Bride.

A surge of deep satisfaction went through him at the idea. Fighting his hunger for her, he drew a bracing inhalation, then made another idle survey of the inn yard in an effort to distract himself. As he did, he noticed something out of place.

Or rather someone.

What the devil is she doing here?

The woman hadn't been readily noticeable at first, seated as she was in a closed, unmarked carriage. But as she leaned forward, Philipa Stockton's cunningly beautiful features came into view, framed inside the square coach window.

Was she meeting a lover?

It was the most likely answer. Yet in spite of Islington having brought Claire here for that same purpose, this country inn seemed an unlikely place for an assignation. Particularly for a woman like Lady Stockton, who valued comfort above all else.

With a mental shrug, he was about to dismiss her and turn away when a dark-haired man strode across the yard at a clipped pace. Edward grew still, recognizing him as Rene Dumont, suspected French spy.

Although Dumont had come over as a young man in the wave of émigrés after the Revolution, he'd never been trusted as completely loyal to his new country. Publicly, he detested republicanism and vocally denounced the revolutionaries, who had killed his parents and stripped him of his holdings and heritage. And yet for the past few months, he'd been suspected of having developed rather pragmatic motivations and a willingness to court favor with Napoleon and the Empire.

From the information Edward had learned at the War Office, it was believed that Dumont was actively working for the French. Apparently, in exchange for his cooperation, he was to receive his family's chateau and a portion of their pre-Revolutionary lands at the end of the war—a war Napoleon would need to win in order for the arrangement to go through.

The War Office was willing to let Dumont continue his activities, since they had no actual proof that he'd betrayed his adopted nation. Yet what was Dumont doing here today? And was he meeting anyone besides Philipa Stockton?

Edward twisted his signet ring around on his finger and watched with interest as the Frenchman walked quickly to her carriage and climbed inside.

Philipa Stockton and Dumont?

Somehow Edward couldn't see them as lovers, since Philipa generally invited much wealthier gentlemen to her bed. Then again, she'd been Jack's mistress, and Lord knew Jack hadn't been swimming in cash at the time of their affair. So maybe there was a real attraction between Philipa and Dumont.

But why here? Why away from the city when no one of import would care if they were seen together?

Could the reason be that Dumont was using Philipa Stockton for information? Or blackmailing her over some sexual peccadillo of hers in order to gain access or information? Perhaps there was even more to Dumont that they'd suspected.

Edward mulled over the possibilities, his eyebrows inching up when he saw Dumont exit Philipa's coach after no more than five minutes inside.

Perhaps they ought to keep an eye out for Philipa Stockton as well? If she was being manipulated, maybe they could turn that to their advantage?

Lady Stockton's coach was pulling away from the inn when Edward heard the click of the door behind him.

Turning, he found Claire standing on the threshold, thoughts of Dumont and Philipa Stockton flying straight out of his head. Smiling, he walked forward. "You look lovely," he said, reaching to take her hand. "Are you hungry?"

Her pure blue gaze met his. "Famished actually."

"Good. Come sit and I'll ring for our meal. I had them keep everything in the kitchen, so it wouldn't go cold."

After assisting her into a seat at the table, he went to pull the bell. On his return, he paused beside her. "I find I'm rather hungry too. For you." Leaning down, he took her lips with a long, leisurely thoroughness that made her sigh in clear happiness. Before he had a chance to deepen their embrace, however, a knock sounded at the door.

In resignation, he straightened and called for the servants to enter.

"Are you sure we're headed in the right direction?" Claire asked Edward nearly two hours later from her seat next to him in the ducal barouche.

The luxurious vehicle in which they were traveling had been driven up that morning from Clybourne House. She'd been pleased to find the comfortable conveyance waiting for them in the inn yard, content to let Edward's coachman drive them home.

Now she was wondering if they were lost, the fields that ranged beyond the window taking on a consistently wilder appearance with each mile that passed.

"Maybe we've taken a wrong turn. This doesn't look like the road to London," she observed, eyeing a stone mile marker with a 53 on it that was half hidden in the weeds.

Lounging in the opposite corner, Edward sent her a reassuring smile. "That's because it's not."

Her eyes widened. "But what do you mean? Aren't we going back to Grosvenor Square?"

He shook his head. "Not at present. We're on our way to my estate in Oxfordshire."

"We are? But why? And when exactly were you going to tell me we're not going back to Town?"

"I thought I'd surprise you."

"Oh, did you now? Me and everyone else, then." She paused as a sudden thought occurred. "But Edward, we have to go back. What will they all think if we suddenly disappear together? There'll be such talk!"

Reaching over, he took her hand and raised it to his lips. "And what do you care about talk, my dear Claire? Last night you were prepared to face complete social ruin. I hardly think a trip into the country with your fiancée will do you greater harm."

"Yes, but that was for another reason entirely—"

"And so it was." Sliding his arm around her waist and legs, he lifted her so she sat on his lap. "A reason that no longer exists."

"Edward—"

"Tell me again." His hair brushed her cheek as he bent to feather his lips over her neck, then up to catch her earlobe between his teeth for a tiny nip.

She shivered and closed her eyes. "Tell you what?"

"That you love me." He closed his palm over her breast and caressed her with gentle yet devastating strokes. "At least that's what you said last night. Did you not mean it?"

"Of course I did."

"Then say it." His mouth pressed against hers in soft, gliding touches. "Tell me you love me."

She hesitated, reluctant to repeat the words that would give him a last irrevocable measure of control over her. But he had it already, didn't he? Her secrets had all been laid bare. "Yes, Edward. I love you."

He smiled, his mouth crushing hers with an ardor that sent her heart beating as fast and light as hummingbird wings.

"Good," he said, when he let her come up for air. "Then you won't mind marrying me today."

She wiggled slightly against him. "Today? But that's impossible."

"Not with the special license I have in my pocket, it isn't."

Her lips rounded with surprise.

"I've sent ahead and the arrangements are already under way," he continued. "We'll be married at six this evening and have our wedding supper afterward." He kissed her temple, his fingers sliding purposefully against her breast. "And then to bed."

"And what if I would rather wait?" she said, even though she was intrigued with the idea of a hasty ceremony.

He sent her a fixed look. "Then we'll both look like fools, since I've sent word to the family about our nuptials and where we'll be staying for the next few days. I also sent notices to the papers to announce our marriage. They'll be on the breakfast tables of everyone in the Ton come morning."

"Well, you were certainly sure I'd agree," she retorted.

His features took on a serious mien. "No, I wasn't. That's

why I didn't tell you earlier and why we aren't waiting. Consider yourself kidnapped, madam, since you're coming with me."

She softened. "I said yes last night."

"You said yes weeks ago. I'm just making sure you don't reverse your decision again."

"I won't."

How could she when she'd lain with him last night? When she'd given him her innocence? How could she when she loved him beyond all reason, so that matters of logic and common sense no longer held any sway?

Laying a palm against her cheek, he kissed her again, his touch coaxing yet uncompromising at the same time. "I'll give you a grand wedding at Braebourne, if it's what you want. But know this, Claire, we're getting married tonight. I'm done waiting for you."

She curved a hand around his wrist. "Then we shall wed. I don't care about a big wedding, I never have. A quiet ceremony will be lovely, just us two."

Relief shone on his face, pleasure gleaming in his midnight blue eyes.

"Although I have to confess that I wish I had something to wear besides this spotted muslin," she said. "But I suppose it will have to do."

"Not a bit." He smiled. "Do you think I wouldn't arrange for a gown? You'll look like a bride, don't worry."

"Oh, Edward. What did you bring me?"

His gaze twinkled. "You'll see."

Then he kissed her again and she forgot about everything but him for the rest of their journey.

Chapter 23

Evening summer sunshine bathed the quaint parish church in a warm golden light, lambent rays shining through rows of leaded glass windows set in the old grey stone walls. A few lighted candles dispelled the remaining shadows in the interior, the scent of beeswax fragrant in the air, the atmosphere still and peaceful.

At the altar, Claire stood with her palm clasped inside Edward's, listening to the words that would soon join them in holy matrimony.

The kindly eyed, white-haired rector Edward had mentioned was officiating the ceremony. The clergyman's wife and daughter were acting as witnesses, the two women clearly awestruck at being asked to take a role in the wedding of such illustrious personages as the Duke of Clybourne and his bride—or so Claire had overheard them whisper to each other.

And just as Edward had promised, he'd provided a dress that was more than suitable for the occasion. When they'd arrived earlier at his Oxfordshire estate, her breath had caught as she'd walked into her bedchamber and seen the dress he'd chosen. She remembered her heart beating in heavy strokes, dazed and dazzled as she recognized the outrageously expensive cream sarcenet gown she'd purchased so many weeks ago.

The dress literally sparkled from the diamonds encrusted in the square-cut bodice, and the leaves and flowers sewn into the skirt using real gold thread. He'd even remembered to have her maid pack the matching shoes—cream satin slippers that glittered with gold and diamond buckles.

She'd never worn the ensemble before, finding the dress far too elaborate for an ordinary ball, even one held in London.

But for a wedding . . . for *her* wedding . . . well, that was another matter entirely.

In fact, as she'd let a housemaid help her into her finery, she'd known that Edward couldn't have selected a gift better designed to please her. She'd wiped a tear from her cheek, more touched by his thoughtfulness than she could say.

She had no veil—there hadn't been time to procure one. But a handful of pink rose buds, freshly picked from the garden, more than ably adorned her short curls.

By the time she descended the stairs to join Edward for the carriage ride to the church, she truly felt like a bride. And when she caught the intense look of heavy-lidded admiration on his face, she knew she was finally ready to become his wife.

For better or for worse . . . till death us do part.

In his clear, commanding voice, she heard Edward repeat those words, speaking the vows that would bind them forever. He slid a wide gold band onto her finger—more of his amazing last-minute planning—then it was her turn.

Meeting his gaze, she repeated the words, not at all sure how she managed with blood thundering like the sea in her ears and her heart drumming loudly in her chest. He'd arranged for a gold wedding band for himself, and with trembling hands, she fit it onto his finger.

Suddenly the ceremony was over.

Suddenly she was Edward's wife.

The rector and his family invited them to share a celebratory glass of wine while they signed the register. Edward accepted with gracious aplomb, carrying much of the conversation, since she could no longer seem to find her voice. Then, before she quite realized, she was being led back to the carriage, stepping inside for the first time as the new Duchess of Clybourne.

But Edward didn't grant her more than a few moments to think, dragging her into his arms to indulge in a ravenous kiss. "I wanted to do this on the altar," he told her, "but I thought we might shock everyone."

Claiming her mouth in fervid, passionate draughts, he showed her exactly what he meant. By the time they reached the house, she was breathless and aching, the lovely two-story redbrick manse naught but a blur as he led her inside.

She half expected him to take her straight upstairs to bed, but to her chagrin, they found the small staff of servants assembled in the hall. The servants showered her and Edward with warm, heartfelt congratulations, beaming with pride at being chosen to serve her and the duke on this most special of occasions.

An elaborate wedding supper had been prepared, they were informed, despite the short notice. Cook had even baked a three-tiered cake, frosted with creamy white boiled icing and decorated with sugared fruits.

Not wanting to take the chance of ruining her beautiful gown, Claire reluctantly trailed upstairs to change. She assumed she would return downstairs to eat in the dining room. But once she was dressed in an airy gown of cool, pale blue silk, she was led along the corridor to a room at the end of the hall.

Edward's bedchamber.

He was waiting inside, looking wickedly debonair stripped down to his shirtsleeves, waistcoat and trousers. "Champagne?" he asked, handing her a glass.

Accepting, she took a long swallow, soothed by the refreshing slide of bubbles that tickled her nose and delighted her tongue.

A wide table was set with china and crystal, and on another an array of appetizingly scented dishes that waited ready beneath their covers.

She and Edward took their seats, with only a single footman to serve. As soon as he'd laid their plates before them, Edward waved the man out, informing him that his services would no longer be required that evening.

Claire's heart sped faster as the door closed behind him, vibrantly aware of the huge mahogany tester bed that waited on the other side of the spacious room. Part of her wished Edward would just take her there now, lay her down amid the sheets and make love to her.

Instead, he encouraged her to eat and drink, pausing to refill her wineglass whenever the contents dropped more than an inch. She was scarcely aware of what she ate or what she said as the minutes slid past. She only knew that she was carrying on a conversation, since Edward responded in his turn.

Time took on a fluid texture, leaving her uncertain how late the hour had become. Then the meal was finished, except for dessert. Slices of the delicious-looking wedding cake had been cut and waited on a pair of plates.

Edward placed one in front of himself. Reaching over, he drew her out of her seat and across to him, angling his chair to one side, as he pulled her onto his lap. Cradling her close with an arm around her waist, he dropped a pair of heated kisses against her throat.

"I thought we'd share," he suggested.

She didn't answer, unsure why she'd become so shy, particularly after last night. Or maybe it was because of last night and all the stunning pleasure she knew awaited her in his arms.

Then she frowned.

What if our passion for each other isn't the same now that we're wed? What if Edward doesn't desire me like he did, knowing the game between us is over and that he's won?

But then her gaze locked on his and she saw the fierce hunger smoldering in his eyes, and knew she was being foolish. More than foolish, she realized, becoming aware of his iron-hard arousal pressing with insistent demand against her hip in a way that proved his need more fully than words.

Taking a forkful of cake, he raised it to her lips. "Try a bite," he said on a husky command.

Opening her mouth, she let him slide the tines over her lips, the sugary confection melting against her tongue. She swallowed. "Delicious."

"You've got a bit of icing on your mouth," he remarked. Before she could attend to the matter, he stopped her. "No. Allow me."

Using a tantalizing sweep of his tongue, he bathed away the sticky sweetness, pausing afterward to take her mouth in a torrid kiss that left her shaking and hungry for things that had nothing to do with food.

Slowly, he leaned away. "Your turn." Taking up the fork, he cut a bite of cake. But instead of handing it to her on the utensil, he put the sweet directly into her hand. "Feed me."

Her nerves leapt. Fingers trembling, she moved to obey.

Holding the offering between her thumb and forefingers, she let him eat the dessert from her hand. Curving his fingers around her wrist, he began licking the crumbs and icing off her skin. Abruptly enslaved, all she could do was whimper against the flood of heat that poured through her limbs as he drew one of her fingers deep into his mouth. With an inventiveness she couldn't possibly have anticipated, he swirled his tongue around each digit in turn, suckling with a thoroughness that roused an answering moisture from between her thighs. On a moan, her eyelids fell shut, air growing thin and unsteady in her lungs, as he showed her that even hands and fingers could be erotic.

Once he released her, he sought out a single candied cherry from the cake plate. Pressing the sweet to her lips, he rubbed the sugary fruit across her skin. Then he licked her, doing to her lips what he'd just done to her hand. All the sugar gone, he popped the tiny fruit into his mouth and chewed. After swallowing, he captured her mouth, taking her with a raw carnality that sent tremors radiating along her spine. The sweet, tart flavor of cherries suffused her lips and tongue, her toes curling, fingers lifting to spear into his thick soft hair to drag him closer.

Wild need burst inside her, fiery longing that drove her to take more and give more as well, meeting his every demand with a craving of her own. Her thoughts spun in dizzying circles, the alcohol she'd consumed merging with the intoxication of his touch to make her drowsy and dazed.

She sighed as he stood them both on their feet, then bent to sweep her high into his arms. Her head went to his shoulder, her hands to his chest, stroking there as she absently began unfastening the top buttons on his waistcoat.

Laying her on the bed, he kissed her again, crushing her mouth to his with avid and unmistakable possession. His hands roved over her body, stroking and caressing, as he loosened ties and undid buttons in a progression that soon had her bared to the skin. Dress, stays, shift and shoes, everything was stripped away, everything except her stockings and garters—those he left in place.

Kissing his way down her body, he roused her passions higher. She writhed, aching in an agony of need. Reaching her thighs, he stroked the sensitive insides, kissing her there with tormenting slowness before parting her legs to take an even deeper kiss.

Her back arched, nails digging into the sheets, as his mouth closed over her. She thought she might die from the pleasure, each warm, wet swipe of his tongue bringing her closer and closer to what she knew must be nothing less than madness.

Breath panted in labored draws, a keening moan rising in her throat that she was helpless to silence. But he didn't seem to want her silent. Quite the opposite, forcing her to the brink and beyond until he controlled everything she was, dictated everything she would ever be.

Then she was soaring, dark waves of rapture breaking over her like a storm. Buzzing and blissful, she let herself float, a smile on her mouth that she couldn't contain. Eyes closed, she felt Edward rise from the bed, heard the soft rustling movements as he yanked off his clothes.

The mattress depressed beneath his knee as he joined her again in the bed. Taking her in his arms, he stroked one of her breasts, playing with the nipple before enfolding his lips around it. He suckled, her hand gliding over his bare shoulders in a long, drowsy caress as he did.

It was a caress that grew drowsier with each passing second, sleep a call she found nearly impossible to resist.

Sliding higher, he kissed her mouth.

"Edward," she sighed.

"Yes, dear Claire?"

And then, without even knowing, she dozed off.

*   *   *

For long agonizing moments, Edward stared, waiting for a reply that never came. In a futile hope that he might rouse her again, he pressed his lips to hers. But there was no response, her mouth slack and unresponsive beneath his own.

Bloody hell! She's asleep!

His shaft throbbing with unsatisfied arousal, he groaned, then flopped onto his back.

I should never have given her all that wine.

But in spite of last night's intimacy, he'd known she was nervous, her fair skin pale with nerves and the surprise of their impromptu wedding. When he'd promised to rush her to the altar, that was exactly what he'd done. He'd thought the wine would relax her. Apparently the liquor had more than done its job.

That and the aftereffects of the climax he'd just given her.

Then too there was the fact that she'd barely managed any sleep last night. His fault again, he supposed, since he'd not only kept her awake making love, but roused her a couple of hours later for another energetic bout.

Groaning, he flung an arm over his eyes and fought his body's insistent hunger. He could probably wake her again, he realized. A few well-placed touches and he could have her up and begging to be taken. But she was exhausted and clearly in need of rest. Much as it pained him—quite literally—he knew he should, and would, wait.

Rolling onto his side, he watched her sleep. Ever so gently, he brushed a lock of hair from her face, marveling for a moment that she was finally, irrevocably his wife.

Claire.

The girl he'd known for such a very long time, but whom he hadn't really known at all.

The woman who drove him to distraction, yet made him want her with an intense, single-minded obsession.

She says she loves me. But how do I feel in return?

He frowned, unsure, having never been the sort to believe in romantic whimsies like love. Such emotions were for those who could afford to be indulgent, who weren't burdened by duty and responsibility and the need to always do what was right.

Stroking the back of one finger over her cheek, he watched her dream and knew that, for now, this was enough.

Moving closer, he turned her so he could slide up behind, angling them together like spoons. Inserting one of his thighs between hers, he cupped a breast in his hand and tucked her near.

With a contented sigh, she snuggled back.

Groaning, he closed his eyes and prepared for a long, frustrating night.

Early morning light flooded the bedroom, Claire's eyes flying open with a sudden snap. But it wasn't the sun that brought her awake. Instead, it was the fierce need assailing her body and the passionate, burning slide of Edward's touch.

Shifting restlessly against the tangled sheets, she moaned, desire riding her with an ache that was utterly impossible to ignore or control. Which was precisely how Edward wished it, she was sure, his hands and mouth moving over her body with a merciless demand.

And yet the sensations were sweet, nearly too sweet, making her crave him with a hunger that ought to have shocked her but didn't. He turned her brazen, her body warm and ripe for his possession, a claiming she wanted more than her next breath.

Needing to touch him, she reached out and slid her palms over his naked body. His muscles rippled beneath her gliding stroke, conveying his pleasure without the need for words. Leaning up, he caught the back of her head in his palm and dragged her to him for a searing, openmouthed kiss. She matched him, returning his embrace with all the eagerness she possessed. Easing a hand between their bodies, she trailed her fingers across his powerful chest, over his sleek, hard stomach to his hip and muscled thigh.

He tangled his tongue with hers, reaching down to palm her breasts and finesse the tender peaks with a skill that drove her wild. She quivered, her fingers inadvertently brushing against his erection. His shaft jerked, a hoarse moan rumbling in his throat.

In her inexperience, she almost drew back, but curiosity prevailed, persuading her to continue. As did Edward, whose hips arched forward in obvious hunger and anticipation.

Wrapping her fingers around his length, she felt him shudder, then again as she began to explore with breathless wonder. He pulsed warmly inside her grasp, thick and hard yet velvety soft. After a first few tentative touches, he covered her hand with his own and guided her fingers over his erection with patience, as he showed her exactly how he liked to be touched.

Learning quickly, she soon had him quaking beneath her strokes, pleasuring him from root to tip. She paused and rubbed her thumb over a bead of moisture she found gathered there, aware of an answering ache that throbbed wet and willing between her legs.

Abruptly, as if he couldn't bear another instant, he rolled her onto her back and parted her legs. In one swift thrust, he was inside, burying himself as deep as he could go.

Or so she thought until he began to move, his heavy penetration making her gasp, as blinding pleasure shot straight through to her core. Arching, she took more of him, yielding fully to his intimate possession. Her inner muscles clung to his every stroke, blood beating violently in her temples and behind her closed eyelids.

Clinging, she pressed her cheek against his neck, her fingers buried in his hair, as she writhed beneath him. Each stroke was better than the last, each thrust like the beat of a second heart hammering frantically in her loins. Need poured through her, hot and insatiable, demanding to be appeased. He kissed her then, wicked and wet, raw with sensuality and unleashed passion.

Consumed, she couldn't think, fully abandoned to the beauty of his touch. The world tipped off its axis, her senses spinning as he slid his wide palms beneath her bottom and angled her higher. She took him then, all of him, rapture breaking over her with a keening wail as she reached her peak. Holding tight, she absorbed the wonder and bliss of every divine sensation.

He claimed his own release seconds after, pouring himself inside her as he came on a rough, ragged shout.

Cradling him near, she let herself drift, cast away on a sea of pure heaven. Kissing his shoulder, she stroked his damp hair, giddy and glad and pleasurably weary all over again.

Lifting his head, he met her gaze. "Good morning."

She smiled. "Good morning."

"I must be crushing you."

"No," she rushed to deny. "I like you crushing me."

"Well, I don't." Bracing himself on his forearms, he began to move away.

Tightening her legs, she held on. "Don't go," she whispered. "Not yet."

"Don't worry. I'm not going anywhere," he murmured. "Just a change of perspective." Clasping her close, he rolled them over so that she lay on top, their bodies still connected. "Good?"

Contented, she snuggled nearer. "Very good."

He caressed the back of her thigh with one broad palm in a slow, sweeping glide. "Hungry?"

"No."

"Tired?"

"A little," she admitted, covering a sudden yawn with her hand.

He laughed, the movement jostling him inside her.

She gasped, then gasped again when she felt his arousal reawaken, swelling to noticeable proportions.

"Do you want to rest?" he asked, his hands moving in leisurely passes. "Feel at your leave to fall asleep on me again."

Again? Only then did she remember the night just past. "Heavens, I did, didn't I?" Heat rose into her cheeks.

Another laugh rumbled from his chest. "Yes, much to my chagrin. A man of lesser self-esteem might have taken affront."

She stroked a palm over his unshaven cheek, his whiskers scratchy against her skin. "There's nothing lesser about you, not your self-esteem or your . . . your . . ." His shaft swelled more, stiffening fully. "Oh God, Edward. Oh, that feels so good."

Shimmying against him, she drew an answering moan. "It certainly does," he said.

Leaning up, he claimed her mouth, his movements forcing him deeper. "So, what's it to be?" he asked, breath panting from between his lips. "Sleep or me?"

"You," she sighed, accepting his first powerful thrust. "Definitely you."

Chapter 24

Over the next five days, Claire and Edward rarely left the bedroom—sleeping, eating, and making love to the exclusion of all else.

Claire laughingly told him on the third day of their honeymoon that she didn't really even know what the rest of the house looked like, let alone the estate. Edward said he'd take her on a tour, but somehow they never seemed to find the time.

Most days they didn't even get dressed, slipping on dressing gowns for modesty's sake when the servants brought them a meal or carried in a great copper tub and hot water for a bath—which they enjoyed taking together. Otherwise, she and Edward lay in bed naked, the days drifting past in a lazy haze that made her feel as though time were standing still.

Now, on the morning of the sixth day, she awakened to the sound of servants' footsteps hurrying throughout the house. Opening her eyes, she realized that Edward wasn't next to her.

Instead, she found him across the room, attired in neatly

pressed tobacco brown trousers, a pristine white shirt and a cream waistcoat. Standing before a large mirror, he tied a final knot in the cravat at his neck. Next, he reached for a dark green coat hanging in the wardrobe and slipped his arms into the snug-fitting garment. Despite his lack of a valet, he looked as dashing and urbane as ever by the time he turned her way.

"Claire," he said, catching her watching. "You're awake."

"I am." Sitting up, she pulled the sheet over herself for the first time in days. "Are you going somewhere?"

A brief silence descended. "London. We're going back to Clybourne House. As much as I'd like to stay here indefinitely, duty demands that we return."

Duty.

Of course. Edward never neglected those things that must be done, even at the expense of his own pleasure. But he was right, she supposed; they couldn't stay here forever as much as she might wish otherwise. Still, he might have told her before now.

Rather than argue, she swung out of bed and crossed to take up her discarded dressing gown. "I'll get ready."

"I'll send in the maid."

Nodding, she turned away so he couldn't see the sudden distress she knew must be visible on her face. She waited, assuming he would leave in a moment.

Instead, he walked up behind her. Laying his hands on her shoulders, he swung her gently around. "What is it?"

"Nothing." She fixed her gaze on his cravat.

Tucking a finger beneath her chin, he urged her to meet his gaze. "I would have told you sooner, Claire, but I didn't want to spoil our last night here. We've had a lovely time."

"We have." One of the most beautiful times of her life.

"But we must leave."

"Of course," she agreed. "I just assumed we'd have a few days longer, but it's of no matter."

Catching her around the waist, he drew her close. "We'll have a proper honeymoon later, I promise. Two or three months, at least, wherever you'd like. Scotland, maybe? Or Wales? I have lovely estates in both places. Or the Continent. Assuming the seas aren't too dangerous, we could take in Italy or even Greece. Would you like that?"

She nodded, a faint smile curving her mouth. "I suppose you have villas there as well? Is there anywhere you don't have property?"

A grin shot across his face. "France, I believe, and the Americas. My father lost our holdings there during that confounded revolution of theirs. Upstart Yanks. As for the Frogs, my opinion is better left unsaid."

A laugh escaped, her smile growing wider.

Smiling in return, he cupped her cheek in his palm. "All will be well, Claire. You'll see. Nothing that matters between us will change once we're back in Town."

Closing her eyes, she leaned into his embrace and prayed he was right. Prayed she could hold on to him once their normal routine resumed and the real world and all its difficulties interfered again.

His lips met hers, tender and infinitely sweet, his gentle kiss easing the tension from her limbs, dissolving the jittery pressure trapped like bubbles beneath her ribs. Deepening their kiss, she wrapped her arms around his back and gave herself over to the sizzling pleasure. His mouth slanted over hers, passion blazing higher and hotter.

Suddenly, and with clear reluctance, he tore himself away. "I'd better go while I still have the strength," he said on a husky tone. "Now get dressed, madam, before I change my mind and tumble you down onto the bed again."

"You may tumble me whenever you like, Your Grace," she murmured.

His eyes sparkled with a wicked light she'd come to know

well over the past few days. "Be careful what you promise, dear girl." As if he couldn't help himself, he gave a half groan and bent to claim one last ravenous, soul-stealing kiss.

Then he let her go.

"I'll send the maid to attend you," he said. "Breakfast will be sent up as well. When you're ready, we'll be off."

Curling a hand against her pounding heart, she nodded and watched him stride from the room.

"Welcome home, Your Graces," Croft said later that afternoon, as Claire and Edward entered the town house. "On behalf of the staff," the butler continued, wearing the widest smile Claire had ever seen on his unflappable face, "I would like to extend our heartfelt good wishes on your marriage. Everyone is truly delighted by the happy news and looking forward to being of service in whatever way either of you may require."

Edward inclined his head. "Thank you, Croft. The duchess and I are most touched by your warm regards on this special occasion. Please convey our deep appreciation to the staff."

It took Claire a few seconds to realize that she was the "duchess" to which Edward had referred. Despite having been raised with the prospect of one day becoming the Duchess of Clybourne, she'd long since convinced herself she would never assume that particular title.

And yet here she was, Edward's wife. Edward's duchess.

Heavens.

Recovering quickly, she smiled at Croft. "Yes. You are all so wonderfully kind and keep the house running as smoothly as one of Mr. Perigal's best timepieces. I know I shall be in excellent hands and scarcely have need of managing the household."

Croft's smile deepened, his wizened eyes taking on a gleam. "Thank you, Your Grace. And please excuse me for not saying so immediately, but the family is waiting for you in the upstairs drawing room."

By "family," Claire assumed Croft meant Mallory, Drake, and Cousin Wilhelmina, but after preceding Edward up the stairs and down the long corridor, she quickly discovered her error.

"Ned!" exclaimed a tall, stalwart gentleman with forest green eyes. One of Edward's brothers, she assumed, noticing the strong resemblance between the two men. "It's about time you arrived," he went on. "We had your note and thought perhaps you had run into some sort of delay."

"Told you they'd be along at their leisure," remarked another man, equally tall, handsome and unmistakably a Byron. "And why should they not when they've just come from their honeymoon bed?" He flashed a devilish grin and wagged his eyebrows, earning a nudge from the comely, statuesque redhead at his side.

"Jack," she admonished in a quiet voice. "Behave yourself."

"I could," he drawled, "but only think how dull things would be if I did?"

Her lips twitched as though she were trying not to be amused, while Jack chuckled, clearly unabashed.

"If my brother is done making his usual outrageous remarks, allow me to introduce myself," said the first man. "I'm Cade and this is my wife, Meg." He laid an obviously proud and possessive hand on the shoulder of the beautiful blond woman seated in a chair before him.

Claire returned their smiles, then exchanged introductions with Lord Jack and his wife, Grace.

As she'd assumed, Drake, Mallory, and Cousin Wilhelmina were there as well. Mallory rushed across to give her an exuberant hug, while Drake bussed her on the cheek and Cousin Wilhelmina fluttered a handkerchief in the air.

Apparently, the sentimental lady cried even at the notion of weddings and honeymoons.

Next she met Edward's twelve-year-old sister, Esme, a bright-eyed girl, who had a pad of paper in her small hand and a smudge of what looked to be drawing ink on her right cheek. She piped out happy words of welcome and congratulations. And then there was Edward's mother, Ava Byron, who looked every inch as regal and lovely as Claire recalled.

Claire had been younger than Esme on the one and only occasion when they'd met—at least the only one Claire recalled, that is. Even now Claire remembered the duchess's gentle smile and the kind words she'd murmured the day she'd visited the Marsden nursery when Claire was ten.

Approaching her now, Claire saw that the dowager duchess's eyes were their same clear, luminous green, her hair still brown with only a few strands of silver to show the intervening years. As for her smile, it was every bit as warm, gentle and inviting as Claire recalled. With their reintroduction at hand, Claire had to admit she was mildly concerned over the thought of meeting Edward's mother again after all these years.

What if the dowager didn't like her, now that she was grown?

What if Ava Byron had heard, and disapproved, of all the gossip surrounding Claire, and was sorry Claire had married her son?

But I did, so there's nothing for it now, Claire told herself, smiling as she sank into a respectful curtsey.

"How do you do, Your Grace?" Claire said.

"I am very well, thank you. And aren't you lovely. Even prettier than I remember you being as a child."

So the dowager duchess remembered her visit as well. The thought warmed Claire.

"I trust you had a good journey on your drive down from Oxfordshire today?"

"We did. Thank you for inquiring."

"Good. I am glad to hear it." Ava walked forward, stopped and turned her gaze on Edward. "Perhaps, then, you'd like to explain just what pair of you were thinking, running off to get married, as though you had eloped? There I am, visiting with Jack and Grace and baby Nicola, when a messenger rides up with a note informing us that you have gotten married. The very next day, I received another letter, several pages long, I might add, from Claire's parents demanding an explanation. Naturally, I could give them none."

"Now, Mama—" Edward began.

"Don't 'Mama' me," interrupted the dowager. "Given your behavior, one might think you had reason not to wait to have a traditional wedding in a church with guests in attendance."

"We *were* married in a church," Edward clarified in a calm tone of explanation.

Ava cut him off with a slash of her hand. "Pish-tosh. I don't care if it was in a cathedral, since none of your loved ones were with you. Just tell me the two of you weren't . . ." Pausing, she cast a glance toward Esme, who had found her way into a chair some feet away and sat drawing. Ava lowered her voice. "Just assure me the pair of you did not *have* to wed."

Claire's lips parted, color flooding into her cheeks at the duchess's implication. Edward, on the other hand, tossed back his head and laughed.

"You may put your mind at ease, Mama," he said, recovering enough to speak. Reaching out, he wrapped an arm around Claire's waist and tugged her against his side. "Claire and I didn't have to marry, we wanted to marry. And don't blame her in any way. The whole affair was my idea, and once I'd made up my mind, there was no stopping me. Is that not so, dear?"

Claire met Edward's gaze. "Yes. He's most obstinate. Some might even say pigheaded, if it weren't so impolite."

Laughter rippled around the room. Edward's smile widened with a lack of repentance that put her in mind of his younger brother Lord Jack.

"She's obviously got our Ned figured out," quipped that same gentleman. "And has him wrapped around her little finger, if I don't miss my guess."

On that second point, Claire knew, Lord Jack was mistaken. Could he not see that she was the one all wrapped up and not the other way around?

Playing into his brother's remark, Edward continued, "That's right. Once I got her to say yes, I wasn't wasting another minute until I put my ring on her finger."

Ava's delicate brows furrowed. "But I thought she had already said yes? You've been engaged for months."

"I meant yes to not waiting," Edward said, making a swift recovery. "And you're right, it has been months and we didn't want to wait another year, just so we could invite half the Ton to the ceremony."

"You might have waited long enough at least to invite your family members," the dowager said. "The countess is quite put out. Apparently she had plans for a grand round of parties in the neighborhood that must now be canceled."

Poor Mama, Claire thought. Then again, just think how distressed her mother would have been had Claire's plan succeeded and Edward had jilted, rather than married, her. The thought swept away a large measure of her guilt. She was sorry, though, about her sisters not being bridesmaids. They must be mortally disappointed. She would have to think up some way of making recompense. New bonnets perhaps? And maybe a smart London frock or two. That ought to work wonders.

"As I've already told Claire," Edward said, "I'm perfectly

amenable to having another ceremony at Braebourne, but that shall be entirely up to her. We shall do as she wishes."

Ava gazed between Claire and Edward for a long moment, then she smiled. "Well, of course we shall. Claire is the Duchess of Clybourne and her word is gold. Now come kiss me, both of you. And no more 'Your Graces,' Claire. You are to call me Mama from this time forward."

Claire found herself enveloped, first by the dowager, and then by all the others in turn. By the time the hugs and congratulations were done, she was breathless and wreathed in smiles.

Just then a resounding, distinctly canine bark sounded from the hallway. Paws drummed over the hall runner before a large black-and-white spotted dog darted into the room at a near gallop.

The animal's whip-thin tail was on full wag, his pink tongue lolling out of his mouth with keen excitement. He barked again, as his sherry brown eyes locked on Edward, his joy uncontained. Bounding forward, he seemed ready to leap on his master and smother him with dog kisses.

But Edward stayed him with a look. "Zeus, heel."

The dog froze, body quivering as he struggled to contain his exuberance and do as he was commanded. Padding to Edward's side, he turned and sat.

Edward waited only a moment before bending down to stroke the dog's head and give his sleek back a hearty, two-handed rub.

The dog was clearly in heaven.

"Good boy," Edward praised. "Good Zeus. I've missed you. Have you missed me?"

The Dalmatian gave a loud bark, his tail wagging at top speed again.

Everyone laughed, Claire gazing on the tableau with melting affection. She loved animals. It would be good to have a dog in the house again. And from what Edward had told her, Braebourne was overrun with a variety of furry creatures. She looked forward to meeting them.

Footsteps pounded to a halt on the threshold, all eyes moving toward the footman standing in the doorway. "I'm ever so sorry, Your Grace," the man said, his chest straining for air, hands frantically trying to tug his livery into place. "He got away just after I came in from walkin' him. Must have heard you, since he lit out like a rocket. Never seen the like."

"Well, there's no harm done," Edward told the footman. "Zeus is behaving himself quite nicely now."

Realizing he wasn't in trouble after all, the footman bowed and withdrew.

Esme, having abandoned her drawing paper, ran across the room and dropped onto her knees next to the dog. Her blue muslin skirts fanned around her like a flower. Zeus gave her a welcoming lick as she wrapped her arms around his neck.

Giggling, Esme pressed her face to his side, then gazed up at Edward. "Thank you again for letting Zeus stay with Mama and me while we were at Jack and Grace's house. Even Ranunculus likes him and he's a cat! Zeus is the very best of dogs and you're the very best of brothers."

Edward smiled and briefly laid a hand on her head. "You're quite welcome, sweetheart. I'm glad he was such good company."

"What's this now," declared Jack, fists on his hips in mock indignation as he regarded his little sister. "I thought *I* was your favorite brother?"

"Oh, you are!" Esme declared with complete sincerity. "And Drake and Cade and Leo and Lawrence. You're all my favorite."

"That's one way not to hurt any of our feelings," Drake shot back with a laugh. "What a diplomat!"

"Indeed," Cade agreed. "Mayhap we should loan her out to the foreign service in a couple years. Or else find a worthy ambassador she can marry."

"I'm not marrying anyone!" Esme declared.

A fresh ripple of laughter went through the room at her impassioned statement.

Seeing the mutinous tilt to the girl's lower lip, and remembering her own recent opinion on the subject of marriage, Claire sent Esme a smile. "Of course you are not. Although you may come to change your mind in time, should you be fortunate enough to meet the right gentleman."

Esme sent her an inquiring look. "Is that what happened with you and Ned? He was the right gentleman?"

Claire paused, her gaze colliding with Edward's before moving away again. "Yes. Exactly so."

The girl smiled and stroked a palm over the dog. "I'm glad Ned married you. I'm going to enjoy having you for my sister."

Warmth blossomed in Claire's chest. "As shall I, Esme. As shall I."

After that, the conversation turned to more general subjects, family members breaking into smaller groups with Esme pulling Edward after her to show him several of her recent sketches. Zeus followed the pair, his tail starting up a new round of wagging.

Moments later, the dowager appeared at Claire's side. "I must tell you, child, how utterly adorable your hair is, even if it is a tad risqué."

"Oh. Thank you, Your Gr— Mama."

The dowager sent her a gentle smile. "I hear you cut it in order to take part in a prank. Do tell me all about this sojourn you and the twins made to Brooks's Club. The one that got them banished to Braebourne."

Claire's jaw dropped.

"Oh yes, I've heard the tale," Ava said. "News travels, even to the countryside, so I know perfectly well why my youngest sons aren't here with us all today. Not to worry though, they're scamps and the temporary set-down will do them nothing but good."

Claire closed her mouth, realizing the dowager was even shrewder than she had assumed. *What else*, Claire wondered, *does Ava Byron know? Good heavens, what do my parents know?* She would have to write again as soon as the opportunity presented itself.

"So, do tell?" the dowager said. "I understand you quite set everyone on their ears. Sounds like me as a girl, when I was still up to my old wild ways."

Old wild ways? How astonishing.

Suddenly Claire knew she was going to love her mother-in-law. With a relieved laugh, she began her story.

The next week floated past as though it was borne aloft on wings. The Byrons were a merry crew and kept Claire busy and entertained from morning until night.

On that first evening after her and Edward's return from Oxfordshire, everyone gathered for a rousing dinner party at home. Cook outdid herself, preparing a selection of viands fit for the King himself. And for dessert there was another gorgeous wedding cake, served amid a wealth of champagne toasts that celebrated her and Edward's happiness and health.

The meal concluded, they adjourned to the drawing room, where Mallory and Esme played and sang, and Cade enthralled them all with a masterful reading from *The Arabian Nights*. In honor of the occasion, Esme had been allowed to join the adults for dinner and stay up far later than usual. By the time Cade finished, she was dozing off, despite her best attempts to stay awake. Seeing her weariness, everyone agreed they ought to retire for the night.

With that in mind, Ava announced that she was removing from the duchess's quarters immediately. "Those rooms belong to you now, Claire," the dowager said. "I shall be quite comfortable elsewhere." Ava went on, informing everyone that she and Esme would reside with Jack, Grace and baby Nicola in their town house on Upper Brook Street—for the time being at least.

It was decided that Mallory would remain with them at Clybourne House, since it was far too much bother for her to move so late in the Season. As for Cade and Meg, they too had their own town house but would be within easy reach, since their residence was only four blocks away.

"Don't worry," Ava laughingly told Claire and Edward, when they urged her and Esme to stay. "We'll all be dropping in on you so often that you'll think we're still living here."

As the days slid past, Claire found that Ava was right. Meg and Grace, with whom Claire immediately became friends, often stopped by in the afternoon. They usually brought the babies along to coddle and admire, which Claire did with the eager affection of a devoted aunt.

Claire developed a strong fondness for Edward's brothers as well, the men as dangerously charming as their eldest sibling, and not at all abashed about turning that charm to good purpose when it suited them.

But it was Edward she loved. Edward who held her completely in thrall, particularly at night when he came to her bed.

To her great joy and relief, they never slept apart. Despite her original fears, Edward was every bit as passionate as he'd been in Oxfordshire. Often during the day, he would find some excuse to steal several kisses or lead her off where they could do quite a bit more. And in the privacy of their bedchamber, he was nearly insatiable, taking her every night and usually again in the morning just as she was awakening.

Seated now in the Clybourne House breakfast room across from Mallory, she couldn't help but smile as she bit into a square of buttered toast. Her body was still limber and glowing after a delicious bout of love play early this morning. Forcing down a blush at the memory, she reached for her tea.

"So what do you say to ices at Gunter's this afternoon?" Mallory suggested. "I thought we could do a bit of shopping first, then stop there for a treat. I'm sure Meg and Grace would be happy to join us, and Mama if she hasn't already made plans with some of her friends."

"That sounds delightful and will give us plenty of time to relax and have dinner before the theater tonight."

Edward was escorting them to Drury Lane this evening, and Claire was looking forward to the excursion. Despite the dozens of invitations that had been pouring in, she'd accepted very few of them. The Ton was in a near foment over her and Edward's hasty marriage, but rather than satisfy their curiosity, she'd been content to exercise her right as a new bride and stay home.

She'd just finished eating a spoonful of fresh blueberries when Croft gave a quiet tap on the door and strode inside bearing a silver salver.

"These just arrived for you, Your Grace. And there is a letter for Lady Mallory as well."

Accepting the small stack of correspondence with a nod of thanks, Claire handed Mallory's letter across to her. "More invitations, I suspect," Claire said.

Resigned to the task, she opened the first missive and began to read the enclosed correspondence. A laugh escaped her, as she reached inside to withdraw a pair of engraved note cards. "Look, Mallory, my Almack's vouchers have been restored. Apparently the patronesses have had a change of heart now that I am a duchess. Edward predicted as much, but I never imagined they would rescind their edict quite so quickly."

Glancing up, she expected to find Mallory grinning in shared amusement.

Instead, Mallory's face was set like a mask, fixed as stone and drained of every hint of color. Unblinking, she stared at the letter in her hand, a dull, glassy expression in her aquamarine eyes that made Claire's chest squeeze tight with fear.

"What is it?" she asked. "What has happened? Mallory, are you ill? What's wrong?"

But Mallory didn't answer or move, her body stiff and lifeless.

Standing, Claire circled the table. She laid a hand on Mallory's shoulder and realized that her friend had turned frigid with cold. "What is it, dear? Tell me, please. Mallory, do you hear me?"

Suddenly, as if only then becoming aware of her surroundings, Mallory gave a raw, keening cry. Crumpling in on herself, she let the letter fall to the floor.

Trembling and more worried than she could express, Claire retrieved the missive. She gasped softly as she read the words, a tear sliding over her cheek.

Major Hargreaves had fallen in battle.

Mallory's fiancé was dead.

Chapter 25

"Write as soon as you reach Braebourne," Claire told Ava three days later as they stood in front of the coach parked outside Clybourne House. "I want to know you're safe and had no difficulties on your journey."

Breaking off, she frowned over at Mallory, who stood in solitary grief not far away, her skin white as alabaster against the stark black of her mourning gown and bonnet. She'd barely spoken a word since receiving the news of Hargreaves's death, taking to her bed to weep in jagged, agonizing bouts before lapsing again into long spans of silence.

Wiping moisture from her own eyes, Claire turned back to Ava.

"We'll be fine, I'm sure," the dowager said in a low, sorrowful tone. "I think home will do Mallory a world of good. She thinks of him too much here. The country air will help, that and time."

"I would come with you," Claire told her, "but Edward

says he can't afford to leave Town right now. Business concerns, I am given to understand."

What business concerns specifically, he hadn't shared with her, only the fact that he needed to remain in London for the time being. They would join Mallory, Ava, and Esme at Braebourne in a few weeks, once his obligations were satisfied.

Newly married, and still unsure at times of the strength of their relationship, Claire didn't feel right about leaving without Edward. Not when they hadn't even been married a month. Not when her place was here at his side.

"There's nothing you can do," Ava said on a murmur quiet enough not to carry to Mallory. "She has to grieve in her own way and get over the shock of losing him. We're to stop at his family home for the service on our way to Braebourne. Mallory will bear up somehow, but it's going to be hard."

Claire nodded, swallowing past the lump in her throat.

"I thank God every day that my Cade came back, despite his injuries," Ava continued. "And that Edward knows his duty too well to go off and get himself shot. I've told the other boys I won't have them buying commissions and chasing after glory. Perhaps it's selfish of me, but I want them close and safe, not bleeding and dying in some benighted foreign land."

Claire nodded, fiercely glad for once that Edward took his responsibilities so seriously and that she wouldn't need to fear losing him, at least not the way Mallory had lost her major. Her chest ached at the thought. "I wish there was something I could do for her. I don't know how to help."

"Just love her and be her friend. That's all any of us can do. Now, I want you to stay and enjoy the rest of the Season." When Claire opened her mouth to protest, Ava hushed her. "No, I insist. We shall all need your most cheerful letters telling us of the best doings here in Town, and all the latest scandals and gossip. The distraction will do all of us good, particularly Mallory."

Nodding, Claire agreed. "Then I shall strive to make my correspondence as exciting as Scheherazade's tales to the sultan."

Amid tearful hugs from the whole family, who'd gathered there to say their farewells, the three Byron ladies and Zeus climbed into the coach. Mallory seemed almost like a sleepwalker, the gentle sunshine gone from her eyes.

Claire was grateful for Edward's arm around her shoulder as they drove away, crumpling against him the minute the coach was gone.

With Mallory absent, an unfamiliar quiet settled through Clybourne House over the following two weeks. A mourning wreath was hung in honor of the major and notes of sympathy sent to his nearest relations. As promised, Claire kept up a faithful correspondence, writing daily letters to Mallory and Ava, as she informed them of the latest news about Town.

Ava replied.

Mallory did not.

Claire also exchanged letters with her mother and sisters, who were uniformly disappointed that she hadn't had a wedding. Ella, however, said she thought the whole thing was frightfully romantic and hoped someday soon to meet a dashing lord and be swept off her feet. In another missive, her mother gave her a rather harsh rebuke, expressing concern over some reports she'd received of Claire behaving in a most shocking manner. Mama said, however, that if the duke didn't mind, then she supposed she couldn't either. Still, she found it mortifying to be the subject of local talk and hoped this would be the last.

Claire's father wrote a single note. It said:

Relieved you came to your senses and married Clybourne. Now give us a grandchild and stop upsetting your mother.

With promises to visit as soon as convenient, Claire smoothed over any remaining difficulties with her family.

As for herself, she joined in what remained of the Season with as much enthusiasm as she could muster. Despite the mid-July heat, there were plenty of entertainments from which to choose, garden parties, routs and balls. Soon, it would be time to depart for the country, and the Ton was making one last push to wring every last bit of merriment out of the days that remained.

Cade, Meg, and little Maximillian had already departed for Braebourne with promises to see everyone soon. To Claire's delight, Jack and Grace remained. Often they accompanied Edward and her to whatever evening function they had all decided to attend.

Tonight was the Throcklys' ball, Claire attired in a gown of amethyst silk with tasseled, Vandyke half sleeves. In her cropped curls, she wore jeweled hair clips fashioned in the shape of wood violets.

Although the windows had been thrown open to let in the stale air that passed for a breeze, the ballroom remained warm, a crush of perfumed bodies and hundreds of burning candles making it nearly oppressive.

In need of a respite, Claire withdrew to a safe corner and opened her silk fan. Waving it in front of her face, she let the tiny draught ease her flushed cheeks. For the briefest moment, she closed her eyes.

"You looked in need of refreshment," said a gentle, feminine voice. "So I brought you this."

Claire's eyelids opened to find Grace standing at her side. Glancing up, she smiled, not at all minding her sister-in-law's impressive height. It put some people off, but Claire thought the additional inches gave Grace a refined, almost goddesslike air. Jack certainly seemed to agree, an expression of adoration on his face whenever he gazed at his wife.

"Lemonade!" Claire said. "Oh, you are too good." Taking the glass, she drank enthusiastically. "And it's so wonderfully cool. Are those ice chips?"

Grace nodded and took a sip from her own glass. "The servants just brought out a new pitcher and I was happy to spirit away the first two glasses. Come, why don't we have a seat."

"You aren't dancing?"

"No," Grace said. "I never really enjoy standing up with anyone except Jack and he's in the card room. No doubt he's winning every hand too, even if they are only playing for penny stakes."

Claire had learned that Jack had quite the affinity for cards. She would have to play him one of these times to see just how good her brother-in-law really was, and if she could hold her own against him.

Finding chairs, they sat down.

"I shouldn't ask, since it's really none of my business," Grace began. "But are you feeling all right?"

"Of course. I'm a little tired, but that's because of so many parties, I'm sure."

"Quite likely. Then again, it could be something else."

"Something else? What do you mean?"

"Nothing." Grace sipped her lemonade. "But if you start feeling queasy in the mornings, we should talk again. Before I had Nicola, I was lamentably ignorant about such matters. It took me weeks to figure out I was enceinte."

Stars above, does Grace think I'm with child? But no,

it's impossible. Well, not impossible, she amended, thinking how often she and Edward made love. *But far, far too soon.*

"I'm not," Claire told her.

Grace gave her a look, then smiled. "Probably just this stuffy room. Still, if you have questions, remember my offer."

"I shall. Thank you."

A baby, Claire thought. The very idea made her giddy and nervous. Did she want Edward's baby?

Yes, came the resounding answer. She would like to have his child, his heir. If she was expecting, she hoped it was a boy in spite of Edward's earlier assurances that the baby's gender wouldn't matter. Even so, she was certain Grace's concerns were premature and that she wasn't with child.

Without realizing, her gaze went in search of Edward, scanning the thick crowd for his familiar dark head and powerful shoulders.

A smile curved her lips as she found him. Then fell away seconds later when she noticed him deep in conversation with a beautiful brunette. But not Lady Bettis, who she knew had left for the country some days ago.

Since her marriage to Edward, she'd come to realize that she had no reason for jealousy on that score. Felicia Bettis might still want Edward, but he'd made it plain he didn't return her feelings. In fact, when Lady Bettis had approached one evening to offer congratulations on their nuptials, he'd seemed bored at first, then annoyed when she lingered longer than ordinary manners demanded. To Claire's delight and relief, he'd given the other woman the cut direct, abruptly turning his back to lead Claire away.

But now there was another brunette, a woman she did not know. An unpleasant tightness lodged in her chest as she watched him smile at the other woman. *But I am only being ridiculous*, Claire told herself. They were at a ball. It was only natural he would talk with any number of women, no matter how attractive they might be.

Still, that didn't mean she had to like it.

"Grace," she asked, striving for a casual tone. "Who is that woman chatting with Edward?"

Claire watched as Grace sought him out. Suddenly Grace's back grew stiff, an expression of intense dislike crossing her face. "*That* is Philipa Stockton, and I can say without reservation that you do not want to make her acquaintance."

"Oh, I see."

Grace met her gaze. "I am sure you do not, but since you're bound to hear the news at some point, I might as well tell you that she used to be Jack's mistress. It was before he and I were married and makes no difference now. Jack loves me and I trust him implicitly, but still, I can't help but detest her."

"Of course you do." Reaching out, she patted Grace's hand. "If I were you, I'd scratch her eyes out."

Grace stared for a moment, then laughed. "I like the sound of that."

Their conversation moved on to other subjects, and outwardly Claire relaxed. All the while, though, she couldn't help but be aware of Edward and Lady Stockton. What were they talking about? For that matter, why was he talking to her at all? Unless there was something between them. It wasn't unknown for a pair of brothers to be attracted to the same woman. Once Philipa Stockton had broken up with Jack, had she gone into Edward's arms instead? Claire had always suspected he had a mistress, but she'd assumed the liaison was over.

But what if it wasn't? What if they'd only been taking a break while he got married and attended to his duty?

Abruptly, nausea churned sickeningly in her stomach, the lemonade she'd drunk burning beneath her breastbone.

Grace gave her a probing look. "Are you all right? You seem awfully pale of a sudden."

"I'm fine."

"You're sure?" Grace didn't look convinced.

Claire nodded.

But suddenly, she realized, she wasn't sure of anything. Not anymore.

A few hours later, Edward sat on the pale almond green velvet divan in Claire's dressing room and watched her brush her hair.

She wore a pink, summer-weight dressing gown with a matching diaphanous silk nightgown underneath. He was also dressed for bed, attired in a dark blue silk robe that Claire had once said she liked because it complemented his eyes.

After he'd strolled through the door that connected their rooms, she'd sent her maid away, saying she would finish her toilette on her own. Her cropped locks had grown about an inch this past month, but were still short enough that a few brushstrokes were all that was required to tame them. Even so, she kept brushing, as though she was using the rhythmic movement to calm herself.

"You're awfully quiet tonight," Edward observed, as he lounged against a pair of the decorative feather pillows that matched the divan. "Is anything wrong?"

The brush hesitated for a fraction of an instant before she resumed the stroke. "Only tired. It's late," she said.

"So it is. Although no later than it often is after we've returned from a ball."

She didn't reply.

Taking five more strokes, she stopped and laid the brush

on her satinwood dressing table. Her hair settled in short, luxurious waves, shiny and gleaming with the warm, rich color of the sun.

Getting to his feet, he moved behind her, then ran his fingers over her hair, savoring its full, silky texture. Bending down, he placed his lips against her neck to nuzzle a spot just under her jawline where he knew she loved to be touched. An answering shiver rippled over her skin before she leaned slightly away.

"I saw you talking to a woman tonight," she said.

He paused, gliding his thumb over the delicate curve of her ear. "Did you? And who is it you mean, since I believe I spoke with any number of ladies this evening?"

"Don't be flippant, Your Grace. I was told her name is Stockton. Philipa Stockton."

His fingers paused ever so briefly. "I may have spoken with her for a few minutes."

"About what?"

He paused again. "Nothing of any particular interest. Small talk, as I recall."

Actually, he'd been probing for information, using a variety of conversational gambits in an effort to persuade Philipa to reveal something about her association with Dumont. But she'd proven irritatingly closemouthed, leaving him unable to garner anything useful—at least not without having to completely tip his hand. All in all, their conversation had been an utter waste of time.

"Just small talk, hmm?" she said.

"Yes. Why do you ask?" Gliding the edge of one finger over her cheek, he pressed a kiss to her temple.

She shrugged. "No reason. Curiosity, I suppose." A small silence descended. "She's very comely, isn't she? Some might even say beautiful."

"Some might, I suppose."

"But not you?"

"No, definitely not me." Straightening, he turned her to face him. "What is this all about, Claire?" When she wouldn't meet his gaze, an absurd thought occurred. "Surely you're not jealous?"

"Me, jealous!" she retorted. "Of course not. Don't be ridiculous."

"My God, you *are* jealous!"

Tossing back his head, he laughed. From her expression, though, he could tell that hadn't been the right thing to do.

"I see nothing the least bit humorous about this." Her blue eyes blazed with temper.

"Well, you would, if you knew what I thought of Philipa Stockton."

Jumping to her feet, she moved away. "Oh, and what is that?" Swinging toward him, she folded her arms across her chest and locked her gaze with his.

"That she may bear the title of lady, but that she doesn't often behave like one. She has the morals of a cat and the claws to go with them, however pleasing a façade she may try to present to the world."

Claire gave a delicate sniff. "Some men like that, I'm sure."

"Yes, some do. Quite a few, in fact, if the rumors about Lady Stockton are to be believed." Reaching out, he tugged her into his arms, her body rigid against his own. "Claire, I don't know why you've gotten this maggot in your head, but you have nothing to worry about. The only thing between Philipa Stockton and me is the fact that we occasionally attend the same balls and share an infrequent bit of mundane conversation."

A measure of the starch came out of her shoulders, her fingers lifting to slide over the lapel on his robe. "You just seemed rather . . . attentive to her."

Did I? Claire is far too perceptive for her own good, Edward thought.

He wished he could simply tell her the truth, but his secret dealings on behalf of the War Office were not something he was at liberty to discuss. Nor did his work for the government have anything to do with his marriage—or at least it wasn't supposed to.

Catching hold of her hand, he pressed a kiss against the center of her palm. "If I did seem attentive, it was only because I was trying to listen politely. With some people, that takes more effort than others."

Her lips twitched, and before she could quash the impulse, she smiled. "I suppose that makes sense."

The corners of his own mouth curved upward, his hands moving slowly over her supple curves. Angling his head, he dropped a line of kisses across her cheek and down the slim, soft column of her throat.

"Anyway," he murmured, cupping her lush bottom to pull her against the hard length of his erection. "When would I have time to be with anyone but you? Or the energy?" Capturing her mouth, he gave her a long, decadent kiss that made the blood rush straight out of his head. Need throbbed insistently in his groin, tempting him to take her right where they stood.

"Oh, I don't know," she said on a low, breathless sigh. "You can be awfully energetic when the mood suits you."

Slipping her hands inside his robe, she stroked his bare chest, pausing to play with his flat nipples in a way that drove him wild.

"Well, it suits me now," he told her, his voice rough with desire.

Sliding the dressing gown off her shoulders, he let it drop to the floor. Her nightgown followed seconds later, together with his robe, leaving both of them naked. Sweeping her into his arms, he carried her across to the bedroom in a few long strides.

Lowering her onto the mattress, he came down next to her, taking her mouth with an amorous passion that left both of them shaking. He caressed her, glorying to the sensation of her small hands as they roamed over his skin with the same abandon as his own.

Then he couldn't wait a moment more, want pounding inside him, leaving him gasping beneath its merciless grip. Parting her legs, he thrust inside, sighing as her sleek, wet warmth closed around him.

Setting a relentless pace, he plunged deeper, harder, faster, listening to her pleasured cries as he drove her higher, then higher still. She was moaning, her nails digging in painful half moons into his back, when she claimed her release.

He followed quickly after, thoughts dimming as the most profound pleasure swept through him, pulling him down like an undertow from which he had no will to escape.

Lying together in a tangle of limbs, he fought for breath, for sanity, hearing Claire do the same. Rolling her over so she lay on top of him, he lay with eyes closed.

Five minutes passed.

Then ten.

In spite of the late hour, neither one of them fell asleep. Neither did his body, which began to stir again, seemingly as hungry as ever.

"Apparently, I *am* full of energy," he remarked.

Smiling, Claire arched against him. "In that case, I think we should find out how much fire you've got left."

Grinning, he showed her.

Chapter 26

Claire settled into a happy routine over the next couple of weeks, content in the knowledge that Edward wanted her—and only her—even if he still never made any mention of love.

But surely he must feel some deeper regard for me, she found herself thinking as she dressed for the evening. After all, how could a man show such sweet devotion and not care? How could a man make such tender, soul-stirring love and be without real affection?

That was the problem, however. Did he feel only affection? Or was it possible that he might finally be falling in love with her? With all her heart, she wanted to believe he loved her. But cowardly as it might seem, she couldn't bring herself to ask him.

Every day the question rose to her lips. *Do you love me, Edward?*

But what if he said no?

What if he looked at her with regretful resignation and told her to be a good wife, a dutiful duchess, and not worry herself over such foolish emotions as love? They were getting along well these days, he would say. What more did she need?

And so, rather than confronting him, she remained silent, patient and secretly hopeful, allowing herself to drift in a pleasant limbo that demanded no more than what each day might bring.

This evening, for instance, Edward was taking her to the opera, an outing she'd been anticipating for days. Once there, they would be able to sit together in the ducal box, listening and relaxing, and if she had her way, holding hands beneath whatever concealing shadows they might find.

For the excursion, she'd chosen an elegant gown of dramatic ruby silk that revealed a rather shocking amount of bosom. When she'd purchased the dress as part of her trousseau, she'd worried it would be far too sophisticated and revealing. But tonight the gown seemed exactly right. Just what she wanted in order to earn Edward's admiring, sensual gaze.

Drawing on her long white opera gloves, she crossed to pick up her gold opera glasses and slip them inside a tiny beaded reticule. She wore a small diamond tiara, the piece one of a multitude of stunning jewels that belonged to the Duchess of Clybourne. She was just turning to go downstairs when a quick tap came on the connecting door and Edward strolled inside.

Claire barely noticed her maid quietly depart, her attention focused squarely on Edward. Stopping, he took a moment to rake her with a hungry gaze she'd come to recognize and enjoy.

"My, don't you look exquisite," he said in a throaty voice. "Delicious enough to eat."

Her smile widened, her body growing loose and warm despite all her exposed skin—or maybe because of it. But then she noticed his attire. As usual, he was elegantly turned out. Instead of black evening attire, however, he wore a brown superfine coat, white linen shirt, cream waistcoat and fawn trousers—smart-looking, but in no way appropriate for the opera.

"Why aren't you dressed?" she asked, approaching him on a sibilant rustle of skirts. "We'll be late, if you don't hurry."

His features grew even. "About the opera, I'm sorry, my dear, but I'm going to have to beg off this evening."

Disappointment wiped the smile from her lips. "But why? I thought everything was arranged."

"And so it is." Reaching out, he took her hands in his. "Jack and Grace will be here any minute, and Drake has agreed to act in my stead as your escort."

Drake?

She liked Drake a great deal and under any other circumstances would be very glad for his company. But she'd planned to spend the evening with Edward, and she certainly hadn't worn this dress for Drake.

"And where will you be?" she asked.

"Out on a matter of business."

Her brows drew tight, wondering what could be so urgent that it couldn't wait until morning. "What sort of business?"

"The unavoidable kind." Tugging her closer, he claimed her mouth for a kiss that was both slow and sultry. "Have a good time," he said, as he eased back. "And I truly am sorry that I won't be with you this evening."

"It's all right." She forced a smile. "How late do you expect you'll be?"

"I'm not sure, so don't wait up."

"You'll join me though, when you get home?"

He kissed the center of her palm. "Of course. There's nowhere else I'd want to be."

Abruptly reassured, she sent him on his way.

Of course Edward has business concerns, she told herself. In addition to the substantial number of landed interests and estates he owned, she knew he had an extensive portfolio of investments. She'd even heard him mention interests in a few plantations in the Caribbean and South America.

She imagined that while she was at the opera listening to arias, he would be at one of his clubs. He and several stuffy gentlemen would sit around a table, smoking and drinking port as they pored over a variety of dry facts and figures.

Realizing the two of them couldn't live in each other's pockets, she determined to enjoy herself in spite of Edward's absence. Forcing a new smile, she left the room.

Hours later, Edward let himself into Clybourne House. Covering a yawn with a hand, he started up the stairs, glad to be home after spending half the night in the Seven Dials neighborhood, one of London's most notorious and dangerous slums.

Earlier, he'd received a report about fresh activity going on in the row house on St. Giles Street, the one known to have once hidden French operatives. For months it had remained abandoned. But all that had changed two nights before when the bored team set to watch the place had suddenly noticed candlelight coming from within, and the shape of shadowy figures moving behind the ragged curtains.

Before notifying him, they'd made sure the individuals going in and out of the property weren't simply vagrants or prostitutes who'd decided to use the space without the bother of paying rent. Assured the house was indeed being employed as a rendezvous point once again, they had sent word Edward's way.

Hoping he might see something—or someone—of interest, Edward had made the trip across Town. Seated this evening with one of the men in an upstairs room across the bleak street that stank of refuse and other unmentionables, he'd watched for renewed signs of life. But to his frustration, no one came. Only desperate, hollow-eyed doxies walked the streets and alleys, along with drunks, thieves and other unsavory types, who weren't up to anything good at that time of night.

At four in the morning, Edward decided to give up and come home.

Yet his gut told him he'd been close tonight and that the revived activity in the house had something to do with his search for the mysterious Wolf.

And the mole?

With persistence and a bit of luck, perhaps he would soon find them both.

Inside his bedchamber, Edward stripped off his clothes, then washed with the water his valet had left out for him. Toweling his face and hands dry, he pulled on his robe and walked barefoot and silent to Claire's room.

Slipping into bed beside her, he tugged the covers over them both before easing an arm around her to pull her close.

"You're home," she murmured, rousing slightly.

"Shh, go back to sleep." Brushing a gentle kiss across her forehead, he stroked a hand along her arm.

She rested her head on his chest and snuggled closer. "How was your meeting?"

"Long and boring. How was the opera?"

"Long and boring too, without you there."

"I'm sorry I was away," he said.

And Edward realized that he genuinely was sorry. Always before when he'd returned from conducting surveillance and hunting spies, he'd been left with a deep sense of excitement and satisfaction. He was doing something worthwhile for his country. But more, he was doing something for himself, the game and the chase providing a kind of thrill he'd never found anywhere else.

Yet tonight, he realized he would rather have spent the evening with his wife at the opera than sit in that lonely room in a depressing section of London, watching for potential French spies.

Of course, he wasn't about to give up this assignment; he'd invested far too much of himself in it to quit now. He wanted to see it through with as much haste as possible.

But if there was no assignment, if he was free to leave Town, he knew he would close up the house tomorrow and take Claire away. They'd go to one of his estates in the north to enjoy the rest of the honeymoon he'd had to cut short. Then he would take her to Braebourne and let her enjoy the beauty of her new home.

Their home.

Needing her with a sudden, almost violent ache, he rolled her to her back, his hands sliding beneath her nightgown to pull it up and off her body. She gave a murmur of surprise, then pleasure, sighing as he caressed her with ardent strokes and frenzied kisses that quickly roused her desire to a fevered pitch. Sheathing himself inside her with a deep, penetrating thrust, he wrapped her securely in his arms. Then to his delight and hers, he proceeded to make up for every moment he'd been gone.

The final days of the Season arrived with a wave of oppressive early August heat that persuaded many of the Ton to pack their bags and depart for their country estates.

Claire and Edward remained at Clybourne House, however—Edward's continuing business concerns keeping him in the city.

Far too frequently for Claire's taste, Edward would

excuse himself from whatever evening entertainment had been scheduled and be gone late into the night. When she pressed him for more details, his answers were often vague and unsatisfying.

Even when he did attend a ball with her, as he had this evening, he seemed distracted, as if his thoughts and interests lay elsewhere. At first, she hadn't let his absences trouble her, but now she was beginning to wonder, and worry.

Where was he going?

Worse, with whom?

She waved a fan over her face, savoring the small breeze the painted silk-covered staves made. She ought not to have come tonight, since she was feeling less than her usual robust self. Of course, she suspected the cause, and if the advice she'd ended up seeking from Grace and her own calculations proved true, then she was with child.

She'd missed her menses this month and her breasts were unusually tender, both signs, Grace assured her, of early pregnancy. Bursting with excitement over the news, she'd wanted to tell Edward. But he'd been away again the evening she'd realized she might be enceinte, and in the couple of days that followed there never seemed a good time to share her thoughts. So she hugged her speculation to herself, even as she concealed her increasing worry over Edward and his nighttime sojourns.

Gazing at him where he stood across the room, conversing with a trio of gentlemen, she wondered if tonight might be the right time to try again. He'd been in a good humor on the carriage ride over. Maybe she would tell him on the way back.

Accepting a drink from a passing servant, she took a sip and was instantly sorry. The beverage was far too sweet, almost sickeningly so. Turning to set the punch aside, she noticed a footman approach Edward and hand him a note.

Excusing himself, Edward moved away to read the missive. Without a change in expression, which oddly enough she found disconcerting, he tucked the note inside his coat, then rejoined the others.

When the time for supper arrived, Edward approached her to ask if she would very much mind leaving early.

"No, of course not," she said. Actually, she would be relieved, since a few extra hours' sleep sounded wonderful.

Inside the coach, she thought again about telling Edward her news, but each time she opened her mouth to speak, she closed it again. Edward's mood was quiet and preoccupied, as if he was deeply lost in his own thoughts. Unsure what sort of reception she might get, she decided to wait a bit longer.

Rather than stop in the family drawing room for a dish of tea for her and a glass of port for Edward, as was their usual custom, they instead each went to their respective bedchambers. She half expected not to see him again that night, but he came to her right after she'd climbed into bed.

Moments after he joined her, he pulled her nightgown over her head and tossed it toward the foot of the bed. "I don't know why you bother with these, since I just take them right back off," he murmured.

Then, before she had time to respond, he was kissing her, his hands and mouth moving over her body with a skill that made everything but him fade away. Breathless and floating on a surfeit of pleasure a while later, he spooned in behind her so they could both go to sleep.

She'd just drifted off, when she awakened again to the sensation of him easing slowly from the bed. Her lips parted to call out, but she held back, listening as he gathered up his robe and left the room.

Getting to her feet moments later, she pulled on her nightgown, robe and slippers, then moved silently across the room. Cracking the door open just enough to see into the hallway beyond, she waited. She was beginning to feel like a complete simpleton and was about to return to bed, when Edward appeared, exiting his bedchamber dressed in dark trousers and coat.

So he is going out! she thought with a lump in her throat.

Waiting until he was far enough ahead that he wouldn't notice her, she followed, tiptoeing after him on silent, slippered feet. Her pursuit led her to a quiet side entrance that went out to the mews. Watching him through a small window, she saw him stride into the stable. A few minutes later, he rode out, Jupiter's hooves clattering against the bricks.

Whirling, she pressed a hand between her breasts and drew in a ragged breath.

Where has he gone?

And who is he meeting?

Two questions whose answer she wasn't sure she wanted to know.

Trembling, she returned upstairs.

A short while before dawn, Edward let himself into his bedroom. Striding into his dressing room, he peeled off his clothes and washed, bathing away all traces of horseflesh that might linger from his evening ride. Flinging his used towel into a corner, he reached for his robe and pulled it back on.

Yawning, he walked barefoot toward Claire's room.

At least the night had proven productive.

Earlier at the ball, he'd received word that his men had intercepted an operative coming out of the row house on St. Giles. In the agent's possession, they'd discovered a leather pouch containing a thousand pounds in Bank of England notes, instructions that appeared to be a wish list of sorts requesting intelligence on British troop strengths and officers' lists, and the partial coordinates to a rendezvous point.

A bit of forceful persuasion yielded the fact that the rest of the coordinates were scheduled to appear in code in tomorrow's *Morning Chronicle*, and that once they were retrieved, the operative was to ride to the meeting place for an agreed-upon exchange.

His contact's name was Wolf!

Finally, the break they'd been seeking, Edward thought, as he opened the door to Claire's bedchamber. Right now, though, he didn't have time to indulge in further speculation. Instead, he needed a few hours' sleep, since tomorrow—today now—was sure to be a busy one.

Claire was lying on her side, turned away from him. Taking care not to disturb her, he slid into the bed.

"Edward?" she asked in a thick, quiet voice.

"Sorry to awaken you."

A small silence fell. "Where have you been?"

He paused for a long moment. "Just downstairs. I couldn't sleep, so I went to the library to read."

"Oh," she whispered.

When she said no more, he assumed she'd fallen back to sleep. Curling up behind her, he did the same.

Claire pressed a fist to her mouth to keep from making any sound. A pair of tears slid over her cheeks, but she refused to let herself cry in earnest. Later, she would give way, but not now, not with Edward sleeping only at her back.

He lied to me, she thought, pain wedged like a knife between her ribs.

She'd always thought Edward told only the truth, but apparently she'd been mistaken. Not only did he lie, he did it with a smooth and confident ease. And if he'd lied to her about leaving the house tonight, what other tales had he spun? What other deceptions had she so trustingly believed?

She could confront him, shake him awake and demand to know where he'd gone and with whom. But he would probably just lie again. And even if he didn't, did she really want to hear the truth?

For in spite of his previous assurances, she couldn't help but wonder if he did keep a mistress here in Town.

Was it Philipa Stockton?

Or another woman?

Yet even if he'd been honest in that regard and he wasn't having an affair, it didn't take back his false words. Or fix her broken faith in him—and their marriage.

Choking back a sob, she bit her lip to keep from crying aloud. Fearing she might wake him, she curled in upon herself and held as still as she could.

Why had she ever let herself weaken? Why had she married him when she'd known where it could lead?

I always knew he'd break my heart, she thought.

And now he has.

Chapter 27

Without pausing long enough to do more than take a cup of coffee, Edward dressed the next morning, then went in search of the newspaper.

He'd left Claire sleeping, her winsome face pressed with a kind of weary peace against the pillows. He told her maid not to wake Claire and to let her sleep as long as she liked.

Carrying the *Morning Chronicle* into his study, he closed the door, then took a seat at his desk. Methodically, he began scanning each page, looking for an announcement or other likely item that might contain the encrypted message.

Finding one, he unlocked his top desk drawer and withdrew a small black book, which contained the cipher key Drake had created. Opening it, he set to work.

His first try proved useless and his second as well. But then he used the key on an advertisement for ladies' skin lightener—guaranteed to erase blemishes and freckles in only five applications—and he had something viable. When he put his new find together with the decoded message obtained from the agent, the date, time and location of the rendezvous suddenly came clear, along with a great deal more.

For long seconds, he stared, his mind racing over what he'd revealed. Puzzle pieces began clicking into place, new possibilities taking shape as a flood of answers sped through his mind.

And suddenly he knew.

Suddenly he felt sure that tonight he would catch more than a Wolf, he would catch a mole!

"I'm sorry, my dear," Edward told Claire later that afternoon, as she sat on the drawing room sofa, "but another matter of business has come up. I'm afraid I shall have to beg off from our dinner at the Mortons this evening."

Without glancing up, Claire drew a length of blue silk thread through her sewing. "Oh, that's a shame. Especially since I hear they are going to be serving fresh peach ices, the best of the Season."

He smiled. "Then I shall be doubly sorry to have missed such a treat. Mayhap Cook can make some ice cream for us one evening when we are at home?"

She pulled another stitch through her embroidery. "I'll be certain to add the sweet to next week's menu."

"I cannot wait until then. Well, I have a few matters I must see to before I leave. I may be very late tonight, so don't wait up."

She sent him a smile. "All right. I hope your meeting isn't dreadfully dull."

He laughed. "I'm sure it shall be both dreadful and dull."

Walking to her, he bent down for a kiss. Her mouth was stiff at first, but then she closed her eyes and kissed him back. He was considering the pleasure of indulging in a second buss when he decided he'd better stop while he still had the willpower. "Have a good evening," he said, "and I'll see you in the morning."

Turning, he strode from the room.

Claire stabbed her needle deep into the cloth, her jaw clenched with anger, as she shot a narrow-eyed glare after him.

Mendacious cur!

How dare he lie to her again, and with such an affable smile on his face while he did it. There wasn't any meeting tonight, she knew that much. At least not one that had aught to do with business. As for his real destination, the possibilities made her stomach flip over with a sick twist.

How dare he kiss her as well, as though everything between them was fine. Although she supposed it was for him. When he'd bent down and covered her lips with his, she'd wanted to give him a good, hard slap across the face. Instead, she'd held still. Then she'd turned weak and wanting, responding to the undeniable pleasure of his touch in spite of her fury and despair. Even aware of his lies, she still wanted him, still loved him too.

But that didn't mean she wasn't hurt and furious. Nor did it mean she had to sit quietly and accept the situation as meekly as a lamb. Suddenly she realized that no matter how much pain it might cause, she had to know where he was going tonight.

Assuming she could find out, that was.

She waited patiently for Edward to depart, using the time between to pen her excuses for the Mortons' dinner. He wasn't the only one who could change his plans.

At a few minutes past six, she saw Edward leave, watching through the window as he drove away. Only then did she ring for Croft.

"There is something I forgot to mention to His Grace," she told the butler with a casual smile. "He's meeting on business tonight. Did he happen to mention where?"

"No, Your Grace. I can try sending a man after him, but I'm not sure if it will serve."

She kept the smile on her face despite her disappointment. "No matter. It can wait after all, I'm sure. Would you see that this note is delivered immediately?"

"Of course, Your Grace."

Taking the missive, Croft bowed and withdrew.

Hands tightened into fists at her sides, she considered what to do next. There had to be some other means of discovering where he'd gone. Suddenly she thought of his study. Mayhap she would find something there. Letters perhaps, or a bill.

The idea made her cringe, but she decided she had to know the truth.

Striding quickly downstairs, she moved along the hallway to Edward's office. Closing the door behind her, she didn't waste any time crossing to his desk. If he'd left anything behind, it was sure to be there.

She searched the papers and books on the top of his desk first, but found nothing of interest. Next she moved on to the drawers, or tried to, a tug proving them all to be locked. Knowing Edward was far too careful to leave the keys out in the open, she decided to take a more direct approach.

Sliding a hairpin from her short curls, which her maid had only just started putting up for her again, she twisted the metal into a new shape. Growing up, she'd learned how to put a hairpin to good use, since Marsden Manor had any number of stubborn old locks in it. Those skills came in handy now as she angled the pin just so and inserted it into the lock.

As she began to work the tumblers, her gaze fell on a framed miniature she hadn't noticed in her earlier search.

Staring, she realized a painting was of herself as a girl. She even vaguely remembered sitting for the work. How unexpected that he would have such an item. Even more, that he would keep it here on his desk as though it was something to cherish.

Knowing that not to be the case, she had no difficulty turning her thoughts back to the matter at hand.

She searched, opening and looking through another pair of drawers before she found what she was seeking. Oddly enough, the information was on a page of today's *Morning Chronicle*, where Edward had scrawled a block of notations.

August 3
11:00
Danberry Hall

Wherever the devil that is, she thought, a scowl creasing her forehead.

Just then a footfall came at the door.

She glanced up and found Mr. Hughes standing on the threshold, a look of astonishment on his face—as well as disapproval, if she didn't miss her guess.

"May I help you, Your Grace?" he said, striding into the room. "Was there something you required?" His tone bordered on the accusatory, as though she were doing something she shouldn't. Which, of course, she was, depending on one's point of view.

Ignoring his remark, she gave him an imperious look, an expression more than worthy of the Duchess of Clybourne. "Have you heard of Danberry Hall?"

Her question threw him off guard. "Well, yes, I think I have."

"Where is it located?"

"South of Guildford in Surrey, I believe. An old estate that fell on hard times after the last earl passed away. Went to a cousin, though I don't think he's in residence very often."

"Thank you, Mr. Hughes. You've been most helpful." Placing the newspaper back inside the desk, she shut the drawer.

He blinked with confusion. "You're welcome, Your Grace." Then he frowned. "A-About His Grace's desk—"

She strode toward him. "I suggest you lock it back up, assuming you have a key. If not, use this. It works astonishingly well."

With his mouth hanging open, she handed him the bent hairpin. Going out into the hall, she called for Croft and ordered the coach.

"They're in there right and tight, Yer Grace," Edward's lead man whispered in a voice too low to carry. "The boys er in position and ready at yer command."

"Excellent, Aggies," he told the wiry, baldheaded ex–Bow Street runner, who Edward had convinced some while ago to do a bit of business for the government instead. The whole team, in fact, were former runners with a knowledge of backdoor dealings and underworld activities. He'd seen their skills at work and knew he could trust them with his life.

Edward checked his weapon, then secured the gun at his waist. He didn't plan to fire the pistol, but there was no sense going inside unarmed.

Glancing up, he surveyed his surroundings once more, the stone walls of Danberry Hall rising up like a looming grey shadow against the nearly moonless night sky. Insects hummed brightly in the moist summer air, frogs belching out deep-throated songs in the tall, unmown grass.

"I'll go first," Edward said. "You and Brown come in behind."

Aggies grinned, then raised his head to give the signal—two owl's hoots that let the others know the mission was in play.

Edward moved toward the house with fast, purposeful strides. Rather than burst through a side door or window, which seemed unnecessarily troublesome and dramatic, he walked straight up to the front of the house and knocked, careful to keep to the concealing night shadows. After all, the courier from St. Giles Street was expected, so someone inside was certain to answer.

A minute passed before he heard the metallic click of a lock being pulled aside and the creak of the old wooden door as it opened. "Haven't I told you not to use this entrance," came a censorious male voice. "And you're late. Again. Do you have the items?"

Edward gave a muffled assent and the door opened wider to admit him. He stepped inside. Low candlelight illuminated the worn interior of the once proud hall with its threadbare carpets and scuffed furnishings.

The other man turned, his eyes rounding as he caught sight of Edward. "What are you . . ."

"Not who you were expecting, eh, Dumont? So sorry to disappoint. I, on the other hand, am delighted, since I was hoping I'd find you here tonight. Seems I'm in luck. So, where's your partner?"

Recovering quickly, the Frenchman assumed a casual stance. "Partner? I don't know what you mean. I am here alone."

"No, you aren't. And you can drop the act, since we have your man in custody."

Dumont didn't react, only a small twitch near his right eye betraying his true emotions.

"Had quite a lot to say, your man, once we managed to loosen his tongue," Edward continued. "So, do you care to add your remarks now or would you rather wait until you can do it from prison?"

Dumont's brown eyes flashed with a mixture of anger and fear. Without warning, he shoved past Edward and bolted for the door. He made it outside, but was just as quickly marched back in, Aggies prodding him forward with a loaded pistol in hand.

"Got us one of 'em, Your Grace." The runner flashed a gap-toothed grin.

"Back so soon, Dumont. Once again, where is your associate?"

"I told you. I'm the only one here."

"How noble. I wouldn't have thought it of you under the circumstances."

Striding deeper into the house, he looked into two rooms, both empty. Turning around, he raised his voice, calling out at large, "I know you're here, so you might as well show yourself. I have men surrounding the house. There's nowhere for you to go."

When no answer came, he called again. "I *will* search if you put me to the trouble. Come out now and save us both a lot of bother."

Long moments passed again, and just when Edward thought he and his men would have to comb the house, the soft tread of footsteps came from the landing above. "What is all this, Clybourne? Or are you often in the habit of invading private homes in the middle of the night?"

"Only when I'm hunting for spies, Lady Stockton."

Philipa Stockton became visible as she moved out of the dim shadows and walked down the stairs. "Spies?" She laughed. "How absurd. And what are you doing to poor Dumont? He's my houseguest and you should be more polite."

"Oh, you may be sure I'll be especially polite when I'm

questioning him. And you too, Lady Stockton. Or should I call you Wolf?"

Her eyes widened, unable to hide her surprise.

"Yes, I figured out the connection," Edward told her. "Although the spelling threw me off until today when I realized I'd omitted the 'e.' Your maiden name is Wolfe, is it not? Philipa Wolfe, whose father owned Danberry Hall until he ruined himself with gaming and drink."

Her insouciant façade cracked, her lip curling along one edge. "Yes, that would be my father, who squeezed every last cent out of this place, and out of me as well when he married me off at sixteen to that reprobate Stockton. The only good thing my father ever did was to break his neck when his horse refused a jump."

She strolled deeper into the hallway. "But having a bad father and an even worse husband doesn't make me a spy. Nor does the last name of Wolfe."

"Oh, but it does," Edward stated. "Not only do we have the money and papers we retrieved from the courier, we have this house as a coded rendezvous point and you as the contact."

"I'm afraid you have the wrong person," she defended. "As for the name Wolfe, it's no more than an interesting coincidence. The items you mentioned are for Dumont. He's the spy." Her lovely eyes brimmed with sorrow and regret as they turned toward Dumont. "I'm sorry to give you up, Rene. I tried, but it's no use. Surely you must see that?"

She looked back at Edward, pleading. "Clybourne, you have to believe me when I tell you that he forced me to let him use this house. He blackmailed me and left me with no other choice."

"Why, you lying little bitch!" Dumont spat back, clearly enraged.

"See how abusive he is? What else was I to do?"

Edward gazed at her, studying her beautiful, supposedly innocent face, and knew why her schemes had worked so well. She was a master at lies and guile and seduction.

"I might be inclined to believe that," Edward told her, "if not for the conversation I had with Lord Lymehurst today. I understand he caught you going through his office one night while he was supposed to be sleeping. Cut you off afterwards, I believe."

Philipa shrugged. "I was merely looking for pen and paper. He completely misunderstood."

"Did he? He knows now that he ought to have reported the incident, but he was too embarrassed at the time. In hindsight, he realizes how badly he erred, not only about his own judgment, but for his trust in you."

He fixed her with a hard stare. "How many men have you taken to your bed to get their secrets? How many lives have you cost with your lies? I'm certain once I have a chance to talk to more of your lovers, an interesting pattern will emerge. Particularly since so many of them have connections to the War Office."

Her face drained of color.

"Secrets have been going astray for quite some time," Edward continued. "We assumed there was a leak high up in the government. We just didn't realize how many someones it was and that they didn't even realize they were passing information. Very clever, Lady Stockton. A location here, a name there, who would ever connect all the small bits into a larger whole?"

Abruptly, her façade fell away. "It was a good plan," she admitted, a look of pride on her face.

"You did it for the money, I presume?"

"Of course. I care nothing for this war. It's all a great lot of nonsense thought up by men who like to squabble and fight. What do I care who wins or loses?" She set her fisted hands at her waist. "What *does* matter to me, though, is maintaining the style of life to which I am accustomed. The miserly widow's portion Stockton left me barely covers my basic necessities. Other women may be willing to accept reduced circumstances, but I'm not among them."

"Another woman would have remarried," Edward observed.

"Remarry! Why would I want to enslave myself again when I'd just managed to throw off the first set of shackles? Thank you, but I have no interest in marriage."

"Just in bedding men for their secrets?"

She cast him a look of derision. "You don't actually think I wanted to sleep with those men, do you?" Her pretty mouth curled in distaste. "Particularly Lymehurst. You may tell him that for me. He's a dreadful lover." Glancing away, she sighed. "No, out of them all, your brother's the only one who—"

"Who what?" Edward asked, his voice softening. "Who mattered? I believe you on that score, since Jack didn't have any secrets worth stealing, did he?" He studied her for a long moment, almost feeling sorry for her. Then his sympathy fell away. "Who is responsible for Lord Everett's murder? Was he your lover too?"

She arched a dark eyebrow. "On occasion, but if you're looking for his killer, you have him already." Lifting a finger, she pointed at Dumont. "How did Everett look again, Rene, when you stuck the knife through his heart? Stunned was the way you described him, if I remember correctly. Everett always did have a rather overinflated opinion of his own worth. He never imagined he might one day become expendable."

Dumont's lips rolled up over his teeth. "As do you, madame. You would do well to watch your back from now on." Realizing he was well and truly caught, he struggled inside Aggies's hold. But his efforts were useless, especially when two more of Edward's men arrived to assist.

"Take him away," Edward ordered. "Make sure he's well guarded until we get him in a cell."

"What about that one?" Aggies asked, nodding toward Philipa.

Edward turned a look her way. "Oh, I believe I can handle Lady Stockton. You're not going to be a problem, are you?"

She gave a faint smile and shrugged. "What would be the use?"

The matter settled, Aggies and one of the men led Dumont away, French curses rolling volubly from the émigré's tongue.

"Is there anything you would like to take with you?" Edward asked Philipa.

"A few clothes, some books, a toothbrush perhaps. What else does one require in prison?" she questioned with a self-deprecating smile.

Edward told the remaining man to go upstairs and gather Philipa's belongings. Once he'd departed, they stood for a couple of minutes in silence.

"Would you care for a seat?" Edward asked, indicating a nearby chair.

She shook her head, her hands folded at her waist. "No. Although I ought to thank you for not rushing me off straightaway. It's most kind of you to allow me to take a few belongings."

"I can't see the harm. You are a woman, after all, even if you're—"

"So this is your dull business meeting, is it?" declared a lilting voice from just inside the doorway.

Edward's heart leapt, his gaze flying forward as shock shot all the way to his toes. "Claire!"

"Seems a rather small gathering with just the two of

you. But then I'm sure you planned it that way. So, are you on your way upstairs or have you only just come back down?"

Lines dug gouges on his brow, his gut tightening with a slick twist. "What are you doing here? You're supposed to be in London!"

Her mouth firmed into an angry slash, blue eyes flashing like lightning, as she strode farther into the room. "So are you, Your Grace."

A new thought occurred to him. "How in Hades did you even know where to find me?"

"I broke into your desk. It proved most illuminating."

Lady Stockton gave a delicate snort of amusement.

Edward's jaw went slack. "You did what!"

"It seemed only appropriate considering your lies," Claire retorted. "How dare you! And to think I believed you when you assured me she wasn't your mistress."

"Oh dear," Lady Stockton remarked, finally entering the conversation. "So she thinks we're having a tryst?" Eyes dancing, she began to laugh. "Dear girl, you are badly misled. Actually he's here to—"

"Be quiet!" Claire told her before rounding again on Edward. "And you, I don't ever want to speak to you again. When you return to London, I'll be gone. You may forward the divorce papers to me at Marsden Manor, since I'm going home to Mama."

Incredulous anger burned through his veins, a panic unlike any he'd ever known hitting him like a roundhouse punch. In the blink of an eye, his entire life had been turned upside down. "Your only home is with me," he said through clenched teeth. "And you aren't going anywhere."

She set her fists on her hips. "Oh yes, I am."

He was glaring back, a rejoinder on his tongue, when Philipa Stockton suddenly lunged at him. Before he could prevent it, she reached down and snatched the pistol from where he'd secured it at his waist.

Claire let out a squeak. "Oh my God, is that a gun?"

Having forgotten all about Philipa in his argument with Claire, he whirled around to face Lady Stockton. "Put that down. It will do you no good."

"I think it will," Philipa stated, stepping back to aim the loaded weapon directly at his chest. "I think this will do me a world of good. You're not taking me to gaol, Clybourne."

"Gaol?" Claire said in obvious confusion.

"That's right, Duchess. Your husband is here to arrest me for espionage, not to conduct an affair. You should have a better opinion of him, you know, since he's as loyal as a hound. Anyone with eyes can see he's besotted with you."

"I'm also tenacious," Edward said, wondering how he could get the gun out of Philipa's grasp. "You won't get away, you know."

"Oh, but I will. I have a store of hidden cash, enough to find my way to France and then on to who knows where. America, perhaps? I hear people can get lost there quite easily. I understand one can even establish a new life with no questions asked."

"You'll be found," he told her. "Your crimes are such that they'll never stop looking."

"They will if I'm half a world away. Now stand aside, so I can leave."

He shook his head. "No. Now give me the gun. It'll go easier on you if you do."

"Never!"

A creak sounded from above, the man he'd sent to pack Lady Stockton's belongings creeping down the staircase, his own gun drawn.

Philipa turned at the disturbance. As she did, Edward sprang forward and grabbed for the weapon in Philipa's hand. But she fought him off, displaying a surprising amount of strength. They wrestled for long moments, the gun firing out into the room.

With that single bullet expended, the battle was done. Wrenching the smoking weapon from her grasp, he turned her over to the runner, who received her with an iron grip. "Lock her up tight," Edward told him. "And be sure not to listen to a word she says."

"No!" Philipa cried, tears streaming over her cheeks as she was led from the house. "No, please!"

But he was deaf to her pleas. He had other more important matters on his mind. "Claire," he said, turning to find his wife. "Let's go home now. Let's be together where we can talk."

Rather than agreeing, she just stared, her face oddly devoid of color, her lips pale as winter frost. "Edward, I . . ."

Terror rippled over him, raising gooseflesh on his skin. "What is it? What's wrong?"

She met his gaze, her blue eyes glassy. "I . . . I think I've been shot."

Rushing forward, he caught her just as she crumpled to the floor, her cloak falling back to reveal the wide red bloodstain spreading wetly over her chest.

Cradling her to him, he gave a hoarse shout.

Chapter 28

I love you, Claire.

Don't leave me. Don't you dare.

You're going to be all right, do you hear?

I can't live without you. Please, sweetheart, please don't die.

Claire . . . I love you . . . love you . . . love you.

Claire knew she must be dead and on her way to heaven. Either that or she was having a really amazing dream. She'd just heard Edward say he loved her. Smiling, she drifted, savoring the words she'd yearned to hear for such a very long time.

Yes, she thought, *I must indeed be dead.*

Then the coach hit a rut and she cried out against the agonizing stab of pain that went through her left shoulder, just above her breast. Surely no one could hurt this much in heaven.

Which means I must still be alive. That or I'm in hell?

"You're not in hell," Edward said in a gruff voice. "You just hurt like you are. Hang on and we'll be home soon."

"Home?" she whispered, rousing enough to realize she was lying cradled in Edward's arms.

"Clybourne House. I've sent a man ahead, and the doctor will be waiting to meet us when we arrive. I didn't want to stay in the country and risk putting you in the hands of some inferior quack."

She bit her lower lip against the pain. "I was shot. You and Philipa Stockton were fighting over the gun."

"Yes," he said, his voice heavy with anguish.

"And she's not your mistress."

"No. I told you before, you're the only woman I want." His lips brushed across her forehead, then over her cheek with a gentle touch that was almost reverent. "The only woman I'll ever want."

How lovely, she thought, fighting the dizzying haze of pain. Leaning closer, she pressed her face against his chest, finding his skin warm and bare, his scent deliciously reassuring. "Why aren't you wearing your shirt?"

"You needed it more. I used it as a field dressing to help stanch the bleeding. Hush now and rest. We'll talk later."

Later? Yes, later sounded good.

But first there was something she had to know, something urgent, something vital. "Did you mean it?" she whispered.

"Mean what?" he asked, stroking a caressing hand over her hair, her cheek.

"I heard you say you loved me. Do you? Do you love me, Edward?"

She gazed into his beautiful midnight blue eyes. As she did, the world began to spin, and before she could hear his answer, everything went black.

Claire came slowly awake. The bedroom was swathed in shadows, the curtains drawn against the brilliant summer sun trying to steal in around them.

Long, indistinct hours had passed since the coach ride home, her memories fraught with flashes of unremitting pain, blood and fear. Yet through the ordeal, Edward had been with her, never wavering as he did everything he could to help her fight the agony, to keep her safe as she fought for her life.

She remembered the steady grip of his hand, the comforting salvation of his voice as the doctor pried the bullet from her shoulder, the tender warmth of his kiss on her cool, trembling lips when it was finally over. Edward had wiped the tears from her face with a damp cloth and told her to sleep.

She had, though for how long, she had no idea.

A heavy ache roused her again now. Glancing down, she discovered a thick white bandage wrapped across her shoulder and another tied across her chest to bind her left arm to her side. Not that she had any interest in moving her arm or shoulder, since she knew it would hurt like the very devil.

Sighing, she turned her head on the pillow, and there was Edward. He was seated in a chair beside the bed, sound asleep as he lay slumped over so his head rested near her hip on the mattress. Even in repose, he held her hand, his fingers linked with her own. She squeezed them, tears of gladness moistening her eyes to find him so near.

"Claire?" He sat straight up, blinking against his disorientation.

"It's all right," she said. "I didn't mean to wake you."

"No, no, I'm glad you did," he said, his words a bit slurred as he worked to shake off his exhaustion.

And clearly he was exhausted, his eyes ringed with dark circles, hair disheveled, his cheeks covered in a heavy swath of black bristles that gave him a rather swashbuckling appearance.

"You look terrible," she said.

He smiled and raised her hand to his lips. "But you look better. Your color's back and your lips aren't white anymore. You gave us all quite a scare."

"Have you been here all morning?"

"And all night. An entire day has passed."

"A day?" she repeated, shocked. "And you've been here all that time?"

He gave a solemn nod. "I couldn't leave you. I won't. Not until I know you're safe." Standing, he leaned over and laid his hand across her brow. "The doctor said you might have a slight fever, but you don't seem too warm."

"I'm going to be all right." And she knew that she was. The worst was over, physically at least. "Are you really a spy?"

One brow arched high. "Those of us in the service prefer 'intelligence agent,' but yes, I do an occasional favor for the War Office."

"Given all your recent business meetings, it seems more than occasional. So that's where you've been? Doing work for the government?"

"We've had a leak for the past couple years that I've been tracking down. As of the other night, I've succeeded in eliminating it."

"Lady Stockton."

"Yes, Lady Stockton and another man with whom I don't believe you're acquainted."

Claire lay for a long moment, considering all she now knew and all she still did not. "Why didn't you tell me? How could you let me think the things I did?"

With great care, he lowered himself onto the bed next to her, taking her hand again. "I was sworn to secrecy and wasn't at liberty to reveal my activities, even if it would have been a great deal easier to do so. And how, may I ask, was I to know what you were thinking? By God, Claire, I still can't believe you rifled my desk drawers, found my location and came after me. You could have died."

"But I didn't."

"No, thank God," he said, closing his eyes on a heartfelt prayer. When he opened them again, his gaze shone with an expression that made her breath catch on a heady rush.

"I should have read you better and realized what you might try," he said. "I should have done the same with Philipa Stockton too. If only I'd been more careful. If only I'd realized the extremes to which she might go." He pressed her free palm to his cheek. "Don't ever put yourself in danger like that again."

"It was never my intention to do so. But I had to know where you'd gone and what you were doing. I had to know why you'd lied. I saw you ride out that evening when you told me you'd been downstairs in the library, reading. You weren't."

He had the grace to wince. "I'm sorry, Claire. I couldn't—"

"Tell me. Yes, I know. However, in future, if you insist on doing more favors for the government, I want to know that's where you are. You don't have to give me all the details, but enough so I won't worry. Frankly, I don't care if Prinny himself swears you to secrecy, I want your word that you'll never lie to me again."

"You have it, Claire. On my honor."

Relief poured through her, knowing that Edward's honor was his bond.

"So you're staying then?" he asked. "As I recall, you mentioned something about going home to your mother."

"I was upset—"

"Not that I would let you leave, mind, because I wouldn't," he continued, "but I want to make sure these things are straightened out between us." Lowering her hand to his thigh, he stroked the sensitive skin along the inside of her wrist.

A curious lethargy stole over her.

"And you're right about secrets," he said. "I don't want any between us ever again. Only the truth."

"Only truth," she pledged.

He met her gaze with an open earnestness that made her throat swell. "You asked me a question back in the coach," he said. "Do you remember?"

She gave a shaky nod, her heart suddenly pounding in swift, hard beats.

"Good, because the answer is yes." Leaning closer, he smoothed a strand of hair away from her face. "Yes, I love you, so very dearly. When I thought I might lose you, I realized exactly how much. You're my life and my heart, Claire Byron, and I cannot do without you. I don't think I could bear it if you were ever to go away."

"Oh, Edward, I love you so much. I never thought, I couldn't let my dream that you . . . that you would . . ." A tear slid over her cheek.

He brushed it away. "Love you too? Well, I do. I'm only sorry I didn't tell you sooner and that I was too stubborn to admit the truth, even to myself. Remember when I said that we seemed fated for each other?"

Gazing at his features, handsome even in his weariness, she nodded.

"On the day your father laid you in my arms when we were children, you became mine. I should have known then what a prize he'd given me. You're my love, and I shall cherish you all the rest of my days."

Bending, he pressed his mouth to hers, slowly, softly and with such sweet tenderness that she didn't know how to contain her joy. Letting her eyelids slide closed, she gave herself over to the rapture, kissing him back with a gentle fervor, a devotion and adoration so wide it knew no bounds.

"You know, Lady Stockton was right," he murmured against her lips.

"A-About what?"

"Me. I am utterly besotted with you and I don't mind who sees."

Laughing, she reached to pull him back down, but a sharp pain jabbed her shoulder. "Ow," she cried.

"Claire." His face turned white. "Have I hurt you? Are you all right?"

"I'm fine, just trying to do too much, too soon."

"I should never have kissed you."

"Of course you should. And you will, again. Just don't let me move my arms when you do it." She grimaced. "*Ow*, that really hurts."

"The doctor left some laudanum. I'll get you a draught."

"No," she said, stopping him before he could leave the bed. "I don't want any."

He frowned. "But you're in pain. You need to take something."

"I'll muddle through without it. I think it's for the best."

"Why? Surely you don't want to hurt?"

"No, but I don't want to harm the baby either."

He stared, his dark brows knitted in confusion. "Baby? But—"

"I've been trying to find the right time to tell you, but you've been away so often at your *meetings* that it just never seemed right."

His jaw went slack. "But you can't be . . ."

She raised an amused brow.

"Well, of course you *can*, but you shouldn't be. It's too soon."

"Apparently not. Or at least I don't think so, since I'm late now for a second month in a row. I believe you must have managed the deed almost immediately, maybe even that very first night."

"Good Lord."

"Are you happy?" she asked, giving him a suddenly uncertain look.

Then he smiled and her worries fell away.

"Of course I'm happy!" He grinned. "How can I not be happy that you're with child. It's only that I thought I'd have you all to myself for a while more."

Careful not to jar her shoulder, she reached up with her good hand and stroked his cheek. "There'll be plenty of time together. We have our whole lives ahead of us, after all."

Gently, he kissed her again. "Our whole, very long lives. I can't wait to spend each one of those days with you."

"Nor I. I love you."

"I love you more." Suddenly a yawn caught him, renewed exhaustion spreading across his face again.

"You're tired," she said. "You should get some rest."

"You should as well. Close your eyes, I'll be here."

"Where?"

"In the chair."

"Don't be silly. Come, lie down with me."

"But I might jostle you."

She shook her head, secure that she'd find no safer rest than held inside his arms. "Sleep with me, love. I need you."

And with that, he stretched out at her side, wrapping her in a gentle, caring embrace.

Smiling with contentment, she forgot her pain, happy in the one place she would always most long to be. Threading her fingers through his, she watched him sleep. Slowly, she dozed off too, knowing he would be with her when she awakened—today, tomorrow and forever.

Look for the next book in
The Byrons of Braebourne series
WICKED DELIGHTS OF A BRIDAL BED
Coming September 2010
From Avon Books

NEW YORK TIMES BESTSELLING AUTHOR

Tracy Anne Warren

Meet the Byrons of Braebourne!

Tempted by His Kiss

978-0-06-167340-5

When orphaned beauty Meg Amberley is stranded in a snowstorm, she takes refuge at Lord Cade Byron's estate. To save her compromised reputation, Cade proposes a pretend engagement and a London season where she can find a husband.

Seduced by His Touch

978-0-06-167341-2

Marry a young woman because he lost a bet? Unreformed rake Lord Jack Byron would do anything to get out of it. But the rich merchant who holds the debt insists he marry his on-the-shelf daughter. Luckily the sensuous Grace Danvers isn't the closed-in spinster he expected.

At the Duke's Pleasure

978-0-06-167341-9

Lady Claire Marsden has longed for Edward Byron, Duke of Clybourne, since she was sixteen. But how can he expect her to agree to an arranged marriage to him when he barely knows her and doesn't love her?